"... a gripping courtroom drama that you won't want to put down! ... full of devious characters, dramatic action and authentic legal dilemmas .... outshines anything currently available in lawyer novels, or on the large or small screen, in terms of suspense and true gut-grabbing, edge-of-the-seat excitement!"

— *Paul Rothstein*
Commentator on Legal Affairs, Cable News Network (CNN)

"Much like a real jury, the reader follows the twists and turns of the proceedings, until reaching a very surprising conclusion."

— *Barry Scripps*
Executive Director, Scripps League Newspapers

"... *Conflict of Interest* was so much fun to read—a real page turner with no end of tension and excitement. I read it practically nonstop. ... Any person who has never tried a jury case from start to finish can see it exactly as the lawyers in the courtroom do."

— *Terry Ney*
Past President, State Bar of Virginia

"The writers of *L.A. Law* have nothing on David Crump. He captures all the characters of a litigation drama as only an experienced lawyer can. But unlike most lawyers, he can really tell a tale the way it should be told."

— *Mark Obbie*
Former Editor and Publisher of *The Texas Lawyer*
(pub. by American Lawyer Media, a Time-Warner Affiliate)

Other Books By David Crump

Law School Texts and Case Books
(co-authored)

Cases and Materials on Civil Procedure
Cases and Materials on Constitutional Law
Cases and Materials on Texas Civil Procedure: Pre-Trial Litigation
Cases and Materials on Texas Civil Procedure:
Trial and Appellate Litigation
The Story of a Civil Suit: *Domiguez v. Scott's Food Stores*
The Biography of a Criminal Case: *The State v. Albert Delman Greene*
The Anatomy of a Real Property Transaction
Evidence in a Nutshell: State and Federal Rules

General Audience

Capital Murder: How Today's Death Penalty Crimes are
Committed, Investigated, Prosecuted, and Defended
(co-authored)
If Kids Could Vote Before They Were Ten:
Fun Poems for Adventurous Children

Conflict of Interest

A NOVEL ABOUT TRIAL LAWYERS, GREED, PASSION, POWER, REVENGE . . . AND JUSTICE

David Crump

Strawberry Hill Press

Strawberry Hill Press
3848 S.E. Division Street
Portland, Oregon 97202

This is a work of fiction. The characters, names, events, dialogue and circumstances are imaginary or are used fictionally. Any resemblance to real persons or actual events is purely coincidental, fictitious or imaginary.

Edited by Kristi Burke
Cover by Ku, Fu-sheng
Typeset and design by Wordwrights, Portland, Oregon

Manufactured in the United States of America

Library of Congress Cataloging-in-Publication Data

Crump, David.
    Conflict of interest : a novel about trial lawyers, greed, passion, power, revenge, and justice / David Crump.
        p.   cm .
    ISBN 0-89407-122-X (trade paper : alk. paper)
    I. Title.
PS3553.R783C66   1997
813' .54—dc21   97-13272
                                                                      CIP

1
DISASTER

The headlines called it the Propane Truck Disaster. For years, it was front-page news. Maybe that was because of the place where it happened, or because of how violently it happened, or because of the carnage that was left behind. Everybody saw those gruesome pictures on television. There wasn't much for the medical examiner to work with when he tried to identify the bodies.

A few days after it happened, the lawsuits started to hit the clerk's office. They made the front page, too. And every time, the newspapers reminded their readers about the reckless, just plain inexcusable negligence of the man who drove the propane truck. He was pushing his rig too hard on the home stretch, and he got in too much of a hurry.

But maybe it wasn't fair to blame the whole thing on the truck driver. Some people pointed the finger at the construction companies—those billion-dollar corporations that had built the roadway. That overpass was a death trap, designed by white-collar criminals who sacrificed lives to boost their profits. It was an accident waiting to happen!

Now, at last, it was almost time for the real verdict. The television anchors exploited it breathlessly: "A battle between giants of the legal profession! Over the greatest tragedy this city's ever seen!" On the Internet, the chat groups grew from five to twenty-five. And finally, a talk-show host unleashed the ultimate hype: "This thing's gotten bigger than the O.J. Simpson case!"

The lawyers felt their adrenalin surge, and reporters fought for courtroom assignments, because the trial of the propane truck disaster was about to begin.

2
THE JURY

All right, Mister Bailiff. Bring them in!"

"Yes, your honor." A buzz of excitement arose from the spectators. Robert Herrick scrambled to his feet the moment the jury panel started to enter the courtroom. His stomach twitched and bubbled, and the custom-tailored hundred dollar shirt he'd chosen for this trial was soaking wet. "My God," he murmured to no one in particular, "I've already sweated through my clothes."

He knew that it was his fear that made him sweat. He tried to settle himself by remembering that he was the immediate past president of the bar association, chairman of a blue ribbon committee appointed by the Supreme Court, and leader of the local bar's project to represent the poor. He had a brilliant career. His clients adored him. He was rich beyond most people's imagination.

But nothing could erase the memory that he had lost three of his most recent jury trials. He was afraid he had lost his touch—and his luck. His hands started to shake, so he jammed them into his jacket pocket, hoping no one had noticed. As he watched the line of randomly-selected citizens shuffle in, he struggled to project confidence, because that could make the difference for his clients between winning and losing.

The bailiff pointed. "First ten of you on the front bench, please. And then let's start the second row."

These were the sixty citizens from whom the final twelve jurors would be selected to try the propane truck case. Not only his clients' fate but Robert's whole career rested in their hands. And that was what terrified him.

"It's not surprising that you're nervous." Tom Kennedy was a five-year attorney, here to assist with the trial. "But Robert, you're the best lawyer for this case."

"Thanks, Tom." He managed a tight smile.

Across the courtroom, his arch rival, Jimmy Coleman, also stood. "Look at Coleman." Kennedy's whisper was heavy with disgust. "Biggest Rambo lawyer in town. Mister Slash and Burn. But here he is, smiling and looking cuddly for the jurors, like an overgrown teddy bear."

Robert usually managed to stay on friendly terms with his opponents, but he couldn't help disliking this one. Jimmy Coleman was the head of litigation at the biggest firm in town, the gigantic Booker & Bayne, with almost five hundred lawyers. He carried a map of his life on his face, punctured by eyes so pale and dead that witnesses turned away when Jimmy cross-examined them.

"Guy's a real street fighter," Robert agreed. "But you're right. He'll make sure the jury doesn't know it."

There wasn't any rule of courtroom procedure that required the lawyers to stand, but Robert stretched to his full six-foot-two-inch height, because he was trying to read as many of the sixty faces as possible. Women jurors usually responded to his youthful looks, with the shock of dark brown hair that fell over his forehead, and the men were impressed when he could speak without notes for hours at the end of a long case. Still, he wished he didn't always feel nervous— not just nervous, but scared!—at the beginning of every trial. His blue eyes grew dark, now, as he searched every juror for some kind of omen.

The first citizen wore a gray suit, gray shirt, gray tie. "Look at that, Tom. The guy's an accountant, of all things. And all dressed in gray." This wasn't the sign Robert had hoped for.

"He wouldn't be a good plaintiff's juror at all," Kennedy whispered back. "In fact, he'd be terrible."

Then, there was absolute silence—a brittle, self-conscious silence—until all sixty citizens had taken their seats.

"Good morning, ladies and gentlemen." Judge Barbara Trobelo's smile seemed a little bit forced, probably because she had to run for re-election soon. "The case now on trial is the one that the public calls 'the propane truck case.' The formal name is *Gutierrez versus Maxxco Construction Corporation and Louisiana Trucking Company*, but I'll explain what all of that means later. This is a civil case, and it will be tried before a jury."

The lawyers weren't listening. They alternated between scanning the jurors' faces and sneaking looks at the jury questionnaires, and all the while, they tried to look relaxed. But Robert found that it was harder and harder to do that.

"This is an awful jury panel!" He showed the list to Kennedy. "It's not just the gray accountant. The whole front row is crammed with types that the psychologists warned us about." This was the luck of the draw, but he wished it hadn't happened now, in the biggest case of his career.

The judge was still reading instructions to the jury panel. "When you begin your deliberations, it will be your duty to elect a presiding juror." She looked up and smiled. "We used to say 'foreman,' but today we say 'presiding juror,' because it's less sexist."

The feminists in the jury panel beamed at that. The men laughed good-naturedly.

But Robert was too wound up to laugh. That string of losses had hurt him badly, even though he tried not to let anyone see it. His latest defeat was the worst: a medical malpractice case where complications from a broken metal rod in a bone had killed Robert's poor client in a cruel, painful way. And that case, coincidentally, had been against this same opponent. This same Jimmy Coleman! "Thanks, Herrick, for refusing our settlement offer and making us try this piece-of-shit case of yours," Jimmy had exulted after the jury brought in a zero verdict. He'd won the case by pulling one dirty trick after another, all artfully concealed from the jurors.

And now, here was Jimmy again, eager to administer another thrashing. Robert valued his reputation for representing injured people with skill and integrity, but these days, his faith in his most cherished talents was shaken.

He was about to ask the jurors to award his clients a billion dollars. A billion, with a "B." But his stake in this case wasn't tied to the money. He also believed passionately in the power of juries to compensate innocent people for the damage that the careless rich did to them. But this case had hooked him at a level even deeper than that.

"You know, Tom, I need to win this case." He turned suddenly toward his younger associate. "For myself, as well as my clients."

Kennedy's voice was even. "We can do it, Robert. Just take it slow and steady."

The judge was beginning to read aloud the names of all the plaintiffs. Her voice was stern: "If any of you, as potential jurors, are acquainted even slightly with any of these parties, you must raise your hand." There would be more than a hundred names, because Robert Herrick's law firm represented all of the survivors of the propane truck disaster, and yet he listened to every one. He knew their pain, because thirty-three people had been killed instantly, and even more had died later. Robert had had to learn all of their life stories.

His drive to win this case had become a raw and primitive energy.

So far, this was the most bizarre case he had ever handled. The investigation had forced him into contact with all kinds of unsavory characters: heroin dealers, murderers, and prostitutes. It also had carried him into high society: luxurious boardrooms, glittering balls. Along the way, there had been a triple murder, a cop-killing, and a shooting in which Robert himself had been wounded.

The judge was warning the panel, now, about jury misconduct. "Do not mingle with or talk to the lawyers or the witnesses . . . . Do not accept any favors from them, such as rides, food or refreshment . . . ."

"If I lose," Robert thought, "I'll hang it up for good." Maria might be pleased by that. She would love him no matter what. His kids would like to see more of him. "But obviously," he reminded himself, "I don't want to go out with my tail between my legs."

Suddenly, the judge ended her speech. Jimmy Coleman was on his feet. "Your Honor! Before we start the trial, I have a motion to make on behalf of my client, Maxxco Construction Corporation!"

"What the hell's he up to?" Kennedy whispered.

Robert had a sense that he ought to know the answer. But somehow, disastrously, all he could say was, "I don't have any idea!"

"Your Honor, we respectfully ask that you realign the parties." Jimmy's motion was all phrased in high-sounding language. "Otherwise, Maxxco would be denied an impartial trial, in violation of its most precious right—the right to due process of law."

What *that* meant, it turned out, was that Jimmy wanted to renumber the Louisiana Trucking Company as the first-named defendant, instead of his own client, Maxxco. "All Maxxco did was, it built the intersection. Mister Herrick's trying to say Maxxco was negligent, but the fact is, it wasn't. And anyway, the case against the truck driver ought to be the one that gets the jury's attention." This seemed like a waste of breath, because it simply didn't matter which defendant was named first. Robert had never heard of a motion like this, and he was sure the judge hadn't either.

And then, he realized that the sixty citizens were listening to Jimmy with rapt admiration. For them, this must have sounded better than *L.A. Law.* It finally dawned on Robert: "Hey, Jimmy's making a jury speech, disguised as a legal argument to the judge!"

Jimmy's hoarse voice was a bellow and a whisper, both at the same time, like the dignified anger that might ooze over the courtroom if Marlon Brando were to play a big-firm lawyer. His words rose and fell half an octave as he made his real point. "Your honor, at the end of this case, the jury will see that the truck driver was the *only* person responsible for this tragedy. Not Maxxco! *Not* my client! Not anybody but the truck driver. And that's all there is to this case!"

Robert lost control for a moment. "No, your honor! That's not what the jury will see. At the end of this case . . ."

But Judge Trobelo's eyes clouded, as she quickly interrupted him. "The motion is denied. And both counsel are way out of line. I won't tolerate any more of this kind of argument in front of the jury." She chose her words carefully, because Robert's outburst meant that it wouldn't be fair to concentrate her irritation on Jimmy alone.

The jurors smiled and nodded their heads. One or two even clapped.

"I guess these are the kind of legal fireworks they've been looking forward to," Tom Kennedy whispered.

But Robert was disgusted with himself as he stared at Jimmy across the courtroom. "First impressions are going to be all-important in this trial," he whispered back. "The consultants warned me that the jury's likely to form its attitudes sooner than in most cases." And now, Jimmy had struck the first blow. Or rather, the first thrust of the stiletto.

"He fooled me so badly, I just wasn't able to stop him." There was anguish in Robert's voice.

Kennedy nodded. "Typical Coleman! But it looks like the jury fell for it. Isn't there at least something we can do?"

Herrick shook his head. "We make a big fuss, and we'll lose more than we can possibly gain."

And so, finally, when that respected plaintiff's lawyer, Robert Herrick, stood up to address the sixty citizens who held ultimate power over the biggest case of his life, he had the discouraging feeling that he was starting from behind.

The trial had only just begun. But already, he was losing.

And he couldn't afford to feel like a loser. He would need to use every bit of his skill in this case, all the way through to the final witness. He dug into his lungs to take a breath. Then he turned to face the jurors. He stared at them for a long, awkward moment as he got ready to take them back to the beginning.

"It all started more than two years ago," he said slowly, "when a truck driver named Louie Boudreau ended his final run."

Robert Herrick's law firm had spent hundreds of hours reconstructing Boudreau's journey. By the time he was finished, Robert knew much more than the route of the propane truck. He knew the personality of the truck driver better than he knew most of his friends. He had come to understand Louie Boudreau's thinking, his hopes and dreams, as well as if he had crawled inside the truck driver's own skin.

And now, he was ready to draw a picture of that strange, disastrous day for the jury panel. He wanted to put the jurors right there in Louie Boudreau's cab. Or better yet, inside his head.

"Let's go back in time." Robert forced himself to keep his voice clear and calm. "Let's go back, ladies and gentlemen of the jury panel, to that horrible day a little over two years ago. Because that is when this case, this story, really begins . . . ."

3
BOUDREAU'S RUN

He was a tough, street-smart Cajun redneck, Louie Boudreau was, with a longshoreman's shoulders and arms, but at just five-foot-six, he was too sawed-off for that line of work. Instead, he'd gotten his leathery face mostly from working deep offshore on platform oil rigs, across from southern Louisiana towns like Houma and Lafayette. And also, of course, by doing what he was doing right now—driving hazardous cargo for the Louisiana Trucking Company—which he often regretted, because he was built so much like a fireplug that he had to rise up out of the seat every time he made a turn.

In the past, Boudreau had made a good chunk of his living smuggling cocaine, making the trip from Texas to Chicago, which he liked because of the easy money and flexible hours. But he'd given it up. He wasn't very religious, but if you grew up in South Louisiana you got used to talking to the saints, and anyway, like most truck drivers, Boudreau was superstitious. He'd quit selling cocaine because something had told him the next trip would be the one when he'd be unlucky. He didn't have enough patience to keep from getting busted forever. When he was younger, in his early twenties, he'd done a deuce plus six months in the state prison at Angola for aggravated assault. He'd been in a barroom brawl over a woman he didn't know except for the fact that he wanted her because she was drunk and she stood about four inches shorter than he did.

As a matter of fact, Louie Boudreau wasn't in a very patient mood right now, either. The big sign on the side of the tank that said "Louisiana Trucking Company—Hazardous Cargo" was barely visible as the rig plunged ahead in the midday darkness and rain. He'd made his run from Lake Charles all the way down to Laredo, just as he was ordered to do. But after almost two days of driving, he still wasn't finished, because everything that could have gone wrong, had gone wrong.

"Forty hours on the road," thought Boudreau. "Forty straight hours! And judging by this weather, every saint in heaven must be mad as hell." The rain had closed in to make a solid wall at the same time that the clumps of chain restaurants and strip centers had come together to signal his entrance into the city. And now, a strange summer hail pounded the roof of his cab as Boudreau struggled to push his eighteen wheels eastward toward Houston. He was heading back home, to Louisiana, on a stretch of Route 59 that the local population called the Southwest Freeway.

He wiped his eyes with his thumb and forefinger. The instant he opened them, the lightning burst in his face, crackling from the top of the sky to the horizon. Suddenly, a blast of wind pushed his rig sharply rightward, like an invisible hand poking a toy truck. Boudreau grabbed the wheel, and he wasted a few choice expletives while the whole rig shivered. "Lord help me," he thought, "if I shift this load." A skid would make him jackknife, maybe even roll over. And if that happened, it would vaporize Louie Boudreau, together with everybody else who was on the road. He remembered the red-lettered warning plastered on the back of his rig: "Danger. Liquified Petroleum Gas. Contents under extreme pressure."

Then, with that little dance of the tires that lasted a second or two, the trouble was over. Boudreau took one hand off the wheel and jammed it into the middle of his hair. Then he pushed it back through the Vaselined grooves until there were shiny black chunks sticking straight out from his head. The cab was hazy and stale with smoke, but Boudreau chain-lit another Camel. It wasn't safe to smoke around this cargo, but he was tired, frustrated and sick of driving, and he didn't give a damn.

This trip hadn't been a good one. Oh, it had started out well enough when he left Lake Charles two days ago. It was amazing, Boudreau thought, how much he missed Elyse and the kids, and how much he missed the little shotgun house that flaked paint chips under the mildewy air of South Louisiana, after he'd been without sleep for two days.

"Propane to Laredo," the foreman, whose name was Pointevet, had told him in a Cajun accent, back at the yard. "It's a nice day for drivin', so you can have some tacos for lonch and be back to have crawfish for breakfas'."

Well, this particular run hadn't worked out that way. Just west of Orange, when he was barely across the Texas border, Boudreau had begun to hear an unpleasant whine from the engine. He'd tried to ignore it, but the noise had gotten louder, until finally, it was a circular, scraping nightmare. Lou Spoda, at Spoda's Truck Stop, thought it might be the air conditioner belt. So Boudreau had tightened all of the belts and sprayed them with anti-slip compound.

The noise had gone away—for exactly two miles. Then it started again with a scratchy wail. He'd stopped two more times along the road, fiddling with the belts, until finally, somewhere just short of Vidor, Texas, he'd pulled way off the Interstate and limped into Ray's Garage. After two hours of looking, Boudreau had finally found it, with the help of a shade-tree mechanic named Joe Bill Heatley. The distributor rotor was busted.

Joe Bill had a genuine burr haircut, less than a quarter-inch everywhere on his head, and black spaces between his teeth. "Look at them circles in that sorry damn thing," he had said, as they both stared at the inside of the distributor cap. The rotor had dug deeply into the metal points.

But that wasn't even the worst part of the trip. When Boudreau steamed into Laredo, it turned out that the buyer of this load of propane was some company on the Mexican side called Petroliferos y Gas de Chihuaua, and they hadn't put up the letter of credit that was required before Boudreau could drop his load. "It's just typical Mexican business," said the man in charge of the terminal, whose name happened to be Sanchez.

Four hours later, Louie Boudreau had gotten to know Sanchez extremely well, and he had long since jolted Pointevet wide awake back in Lake Charles. "Jus' bring de whole damn t'ing back here," Pointevet had told him finally. "We try to settle up wid dose fucking Mexican bastards later, or else we blackball 'em." And so Boudreau had backed the fifth wheel into place and connected the hoses for the trip back to Louisiana.

"I guess I be goin' home," he announced, "an' takin' my propane 'long wid me!"

Sanchez thought all of this was hilarious. "Haulin' propane back to Lake Charles, as if they didn't have enough of it," he roared. "That's a hell of a note, even for a dumb coon-ass like you, Louie!"

As tired as he was, Boudreau had to laugh when Sanchez went on to suggest various unnecessary cargoes that he might consider importing into Louisiana. Maybe a load of crawfish? A trailer full of Blackened Voodoo Beer, which was brewed in South Louisiana? "Or how about taking back a couple hundred a them doggy-lookin' strippers with the little titties, only when they get it all off it turns out they're these female-impersonator-type guys, instead? Surely they didn't have enough of those down on Bourbon Street," said Sanchez.

Boudreau was cracking up when Sanchez waved him out of the yard, yelling, "Stick with me, Louie, and I'll make you the richest coon-ass in all a Lake Charles, even if you are dumb enough to haul propane to Louisiana!"

Now, Boudreau wasn't laughing, as he pushed the rig toward the city. The hallucinations, he knew, couldn't be far away. Bands of color would focus into red, green and blue figures that would cavort across his windshield like a drive-in movie. The way they always did, after forty hours on the road.

Boudreau came closer and closer to his favorite shortcut. His favorite illegal shortcut, in fact. The lightning crashed again, this time behind him. He would take the long, looping ramp that connected to Interstate 610, and then, a few blocks north, he would turn east again on Interstate 10, and that would take him clear to Lake Charles without another turn.

It was illegal as hell. Boudreau would sail right under the bright green sign that banned hazardous cargoes from the inner city. It was marked on all of the Louisiana Trucking Company's maps, as Pointevet had shown him with the stub of a cracked greasy fingernail when Boudreau first had started driving for the company. But the shortcut would save him a good half hour. "If any cop can catch me in this weather," thought Boudreau, "he deserves to write a big-truck ticket."

The Transco Tower, tallest building in the world outside a metropolitan center, rose out of the darkness on his left. The building was spooky, with shiny black surfaces and a pointed hood. Just past it, Boudreau saw the silhouette of the Galleria Mall. When he turned the corner, he would be a few hundred feet from Neiman Marcus, Tiffany's, and the hundreds of other glittering merchantsto-the-wealthy that linked this patch of Houston to Fifth Avenue and Rodeo Drive. Maybe that was why hazardous cargo wasn't supposed to be here.

But still, Boudreau pressed his foot on the accelerator. His speedometer needle bounced over fifty-five. He downshifted and dodged the concrete blocks that marked the exit ramp off of the Southwest Freeway and onto Interstate 610. Immediately, Boudreau was in a spaghetti bowl of concrete and steel, with a commanding view of Transco Tower. He braked as the ramp began to turn northward, and he coasted under the Hazardous Cargo sign.

On the radio, Don Henley sang about "Forgiveness." "Maybe there's something a little more cheerful on another station," Louie thought. He watched the freeway with half his attention while he turned the dial over to KIKK, which was one of Houston's many country stations. Instantly he was rewarded by Mary-Chapin Carpenter's voice singing, "I wanna dance to a band from Lou-si-anne tonight." For the first time in five hundred miles, Boudreau actually smiled.

And then it happened. The thunder, and the lightning, and the aftermath, so fast that it was all one event.

The thunder was like a bomb; the lightning, white hot and incandescent, seemed to ride right on top of his hood, burning through Boudreau's dilated eyes. Ahead of him was a Toyota painted the same silver color as the rain. It skidded and revolved as the driver panicked. In the instant before he braked, Boudreau rode almost on top of the Toyota. That was when his own wheels locked and his cab began to skid.

As he struck the left side of the Toyota, Boudreau's propane tank burst the railing and sailed off the ramp, the way a child's yo-yo breaks free from its string. He felt his fifth wheel tearing loose as the tank pulled his cab off the ramp. There was a sickening silence as the rig fell, and Boudreau saw Sanchez's face appear in front of him, then his wife Elyse, and the kids, then the foreman Pointevet, followed by red, green and blue figures of the Bourbon Street transvestite strippers that Sanchez had conjured up. Then, for an instant, the images faded, but finally, Boudreau's spinning nightmare came back into focus with the transvestites transformed into all of the saints of heaven, bending over each other in an orgiastic Roman holiday while the clouds shook with lightning and rain.

The propane tank hit first. It slammed across the three inside lanes of the Southwest Freeway. The pressure found a pinhole. Inevitably, there was enough of a spark to ignite the bullet stream of escaping gas. The cab separated and flew to the other edge of the road, but before it did, the earth and sky exploded. The incoming cars skidded and flipped as their drivers desperately tried to stop. But the whole freeway was blocked, and the momentum of sixty miles per hour hurled them into the holocaust.

Later, shaken witnesses would describe a huge orange fireball that they thought was taller than the Transco Tower. And one even insisted—against all of the evidence—that there had been hundreds of cars twisted in the wreckage at its base. On the Southwest Freeway below the ramp, investigators found fourteen vehicles with melted dashboards and tires exploded from the heat. Parts of the cars actually had vaporized, and there were more than thirty human bodies, several of which were impossible to identify by conventional means.

And the last thing that Boudreau had seen, before his cab hit the freeway, was the sweet face of the Virgin.

4
HERRICK

After the propane truck exploded, it was all that people talked about. Endlessly, they speculated about how such a terrible thing could have happened, who was to blame, and whether the victims had suffered.

"Just look at that intersection, Tom!" said Robert Herrick. "You still can see where it's burned, all the way from here."

Two days already had passed since the disaster, but the ugly smudge was easily visible from Herrick's office in the center of the city. Tom Kennedy nodded his head when he saw where his boss was pointing.

Robert Herrick's law firm occupied the entire top floor of the Texas Commerce Tower, Houston's tallest building. His own office was spacious, and the dark parquet floor was covered by the most beautiful oriental carpet Tom Kennedy had ever seen. The furnishings were spare, but elegant: plants and flowers under the greenhouse-style windows, a mahogany desk with three desk chairs, and paintings by Picasso, Mondrian and Wyeth. Outside the window, the downtown buildings sprawled toward the south in shades of gray, brown and white. Off to the west, the lush greenery along Memorial Drive stretched past River Oaks and Tanglewood and away into the distance. The site of the propane truck disaster stood out like a burn in a bright green carpet.

"Thirty-three people." Herrick leaned against the window and stared down at the remains of the holocaust. "Burned alive in their cars. And you know, Tom, there'll be even more who'll die later in the hospitals."

His voice was anguished, as though he'd known the thirty-three personally. Sometimes, Robert Herrick admitted to himself, he wasn't analytical enough. He identified too emotionally with the plaintiff's side. But still, he was phenomenally successful, probably because he felt so strongly about right and wrong when he chose his cases.

"The worst thing is, there's no excuse for that propane truck disaster." Herrick frowned. "The intersection's a death trap. Those humongous construction companies are as much to blame as the truck driver. As far as I'm concerned, Tom, those thirty-three people were killed by corporate greed."

"Now, there you go again, Robert." Kennedy smiled and shook his head. "You haven't even got a client in the propane truck case, and already you sound like we represent the plaintiffs. What if one of those humongous corporate *defendants* hires us, one that we think is innocent?"

Herrick smiled in spite of himself, and he turned to face his favorite associate. "Well, I suppose that could happen. After all, our system depends on a lawyer's being able to argue either side."

"Aw, come on. You don't fool me. You always want to be fighting for the injured plaintiff against those rich, powerful corporations." Kennedy smiled again. "I'll never forget my first day on the job. It showed me just how much you identify with the little guy, Robert. You remember? The thing with Mrs. Polk."

"No. What thing with Mrs. Polk?"

It was a story Kennedy had told many times, but never to the boss. "Well, Robert, you interrupted a deposition you were taking so you could greet your client. Who happened to be a cleaning lady. And the witness in the deposition just happened to be the CEO of a Fortune 500 company that you were suing, but heck, that didn't stop you. 'Hello, Mrs. Polk, how are you? Are you back to a hundred percent again?' And you kept that pinstriped big shot waiting while you talked to this cleaning lady about her grandkids, her church, and her favorite barbecue joint! That was my first day working for you, and I was amazed."

"Yes. I do remember." Herrick was laughing at himself, this time. "But see, I'm tremendously fond of Mrs. Polk. She's not just a client or a cleaning lady, she's my friend. And besides, the whole thing turned out all right, even if it was completely by accident, because when I met with Mrs. Polk, it distracted the big shot in the pinstripes."

"Yeah?"

"Yeah. By the time I went back into the deposition, the whole atmosphere had changed. It wasn't something I planned, but that's when the CEO spilled his guts and decided to tell the truth about everything. It happens sometimes. The guy who thinks he's such a big shot has to wait a few minutes because of somebody he decides is one of the little people, and it disorients his sense of self-importance. Anyway, after Mrs. Polk, that CEO gave me all the truthful testimony I needed against his own company, which was guilty as sin, I might add."

"Sometimes the best justice happens by accident," Kennedy agreed. "So, how'd it all come out in the end?"

"Well, the defense lawyers in that case were from Booker & Bayne. They were pretty sanctimonious, and they refused to admit any fault at all. But after that deposition, they called up and offered to pay five hundred thousand. That was totally inadequate, of course, because Mrs. Polk's husband was hurt pretty badly. He was almost a paraplegic, the poor guy. I decided I shouldn't even make a counter demand."

Herrick turned to face his associate. "But then, they offered a million, and then two million, and that's when Mister and Missus Polk authorized me to counter, at fifteen million. Those Booker & Bayne lawyers knew that if the CEO's deposition came out at trial, the jury would have kicked them all over the courtroom. And we finally settled for twelve-and-a-half-million, which was better than Mrs. Polk or I ever expected to get. It'll pay for her husband's medical care and maybe make his life worth living."

"Gee. Maybe you ought to hire Mrs. Polk to interrupt all your depositions." Kennedy shook his head, as if to say, "That's Robert Herrick!" But he had to admit that his boss was effective, even if he did follow his heart too often instead of his head.

"I just wish I could have given Mrs. Polk back a husband with a healthy body." Robert's voice was more subdued, now. "I'd rather have that than all our financial success."

And of course, the financial success had been amazing. Today, Herrick's law firm, which was called "Robert Herrick & Associates," had seventy-eight employees, including twelve lawyers, twenty paralegals, and an audio-visual studio that made exhibits and videotapes for use in court. And all of it had been built by Robert himself, after he came out of law school with nothing but debts. He had refused the secure salary that every firm in town had offered because he wanted to go it alone.

And now, his firm handled large and small commercial cases right along with large and small personal injury and death cases. The big-firm lawyers treated him with respect when they agreed to settlements that brought millions of dollars to countless injured people or their families. His clients loved him because they knew he didn't just analyze an injury in terms of dollars and his mind wasn't confined to the bloodless words of the law books. He also felt it, the same way they did; and they knew he would fight for them. The way he had for Mr. and Mrs. Polk.

But Tom Kennedy still wasn't finished arguing. He wanted the firm to represent more banks and insurance companies, the kinds of clients who could pay up front. "So, Robert, how come you're already on the side of the plaintiffs in the propane truck case?"

"You're right. You got me. I'm a bleeding heart." Robert laughed good-naturedly. "But Tom, you know what I said is true. The guardrails on that overpass are way too weak, and I'm sure you've driven on it yourself, so you know it isn't banked enough. And it's way too narrow. No wonder that truck fell off."

"I hear a jury speech coming on."

"What I mean is, it wasn't just the truck driver's fault. It was those sorry construction companies who built the overpass, too. And they ought to get sued. Those thirty-three people are dead because of them."

Kennedy grinned. "I rest my case."

Robert shook his head. "You got me, Tom!"

As Robert grinned back, he had to crane his neck around the two-foot stack of accordion files on the desk. Suddenly, he realized that all of these files were about one single case—a pro bono case, in which the whole office had worked hundreds of hours for free on behalf of a minority business that had been cheated out of its contract. Robert had insisted on this crusade, even though he was sure to lose, because he thought the plaintiff was right.

And then, painfully, his mind wandered back to the disastrous string of defeats he'd had recently, most of which should have ended with his clients getting something. And with that, he began to think the unthinkable: "Maybe Kennedy is right. Maybe I do need to pay more attention to the business."

And then, for the tenth time that day, he looked out at the scorched overpass where the propane truck had gone down.

Suddenly, the telephone rang. The sound was unnaturally loud; it jolted Robert back to the present. He reached for the speaker button clumsily because he still was thinking about the propane truck disaster. "Hello. This is Robert Herrick."

The voice that answered was unexpectedly raspy and hoarse. "Hello, Mister Herrick! This is Jimmy Coleman, over at the law firm of Booker & Bayne."

Herrick knew that his face betrayed his feelings. He didn't like Jimmy Coleman, and he had even worse feelings about Coleman's law firm. Booker & Bayne was one of those factory-size behemoths, even though they never hired anyone who hadn't made the law review and ranked near the top of the class. And then, too, Jimmy was the one who'd beaten him in the most recent of his humiliating losses.

But still, he struggled to be pleasant. "Nice to hear your voice, Jimmy! What can we do for you?" "Come on," he said to himself, "you learned a long time ago that you can catch more bears with honey than with a club."

"I want to refer a new lawsuit to your little old firm." Jimmy sounded like a modern-day warlord presenting an opulent gift to a rival chieftain. "And this lawsuit, it's a good 'un. Our firm can't take it because we would have a conflict of interest. Too bad, because this case oughta be worth at least fifteen million bucks, and Mister Herrick, I think you're the man to handle it!"

"Well, that's very nice, Jimmy. Thank you." Maybe Booker & Bayne wasn't really that bad, after all.

And as Jimmy spelled out the details, it became clear that this case was, indeed, a "good 'un." The plaintiff was a little start-up corporation called Paragon Paging Service, and it had been driven out of business by the biggest paging company in town. "The president even wrote a memo to one of his vice-presidents, tellin' the guy to organize a boycott against little bitty Paragon Paging." That was illegal, of course, "and this dumb-shit CEO, he puts it all in writing! A real smokin' gun document."

Jimmy's voice sounded like sandpaper. "It's too bad Booker & Bayne can't keep the Paragon Paging case. But it would be a pleasure to refer such a fine piece of business to a lawyer like you, Mister Herrick."

Jimmy was talking about exactly the kind of David-against-Goliath lawsuit that put Robert into his element. He was at his best in cases that challenged the comfortable world of power-abusing executives by getting an occasional verdict for some poor, disadvantaged little guy who'd gotten destroyed. But why the change in Jimmy's attitude? Robert's face tightened. After the zero verdict in that awful malpractice case, Jimmy had been just plain nasty. He'd gone out of his way to rub it in. Something told Robert that this Paragon Paging lawsuit was too good to be true.

"Sounds great," he said finally. "But let me ask you this. I've never seen a good lawsuit without a few warts on it. I've even had a few supposedly 'good 'uns' that turned out to be dogs, and I had to walk them over to the courthouse on a leash, after which, the jury poured me back out on the street. So, what's wrong with this lawsuit, Jimmy? Or are you saying I can just mosey over to the bad guys' headquarters and pick up a fifteen million dollar check?" He said it with a smile in his voice, because it was nice of Jimmy to think of referring the case, but still, he needed to ask the question.

Jimmy chuckled at that. "No, nothin's wrong with the lawsuit. It's solid gold." But suddenly his voice changed, and he was even more hoarse than before. "It's just that—well, Robert, there *is* one thing that I'd have to ask in return."

"Uh-oh. Here it comes." Robert spoke under his breath, but he realized he'd said it loud enough for Jimmy to hear.

There was a strained silence. And then, finally, Robert asked: "Okay, so what's this 'thing' you want in return?"

"Maxxco Construction Corporation is one of my best clients." Jimmy's voice, now, was like nails scratching a blackboard. "You know, Maxxco is the construction outfit that built that overpass where the propane truck went down."

The propane truck disaster! "I've just gotten through calling the overpass a death trap," Robert thought, "and now, here's this Booker & Bayne lawyer telling me he represents the same company that built that overpass!"

"That's my client," Jimmy repeated unnecessarily. "Maxxco Construction."

"But see, that puzzles me," Robert said. "What could Maxxco possibly have to do with the case you're referring to us? You've got me wondering, Jimmy. I appreciate your thinking of me, but why mention Maxxco?"

He said it matter-of-factly, with the tone of voice that he used for hard negotiations. But he had an uncomfortable feeling about this conversation, and without even thinking, he reached toward the picture of Patricia Herrick on his desk.

Patricia had died of ovarian cancer three years earlier, but before that, she had been Robert's wife of more than seventeen years. Recently, he noticed that he had formed an odd new habit. In uneasy situations, he would touch the photograph of Patricia Herrick, in its heavy gold frame, just as he was doing now.

But Jimmy was oblivious to Herrick's disdain. "To put it bluntly, if I refer you this fifteen-million-dollar lawsuit, I'd expect you to stay out of the propane truck case. Or, at the very least, I'd need your agreement that you wouldn't sue Maxxco. It's actually a fine company, Maxxco. It employs hundreds of thousands of people all over the world."

There was a pause, and then Jimmy appealed to Herrick's honor. "You got to understand, Robert, I can't be referring this case to you if you're going to turn right around and stick everything up my ass by suing my best client."

That made it all make sense. Even with his recent string of losses, Robert Herrick had a reputation as a masterful trial lawyer, and he'd seen plenty of defendants try this tactic. Sometimes, they even tried to hire him themselves, before the bodies were cold—just so they could keep the plaintiffs from having him as their lawyer. Jimmy was trying the same tactic in a different way.

Robert Herrick was muscular and slender, and at forty-four, he looked at least ten years younger than his age. His opponents still called him by an odd nickname: "The Baby-Faced Warrior." But his most striking feature was the dark blue eyes that shined like polished spheres of sapphire when he talked to the twelve common people on a jury and asked them for their trust. In the courtroom, Robert could speak in a voice that went from a shout to a whisper and held the twelve citizens' attention the whole time. All in language that sounded authoritative, but simple; language that didn't talk down to anybody. Jimmy Coleman obviously knew all of this, and that was the reason he wanted Herrick off the propane truck case.

But no one had ever made this kind of proposal sound quite as blatant, or as offensive, as Jimmy had done just now. It might have been perfectly legal, but it sounded like—well, like a payoff.

"Jimmy, this is legalized bribery," Robert protested. "Come on! Don't put me in this kind of position."

But then, the conversation was interrupted.

At that moment, Donna de Carlo knocked on the door and walked across the oriental rug to hand a note to Robert. As Herrick's secretary, Donna was expected to be tough, smart, and professional, even though she always preferred to wear four-inch heels and short skirts. Herrick was self-conscious about looking, but still, involuntarily, his eyes followed Donna step for step across the jagged red, blue and green shapes in the oriental carpet.

Robert looked puzzled. With two fingers, he held up the note and showed it to Tom Kennedy. In Donna de Carlo's big handwriting, it said: "A JUSTICE FROM THE TEXAS SUPREME COURT IS HOLDING!"

A justice from the supreme court? What on earth was this justice calling him about?

"Jimmy, just a minute," said Robert. "I'm going to have to put you on hold."

Jimmy Coleman's loud "Harrumpf!" exploded from the speakerphone just before Robert pushed the button.

"Hello?" said Robert into the second line.

The bouncy, feminine voice that answered him was immediately familiar. "Hi, Robert!" said Maria Melendes. "I'm sorry to announce myself by pretending to be a supreme court justice, but Donna warned me that I wasn't going to be able to get through to you. You work too hard! You need to take a break so you can do something more important. Such as talking to *me*, for instance!"

Robert laughed in spite of himself. She always made him laugh. That was what he liked most about her. "Maria, what am I going to do with you? Someday you're going to interrupt me when I'm doing something that really is important."

But actually, he was glad to be spared, just for a moment, from the "unimportant" business of talking to Jimmy Coleman about that fifteen-million-dollar lawsuit that had turned out to be a bribe. Jimmy was still on the line, and Robert was going to have to give him an answer.

5
MARIA

Robert leaned back in his burgundy leather chair with a look of puzzled amusement. "Telling Donna you're a supreme court justice," he said to Maria. "Can't you come up with something a little less devious?"

But she was unrepentant. "I'm Cuban, and I have red hair. And you know I've got to have chutzpa, because of the strange kind of law practice I do."

She laughed. And so did he.

This was the first woman he'd really been able to care about since his wife's death. It was ironic, since Maria Melendes was an assistant district attorney, and she had the dubious distinction of being known as "The D.A.'s Official Killer." When a murderer got the death sentence and the appeals courts affirmed it, Maria would inherit the gut-twisting responsibility for getting the execution carried out. Sometimes the condemned man would make eleventh-hour claims of innocence, but if his story was fraudulent, her job was to say so, all the way up to the United States Supreme Court.

"Well, Maria, you know I respect you for the way you handle that job of yours." Robert picked up the receiver, cutting off the speakerphone. "I only wonder why you turned out to be a conservative Republican instead of a good Democrat, like every educated person ought to be." He laughed. She was strong enough to be soft and feminine, and she understood what it meant when he teased her.

He stage-whispered to Kennedy: "This'll be just a minute. I need to go ahead and talk to her since she's had trouble getting me."

Kennedy smiled and nodded. "She's a character." He, too, was a big fan of Maria's, and more than once he had told his boss how glad he was that Robert had found somebody "this fantastic," as he put it, to fill the long emptiness after Patricia's death.

"Now, come clean, Maria." Robert grinned as he held the telephone. "The real reason you pretended to be a supreme court justice just now was—you always wanted to be an actress. It's a step up from . . . well, being an exotic dancer."

"A showgirl," she corrected him. "Back in those days in Las Vegas, I was called a showgirl. Try saying that, Robert. It's more dignified."

"Sorry. I guess I forgot." He enjoyed kidding her about her past life on the stage. "But please don't try to get me executed, at least not for that particular crime."

"You're harmless. You're an innocent. And as I've told you, part of my job is to protect the innocent."

It was true. There had been several cases where Maria had joined with the defendant's lawyers in asking for a new trial. She always said the hardest part of her job was knowing the difference—when she should agree with the defense lawyer for one of these brutal murderers, and when she should fight to the end.

"Now, on to something more important," said Maria. "Robert, do you ever go to the symphony?"

Actually, Robert agreed with Kennedy. He was glad to have found someone this unusual after emerging from the years of mourning his late wife. They were a strange couple, but they were opposites that attracted—the successful, self-made boy scout courting the worldly showgirl-turned-assistant-DA.

"The symphony? Sure," said Robert. "Where's it playing? Your place or mine?"

Tom Kennedy rolled his eyes. It was amazing how women acted around Robert Herrick now that he had emerged from the shadow of his wife's death. He was never sophisticated even when the women were, and he used incredibly corny lines, but it always seemed to work.

Maria laughed in her little-girl voice. "No, silly. You're so full of it." She laughed again. "It's at the Wortham Opera House, and it's a whole month off, but I hope you can pencil it into your busy schedule. Anyway, they have a concert that's called Mostly Mozart. As even a guy like you could probably figure out, it mostly will be music by Mozart. And they're going to do the Haffner Symphony, which is my favorite symphony of all time."

"The Haffner Symphony? That's my favorite, too, and just about everybody else's," Robert answered. "The Haffner Symphony in D Major. Written during the last years of Mozart's life, when everything he touched was a masterpiece."

"Wow," she said. "I'm impressed. How did you get to know so much about classical music? And I thought you were like Charlie the Tuna. You know, going to the symphony just to show you have good taste."

"That, too. Just think in terms of all the PR, Maria! If people catch a glimpse of you listening to the Haffner, it'll do more for your image as a high-class Cubana than being seen with Desi Arnaz at a Gloria Estefan concert."

She laughed. And then he wrote it into next month's calendar while they settled on the details.

"By the way," she asked him suddenly, "how *did* a macho guy like you get to know so much about cultural stuff like Mozart, anyway?"

"Okay. I'll tell you the whole story. Only, it'll have to wait until I see you again." Maria always acted as though she loved to hear him tell the "whole story" about anything.

Now, she said, "Good-bye, sweetheart." And the light that was marked "line 2" blinked off.

"Well, I'll say one thing, Robert." Kennedy was smiling and shaking his head. "She always makes you laugh."

"Some of the pranks she pulls, all you can do is laugh." Robert grinned and looked out the window. "I remember talking to her about my baseball team, way back when I pitched in the College World Series. Nowadays, I've got my team picture hanging in my office instead of my law license. She started laughing at me for that. And it wasn't all that funny, but she got me laughing, too. And it was like we couldn't stop."

"Does she ever get serious?"

"Oh, sure."

"So, then, she understands your tenacious dedication to the underdog? And why you're such a maverick?" Kennedy smiled.

Robert laughed. "I don't know if anybody completely understands that. Not even me."

"Well, anyway." Kennedy suddenly was serious. "I understand why you like this lady."

"No question about it." Robert looked away, and his eyes clouded. In those depressed years following Patricia's death, he had gone through a bizarre period when he'd chased women left and right. With the bravado that came from inner emptiness, he had succeeded so often that it surprised him. Back then, all he'd been interested in besides working twenty-hour days was these one-time conquests.

He felt a little silly about it. "Now," he said to himself, "that time I went through, of acting out, has been ended for good. By Maria Melendes."

Robert sat for an instant with his hand on his chin, looking out the window toward the scene of the propane truck disaster. Then he turned, finally, toward Tom Kennedy.

"I want us to start work today on the propane truck case," he said. "Get whichever one of the investigators has the most free time. Tell him to start identifying witnesses."

It was instinctive, not the result of analysis or calculation. He simply felt drawn to the case, and he knew why—horror at the disaster and a desire to set things right for the families. A trial lawyer's sense of justice. But he also felt certain of this decision, sure that it was right, even if he was just going on instinct.

Kennedy's eyebrows went up. "Start an investigation? Now? But we don't even have a client!" As the saying goes, time is the lawyer's stock in trade, and neither Kennedy nor Herrick had gotten where he was by squandering it. "Why should we start an investigation in the propane truck case when nobody's asked us to represent them, and maybe nobody ever will?"

But Robert's mind was made up. "I know it's unusual, but let's do it. The clients will find us, I'm sure, and we'll give them better service by starting now."

"Robert, I don't like this. I've got a feeling that it's going to turn out badly. What makes you so sure that the clients are going to come to us?" There were thousands of lawyers in the metropolitan area.

But Robert already was thinking ahead. "I can't be sure yet of all the defendants we'll want to name, but I know this: The Louisiana Trucking Company isn't the only one. And as for the people that built the intersection, the

Maxxco Construction Corporation or whoever Jimmy Coleman said his client was—" And at that, Robert's voice trailed off. He seemed doubtful, as if he was still weighing Jimmy's offer.

"Speaking of Jimmy Coleman! What about him?" Kennedy asked suddenly. "He's still holding on the phone, isn't he? My gosh! He's still just *sitting* there, waiting for your answer to that god-awful proposal of his!"

"Yes," said Robert, who was shocked to find that he had forgotten, too. "I'd better talk to him." He thought to himself, "Kennedy must be wondering whether I've really got such ice water in my veins that I'm able to ignore the referral of a case that, after all, would bring a multi-million-dollar fee to the firm." And so he added, "I really didn't mean to leave him hanging. I just got preoccupied."

His finger pressed the telephone button, and his voice became professional. "Jimmy, are you still there?"

"You bet." Jimmy sounded earnest. In fact, he sounded eager. "Maxxco Construction Corporation is real interested in your response. And also, of course, I want to refer you this other lawsuit, the fifteen-million-dollar case."

"I'm sorry." On the big oriental carpet, a hundred geraniums bloomed from the floor in shades of red, pink and orange. But Robert looked out past them, toward the smudge left by the propane truck disaster. "I'm sorry, Jimmy, but I can't agree that I won't sue Maxxco if it turns out they're at fault."

Jimmy was flabbergasted. "This Paragon Paging case, the one I'm talking about referring to you, it's worth fifteen million! Cold! You mean to say you'd turn down a case like that, a bird in the hand, for an impossible lawsuit against a fine company like Maxxco?"

"Well, my grandpa once told me, it isn't the easy decisions that count. It's the hard ones. And this is a hard decision, because frankly, I don't object to making a living. And I'd like to be the one to handle your fifteen-million-dollar case. But Jimmy," Robert's voice was carefully controlled here, "I've never agreed in advance that I wouldn't sue a defendant who I thought was guilty. I always thought it would be wrong. And you've got to understand, I just can't agree to it now."

At that, Jimmy Coleman went ballistic. "Well," he shouted, "you're biting off more'n you can chew! If you do sue Maxxco in this frivolous kind of lawsuit, I'll move the court to order sanctions against you so fast it'll make your head hurt. You're not going to believe the heat that'll come down. Because it won't be just in the courts!"

And with that, Jimmy's voice escalated a notch further. "Those union guys at Maxxco, they'll take it as a direct threat to their jobs! I've got no control over them, and they don't play patty-cake!"

At first, Robert was amazed by this outburst. It couldn't possibly work. But then he realized, it certainly could work, if the lawyer on the other side from Jimmy had anything weaker than a cast-iron stomach, or if that lawyer wanted the security of Jimmy's fifteen-million-dollar lawsuit. Actually, Robert's own stomach felt a little wiggly right at this moment, as he thought, "This propane truck case sure is a lot of trouble. I don't even represent anyone yet, but already it's cost my firm several million dollars, plus a threat of violence from a labor union."

But then he thought, "This propane truck case is exactly what I need after the cases I've lost." And then, almost immediately, that thought was replaced by another: "Kennedy's right. No matter how much I want it, I may never get hired by a client in that pie-in-the-sky case." And then, finally, he settled down: "But still, I can't let Jimmy push me into selling out."

The sad thing was, Jimmy probably thought this slimeball tactic was just part of his job.

"I'm sorry." Robert was uncomfortable, but he struggled to keep his voice even. "I may go broke, and I may lose the lawsuit, but I just can't change my answer about suing Maxxco."

"We'll see." Jimmy Coleman unleashed a few more "Harrumphs!" that apparently were a substitute for saying good-bye. And then he hung up.

His telephone call, Robert reflected, had started out as an offer to refer a case, but it had changed into an attempt at bribery. And just now, it had ended in a threat.

6
ANGELA

The Medical Center in Houston is like a separate downtown, almost as big as the center of the city. It has row after row of high-rise hospitals, professional buildings, diagnostic clinics and medical schools. As the Chamber of Commerce might put it, the Med Center ranks with oil and space as an industry for which Houston is known throughout the world.

It was here that the flotilla of life-flight helicopters had brought the injured victims of the propane truck disaster. To the Andrews Burn Center, on the third, fourth and fifth floors of the Baptist Hospital. Actually, there were very few propane truck victims who were merely injured, because those in the range of the fireball had been killed instantly. And the dead were probably the lucky ones. But there were a few who were still alive, and ten-year-old Angela Gutierrez was one of them.

From the start, the docs knew that Angela wasn't going to make it. But doctors are surprisingly poor at delivering bad news, and so it was two days before anyone told the Gutierrez family. The family's first reaction was simple. They didn't believe it. In the waiting room outside the third-floor nurse's station, they held a vigil of hope, which actually was a death watch. But gradually they accepted the facts when they were confronted day after day with Angela's suffering.

Late on the fourth day, two men stood and talked outside the nurse's station. One of them was a tall, emaciated stranger named Esparza, who obviously wasn't part of the Gutierrez family. The other was Pedro, Angela's father. Both of the men wore green sanitary garments over their street clothes because Angela was sealed off in a sanitary corridor to reduce the risk of infection.

"*Está casi muerta?*" the man called Esparza asked. "Is she almost dead yet?"

Pedro Gutierrez should have been offended. Instead, the wiry little man was deferential to Esparza's authority. "*Señor abogado,*" he began. "Honored lawyer . . . ."

He stopped, and then he tried again, with his hand over his eyes. "My beautiful Angela! She is my little girl . . .," and that was all he could say. He was frustrated that he could not concentrate on his lawyer's question.

Behind them, the duty nurse watched a rerun of *Dallas* on a little black-and-white television. For the ten-thousandth time, Pamela Ewing was defending the Ewings against the whiny verbal assaults of her sleazy brother, Cliff. The name tag identified the nurse as LaVonda Hall, and she didn't particularly like this episode of *Dallas*, but she had been on duty for thirty-six hours, and she was glad to be off her feet for a minute.

Suddenly the television's glow grew dimmer, recapturing LaVonda Hall's attention. The scene shifted to a closeup of J.R. in bed with the office receptionist. LaVonda Hall was so exhausted that she barely was able to control her annoyance when the man named Esparza intruded.

"Miss—hey, Miss! What's the word on Angela Gutierrez?" Esparza accosted the nurse in a too-loud voice just as the camera panned across the bedcovers to show J.R.'s ostrich-skin cowboy boots intertwined with the receptionist's stiletto heels.

Esparza sure didn't look like any of the attorneys she'd ever met, LaVonda Hall thought—this tall, skinny stranger with the two-day beard, the mirrored sunshades and the dirty white-on-white shirt. But the man certainly was insistent. "The little ten-year-old girl with the burns from the propane truck. What's the word on her?"

LaVonda Hall hadn't been able to pay much attention to the monitors for the last hour. She could tell immediately if anything was wrong, and then the adrenalin would flow as she ran to the patient. But in a big hospital, you had to prevent burnout by filtering away the things that didn't matter. This included people who wanted to push the nurses around, and LaVonda Hall could already tell that Esparza wanted to do exactly that. She shifted in her chair so that she could see the bank of oscilloscopes that filled the wall behind her. Each one featured a sawtoothed line of light led by a bright point that never stopped in its monotonous course from left to right.

LaVonda Hall found the sign that said "GUTIERREZ, A.," under one of the screens. "Heartbeat looks okay, systolic is good, EEG unremarkable. I'd say she's pretty stable." She wanted to sit still for just a minute and then get back to her patients, and she wanted this strange man not to push her around.

But Esparza didn't get the message. "Where's that guy, Doctor Fahmi? When's he comin' back?"

And now LaVonda Hall remembered. The doctor's instructions were marked "DNR" for Angela Gutierrez. "DNR" meant "Do Not Resuscitate." Doctor Fahmi was the chief resident, and he had personally explained the do-not-resuscitate instructions to everyone on the service.

DNR's were rare in the Baptist Hospital, even in the burn center, where lingering death was an everyday reality. Nowadays, court-ordered "disconnects" were more common. A judge usually would order life support to be discontinued at the request of the patient's family. That way, the judge's order protected the hospital from expensive lawsuits for malpractice, which family members were too ready to file even after signing an "informed consent" on the hospital's form. This legal stuff drove the docs crazy because every state did it differently, and the rules were always changing.

"So when's that doctor, the little guy from India or wherever, when's he coming back?" Esparza was saying.

"I don't know," LaVonda Hall answered. She was struggling to be polite. But then curiosity got the best of her. She had seen only one other DNR during the last year, on a horribly burned man from Paraguay who had been extracting cocaine with ether in a remote rainforest. Angela Gutierrez's case sounded like something equally mysterious. And so she asked Esparza, "How come this patient is just a DNR instead of a court disconnect?"

"Because I said so," Esparza said flatly.

Her eyes got a little bigger as she absorbed that statement. "But why?" she asked finally.

"This girl is part of that propane truck accident out on the Southwest Freeway. Great big lawsuit." For an instant, Esparza showed the gleam of an odd-shaped gold cylinder instead of a tooth, right where his left upper incisor should have been. "They've got a good lawsuit, the family. I don't want anybody messing it up." He smiled and flashed the gold cylinder again. "It's a better lawsuit if the docs don't kill her."

LaVonda Hall stared at this strange man with her mouth open and her eyes wide. The do-not-resuscitate, besides being legally reckless, would prolong the child's suffering. And this man had just explained to her that this was what he wanted, just because it would create a better lawsuit! She blinked and started to say something. But Esparza already had turned his back and walked over to Pedro Gutierrez, who was just out of earshot.

"Come on," he said to the smaller man. "Let's go see the patient."

Inside room 623, ten-year-old Angela Gutierrez lay under a plastic anti-infection tent. The plasticene netting that was known as "artificial skin" covered most of her body, including the ninety percent with second- and third-degree burns. A forest of tubes sprouted from her tiny body, winding through the dressings that swaddled her so that it was impossible to see where they ended, like roots in a carpet of undergrowth. There were two tubes feeding her a heavy mixture of glucose, water and antibiotics. There was an aspirator. An oxygen mask. And the electrocardiogram, connected to the screen behind the nurse's station.

"*Señor* attorney," said Pedro Gutierrez, "this is what they did to my daughter. The Louisiana Trucking Company. You can get them, can't you? This is the Estados Unidos, the United States!"

"You bet I can get them," said Esparza. "But I can't do it until you sign the contract."

The case against the trucking company was very strong. And the damages would be in the millions. Esparza had a videotape of a team of doctors and nurses changing Angela Gutierrez's dressings, which would eventually become an exhibit for the jury. The process was called "debridement," which was a medical term that meant the removal of dead or dying tissue. The videotape was gross and disturbing, with charred or blistered skin sloughing off and lobster-red color underneath.

It had been four days. Long enough. Even Esparza couldn't handle the pain of watching it drag out.

It was time for the girl's ordeal to end. And yet her death needed to be natural, or at least it needed to appear to be natural.

"Hey, listen, Pedro." Esparza's voice was deliberately casual as he created his diversion. "Holler at that nurse and get her in here for a second."

As soon as Pedro reached the door, Esparza reached inside the tent. Skillfully, he located a vein and slid the needle in, then pushed the plunger with a quick, practiced motion.

"Forget the nurse, Pedro." Esparza said offhandedly. "I found what I was looking for."

The heroin would metabolize into opiate derivatives inside Angela's body. It wouldn't be detectable in the autopsy because nobody would know to look for it, and soon it would be indistinguishable from the morphine that her doctors had prescribed. But it would be enough to kill her. This was necessary, from Esparza's point of view. The family would not go along with the DNR forever, and really, neither could Esparza. The child's pain was too palpable. This was the best solution he could think of.

In an instant, Esparza's uncharacteristic act of kindness was completed. The girl would die a little later this evening in a way that wouldn't arouse any suspicion. Esparza fumbled to replace the syringe under the sanitary green overshirt.

Almost immediately, there was a murmur from Angela Gutierrez. Behind the bandages, she repeated, "Papa . . . Papa . . . Papa." A pause. Then, "*Donde está Mama*? 'Where is Mama?'" It was what she had said, over and over again, since Pedro had been by her side.

Mercifully, Pedro's wife had been dead before she arrived at the burn center. "She is sleeping," Pedro Gutierrez said. "*Mama está dormiendo*."

Angela murmured again: "There was the big truck, up in the air, going over the rail and smashing it down . . . . *El camion de fuego*, the truck full of fire. I still see it, coming over that rail . . . ." Esparza grabbed a prescription pad and wrote it down: "*El camion de fuego* . . . over the rail." It might be useful later in the lawsuit. The jury could be told that the last thoughts of this dying child were a nightmare memory of fiery death.

Neither of the two men really could predict the significance that Angela's description of the accident might have, much later, in court. But Esparza was sure that the whole propane truck case, with all thirty-odd victims, would be worth hundreds of millions of dollars, and this child's simple words were just the thing to make an impression on the jurors' memories. He stuck the prescription pad into his pocket. "Come on. Let her rest for a minute. And now's a good time to start our lawsuit. Here's the contract."

"*Si, Señor Abogado*," Pedro answered. "I will sign."

It was a standard, one-page contingent fee contract. Holding it against the wall, Pedro labored to write his name with the hospital ball-point that Esparza had handed to him. The contract said that Pedro would pay his lawyer a fee of one-third of the amount he won, or forty percent if a trial was necessary. Curiously, the contract did not contain Esparza's name. Instead, there was a long blank space that said, "My attorney, _____." But Pedro Gutierrez did not notice the omission.

Esparza finally had the case signed up. He strode down the long sanitary corridor after brief good-byes, with an ebullient spring to his step.

Three miles to the north, Robert Herrick sat in his office and looked at the magnificent view. The Texas Commerce Tower was beautiful, and his own surroundings were the finest, but that didn't help him to feel any better. For the thousandth time, he thought about the painful losing streak he had suffered through. And about the clients who'd gotten nothing because of it.

First there had been that bank fraud suit. Robert had spent three months showing the jury how his client's pension fund got cheated out of twenty million dollars. But as soon as he rested his case, wham! there was a directed verdict in favor of the bank, because the judge said Robert's evidence wasn't even sufficient to let the jury decide it.

His next case was about a hydraulic jack that failed. It turned Robert's client into a quadriplegic, but after more than a month's worth of evidence, the jury came back with a zero verdict. The foreman's explanation was simple. "We thought it happened because that poor guy just don't know how to use a jack, Mister Herrick." But all that meant was that Robert hadn't persuaded them, and his injured client would get nothing.

And then there was the third case, the one against Jimmy Coleman. A rod inserted into a broken femur bone had cracked, and it killed Robert's client. Robert told the jury the case was about a defective metal rod, but Jimmy kept calling it a "medical malpractice case." Every time he said it, Robert winced. And after the jurors had listened to the word "medical" several hundred times, they gave the verdict to Jimmy—in honor of all the poor doctors who are targets of all those frivolous malpractice suits that everybody hears about.

With that, Robert had three heartbreakers in a row. Now, he needed a win in a big case, the same way a movie star who has a series of flops wants a blockbuster at the box office to get back on top.

At times he felt desperate, like a failure. Would he ever get a rematch with Jimmy Coleman? He had more money than he could ever spend, but the question was, could he keep on doing a good job for his clients? Deep down, he was afraid of the answer.

And then, he forced himself to look at the positive side. He was *going* to handle the propane truck case. He was determined. There was nobody else who could do a better job of representing the propane truck plaintiffs. He had spent a lifetime preparing himself for it. He wanted that case. In fact, he needed it. He turned to look out the window again. The spike of the Transco Tower stuck out of the ground like a blackened tooth to help mark the site of the disaster.

Back at the Baptist Hospital, the sanitary corridor where the burned child lay was bustling with activity. But outside it, there was an eerie quiet. Just beyond the double doors at the end of the hall, the man named Esparza found a hospital telephone. And from the worn business card, he dialed the number of a hard-luck lawyer named "Icky" Snopes, who advertised prominently in the yellow pages.

Esparza knew he needed to get a real attorney very quickly to handle Pedro and Angela Gutierrez's lawsuit.

The secretary put him through to Icky Snopes, Counselor at Law. Esparza had wondered about that name, "Icky," and how Icky Snopes had gotten it, because it sure was a strange name for a lawyer. Maybe it was because Icky always was sort of scuffy and dirty. But right now, that didn't matter. Not after Esparza had signed up Pedro Gutierrez as a client.

Icky's voice wobbled when he answered. "Hello?"

"Icky? That you? Listen. I got it, man." Esparza was buoyant. "I got this propane truck case signed up. You remember what we talked about? Well, we can do business right now, if you can get Herrick on board like you promised."

"Hold on," said Icky-the-Yellow-Pages-Lawyer. "I'll call Herrick on the other line."

There was a pause. A long pause, while Icky Snopes telephoned Robert Herrick.

And when Icky finally came back on the line, he was excited, too. "I don't quite know why, but this time Herrick said yes, he'll take your case for Pedro Gutierrez! He doesn't know that an illegal case runner is involved. And I sure as hell didn't make a point of telling him about you, Esparza."

"He said yes? You mean, Robert Herrick said yes?"

"I went to law school with Herrick." Icky sounded inordinately proud of that fact. "Sat next to him in all our first-year classes. And yes, he's gonna handle the propane truck case. Not only does he want the case, but I think he's doing it partly 'cause of me. We go way back, man."

Icky was just a go-between, because Esparza didn't dare call Herrick directly. In fact, Icky's role was just to sanitize the deal. It was best if Herrick never suspected that Esparza was involved. So, let Icky bask in glory, it didn't matter.

Esparza let out a whoop. Herrick's involvement would mean that the case would be worth twice as much money as with any other lawyer in town. He put the phone back on the hook and stuck his fist in the air.

The deal was done.

"*Hola, enano!*" he heard a voice say behind him. "Hello, shrimp!"

Esparza flashed the misshapen gold cylinder. "*Hola,* Tommy," he answered.

Then he added: "Don't bother with this one, Tommy. I already got it locked up."

"Oh, yeah?" Tommy said. "I bet you broke the law and pretended to be a lawyer again, didn't you?"

"Guess," said Esparza. He smiled again. "Anyway, I got this case locked up tighter'n your girlfriend's pussy when you want some action outta her."

"Tell me, *hermano*, little brother. What is making you such a good case runner lately? Have you got the scales of justice printed on those fake lawyer cards you hand out?"

Tommy, like Esparza, had never spent a day in law school, but he made more than two hundred thousand dollars a year. These two case runners were experts at reaching the scene before the ambulance and getting the signature on the dotted line while the tears were still wet in the survivors' eyes. It was illegal. It was as illegal as hell. But it paid well. And it was surprising how often these case runners could command huge fees from marginal lawyers—sometimes even from a few of the well-established lawyers, because they wanted or needed a particular kind of case.

"You got Herrick to take the case?" Tommy was amazed. "Robert Herrick? He's never dealt with a case runner in his life."

"I know. He's got the squeaky-cleanest reputation in town. For some reason, he wants this case real bad. I never met Herrick in person or even talked to him, but I had one of our friendly lawyers named Icky Snopes dangle it in front of him. Only time I ever found a way to crack Herrick's armor."

"Dumbest thing he ever did, dealing with you." Tommy grinned. "Even if he didn't know you were involved, which I'm sure he didn't."

Esparza liked the way Tommy was ragging him. Tommy was envious. "Come on, *hermano*," Esparza said. "I'll buy you a couple shots. I'll buy you the whole bottle. José Cuervo Gold."

Esparza was in a mood to celebrate. "I've peddled this case to the best lawyer in the state, man. He'll make it into a hundred million dollars." The gold tooth flashed even brighter as Esparza's grin widened and he pumped his fist in the air. "I think I just hit the big one!"

Back in the Andrews Burn Center, LaVonda Hall was watching the late movie. It was an Elvis. He was singing "Return to Sender." She had been on duty forever, and she had a minute, now, to sit and rest.

She jumped instinctively when she heard the beeping sound from the monitor. She felt the rush, that involuntary alarm conditioned deep in the body. Run, get the paddles, and try to start that dead, stopped heart again. She actually rose halfway from her chair—but then she sat back down. The name below the flat line was Angela Gutierrez. The little girl with the DNR.

Just past the wall, she knew, the little girl was curled into a fetal position, at least to the extent that her burns would allow it. In hospital slang, the child was "pretzeled." And the life of this small patient hung suspended in the two or three comatose minutes of cardiopulmonary arrest that bridge from shadowy unconsciousness to the brain death criterion, as the line on the EEG scope gradually relaxed under the accelerating weight of anoxic cerebral damage.

But instead of running to her, LaVonda Hall sat still. And then she slowly called for an orderly. Wrapped in artificial skin, and attached to more than a dozen pieces of technology, the tiny, charred lump that once had been a ten-year-old girl named Angela Gutierrez finally was dead.

7
THE KIDS

You pretended you were what? A supreme court justice?" Wendy Bachman frowned over her keyboard. "Oh, yeah, sure, Maria. That's funny as shit. Pardon me, but isn't there some kind of crime called 'impersonating a judge'?"

"Well—it's called 'Impersonating a Public Servant.' Penal Code thirty-seven-eleven." Maria suddenly was uncomfortable. "But it's *not* a crime, unless you intend to make the other person 'submit to your authority!' As I recall, that's the exact words."

"Just the same, Maria—fuckin' A! Don't you think it's stupid, you being an assistant D.A., calling somebody up and pretending you're a judge?"

"Of all the secretaries in the entire D.A.'s office, Wendy, you are the one with the foulest mouth." Maria laughed. "And it's ironic that you also are the one with the strictest morals. You've got that big-print *Bible* on your desk, alongside the *Book of Mormon*, but Wendy, yesterday I saw you reading a *Playgirl* magazine, and so Wendy, don't start in on me."

Wendy laughed, too. "But come on, Maria. There's a difference. Me, all I do is cuss and occasionally flip through *Playgirl*. You, you're a prosecutor. And you can't afford to be involved in these crazy pranks you're always pulling. Some day, somebody on the other end of the line's going to take it the wrong way and call the cops."

She wagged her finger. "And then, Maria, guess what the district attorney's going to do. He's gonna fire your ass."

Maria thought about that for a moment. "Hmmm."

"Listen." Wendy's voice was softer. "You know the reason I'm telling you this. It's because I care about you." Then, just as suddenly, she spoke louder. "It's not the Mormon in me, Maria, it's the friend in me. Listen to this admittedly foul mouth! You keep pretending you're some kind of friggin' actress, and you're gonna get your ass in big-time trouble."

Wendy was very pretty, with blonde hair and innocent features. She looked impossibly young, being just over five feet tall, and it was incongruous to listen to her profanity.

"You're right, of course." Maria pursed her lips. "That's why I appreciate having you to talk to." Then: "Wendy, you're absolutely right! Sometimes I forget I have to act differently as an assistant D.A. than I did in Las Vegas."

It was a huge difference, she thought to herself. She certainly did have an unusual background for an assistant D.A.—so unusual, in fact, that the newspapers had done feature stories about her. One of the articles, which forever embarrassed her, even had a picture. There she had been, right there in the newspaper, smiling coyly from behind a mountain of red hair, feathers, faux pearls, bare shoulders, and blue and mauve and rose eye shadow. The caption had only made it worse: "Maria Melendes, The Showgirl Who Turned Assistant District Attorney." It was all Maria could do to convince her chuckling co-workers that her show had been suitable for families. "We were like the Rockettes," she had found herself protesting.

Now, she thought a moment more about what Wendy had said. This wasn't Las Vegas, and it was easy for an assistant D.A. to violate the unwritten rules.

But then, plaintively, Maria blurted it out. "Look, Wendy, all I was trying to do was get my boyfriend off the phone."

"Sure. And I'm just waiting for you to say, 'I'm a red-headed Cuban.' Frankly, Maria, you use that 'I'm a Cuban' bullshit too often. What if I answered everything by saying, 'I'm a hotblooded Mormon!'?"

"Okay. *Okay!*"

There was a pause. And then, at last, Wendy was a fraction more conciliatory. "Well, I don't want to make it sound like the end of the world."

"No, but you're right. I've gotten into trouble before by having a big mouth."

"Haven't we all," Wendy admitted.

They both stared at the walls, which in the D.A.'s building were a musty milk-white and bare of any pictures. Odd vestibules and halls that went nowhere, sealed-off doors, and mottled brown carpet that sometimes ended in the middle of a corridor—it was that kind of building, a county government building.

"Not to change the subject," Wendy said finally. "Just how is your guy, that famous Robert Herrick, when you get him away from the phone? You know what I mean. Is he any good?"

Maria smiled. "He is *sensational.*" She turned and looked directly at Wendy. "And it's wonderful, because yes, first of all, he's fantastic in the way you're thinking about in that devious mind of yours, Wendy. But that's not all, because—get this—in the second place, he also is worthwhile afterwards. I mean, this is rare. He even is worthwhile outside of the bedroom. And I don't know how you feel, but far as I'm concerned, you can't expect that from the average guy."

"Tell me about it." Wendy was trapped in a depressing marriage with no prospect that her beliefs would permit it to end except by death. Maria knew what she was thinking. Wendy's husband wasn't abusive, but all he ever did was get drunk and race his boat.

"Anyway." Maria's voice was uncertain. "Tonight is a big night for me and my famous guy, Robert. I've met both of his kids, and I get along with them okay. But tonight, I have a command performance, and—well, I don't mean to get overly dramatic, but I'm invited home with both his kids, and his mother."

"His kids? What are they? Girls? Boys?"

"One of each. There's Pepper Herrick. She's the oldest. And 'Pepper' is definitely the name. Call her 'Cynthia' and you're in trouble. Pepper and I went to see the Rolling Stones together. That kid spent the whole three hours talking about what a 'bitchin' body' Mick Jagger had, and his tight trousers. But actually, once you get through the teenage attitude, Pepper's really kind of sweet. Then, there's Robbie. That's Robert Junior, and he's his daddy's little boy."

Maria hesitated. "And also, there's Rosalie. And I'm nervous, because I've never met Rosalie."

"Who's Rosalie?"

Maria rolled her eyes. "Robert's mother."

"Oh."

"Right. It's been a long time since I had to go home and meet my boyfriend's mother." She got up to walk back into her office. "Life is such a strange adventure!"

"Tell me about it," Wendy murmured again. And with that, she turned back to keyboarding a brief that she and Maria both hoped would persuade the federal court of appeals, next week, to permit the lethal injection of a serial killer.

"The pictures of these six dead women—I mean, I've never seen anything like it." Wendy wrinkled her nose as she started typing. "Holy shit, Maria! You've *got* to get this charmer off the streets. Permanently!"

That evening, Robert made trout almondine with au gratin potatoes and artichokes. Alone with him in the kitchen for a moment, Maria was amazed. "Where'd you learn to do that? Was it when you worked at that garage in Rhode Island?"

Robert just laughed. He had told her about his teenage years in Providence when he lived alone with his mother and he'd had to work at a body shop to make ends meet.

"I know," she went on. "You learned it at Harvard." He had gone there on a scholarship.

"No. I didn't have time to do much at Harvard except study. I worked nights so I'd have a little spending money."

"Where, then?"

"In Vietnam." He smiled and shook his head. "Most of the time I was a platoon leader, but between search-and-destroy missions, I was stationed at Da Nang. They drafted me from law school to make me into . . . a cook."

She almost couldn't stop laughing. "But it's not very macho, what with you baking a soufflé and all!"

"Right. Think you can handle it?"

"Definitely. I think I'm gonna give up ever going out again with Cuban guys. Too macho, and some of 'em have a lousy attitude toward women. I'm gonna go for the Cuisinart type, instead. Like you, sweetheart."

He laughed. And they went in to join the others.

Later, after dinner with the Herrick household, everyone adjourned to the family room, and seven-year-old Robbie glued his eyes to the television. He didn't look up from the football game for anything—until he found out that Maria was willing and able to answer his questions.

"See, Robbie, that's what they call a post pattern." She pointed. "The receiver runs straight down the field and then angles in toward the middle.

Toward the post—you know, the goal post. It's hard to make it work, though, if they've got both safeties back. Unless you can split them."

It was the Forty-Niners against the Cowboys on Monday Night Football, and the crowd roar almost drowned out the play-by-play.

"What was it that you called the other pass pattern, the one the Forty-Niners just did?" Robbie was treating Maria like a visiting professor.

"A flag pattern. Same thing, except the receiver angles toward the outside. The opposite way. And the reason it's called a flag pattern, Robbie, is because the guy runs toward the little flag that marks the corner of the field. It's harder for the other team to double-cover him. And it depends on who's throwing, but some people think there's less chance of an interception."

Now it was Robert's turn to be amazed. "Where'd you learn that kind of stuff?"

"Same twists of fate that taught you how to bake a soufflé, probably," Maria laughed. "But Robert, dear, I hate to tell you, you look pretty corny in that 'Kiss the Cook' apron."

"I know. One of my clients gave it to me." He put his boots, handmade with his initials on them, up on the coffee table, as Rosalie frowned. "Some of my clients are grateful but strange, and I never got around to buying a more 'with-it' apron."

"I guess you're 'with it' for a parent," said Pepper Herrick impassively. And everybody laughed except Pepper, who, being fifteen, looked as though she couldn't tell what was all that funny.

And so she added, "Just like Grandma is 'with it' for a grandparent!" hoping everyone would be amused again. But this time no one laughed, and Pepper looked disappointed.

"Speaking of which," said Grandma Rosalie in an effort at graceful transition, "how on earth did you get to be so 'with it' in the United States, Maria, when you came from a different language, different rules, and a whole different country?"

"Her father believed in the total immersion theory of education," Robert volunteered.

At that, Maria's eyes watered imperceptibly, remembering the day her family had washed up on the Florida shore. Dr. Jorgé Melendes had been the respected Director-General of the Hospital at Miramar, until he got crosswise of the communists' national health administration. As soon as he could bribe his way out of Castro's jails, Dr. Melendes had gotten his wife and children out of Cuba. Maria had been twelve and didn't speak a word of English. Such an awful, frightening time!

"Not only that." She smiled and shook her head. "What my father believed in—if you don't mind one more reference to football—was the Vince Lombardi theory of education. Failure at anything was . . . well, it wasn't permitted. And anything less than the best, even second place, was the same thing as failure."

Grandma Rosalie was fascinated. "How do you mean?"

"Well, I remember every time I got a B on my report card, which ought to be considered pretty good, right? Well, he would ask for a full explanation of why it wasn't an A. He would say, in Spanish, 'I've worked too hard all my life to be raising any spoiled kids.' And then he would repeat the same thing in English."

"Hear that, Pepper?" Robert wasn't going to miss this chance. "This is Vince Lombardi speaking. I ain't raising no spoiled kids."

This time the remark struck a spot deep in Pepper's teenage funny bone, and she almost couldn't stop laughing. Except to say, "Daddy, that's so-o-o-o ridiculous!"

"Anyway," Rosalie said after a pause, "your parents wanted you to get absorbed in the melting pot?"

"Not at all." Maria's answer was quick. "We all went through such a—well, such a wrenching transformation that we held on to anything from the old country. I think it was hardest on my mother. She was a proud society lady, and suddenly she's working in places like laundries and hotels. And she would do anything that took her mind back to Cuba. She'd bet on the jai alai games, shop in the open air markets, and most of all, give money to any group that worked for Cuba Libré."

She smiled, and her eyes were shining. "Whenever my parents disapproved of anything they saw in America, they always had a standard line. 'It wasn't that way in Cuba.' They drummed it into me. 'That is where you came from, and you owe respect.'"

The television set roared, again, in response to a Cowboy touchdown.

"I wonder," Robert thought, as he listened to Maria. "She is so *different* from me! Maybe these are healthy differences, but she's pretty opinionated. Me, I'm set in my ways. Used to things as they are. And I don't know that I could change."

He glanced at her: the long, fluffy corkscrews of dusky sunset hair; the big hazel eyes, so shiny and liquid; the near-translucent Hispanic skin, pale and clear, that merged playfully with the light; the soft cheekbones, a shade more rose-colored than the rest; the perfect full lips—

And he wasn't aware that he was staring, until suddenly, Maria looked back at him and smiled, in a way that made the room feel warmer. And made his stomach feel as though there was a puddle in it.

"Where'd you two meet?" Rosalie asked suddenly.

"Well, I hate to tell you this." Maria's eyes were mischievous. "It was in a bar."

"Come on!" Robert laughed in spite of himself. "It was at one of those bar association functions, which happened to be at the downtown Bennigan's."

"Well." Rosalie was having a good time with this. "What did he say to you, Maria, that impressed you so much?"

"Nothing. He just walked up and said, 'Hi. Who are you?'"

"Oh. The direct approach."

"I guess! And he looked first at my ankles, then up at my face, then back down to the ankles again. I don't think he knew he was doing it. Conditioned reflex."

"Okay, Maria, that's enough!" Robert wanted to stop this before she crossed the line. But he had to laugh.

Robbie didn't hear any of it. He was watching football. But Pepper wore an amused fifteen-year-old smile as she said, "Daddy, I'm proud. I didn't know you had it in you."

And at that, they all laughed. But Robert laughed with the puddle still there in his stomach.

8
SQUINT

Don't you think I look just like Clark Gable driving this baby?" asked Robert as he eased his burgundy-colored Duesenberg out of the parking space.

"Yes, but don't get too carried away with Hollywood stuff and drive it off the overpass," Tom Kennedy kidded. "We're supposed to inspect the site, not do a re-enactment."

Robert laughed. "Well, anyway, old Clark had a Duesenberg just like this. He used to cruise up to the set while they were making *Gone with the Wind*, and he had a scarf that matched the color of the car." Robert steered toward the down ramp in the Texas Commerce Garage. "But okay—I'll try not to get too flamboyant on top of the overpass."

The bulging, curved hood of the Duesenberg seemed to go on forever. Underneath it, twelve cylinders stroked in perfect synchronization. It was expensive to keep this car tuned right, but when it was, the twelve cylinders sounded so much better than six. They blended in a purr that was louder and yet lower-pitched, and to Robert far more satisfying, than any of his seventeen other cars, from the Testarossa to the '38 Packard.

"I know you've got a whole bunch of other cars," Kennedy said as they started down the exit ramp.

"I've added on to my garage three times," Robert agreed. "That building costs a fortune. It's got better temperature and humidity controls than you'd have in a wine cellar."

His 1931 Stutz had a fold-down windshield and a genuine rumble seat. The 1930 Bentley was the favorite of James Bond, Agent .007, and Robert had one that was dark green. His 1930 Cadillac had an incredible total of sixteen cylinders that warbled like a bird, but got eight miles to the gallon. Robert usually wasn't ostentatious. In fact, sometimes he was reluctant to spend money even for small luxuries because he didn't want to act like the rich and powerful people he disliked. But these beautiful old cars were something else. "After my two kids," he confided to Kennedy, "I guess they're my biggest indulgence."

The Duesenberg was approaching the first floor. The guard who waved for them to slow down was a new employee. His gray shirt was dark and unfaded, and his policeman's hat was crisp.

"I guess my favorite, believe it or not, is my 1963 Lincoln Continental," Robert went on. "I don't drive it much. What's fun is to watch the convertible top go up and down."

The security guard seemed to have a bad eye, and as he looked over his shoulder, the one with the "Rowland Security" patch, his face was tightly knotted into a permanent squint.

Something was wrong, terribly wrong, but Robert couldn't put his finger on it.

"Anyway," he continued, "I'll show you how the Continental's top works sometime, Tom. You won't believe it. First, this flap comes up, and these two screws come out and start twirling, and they push out the ragtop, and then they retract, and . . . AND . . . LOOK OUT!"

He pushed Kennedy hard, down and to the side, at the same time that the squinting security guard lifted the muzzle of his gun. Instantly, Robert recognized the distinctive clip and barrel. It was an AK-47. All too familiar, from his time in the Mekong Delta of Vietnam. The guard fired, and the windshield shattered. The machine-gun spray told Robert that the weapon had been modified to fully automatic. Suddenly, there was a spidery hole in the glass precisely in front of the place where Tom Kennedy's head had been. The fusillade smacked against the burgundy doors and trailed back along the sides.

For once, as he slammed the accelerator down, Robert was glad about the obsessive pride that made him keep the Duesenberg in perfect condition. The security guard pivoted and fanned bullets across the back of the bulging fenders. Steering from barely above the seat, Robert spun the wheel hard to the left. The right-side tires screamed as he entered the street. The guard's AK-47 made a pincushion of the trunk and sent bullets through the windshield, this time in the other direction.

The Duesenberg roared through the intersection against a red light, but Robert ignored the hard-button horns of the oncoming traffic. Seconds later, he stepped on the brakes in front of the bank building. He yelled "Come on!" to Kennedy and started running for the bank lobby. The Duesenberg had traversed only two half-blocks, and it was dangerous to stop here, but Robert Herrick hadn't gotten where he was by always playing it safe. And right now, he wanted to catch the squinting security guard.

"You're bleeding," said the bank guard who sat at the lobby desk. Robert looked down. A perfect round hole split the pinstripes in his jacket just below the shoulder. He hadn't noticed the bullet that had gone through his arm.

And he didn't want to notice, now. The words tumbled out as he told the bank guard about Squint. The man couldn't have gotten far!

But the bank guard refused to budge from his desk. "What we do in a case like this," he explained calmly, "is to call the police." The bank's policy was for guards to avoid seeking out encounters with armed individuals, and they were under strict orders not to pursue anyone for any reason. "The bank is like everyone else," the guard said, while he dialed the Houston Police Department. "The Board of Directors doesn't want to encourage lawsuits."

When the ambulance arrived, Robert protested. "It's only a scratch." But he finally got in it. He protested even more when the emergency room doctors insisted on admitting him to the hospital and ordered him, firmly, to ride to his room in a wheelchair. A gunshot wound is a nasty thing, they explained. It is easily given to infection, vulnerable to anaerobic bacteria, contaminated by powder, abraded by the searing heat of the bullet, and complicated by embolism of the structures underneath. Robert surrendered.

But when he arrived at his room in the wheelchair to find Maria waiting for him, and she made a fuss over him, he wished he had protested more effectively. "Tom Kennedy called me," she said. "My poor sweetheart! You have to be in a wheelchair?" Her hands went up to her face. "My God! Where *is* it that you got shot?"

And even after that concern was clarified to her satisfaction, Maria still was amazed by the story of Squint and the AK-47. "The guy was a security guard?"

"Well, obviously, he wasn't a real one."

"But I mean, he went to all the trouble to dress up like a security guard. Why?"

"I don't know," Robert admitted. "Who knows why people do things these days? They go to the courthouse armed with automatic pistols and shoot strangers just because they happen to be there. Remember that nut in San Francisco who went up and down that law firm and shot everybody in sight? This guy who shot at me may have just been some kind of nut, too."

But in his heart, he knew it wasn't true. It wasn't a random act. That was the point of Maria's question. And as much as he wanted to reassure her, they both knew he still was in danger. Long after Maria left, he sat quietly and wondered about it. Why did someone want to kill him? And who?

There was a knock at the door. "Good afternoon, Mister Herrick. I'm Detective Derrigan Slaughter," said a huge, courtly African-American officer. He had on a perfectly fitted gray double-breasted suit with a fine blue stripe and a dark blue solid tie, below a carefully trimmed full beard. "And this here is my partner, Detective Donnie Cashdollar."

He gestured toward his partner, who was almost a foot shorter. Cashdollar wore an ill-fitting combination of a light green jacket, a pink shirt with gray stripes, a flower-and-grape-leaf tie, and brown polyester pants. "We're from Homicide," Detective Cashdollar added unnecessarily.

Robert had the good sense not to say out loud what he was thinking, which was: "Well, I certainly can see why a Detective called 'Slaughter' belongs in the Homicide Division. But with a name like 'Cashdollar,' the other guy really ought to transfer to Forgery!" Instead of saying it, he smiled a tiny smile. What a pair!

Detective Slaughter got right down to business. "Please look at this here letter." He held out a transparent evidence bag that had a piece of white paper inside. The envelope it came in was also inside the same clear plastic bag.

"About an hour after you got shot at," Detective Cashdollar explained, "the dispatcher got a call from a Ms. Donna de Carlo. Your secretary. She was all in a panic. Told us this letter showed up on the floor in your waiting room, an' nobody saw who left it."

The paper was dead white. No color in it at all. It had two short lines of jagged words pasted on it in uneven black letters, cut from some printed page like a newspaper. Robert stared at the bumpy print:

StAY awAY

from MAXXCO sHYsTer

The envelope was blank except for two words, "RoBert hERRick," pasted together the same way.

Robert was slow to answer. "I thought they only did this kind of thing in the movies."

"It's pretty smart, actually," Detective Slaughter answered. "Guy didn't want to write it by hand, and he knew he shouldn't use a typewriter, 'cause that's even easier for a documents examiner to trace than it is to identify handwriting. No, our suspect is more eee-lusive than that. If he uses cut-outs from the *Wall Street Journal*, he figures there are several million other people who had access to that same criminal instrument."

"And so anyway, there's no way for you to recognize the type," Cashdollar said. "We just want to know if there's anything in it that you do recognize. A particular word that somebody's used before in your presence? The paper? The syntax?"

Robert was almost amused by that. "Not much to go on, as far as syntax is concerned."

Then, the two detectives took down Robert's statement about Squint and the AK-47. They promised to have an artist come by and draw the suspect. "But don't expect miracles from that," Robert said. "I was way down in the seat. I mean, way down. All I remember is his squint."

"Well, that's too bad, 'cause nobody else saw the guy, neither." Detective Slaughter shook his head. "We been all over that parking garage, and everybody says they saw a security guard. But they can't describe him, and they didn't notice where he went. I'd imagine that's what our suspect had in mind. A guy dressed like a security guard isn't suspicious, even when he's carryin' one a them AK-47's."

"Holy shit, Maria! Somebody *shot* him?" Wendy Bachman's voice sounded astonished and frightened as it came through the pay phone in the hospital lobby.

"Yes. Yes!"

"You're . . . crying. Maria, I–I . . . I'm really sorry."

"I know. Thanks. It . . . took a real effort to. . . keep from getting upset when I visited him. But I figured it was important to stay calm. Important to Robert, that is. So I did manage to stay calm. Cheerful. Upbeat, you know?"

"It's that Cuban discipline. You've got more self-control than anybody. But what about Robert? He's okay, isn't he?"

"Oh, I think so . . . this time. The real problem is, what about next time? As long as he's involved in this propane truck case, he's bound to be targeted for assassination again! I've got to persuade him to get out of it."

"Wait a minute, Maria. Why does it have to be you who persuades him to get out of it?"

"I really love the big dope." Maria was struggling not to cry again. "I'm crazy about him, and I know he's going to get shot again. But he is a big dope, and he's stubborn."

"Guys are like that." Wendy was philosophical. "Sad thing is, the ones that are most worthwhile, seems like they're the ones that are the most stubborn."

"He doesn't even hear it when I talk to him about the propane truck case. I've got to find some other way."

"Maria, be careful. You're going to get your ass in trouble." Wendy didn't like where this conversation was going. She could almost hear Maria thinking on the other end of the line about indirect ways to get Robert to do what she wanted. "Maria, you asked me about Johnny Ray Garrison. Brief's gonna be due next week in the district court."

"I know." The change in Maria was instantaneous. This was business, and Johnny Ray Garrison's case was the worst robbery-murder she'd ever seen.

"Johnny Ray's lawyers screwed up the way they challenged the jury instructions in the state courts," Wendy said matter-of-factly. "It's time for a decision. Do you want to let them challenge it again in the federal courts, or do you want to shove that mistake up that rat-fucker's ass?"

"No." Maria was thinking hard, now. "Insisting on correct procedure is one thing, but using technicalities is another. A prosecutor in a death penalty case can't ever afford to be that heavy-handed. Even if Johnny Ray Garrison deserves his sentence, I want to get there by letting the defense lawyers have their say."

She paused. "I'm still worried about Robert. I wonder what else I can do to keep him from getting killed?"

Wendy's voice was flat. "Whatever method of persuasion you use, Maria, just try not to mess up his life any worse than it already is."

The detectives had been in Robert's hospital room for almost an hour and a half. Still, they talked on. And suddenly, the telephone rang. "This is Carmelita Bueno from the governor's office," said the confident, patrician voice at the other end of the line. "Will you hold, please, for the governor?"

There was a pause, and then the voice of the Governor of Texas came over the telephone. "Robert? Robert Herrick? You doing okay?" The voice was powerful, but the familiar twang was tinged with concern and, at the same time, with a touch of humor. "I don't like having people shoot at any of my constituents, much less one of my biggest contributors."

Robert smiled. "Hello, Governor. I'm doing fine."

"That's good, because you and me go way back, Robert. There aren't that many Democrats out there raising big money for my re-election, like you are."

"Thanks—I think!" He laughed.

The governor suddenly was serious. "I've talked to Colonel Neavitt over at the Texas Department of Public Safety. And I've asked him to see that you have somebody from DPS providing you with security from now on. He figures two DPS officers at a time."

"But, Governor—"

"Now, please don't argue, Robert. They tell me you're working on this propane truck case. Good. I'm just like everybody else in Texas. I want you to get to the bottom of that case. But also I want to be sure you stay in one piece until that case is over. You take good care of yourself, now, you hear?"

And then, a moment later, the governor was gone.

Robert looked dazed. "Two officers? That sounds a little extreme. With three shifts, that's six DPS officers a day. Counting weekends and holidays, the governor's talking about tying up eight, maybe ten DPS officers a week. And it might be a long time before this propane truck case is over."

"Yeah," said Derrigan Slaughter, "but if I was you, I'd take the man up on it."

His partner continued the train of thought from there. "This Squint, he's determined enough to wear a authentic, highly realistic security guard costume. He's sportin' an AK-47, which it happens he managed to get modified into a machine gun. He leaves you a note made out of letters cut out of a newspaper sayin' he don't want you handling this case." Here, Detective Cashdollar paused and frowned before going on. "And I don't know you that well yet, Mister Herrick, but somehow I sense that you're not prudent enough to take Squint's advice and stay off the case."

And then Detective Slaughter finished the thought. "What Detective Cashdollar is trying to say, Mister Herrick, is this. Squint, and whoever else is working with him—they ain't finished." He hesitated. And then, he said it. "Old Squint and his pals—they prob'ly gonna try to kill you again."

9
ICKY SNOPES

cky" Snopes's real name was Clarence. But during his first year in law school, he'd answered a question in torts class by saying, "Well, Professor, I didn't read the case you assigned in the book. But I remember, when I was a kid, I read a story about this guy named Ichabod Crane . . ." Immediately, a chorus of catcalls and laughter had interrupted whatever misguided literary allusion young Clarence Snopes had intended as an evasion of the professor's inquiry, and from that day forward, his classmates called him "Ichabod"—which they soon shortened to "Icky." It fit, since Icky's cutoff jeans were greasy, his grooming was unkempt, and his hygiene never was anything to write home about.

Icky bet the football games with a great deal more diligence than he read his torts and contracts. At times he beat the point spread, and that was when he'd had the wherewithal to discover cocaine. He got through law school by complaining to softheaded professors and persuading them to fudge his grades, and in his senior year, with a bleary smile, he bragged to his more studious comrades, "Without me to be the anchor-man, all of you would've graduated with a lot lower class rank." He got his first job in the city attorney's office, trying traffic ticket cases. He lost it nine months later when he went on a coke binge and didn't show up at work for a week.

But the strangest thing about Icky, everybody thought, was his friendship with Robert Herrick. Robert had laughed harder than anyone in the entire first year class at the Ichabod Crane remark, but he took it for what it was—a sign of Icky's insecurity. He befriended Icky. He actually managed to like him, and the two often drank beer at Grace's Bar late at night, after Herrick had finished studying and Icky had finished God knows what. They ended up in the same study group. Both were delighted when Robert got all A's, but disappointed that Icky got C's and D's. Icky wasn't stupid, just not very focused. After he got into doing drugs, skipping classes to sit through triple-feature movies, and lying about his grandmother's funeral to cover his absences from exams, he and Robert finally drifted apart.

These days, Icky operated out of a one-room office at the edge of downtown, in the ramshackle buildings where the rent was lowest. He occupied it irregularly. Twenty years after law school, he got by on fees from case runners like Esparza, among other sometime sources of income.

And even his own mother called him "Icky."

To prepare himself for today's most unpleasant task, Icky Snopes opened a small envelope of white powder over the dirty glass on top of his desk. He spread it with a chewed-up ball-point pen that said, "Hotel Nevada: On the Strip." Then, he bent over, drew the cutoff plastic straw to his nose and inhaled. He was depressed, and he needed to feel a little more "up." Actually, he admitted to himself, he needed the coke to feel normal again. He was about to call Robert Herrick. The guy had always been a loyal friend in the past, even when Icky had screwed up, and maybe he'd understand this time, even though Icky had screwed up royally.

The ringing noise in the phone receiver sounded like those faraway warning bells in the ship channel. The woman who answered in Herrick's office had to say, "How may I help you?" three different times, before Icky finally told her. But then, at last, he heard Herrick's voice, "Hello? Icky?" sounding warm and pleasant, but foggy and distant, like an echo from the other end of a tunnel.

"Yeah. It's me. Icky."

"Hello there, stranger! How's business? Have you hit it big yet with any of your cases?"

"Just barely edgin' by." Icky hesitated. He knew Robert wouldn't take it well if he acted like he was wired on coke. He tried to concentrate on speaking slow-ly-and-dis-tinct-ly.

"So what's up?"

"You remember that propane truck case I sent you?"

"Yes. You're in it, too. We wrote you in as 'of counsel.' And I'm sorry, old buddy. In the suit papers, we put your name down as Clarence, not Ichabod."

They both laughed. The first year in law school had been like boot camp in the Marines. It had formed an unbreakable bond. This odd couple would always be friends, no matter the distance between them.

But at this point, Icky knew it was time to get down to business.

"There's a problem, Herrick." He was afraid he'd said it much too abruptly.

"Why?" Robert still sounded pleasant. "What's the problem?"

"That propane truck case came to me through a case runner. I never told you, but that's the fact. Now it's time to ante up. They been after me. There's this crazy-ass outlaw, name of Esparza, for one, and there's also another guy named Tommy who's helping him collect. I got to pay their fee. Esparza's case runner fee. And Herrick, I ain't got it."

"Icky." Herrick's mind was spinning. "Icky, you mean you got me involved in a case with a case runner? Without even telling me you were breaking the law? Icky, tell me the truth. Are you messed up again?"

"Oh, no, no! No drugs, no more. I'm *never* doin' that shit again." Bright colors flashed in front of Icky's eyes as he said it, and he struggled harder to make his voice sound straight. "But anyway, Herrick, I'm ass deep in trouble. It's twenty-five grand to me. And those guys, if I don't come up with the dinero, those guys, if I don't—if I don't produce—"

There was a pause.

"Icky! Now, listen, Icky!" Robert was becoming more concerned by the moment. "We've already signed up Angela Gutierrez's family as clients in the propane truck case. And through that, we've gotten cases from a whole lot of other families, too. My law firm's got a *contract* that obligates us to all of these clients! I'd like to be able to go back to the beginning and refuse all the cases if there's a runner involved, but it's too late for us to do that!"

"No shit, Sherlock." Icky sounded irritated, as if he thought Herrick was unreasonably slow to grasp this everyday situation. "Of course it's too late! For one thing, if I'm not real prompt about payin' the twenty-five grand I owe Esparza, you're gonna read about me bein' found in my car trunk, with my epidermal layer a whole lot less intact and unblemished than I'd like to keep it. So here's the deal: I need you to pay me the twenty-five bills so I can pay this runner what I owe him."

"No. I'm not getting mixed up in paying a case runner. I've never dealt with those kinds of people." Robert knew about runners from his term as president of the bar association. They lied routinely, pretended to be lawyers, left unsuspecting "clients" high and dry if they couldn't shop the case, and defrauded their marks at their most vulnerable moments.

"It's my ass, if you don't." Icky's voice was becoming louder and louder, and now it was beginning to sound desperate. "I'm going to end up stuffed inside a refrigerator. Or mailed to your office in multiple containers!"

"Listen, Icky, just slow down. There's got to be a sensible way to resolve this."

But really, there wasn't. Herrick's mind did flip-flops as he considered his options. He could ignore this telephone call, but that option was unattractive because Icky might do something crazy, and besides, Icky was right. The case runners might do something unpleasant to Icky. Another option was that Robert could hang up and call the bar association, and that sounded like a tempting choice, perhaps—until you considered that it might hurt all of the firm's clients in the propane truck case. That, of course, was unthinkable. And then, too, if Icky did end up skewered and stuffed in his car, Herrick would never forgive himself. Finally, there was the option of doing what Icky was asking for, giving him the twenty-five thousand dollars. But that wasn't a very good idea either, since Icky was just as likely to blow all the money at the horse races or use it to buy coke as he was to pay it to the case runner to save his own life.

"Icky, how'd you manage to get me into this mess?" Robert's voice was weary, because he knew the answer. This mess had happened because of his own misplaced faith in human redemption, the unearned faith that he had lavished on his nonconformist law school friend. Robert had never been judgmental about other people's flaws. Sometimes it was a blessing, such as the many occasions when his clients repaid him with simple, pure affection for overlooking their human frailties. At other times, like this one with Icky, it was disastrous.

Anyway, it didn't matter much why it had happened, because by this time, Robert had figured out what he had to do. Unfortunately, he knew it only too well. It was risky, and technically was wrong, but it also was the only choice that had any prospect of coming out right in the end.

Icky heard the change in Robert's voice, and he knew that his friend was going to rescue him. "Thanks, old buddy," he said with smarmy enthusiasm. "I knew I could count on you."

Robert shut his eyes to the blue and green sunlit view outside his office, and silently, he shook his head.

10
BOOKER & BAYNE

The boxy secretarial bays in the law firm of Booker & Bayne stretched down the hall as far as the eye could see. They were made of white birch. The firm had gotten all of the matched veneers for its ten floors of offices from a single growth of this prized wood in Vermont.

The founder of Booker & Bayne, almost a century ago, in 1897, had been Colonel Henry Anderson Booker. Colonel Booker was a confidant of governors and presidents. He kept a spitoon in his office and wore striped suspenders. "The Colonel" had put together the financing to build all of River Oaks, he had qualified the bonds that dredged the Houston Ship Channel, and he even had represented the city council when the Astrodome was built. Every time a client wanted to do a shady deal, The Colonel was famous for asking the question: "Yes, but is it *fair?*" After which, Colonel Booker always found a perfectly legal way to do whatever it was that his clients wanted to do—regardless of whether it happened to be fair, or not.

Today, Booker & Bayne still prospered, even though Colonel Booker had long since passed on to that great partners' meeting in the sky. The firm represented General Brands, First Texas Bank, American Petroleum, Habushita, Spinelli, and a thousand more of the world's largest corporations. It had four hundred ninety-three lawyers, all of them blue bloods, and in addition to the original office in Houston, it had offices in New York, Chicago, Los Angeles, Washington, London, Tokyo and Moscow. Booker & Bayne lawyers had long since stopped handling personal injury cases, unless they were mammoth in size. You couldn't possibly make money by charging those piddling little fees, like a hundred and fifty dollars an hour.

But still, today, Booker & Bayne lawyers lived by the Colonel's original formula for success: "Find out what the client wants, and then do whatever it takes!"

If there was any living person at Booker & Bayne who was the successor to the legend of Colonel Henry Anderson Booker, it was Jimmy Coleman. Jimmy had led the team of lawyers that won the biggest judgment in history—over eleven billion dollars—on behalf of Emperor Corporation, in the Emperor-Newcorp litigation. The lawyers had frequently gotten confused in that case, and accidentally said "million," when they meant "billion." But not Jimmy Coleman. It seemed easy for him to think in terms of making the other side lose billions.

Now, as Jimmy Coleman entered through the huge glass doors with the gold-lettered name "Booker & Bayne," he looked with satisfaction down the long rows of white birch. And as he walked briskly down the corridor, Jimmy smiled. He heard the familiar sound of Booker & Bayne lawyers at work.

From behind the door of Jack Compton, the real estate lawyer: ". . . Yes,

Mister Rossi, but that clause isn't going to help the other side if the deed restrictions say they can't build on top of the easement." Jack was on the telephone, trying to work out a deal to buy an office building in Los Angeles for an Italian conglomerate. More importantly, Jack was bringing in four hundred and fifty dollars an hour. Jimmy smiled again.

Next door, there was Brady McLaughlin. A bankruptcy lawyer known for pushing around his opponents. Brady was on the phone, too, and Jimmy heard him yelling: ". . . So you better be thinking about the creditors' committee, right? Because if you piss them off, you're going to get crammed down on till your butt comes over your head!" Jimmy laughed. Brady's opponents didn't always know that his bite was even worse than his bark.

The next door was Martha Peters. An oil and gas lawyer, and also, the first woman to become a partner in this former male bastion. Right now, Martha was dictating a letter: ". . . the termination clause will only allow you to hold forty acres around each well unless you hold the entire lease by production. Even the landowner would be hurt, because this clause would reduce the allowable . . . ." What that meant, in English, was that the deal gave too little acreage to Booker & Bayne's client, and the other side ought to *want* to tear it up and start over—because they had shot themselves in the foot by their own hard trading.

And at that, Jimmy smiled again. He really enjoyed the kind of stab-your-brother-in-the-back lawsuits that came from broken oil and gas deals.

Finally, at the end of the corridor, Jimmy found the last secretarial bay. "Hello, Lisa," he said. "I'm here."

She turned around. "Hello, Jimmy!" She stood up, all six feet of her.

Jimmy Coleman was constantly being kidded by his partners for hiring Lisa Marshall as his secretary. It wasn't because he liked women taller than he was, although he did. Instead, it was because Lisa could type ten error-free pages in ten minutes, juggle all his telephone calls, and keep from panicking when Jimmy started into a new crooked deal.

Jimmy Coleman wasn't particularly tall. In fact, he was just five foot eight. But he seemed taller. "He looks the way a Mafia godfather would look if a Mafia godfather ever became a lawyer," said one of his partners. The huge mane of white hair, combed straight back. The cold gray eyes. A voice like tractor tires scraping on gravel. The pear-shaped body, with a half-dozen chins. And then there were the qualities that made Jimmy Coleman a charismatic leader in the firm—his brainpower, his long hours of hard work, his give-no-quarter litigation skills, and his plain old-fashioned nastiness whenever the occasion called for it.

Lisa said, "I know you want to meet with Jennifer Lowenstein about the newest plan you had for the propane truck case."

"That's right. Find her."

Jimmy walked into the enormous corner office. It was piled a foot deep with mail, but you still could see the intricate handwork of the Italian *intarsiato* desk against the honey-colored wood. The desk and armchairs had been custom made by craftsmen in Venice so that they matched his prized piece of furniture—the seventeenth-century chest, inlaid all over with white trees, green vines and brown flowers that wound around its glittering gold hardware. Two sides of the office were floor-to-ceiling windows that looked out over the Southwest Freeway, where hundreds of cars, forty floors down, inched past the scene of the propane tank disaster.

Jimmy looked through the stack of papers on his desk for a copy of the case memo that he had asked Jennifer Lowenstein to prepare. When he found it, his jaw dropped. "Holy shit!" he said out loud, as he read the opening paragraphs:

PRIVILEGED AND CONFIDENTIAL
ATTORNEY WORK PRODUCT

Booker & Bayne

Office Memorandum

TO: Jimmy Coleman

FROM: Jennifer Lowenstein

SUBJECT: How We Can Choose Which Judge Gets the
           Propane Truck Case

Following your instructions, I hired a private investigator to conduct a clandestine surveillance of the Robert Herrick law firm. We wanted to find out the exact time when they normally make the "daily courthouse run" to file lawsuit papers.

After doing that surveillance, the P.I. says, quote, you can just about set your watch by when Herrick's messenger departs, unquote. Specifically, our P.I. reports that the messenger leaves Herrick's office at three o'clock sharp, every afternoon, and he walks the five blocks to the courthouse in approximately ten minutes, arriving at the Clerk's Office about 3:10 p.m. to file the papers for that day.

Also, based on pretextual interviews with employees of the Herrick firm, the P.I. predicts that Herrick will file the propane truck case this coming Wednesday. Therefore, that is when the propane truck case most likely will be assigned to a judge. The point is, we should make sure our man in the clerk's office is primed and ready to go at all times between three and four o'clock this Wednesday.

This memo should be kept highly confidential. We deliberately invaded attorney-client privileged information under false pretenses, of course. Specifically, our P.I. identified himself, on the phone, as a contract employee of Herrick's own firm, and that is how he was able to get Herrick's people to talk to him.

Jimmy grabbed his telephone and stabbed at the numbers of her extension. Jimmy had always thought Jennifer Lowenstein had an instinct for the jugular. This proved it, and he was satisfied.

"Where is she?" he yelled when Lowenstein's secretary answered. "Okay, well, go to the library and get her! And tell her to get her ass up here on the double!"

Exactly three-and-a-half minutes later, when Jennifer Lowenstein arrived out of breath after taking the stairs from four floors down, Jimmy Coleman was practically beaming with excitement. "How did you do it?" He asked. "How'd you find out when Herrick's going to file? If we can somehow steer his lawsuit to one of the real conservative judges who favors the defendant—like maybe Judge Dexter Medaxas, my former partner—well, then we'll be halfway toward winning the propane truck case!"

"The P.I. called several people in the Herrick firm," Jennifer answered. "Under pretext, of course. Actually—you're going to love this—our P.I. pretended to be one of Herrick's own investigators. Turns out the papers are all drafted, but they want to review them one more time, and that's why they've scheduled it for Wednesday."

"Well, you did a fine job. And you really got me excited."

"I know. You scared the crap out of my secretary. I kept asking her, 'What exactly did Jimmy say?' and she just said, 'I don't know! But he's mad as hell!'"

Jimmy Coleman laughed. "I wasn't mad. Shit, no! I just get my adrenalin pumpin', little lady, when I think about how we're going to beat the system here and win this lawsuit."

Jennifer smiled.

"Anyway, enough of that," said Jimmy Coleman. "I want to talk to you for a minute about how we're going to use this information in the service of our good client, Maxxco."

Jennifer Lowenstein sat up straight. "I'm all ears."

All of the young lawyers wanted to work for Jimmy Coleman, even though they knew they'd wind up working harder, because they also knew they would make huge amounts of money. Jimmy Coleman earned his two-and-a-half-million-a-year draw by being a ferocious trial lawyer, an eighty-hour-a-week worker, and a consummate field general. As the head of the litigation section of the firm, he supervised a group of seventy-five other partners and more than a hundred associates. All busy, all the time.

And so Jennifer Lowenstein valued this opportunity. With her little round gold-rimmed glasses, straight-back hairdo and navy suit, she almost seemed to be standing at attention while sitting in her chair.

Jimmy Coleman stared at the surveillance memo, and his gray eyes narrowed. "If this Wednesday is Herrick's filing day, that means we've got less than two days. There's not a minute to lose, but if we're fast, we can get the propane truck case in front of a judge who's in our pocket."

His voice dropped until it sounded like hailstones falling through a canebrake. "Listen to me very carefully, Jennifer, because we can't afford any mistakes with our man in the clerk's office. And we sure as hell can't afford to get caught. Get in touch with the deputy clerk whose name is on this card. And then, here's what I want you to do next . . . ."

At the very same instant, half a continent away in suburban Virginia, an FBI chemist was logging in a brown evidence envelope. The postmark was from Houston, Texas.

Carefully, the chemist broke the seal that had the sender's signature across it. He recorded the scribbled name in his report. The envelope came from a Houston detective named Derrigan Slaughter. Inside the brown envelope, there was another evidence envelope made of clear plastic. The chemist stared at the jagged, cut-out letters that spelled out the warning: "StAY awAY from MAXXCO sHYsTer."

And then, the chemist's rubber gloves gingerly opened the clear plastic bag. The "sHYsTer" letter, together with a dirty white envelope addressed to "RoBert heRRick," tumbled onto the black slate surface of the laboratory desk.

The chemist's first move was to collect tiny samples of the newsprint from the cut-out letters. He was careful not to remove any of the typeset characters, because another identification specialist would study the type styles and compare them with suspected newspapers ranging from high-tone news sources like the *New York Times* all the way to near-obscene rags such as *Screw Magazine*. Meanwhile, the chemist's task would be to compare the sulfur dioxide bleaching in his tiny samples to known newsprint papers so that he could estimate the age of the newspaper.

But right now, there was another step for the chemist—which actually was a much more important test. He would use a chemical called ninhydrin to try to develop fingerprints from the surface of the paper. Ninhydrin was one of the great inventions of twentieth century criminology.

Few criminals suspect that their fingerprints can be obtained from paper surfaces, and even fewer know that these prints are persistent enough to be developed long afterward—sometimes even after weeks or months. Actually, fingerprints are merely deposits of oil and impurities that conform to the ridges, islands, forks and whorls of human skin. Ninhydrin reacts with the body oils on the paper, but it leaves the paper clear. If there was a fingerprint on this paper, the ninhydrin would turn a bright orange color along the fine ridges of oil, and bring them into view like the engraving of a postage stamp.

The chemist's excitement grew as the orange color sprang out. Here were two prints from the edges of the paper where the suspect had folded it and put it into the envelope. Next, the orange swirls blossomed near the newsprint letters—probably where the suspect had held the paper down while pasting the message. The orange color was beautiful, as beautiful to an investigator as any painting by any artist that ever lived.

Fingerprint experts have a saying: "Finding a usable fingerprint is the exception, rather than the rule." That was why it was exciting, even to this veteran FBI agent, to see half a dozen places where there might be enough points for a fingerprint identification. The chemist was well aware that he was investigating an attempted murder, and in fact, he knew that this suspect had tried to use murder as an instrument to obstruct justice in the courts. This wasn't just a bloodless laboratory experiment. For this FBI agent, it was a chase, just as surely as a pursuit with bloodhounds is a chase.

Next, high-resolution photography would convert the fine orange lines into sharper black. An optical scanner would translate the lines into digital representations. And then, a Cray computer, capable of tens of millions of operations a second, would compare the digitalized print to each of the tiny electrical impulses in the representations of millions of known prints collected by the FBI—all stored in the enormous fingerprint register known colloquially as part of the NCIC, the National Crime Information Computer.

And that was why the ninhydrin results gave this chemist the same rush that a twelve-year-old feels from a video game. Because now, the law was a giant step closer to identifying the man behind the AK-47, the assassin who wore the security guard's uniform, the suspect who had tried to kill Robert Herrick. The suspect, so far, who was known only as "Squint."

11
TOPLESS

The deputy clerk was nervous. The office was nearly empty, and nothing was happening. Why, he asked himself, is my heart pounding so fast?

Even if he lost his job, it would be all right. They would take care of him.

The call from Booker & Bayne had come about ten o'clock this morning. "Jimmy Coleman told me to call," the young lawyer had said. "Jimmy says you'll want to help us." Her name was Jennifer Lowenstein.

The deputy clerk had been pleased, at first. "Sure! Anything for Jimmy Coleman. What can I do to help?"

"We figure the propane truck case is going to be filed today, and we want to make sure it gets filed in the right court. With the right judge, that is."

The deputy clerk remembered the flutter in his stomach at that.

In Texas, judges had to run for election, just like all the other politicians. And so the judges needed to have billboards, bumper stickers, and postcards, and they needed campaign workers, consultants, and telephone banks. In high-stakes races, they bought radio advertisements. Some of the richest campaigns used television ads. But for all of the judges, money was the lifeblood of politics, and for that reason, Booker & Bayne gave hundreds of thousands of dollars every year to judges campaigning for re-election. That way, the firm's lawyers could count on having their cases heard by judges who remembered receiving whopping contributions. Obviously, that was what Jimmy Coleman was interested in now.

The deputy clerk didn't say anything. He just listened, and he dreaded what was coming.

"Jimmy Coleman would appreciate it if Judge Dexter Medaxas got the propane truck case," Jennifer Lowenstein went on. And again, there was that flutter in the deputy clerk's stomach.

The problem was, the rules in the clerk's office were set up to prevent lawyers from "judge-shopping." Each day, a deputy would tap the codes into the computer that assigned cases to judges in a rotating sequence. The sequence was changed frequently, so that a lawyer couldn't just figure out when his favorite judge would be next in rotation. Otherwise, a friendly judge might let that lawyer exploit all the wiggle room in the rules of procedure. And that was precisely why Jimmy Coleman was trying to beat the system now.

"How could I possibly do what you want me to?" The deputy clerk squirmed. "My hands are tied."

Every employee in the clerk's office was under strict orders not to tell any lawyer the name of the next upcoming judge until after the case was filed. And if a lawyer tried to fool the system by dismissing his suit and re-filing it, the case tracking computer would recognize the names of the plaintiff and defendant.

Automatically, it would transfer the case back to the court where it was filed the first time.

"But it'll be real easy, in this case," Jennifer Lowenstein was saying. "We want Judge Medaxas, and I'm going to explain to you how to do it."

The deputy clerk's nose wrinkled. He knew Dexter Medaxas. Medaxas was the kind of judge who would fudge some technical rule or other just to make the testimony of a whole string of witnesses inadmissible. Because that way, he wouldn't have to bother with hearing them. The man was smart, but he was narrow-minded and lazy. Come to think of it, the deputy clerk suddenly remembered, Dexter Medaxas had started out his legal career at Booker & Bayne! But the future judge hadn't showed much talent at the big firm, and when the time came to edge him out, the partners had bankrolled his election campaign. That was how Dexter Medaxas had become a public servant twenty years ago. And now, of course, Jimmy Coleman wanted Judge Medaxas for the propane truck case.

"We've kept Robert Herrick's office under surveillance," Jennifer Lowenstein was saying. "We wanted to find out when they do their daily courthouse run. And it turns out, they always do it at exactly three o'clock in the afternoon, because that's when your office, the clerk's office, is the most empty. And at three o'clock, there's only one unrestricted filing window open, and so today at three o'clock, the deputy clerk at that window needs to be you."

That conversation with Jennifer Lowenstein had been at ten this morning. Now it was five minutes before three o'clock in the afternoon. The clerk's office was empty, and the deputy clerk was sitting there all alone at the filing window, just as Jennifer Lowenstein had ordered him to. And he was nervous as a cat. As he waited. And waited. In the empty office.

Across town, it was also five minutes to three. And this place, in a very different neighborhood, happened to be the location where two other players in the propane truck case had agreed to meet.

In a topless bar called the Play Mate Club, Esparza the case runner was sitting in a purple plush chair right beside the center stage runway. He was waiting for Robert Herrick. The lawyer hadn't wanted to meet him here, but Esparza had demanded it. These two men were worlds apart, but now they were linked by a secret. And Esparza enjoyed the fact that he could make demands, simply because he had less to lose, and make Robert give in to them.

Suddenly, the door opened. There was a flash of light, and then it closed again. Robert Herrick stepped in, and involuntarily, he hunched his overcoat up around his face. He saw Esparza from far across the room as soon as his eyes adjusted to the darkness. Some kind of unidentifiable rock music with a driving beat was throbbing from speakers everywhere. There were three featured dancers, and each one had multicolored lights shifting over her large round breasts. Each one's body glistened with a mixture of perfume and sweat.

The room was huge. At three o'clock in the afternoon, it was already full. The only women in the place were dancers and waitresses, and the men sat in groups of twos, threes, and fours, drinking scotch, bourbon and martinis. They alternated between peering through the darkness at the shiny bodies of the featured performers, and laughing at their companions who were enjoying couch dances. For twenty dollars, a dancer would wiggle in front of a customer, brushing up and down across his business suit. Visitors from New York or Los Angeles always were amazed at the classy sleaze of Houston's topless bars, which seemed to sprout on every street corner, and every one of them seemed to have lots of red neon and Ferraris in front. Inside every one, there would be a small army of architects, vascular surgeons and oil barons getting couch dances.

The Play Mate Club was expensive, and it advertised itself as a "Gentlemen's Club." There was a big sign: "The Businessman's Bonus for a Hard Day's Work." And if you gave the waitress your Gold MasterCard for whiskey, or for a businessman's lunch, or even for a dozen couch dances, the charge slip would say "BarBQ Restaurant" instead of the Play Mate Club. That way, you could get reimbursed from your expense account and your company could take a tax deduction.

The dancers wore wet lipstick, each one in several shades of red. Their eyeliner was thick but precise, and their eye shadow was an amazing collection of multiple hues. About a third of them were between the ages of seventeen and twenty. The preferred dress was leather wrap skirts and halters, easy to remove, with the hemline barely at the crotch. The three dancers wiggled on top of little stages, with high intensity lamps pointing straight down over them, so that the harsh light glinted—alluringly, they hoped—from their breasts.

As Robert approached, he saw that Esparza was not alone. Two couch dancers were bent over him, both wearing matching T-straps with red and yellow sequins. Alternately, they undulated from a crouch to a semi-standing position. But because the rules of the Alcoholic Beverage Commission said so, the two women avoided actually touching Esparza with their sexual parts, other than an occasional brush-by. Or at least, when they touched, they made sure it was unseen. These two ladies obviously had the artistic skill to achieve the desired effect, while at the same time keeping from getting arrested for what vice officers euphemistically called "lewd dancing."

"Hello, Counselor Herrick!" said Esparza with exaggerated enthusiasm.

"Nice place, Mister Esparza," said Robert. "Tell me, what does a guy do with himself after he leaves here? And so why's he ever going to want to come here in the first place?" Herrick didn't care for topless bars. He had never cared for girls who teased when he was a teenager, and he didn't like them as grownups now, including the professional ones.

"Tell you what," Esparza bristled. "If you think this isn't a good place to do business, next time I'll meet you at the River Oaks Country Club. I just figured maybe you wouldn't want the mayor and about twenty-five judges around."

"You're right, but I wouldn't have chosen this as a place to meet, either. Just as I'd never have chosen to deal with a case runner, if I'd had a choice. Look,

Esparza. The only reason I paid you was to get Icky Snopes out of trouble, and of course, I had to give it to you myself, because I couldn't trust Icky with the money even long enough to pass it on to you."

"Well, anyway, this is Tanya and Tina." Esparza pointed to the two wiggling bodies. "They're a sister act. Known as the Sausage Girls. You prob'ly heard of 'em." Esparza nodded. "Say hello to Mister Herrick, you two babes!"

"Hello, Mister Herrick," giggled Tanya and Tina.

Robert just wanted to find out what Esparza had on his mind and then get out of here. His escort from the Department of Public Safety—the two officers sent by the governor—had started out following him in their dusty Plymouth. It had been like a chase scene in a cops-and-robbers movie, because Robert had tried to lose them in traffic, but he couldn't. Finally, he had pulled over, red-faced, and told them to leave him alone, because this was a "personal errand." They left, and now here he was at the Play Mate Club. He shook his head and tried to appear inconspicuous.

Esparza still didn't get the message. He turned back toward the writhing Sausage Girls. "Okay, so girls, as I was telling you before Mister Herrick interrupted us, there are these two lawyers, and they're standing on the street corner." He turned to grin at Robert. "I know you prob'ly like these lawyer jokes as much as anybody, Mister Herrick, so just see if you can follow along."

The case runner was enjoying himself. "One of the two lawyers sees this beautiful, shapely blonde crossing the street. He says to the other guy, 'Wow! I sure would like to screw her!' And so the other lawyer says, 'You wanna screw her? Well, outta what? Outta *what*?'"

Esparza shifted his eyes quickly back and forth to show that the guy in the joke really was a lawyer.

Tanya and Tina both giggled some more, in unison. Herrick stared off in the other direction. He usually didn't take offense at lawyer jokes, at least if they weren't excessively malicious, because he heard a lot of them from his clients. But that wasn't what bothered him. He didn't like Esparza, or the fact he'd been boxed in about paying him, or this meeting.

"Well, so tell me, Mister Esparza, what exactly is it that we're here for?" Robert asked. "I mean, other than to let these ladies minister to the spiritual side of your nature. What'd you get me over here for?"

Esparza suddenly was serious. "You got the package, and you got it signed up."

"Yes," Herrick answered. "Yes, Mister Esparza, but without knowing that you were involved. And in spite of that, you got a 'package' that consisted of twenty-five thousand dollars."

"I appreciate it, but that's what I want to talk to you about. I need more."

"Look, Esparza, I'm going to tell you one more time. I've never gotten mixed up with you, or with any case runner, ever before. I wouldn't have taken this case if I had known Icky was breaking the law. I only paid the twenty-five thousand dollars to get my friend out of trouble." For the hundredth time, Robert thought to himself, "I wanted the propane truck case too much. Now, what have I done? What am I doing here? And why am I involved with this sleazy Esparza?"

Esparza didn't get the message. "I'm kind of in trouble, Herrick. I need the money, and speaking of money, you're going to make a ton of money off that propane truck case. I even heard you signed up the cases on all a the plaintiffs, after you got that one case on Angela from me."

"Yes. But that doesn't have anything to do with it."

"But all the cases on all those dead people came to you because of me. That's worth a lot of money."

"Listen." Robert's voice was strained. "I paid what Icky agreed to pay you. And now, if I pay you more, I'll be getting myself into this mess. And besides, if I do that, I know you'll just keep after me forever, asking for more."

He looked away, toward something off in the distance. He was working hard to hold his temper. He also was working hard to overcome the cold, sweaty fear he was beginning to feel.

"So, I figure you can treat it all as an advance." Esparza's voice was matter-of-fact. "Sometimes, case runners work on a percentage, and usually I get fifteen percent."

"It's like you didn't hear me. The only reason I paid you the twenty-five thousand dollars was because Icky told me *he* had to, because you were threatening him. And the only reason I paid it myself was that I was afraid Icky might spend the money on drugs. And I repeat: I never would have taken the case if I'd known you were involved."

"Well, but I'm saying, it's an advance. An advance on the fifteen percent. You know you're gonna make somewheres in the millions off this one."

"No, I do not know that," Herrick answered angrily. "This case is *not* an easy one against the real defendants—the ones who can pay a judgment. Oh, I suppose it's a good case against the trucking company, but the trucking company's broke, and it doesn't have enough insurance to cover the damages. And so, I might win the case against the trucking company, but if I don't win against the construction companies, then I'll get less than what I spent."

Robert was sweating like a waterfall, by now. "But anyway, that's beside the point, Esparza, because I never intended to pay *anything* to a case runner! Not fifteen percent, not twenty-five thousand, not anything."

Esparza wasn't impressed. "I need more. And you'd better treat me fair, if you know what's good for you."

Herrick turned to stare into the case runner's eyes. "Look, Mister Esparza. I can't do what you're asking me to do. If I did, you'd be after me again after that, and you'd want to make another deal, then break the deal and get me to pay you more. I'd be buying into a lifetime of blackmail."

Now, Herrick had his hands on the arms of the chair, with his elbows raised. "The only reason I took this case was that I didn't know you were involved. And the only reason I ever dealt with you, at all, was to save Icky's life."

His voice was even. But he felt a desperate chill as he faced this obnoxious character with whom he now shared a deep and strange bond. At this point,

Robert Herrick's connection to Esparza had become a relationship of frightening dependence with a man he didn't know at all and didn't want to know. A relationship that he'd like to erase now, but couldn't. Robert looked, again, at the misshapen gold tooth, and then at the spidery tattoo crawling up the pockmarked neck. And once again, he wondered: "How did I ever let Icky drag me into getting involved with this weirdo?"

Esparza stared back at him. He had no expression. His face didn't change when Robert stood up, turned and walked away.

"That ain't the end of it, you motherfucking son of a bitch," Esparza said quietly to the vanishing figure. His voice was so vehement, and at the same time so cold, that Tanya and Tina both froze for an instant and looked at him in surprise before continuing to undulate.

It sounded as though Esparza intended to kill Robert Herrick.

Meanwhile, back at the filing window in the clerk's office, the deputy clerk sat and waited.

He'd been here, now, for almost half an hour, doing practically nothing, just staring out at the black and white squares in the government-style checkered linoleum in the clerk's office. Just staring. And getting more nervous by the minute.

Suddenly, here was the man from Robert Herrick's office.

The Deputy Clerk recognized Tom Kennedy, Herrick's most trusted associate. If this guy, Kennedy, was doing the filing of the suit papers instead of a messenger, it must be an important case. "It must be the propane truck case," the deputy clerk thought. "That's probably why the guy is later, today, than usual."

Tom Kennedy's kiltie-tassel loafers clicked on the faded linoleum as he entered the system of posts and cords that, earlier today, had held a queue of twenty-five or thirty lawyers, all waiting to file papers. But Kennedy walked right through, because the office was almost empty.

"Hi," was all the lawyer said, and he smiled at the deputy clerk.

"Good afternoon," the deputy clerk answered. He struggled to sound nonchalant.

Booker & Bayne had found a flaw in the system of the clerk's office, and now it was up to the deputy clerk to perform the simple plan that Jennifer Lowenstein had explained to him. He reached down to the floor and picked up a cover sheet with Judge Medaxas's court number on it.

It came from a large stack of mail-in filings, which were there because one of the deputies at the window was supposed to work on these during slack periods. But today, instead of filling in the cover sheets first, the deputy clerk had left each of them blank, until after they were file-stamped. And when Judge Medaxas's court number came up, he filled in all the other "mailers," but he left that one blank.

Now, he had a blank cover sheet that he could use to assign the propane truck case to Judge Medaxas's court.

"File-stamp this extra copy, please," said Tom Kennedy pleasantly. "And give it back to me so we'll have proof of filing."

The exact hour and minute on this file-stamp would be different from the stamp on the cover sheet, but the odds were a million to one against anyone ever noticing. Even if someone did notice, there could be a hundred innocent explanations. The deputy clerk filled in the blank, "topless" cover sheet—the one he had saved from the mailer—with the names of the plaintiffs in the propane truck case, starting with Pedro Gutierrez. It looked as though Herrick had signed up most of the families, by now. There was a long list of plaintiffs. Next, the defendants. There were more than a dozen of them: the trucking company, the estate of the dead truck driver, the architects, the engineering firms. And the construction companies.

Maxxco Construction Corporation was included. The deputy clerk wasn't surprised to see Maxxco named as a defendant, because Jennifer Lowenstein had told him to look for that name. But he was surprised to see where Maxxco's name appeared on the suit papers. Maxxco Construction was the first defendant on the list, and it was listed even before the trucking company. That probably meant that Herrick intended to make Maxxco the target defendant.

"Thanks," was all that Kennedy said as he reached for his file-stamped copy. The deputy clerk let out a long breath of air, and he turned back to his business. Now, he would go ahead and file the "mailer" that he had taken the cover sheet from; it didn't matter what court the mailer case got assigned to.

Almost immediately, he heard the sharp intake of Kennedy's breath. Then, softly, he heard the lawyer say, "Oh-h-h, no!" That meant that Kennedy must have seen the court number and instantly made the connection to Judge Medaxas. Probably the last judge that Kennedy and Herrick would have wanted for the propane truck case.

The deputy clerk waited a few minutes, and then he shakily dialed the telephone. "It's done. No problem."

"Good man," said the raspy voice at the other end of the line.

Three years ago, this deputy clerk had had a very large insurance claim for the medical expenses of his infant daughter, who suffered from an unusual liver disease. The insurance company hadn't wanted to pay, because the deputy clerk still was a probationary employee. If push had come to shove, the insurance company probably would have won, because it was legally correct. It didn't have to pay, under the law. The deputy clerk was frantic. He couldn't get his daughter admitted back into the hospital. That was when Jimmy Coleman had agreed to represent the deputy clerk and the baby, for free, and with one phone call, that wonderful Mr. Coleman had gotten the insurance claim paid in full. He had saved the baby's life. Today, the baby still wasn't cured, and so now the insurance money was a flowing stream, month after month, as essential as blood for keeping the little girl alive. The deputy clerk's gratitude to Jimmy Coleman was immeasurable.

But actually, the deputy clerk felt a mixture of gratitude and fear. Mr. Coleman had subtly hinted that he also was powerful enough to get the insurance money cut off, just about as easily as he'd gotten it turned on. Of course, the deputy clerk also was afraid of what he had done for Mr. Coleman, because he could get fired for favoritism to lawyers. This particular shenanigan had put the deputy clerk in a difficult and dangerous position. And the danger had at least a small chance of coming home to roost at Booker & Bayne. That was why Jennifer Lowenstein had been careful. Jimmy Coleman had insisted on protecting Booker & Bayne with the utmost care, by keeping the deputy clerk from even becoming the object of suspicion.

12
THE MULE

Está perdido mi pájaro," said the strange woman who appeared at Esparza's front door. "My bird is lost."

She stood in the doorway holding two battered suitcases, one red and one black. She wore a cheap polyester blouse and a plain black skirt. A fringed shawl woven in nubbly colors was wrapped around her shoulders.

Esparza the case runner opened the door for the woman. He showed the gleaming gold cylinder that substituted for a tooth. He had never seen the woman before this knock on his door, just past midnight, but he had been expecting her for nearly four hours. He had rehearsed his own counter-password over and over again throughout that time, as he nervously looked at his watch and wondered what could have gone wrong. Now he was relieved to see that nothing was wrong, and that finally, she was here.

"*Yo pienso que se perdió porque usted está borracha,*" he replied. "I think he got lost because you are drunk."

The fact was, actually, the woman did not in the least appear drunk. She was disheveled and tired from the long flight, and she was nervous. But not drunk. It was just a code. And now that Esparza had answered with the password, the woman relaxed a little.

Esparza regained his smile. "Come in, Luisa," he said. The identification process was completed.

The woman named Luisa entered the tiny living room. The walls were a bare white except for a plastic-rimmed mirror beside the window and a hole the size of a fist near the opening to the hallway. Luisa had the fleeting thought that a man who did a lot of big drug deals ought to be able to afford something a little more luxurious, but she left the idea unexpressed. Esparza flopped onto a couch covered with blue and red velveteen. When Luisa asked, he pointed to the bathroom. Without another word, she walked into it and closed the door.

She called out five minutes later to tell Esparza that she had passed the first packet.

"Go ahead and pick it up," Esparza said sharply. There weren't any social graces in this kind of operation. Esparza remembered one mule who had absentmindedly pushed the plunger and lost several thousand dollars worth of precious contraband, setting off a frenzied effort by both Esparza and the mule to fish out the remaining packets before they swirled and disappeared.

With thumb and finger, Luisa held up the prize. Two gleaming condoms, one inside the other, to provide a minimal measure of safety against the certain death that would follow from rupture. There was a shifting, powdery substance inside. It was heroin. Very high in purity. So fine that it seemed almost liquid in consistency inside the rubber container.

She hung her head in weariness and pain for another forty-five minutes as the long journey of the heroin neared its end. First there had been the bright field of poppies in the high mountain forest of northern Thailand. Harvested by hand, the bulbous fruit ran milky white when it was cut. Refined into opium, the quantity shrank, and the potency increased threefold as chemists and cookers transformed the raw mix into heroin. Then over the ocean and across the mountains it went, into Ecuador. The Quito airport had the right combination of primitive security and proximity to the United States so that swallowing mules, like Luisa, could do their work. Esparza didn't think about it much, but he knew she would take home less than a hundred dollars for her trouble. A good mule could swallow upwards of a dozen condoms, each one loosely filled with several ounces of the pure opiate derivative. A break, of course, would be undetectable at first, but it would flood the mule's intestines with many multiples of a lethal dose, which would be absorbed before the most determined surgeon could do anything about it—even assuming there was one on board the aircraft, and for that matter, a fully-equipped operating room. A leak in any one of the rubber packages would mean death for the mule.

Now, in her position of safety, Luisa the mule laughed as she told Esparza about "*los perros que huelen drogas*," the drug-sniffing dogs, that Customs had used at both ends of the flight. Esparza's gold cylinder flashed in derision as he heard how the passengers were separated from their luggage, and a cocker spaniel trotted through the empty aisle in between and sniffed first the people, then the bags. "But of course the dog could not smell *las drogas* inside me!" Luisa said, and she and Esparza laughed.

"*Atiende el trabajo, hermana*," Esparza said finally. "Pay attention to your work."

By one-thirty in the morning, Luisa had passed all ten of the condoms she was carrying. The one pound and thirteen ounces of heroin that Esparza retrieved and weighed would have a street value, when cut and finally sold, of more than half a million dollars.

Esparza needed the money. Once again, he felt white-hot hatred toward Robert Herrick, and toward the hundred-millions he was sure the lawyer would make from the propane truck case.

At last, he slept. He didn't wake when the sun rose.

The next morning came early for Robert Herrick. At five-thirty he was up, and before breakfast, he was working on interrogatories to send to Jimmy Coleman.

His whole day was consumed by the propane truck case. First, figuring out who he needed to take depositions from. Then, trying to guess which construction documents to subpoena from Maxxco. Robert made the big decisions, with Kennedy's advice. Now, Kennedy's job, as associate, would be to get it all done.

❖ ❖ ❖

It was just before ten o'clock at night when a tired Robert Herrick dragged himself home and met his children at the kitchen door.

It was time for him to dig deeply into what was left of his energy, so that he could do a good job as a father to these two kids. That was even more important, he reminded himself, than doing a good job as a lawyer.

Robbie immediately started in on the evening's most recent event: "She hit me." He pointed to his sister, Pepper.

"But only after he snuck up behind me in his Ninja Turtle costume and whacked me with his sword." The look on fifteen-year-old Pepper Herrick's face was philosophical. Both children looked at Robert like two anxious subjects in front of King Solomon.

During the day, Robert's mother usually stayed with the children. In fact, she lived under the same roof, with a separate entrance that gave her privacy, which Robert had constructed after his wife had died. But there was a problem when he worked late, because Grandma Rosalie needed a nap after a long day. There were times when fifteen-year-old Pepper was in charge. "And," Robert thought to himself, "I'm used to being a more active parent than these eighteen-hour days will allow."

And so he struggled, after his total absorption in the propane truck case, to shift gears. To become a father.

But then, he heard the television set spit out that squiggly electronic music that always introduces the ten o'clock news. For a moment, at least, he would have to postpone the agony of another biblical-style judgment. "Wait, kids. I've absolutely got to watch the news tonight."

He turned up the volume, and the TV set blared. "Good evening, friends! I'm John Moreno, and THIS . . . IS . . . *ACTION NEWS*!" There was a kaleidoscopic series of city skylines, followed by grinning portraits of the news, sports and weather anchors. And then, suddenly, the toothpaste-ad smile of the news anchor disappeared. It was replaced by a pencil drawing of a round balding face with a permanently squinting eye. Robert Herrick stared at the composite drawing of the man known as Squint, there on the TV screen.

"Have you seen this man?" asked the news anchor's voice, excitedly. "He's a prime suspect in the shooting of prominent Houston lawyer, Robert Herrick. If you do know him, call our ACTION NEWS HOTLINE. Because there must be SOMEBODY who can help solve this crime . . . and maybe, . . . just MAYBE, . . . that SOMEONE . . . is *YOU*!"

Robert Herrick stood mesmerized, as though he was staring at death itself. He relived the moment when the sketch artist had flipped his sketch pad over. Robert remembered his astounded reaction: "That's Squint! That's the man who shot at me."

"He looks just like Vanilla Ice!" Pepper Herrick said excitedly.

And Robbie's voice was full of seven-year-old wonder. "Can he do anything with that eye of his, like the X-men? I mean, like the one called Cyclops, who has the heat ray coming out of his head?"

But Robert didn't hear them. "Maybe now we can catch this guy," he thought to himself. First there were the fingerprints from the "sHYsTer" letter, and now, Squint's face was on a million TV screens.

Then that thought gave way to a weary reality. "I've got to keep my eye on the ball. I've got dozens of clients who are counting on me in the propane truck case. And none of those clients understands how hard it's going to be, because I've got to win against the defendants who are solvent. The construction companies, like Maxxco. Not just against the trucking company.

"And, also," Robert reminded himself, "I'm trying to be a single parent to my kids." He understood, these days, the plight of other parents—mostly single women—who barely scraped by on low incomes and exhausted emotions, like the secretaries in his office who always got year-end bonuses and who always were dealt with sympathetically when they missed work because of sick kids. Robert made sure of it. He didn't have quite the same financial burdens, but he sure had enough of the emotional and career difficulties to understand how hard it was for his employees who were single mothers.

And there were two other complications. Robert's thoughts on this were very clear: "Squint wants to kill me. Then, there's Esparza, and he probably wants to kill me, too."

He sat down, heavily. "Okay, Robbie. Is it true, what Pepper says, that you hit her before she hit you?"

At the same time Robert was staring at the image of Squint, Esparza had arranged his heroin deal. It was best to move the stuff out fast.

And now, after three o'clock in the morning, Esparza sat waiting in a 1988 Thunderbird, parked in a half-empty lot. He was sitting with two other men named Puerco Rodriguez and Jimmy Ybarra. It was a pitch black night. No stars, no moon. That was fine with Esparza. He liked the fact that it was dark and hard to see anything. He was waiting for the guy named Almanza.

Suddenly, an ugly green 1985 Plymouth pulled into the opposite corner of the lot. It shook and rumbled every inch of the way. "There's those guys, right there," said Puerco Rodriguez sharply. "That Plymouth still scares the shit out of me."

Esparza felt the pang in his stomach that he always felt on the edge of a deal. Plus, he felt annoyed at Almanza, because Esparza had insisted that his group—he and Puerco and Jimmy—would get to the drop point after the buyers. If you get caught holding fifty thousand dollars in a shopping bag, you don't go to jail, but if it's a pound thirteen of heroin, you do. Here was Almanza showing up late, when he was supposed to get there first. It wasn't good. But Esparza conjured up what was left of his patience, and he let it pass. Almanza was just late, that's all, and what was he going to do about it? Sue him?

Esparza had used this drop site a couple of times before. It was the parking lot of a complex called the Gallery Apartments, at the corner of Richmond Avenue and Quick Street. The neighborhood was eclectic, to say the least. Just to the east was Montrose Boulevard, hub of one of the largest gay communities in the United States. The Montrose area historically had been a high-crime district, although not because of the gays, who were far more law-abiding than the average citizen and who voted conservative on most issues other than gay rights. To the southeast of the Gallery Apartments was a Latino community, and there was a predominantly black area to the west. The Gallery Apartments themselves catered to a shifting mixture of students, downtown secretaries, and artists, and recently it had also begun to attract some of the upper-middle-class members of Houston's large Vietnamese population.

None of which had much to do with Esparza's selection of the site. Instead, his reason was that the Gallery Apartments had a large square parking lot on the back side, away from Richmond Avenue. They wouldn't attract much attention in this area, particularly at three-thirty in the morning.

Each party would park at an opposing corner of the lot, diagonally across from each other. They would walk toward each other and meet at the corner where the two streets met. There, they would exchange shopping bags. The seller would check the money, the buyer would check the heroin. And both groups would walk back, extremely carefully, and drive away.

"This deal, it's always seemed fishy to me," said Puerco. His name in English was Porky, and he weighed roughly two hundred and sixty-five pounds, very little of which was muscle. He was carrying a shotgun, cut off so that it was just under two feet, with a pistol grip. It easily fit under the folds of his bulky, flowing overcoat.

Esparza had been concerned about the Plymouth, too. Always. But consciously and with effort, he had decided to put his fear aside. "It's all right," he said with a trace of annoyance. "I been through the wars with Almanza, and I ain't about to run out now."

It was true. He and Almanza had joked at first about the ugly green Plymouth. "Not a cool car," Esparza had said doubtfully. "Cool" was cop talk for "undercover"—a Lincoln was cooler than a Plymouth, and a Corvette was probably cooler still, unless you were one of the actors in *Miami Vice*. "But it's what I drive, this Plymouth," Almanza had said. "If I was a cop, I'd drive a Mark or a 'Vette, I guess, forfeited out of some bust. 'Course, I guess I could go out and spend thirty thousand on a rig like that just so you'd feel like less of a squirrel." Esparza had laughed, and they had done some business. Then later they did some more business, and then it got past the point where Esparza could raise a question about the Plymouth again.

Sure, Almanza and the Plymouth always gave Esparza a twinge. But so did everyone else when it came to selling heroin. In the end, it came down to this: The Plymouth was too obvious. Almanza was right. He couldn't possibly be a cop and still try to do undercover drug deals in this silly-ass car. It wasn't just uncool, it was so uncool that no cop would ever drive it.

Across the lot, there was the sound of a car door opening. Almanza had curly black shoulder-length hair. He always wore a black cowboy hat with the brim turned down in front and a huge silver band, with the top coming up in a peak like Tom Mix. He had two guys with him that Esparza had never seen, both in jackets made out of heavy black leather, both with burr haircuts. "Fine," Esparza thought, "except they look too clean cut to be hanging with Almanza."

Everybody started to walk slowly toward the point.

Jimmy hung back. He always did. "Come on," Esparza said to him impatiently.

"Look it them two skinheads!" Jimmy answered in a disgusted voice. But he came on.

The actual deal was an anti-climax. At the point, Almanza smiled an easy smile. "Here you go, tough guy." He handed Esparza the shopping bag.

"Just what I always wanted. Some piece of shit from K-Mart," Esparza answered. He flashed the gold tooth and edged away a few steps with Jimmy and Porky covering him. Meanwhile, Almanza squirted a drop of Marquis reagent to test the heroin. Immediately, the little purple spot told him the goods were real. Meanwhile, Esparza counted the fifty thousand. Then, in a long, slow ballet, everybody backed away from the point. When they got closer to the cars, they hustled.

Three short beeps of the Plymouth's horn signaled that Almanza had found everything in order. Esparza answered with the same signal. Jimmy and Porky breathed easier.

Then, boom! It happened, all at once. The sound of the bullhorn wasn't just something that they heard. It exploded over them, from nowhere. "Freeze! FREEZE, you muthafuckas! POLICE! You're UNDER ARREST!"

The car wouldn't start. The police must have disabled it somehow. Esparza turned the key and panicked when he realized it wouldn't turn over at all.

Riding shotgun, Porky cracked his door, swung his bulk, and got ready to run. The black barrel of his enforcer stuck out. He was trying to aim it, it looked like, but maybe it was just sticking out. There was a "boom," and Porky had a puzzled look on his face. He fell back into the dashboard, splattering blood and brains. There was a cavity the size of a fist in the back of his head, pink and pulsing.

Esparza sat rock still. He couldn't see a thing, and he didn't know how many cops were out there.

But he had forgotten about Jimmy. Jimmy was always skittish, and always a hothead. Now, the chubby little man panicked and ran out of the back seat firing his Uzi, just like in the movies. But unlike the movies, this time it was incredibly stupid. There was a chorus of booms. Jimmy fell down before he made ten steps. His sweatshirt was shredded, and it started to leak. The garish red color puddled and ran in several directions, like the legs of a spider.

Esparza was still motionless when three uniformed officers ordered him out, put his hands on top of the Thunderbird, and frisked him tightly and thoroughly. All the while, they shouted crisp orders laced with liberal obscenities. Then

Almanza was there to read the Miranda card to Esparza. ". . . If you want an attorney and are unable to afford one, an attorney will be appointed for you by the court before any questioning."

Almanza faced Esparza close. "Do you understand these rights, shithead?"

"Yes."

"With these rights in mind, are you willing to discuss the charges against you?"

"No, sir."

"It don't much matter. We got the heroin, we got you holding the money, and we got the whole fuckin' thing on videotape."

Then there was a shout. And a lot of screaming. Just outside the second floor of the Gallery Apartments, one of Jimmy's bullets had pierced the aorta of a nineteen-year-old woman who was a freshman at the University of St. Thomas. Her next door neighbor had slipped on the blood after coming to the landing to see what all the commotion was about.

"A person dead during a felony," said Officer Almanza finally, when the scene was under control again. "Actually, three people dead during a felony, if you count those two turds you so kindly brought along, Esparza. Are you intarested in knowin' what that means? It means it's a murder case. Three murders. That's called the felony-murder rule. You are guilty of murder under the felony-murder rule. Now are you willing to discuss the charges against you, shithead?"

"No, sir."

It was his own fault, Esparza thought for an instant. He wasn't careful, and getting busted was his own fault.

Then, that thought was replaced by another. It was Robert Herrick's fault.

13
JUDGE TROUBLE

It was seven fifty-two in the morning when Judge Barbara Trobelo smoothed the salt-and-pepper in her hair, put on her little gold glasses, and stepped out of the elevator in the Family Courts Building.

As a divorce judge, this was where Barbara Trobelo worked. The Hall of Broken Dreams; the Palace of Matrimonial Misery! Already the courts were filling up with austerely dressed women holding crying babies and hoping, against the odds, that they might collect a fraction of the unpaid child support.

She smoothed her hair again as her feet touched the dirty linoleum. Unlike many judges, Barbara Trobelo kept up her appearance—even though it didn't matter as much as it had when she was a trial lawyer. She wore more dresses, in pinks, reds, and greens, and fewer of those severe gray suits. Her husband was an aerospace engineer at NASA and had a good-natured distrust of lawyers, and so he applauded the difference. But he liked her best in jeans and cowboy boots.

A lawyer in a tan polyester suit almost ran into her, right at the elevator door.

"Judge, I don't mean to break the rules by talking to you without the other lawyer present," he began. But then, this polyester lawyer proceeded to do just that. "All I want to do is to tell you the facts, so you'll see why I need an emergency hearing . . ."

These were the busiest courts in the state. A divorce judge had to accept frequent injustices because of the raw human tide that flowed through every day. Not to mention having to put up with lawyers like this one, who continued to talk as Judge Trobelo opened the heavy oak door to her courtroom. By the time she reached her chambers, she had picked up an entourage of three more lawyers. The bailiff, Pete Bonaventura, stood there in his uniform to ward them off.

"Thanks for your time, your honor!" said the polyester lawyer happily. "Now I can tell my client I have special influence with the judge!"

Inside her chambers, Judge Trobelo shook her head. The rules said you couldn't claim special influence with the judge, but this guy was so blissfully ignorant that he had almost quoted what he could get disbarred for doing. She sighed. Don't sweat the small stuff.

Everybody knew Barbara Trobelo was bright, hard-working and intellectually curious, and she didn't intend to stay in the divorce courts forever. It would be much more interesting, she thought, to be judging big civil damage cases with good lawyers. Like that propane truck case that's all over the newspapers, for instance. "I'd love to be the judge in that one," she said to herself.

Pete, the bailiff, interrupted her thoughts. "Did you remember this is the day the magistrate isn't going to be here?" The magistrate usually handled the uncontested divorces, but today Judge Trobelo would have to hear them all.

"How many?"

"So far, I've got nine. But I'm guessing there'll be twenty or so when they're all lined up, not counting twelve on the auxiliary docket, and those are mostly about who gets to live in the happy couple's mobile home until the divorce."

With that, Judge Trobelo put on her robe and stepped into the courtroom to start the day.

Thirty minutes later, Judge Trobelo had forgotten about the polyester lawyer, and she had signed judgments in seven uncontested divorces. Now, in case number eight, the lawyer was addressing his client in the monotone reserved for the standard questions. "Have you been a resident of this county for the last six months?"

"No, I didn't get arrested in this county." The client was a large woman with red bouffant hair. "I got arrested in Tennessee, but I wasn't drunk enough for that little machine to show it."

"No, no, no!" said the lawyer. "I explained to you, Mrs. Eads, about the residency requirement." The lawyer gave the word a careful enunciation: "Have you been a REZ-EYE-DUNT of this county for the last six months?"

"Mrs. Eads," Barbara Trobelo interrupted, "how long have you lived here?"

"All my life, ma'am," said Mrs. Eads.

The lawyer smiled, and he started to go on to the next question, but Judge Trobelo interrupted. "Wait just a minute." She had heard the "ping" sound of the telephone mounted beneath her bench.

"It's Carmelita Bueno," the clerk said. "She's the governor's assistant for judicial appointments."

Barbara Trobelo smiled as she held the phone. "Hello, Cappy."

"Well, hello there yourself, Judge Trouble!" said Carmelita Bueno. She always sounded warm and confident, and yet her voice bordered on amusement.

"Everybody calls me that," Barbara Trobelo sighed. "Judge Trouble. I guess it goes with a name like Trobelo, that nobody ever heard before. Nowadays, I even encourage it." She laughed. "I want people saying, 'Listen, boy! If you pull any kinda dirty trick in that courtroom, Judge Trouble gonna have yo' ass!'"

This time, both women laughed.

"Okay, Cappy. When are you going to get good old Judge Trouble out of this place? It's a zoo." Barbara Trobelo wasn't laughing, now. "I've done a good job, and I need a promotion to a regular court that doesn't do divorces."

"Well, that's why I'm calling, but I've got bad news. When Judge Dexter Medaxas announces his retirement today, the Governor's decided to appoint Harmon Bilandic to replace him."

Judge Trouble bit her tongue. She had to go with the flow. "Not a bad idea, with Bilandic being chairman of the party."

"Well, yes, Barbara. But I know you want to move up to a regular court, and

I want you there, too. There'll be another judgeship, and you're at the top of my list. Us Latinas have got to stick together."

"Well, thanks. 'Bye, Cappy. You're a sweetheart."

She suddenly realized that Mrs. Eads was still standing there. This divorce was one of the most traumatic events in Mrs. Eads' life. "Let's go ahead and hear the rest of the case from this nice lady," she said, and smiled.

"Well, your honor," Mrs. Eads' lawyer puffed up his chest. "I never heard anyone call you Judge Trouble. And I guarantee I never called you that myself!"

"What a brown-noser this guy is!" Judge Trouble thought. But all she said was, "You may proceed with the questions to Mrs. Eads, counsel."

Judge Trouble didn't know Jimmy Coleman. But at this moment, Jimmy was meeting with his favorite associate, discussing the propane truck disaster.

It was ten o'clock. And far away from the grimy sadness of the divorce courts, in the elegant white birch offices of Booker & Bayne, Jimmy was in a celebratory mood. Sitting in the middle of the flowering vines inlaid on his resplendent Italian furniture, Jimmy showed his cigar-stained teeth.

"Hot dog! It worked, and we got our judge!" Jimmy's grin was so wide that it gave him a couple of extra chins. "My old buddy, Dexter Medaxas, will help us beat the crap out of Robert Herrick. It'll be like there's an extra DEE-fense lawyer at this trial, except this one is gonna be wearin' a black robe."

"Well, it sounds like overkill to me." Jennifer Lowenstein sat at attention, again. "Our client, Maxxco, didn't do anything wrong. How come we needed to go to all that trouble and take all those risks, just to get a friendly judge?"

"I'll tell you why."

"Okay, why?"

"Conflict of interest," said Jimmy matter-of-factly. As though it answered all the questions.

But Jennifer was used to Jimmy not getting to the point until he was ready to. And so all she said was: "Okay. Conflict of interest. What does that mean?"

"Well, let's think it through. The Louisiana Trucking Company is the easiest target for Mister Herrick. But that won't be his real target." Jimmy held up a thick index finger. "I've never seen an insurance company that would give a trucking company enough insurance to cover a disaster like this."

"And so you don't figure the trucking company has more than a few million. Not a big enough pot of gold in a case like this." And Jennifer thought, "This is so much like Jimmy. For all his faults, he's a wonderful teacher. He's vindictive toward his adversaries, but he's patient and protective toward his junior lawyers."

"Right," he grinned at her. "So Maxxco will be the real target. Maxxco's good for several billion, and Herrick knows it."

"But Jimmy, if this truck driver was going way too fast, and he drove off the overpass and into kingdom come, how come our client has to pay?"

"Well, truth is, I'm afraid our good client Maxxco does have some—exposure." He dragged the word out and savored it: "Ex-PO-O-O-O-sure."

"Some—exposure?"

Jennifer was new, but she had learned to translate this kind of lawyer talk. Saying that Maxxco was the firm's "good client" meant that it paid its bills to the tune of millions every year. And Jimmy's reference to Maxxco's "exposure," in plain English, meant that Maxxco was guilty as sin of exactly what it was charged with. At Booker & Bayne, the lawyers never talked about the rightness or wrongness of a client's actions, or about its responsibility for whatever calamity was behind a given lawsuit. Instead, they just muttered, "Well, I'm afraid our good client—the Amalgamated Worldwide Widget Holding Company—just might have a little bit of—well—ex-po-o-o-o-sure, even though officially we're going to deny it."

"Yes. Maxxco has a lot of exposure, frankly." Jimmy sounded noncommittally cheerful. "A lot of ex-PO-O-O-O-sure."

Jennifer waited.

"They built the intersection the best way they could," Jimmy said finally. "But back then, Maxxco had cash flow problems. They had to bring in this project way under budget. They skipped a lot of the compaction tests, that kind of thing. And as for Mister Herrick's claims about the narrowness of the ramp, and the curve being inadequately banked, and the too-skimpy guardrails—well, I'm not saying I agree with him, or that our client was exactly negligent, really . . ."

His voice lowered.

Jimmy looked out the window and stretched before going on. "Anyhow, some of Maxxco's engineers definitely were opposed to it. They wrote a bunch of memos showing how this intersection was dangerous. We'll try to bury the memos, much as we can, but it's impossible to bury every one of 'em, because there are so many that are incriminating. And that's why I say—well—Maxxco's certainly got some . . . well, lots of—exposure."

He grinned.

"Well, Jimmy, can't you beat Herrick by hiding the evidence and persuading the jury that it was safe? You've beaten him before."

"Don't underestimate Herrick."

"Why do you say that?"

Jimmy frowned. "Because Herrick is good with juries. He chooses cases he believes in, and the jury always can tell he believes in his client's case."

"How is it that he does that?"

"He will have three simple themes." Jimmy's voice sounded like a cement mixer. "First, he'll say that this was a dangerous overpass. And unfortunately, he'll have evidence to prove it. Second, he'll say that Maxxco knew it was dangerous. Maxxco does have some exposure on that. And third, he'll say that Maxxco covered up the danger."

"How can you know he's going to say those things?" She was shocked. "I can't believe the top guys at Maxxco even thought the overpass was dangerous, in spite of a few engineers who disagreed. And on top of that, they covered it up?"

"Look, everything is dangerous. Overpasses, bathtubs, even your hair dryer." Jimmy shrugged. "And Maxxco's files will have hundreds of documents trying to reduce the danger. But to Robert Herrick, those memos won't mean our guys were trying to do it right, especially since they didn't do it right, frankly. Instead, he'll use all that paper to show we knew this overpass was dangerous, which of course we did. And since we didn't follow our safety memos and we didn't make 'em public, there's a cover-up. See?"

"That's the cover-up?" She was fascinated. "Will it work?"

"In front of a jury? Yes. And that's why we need a judge who's on our side."

"But, wait! You said this case was about a conflict of interest. How's that?"

"That's what motivates most trial lawyers," said Jimmy. "Conflict of interest. You see, there has to be a conflict over a large amount of money, or else, most of 'em are just not interested!"

Jennifer laughed. Jimmy could be charming, and in fact he could be downright cute. She liked working for him.

They said Jimmy practiced law like a street fighter—precisely because, when he was a kid, he actually had been an accomplished street fighter. Supposedly, he had a juvenile conviction for burglary or something. But it was sealed. It was said, too, that he had been small and skinny, but he made up for it by being meaner than anyone else. If anybody picked on him, Jimmy wouldn't stop after he'd kicked the guy's ass. He'd roll him over and knock his teeth out, just to keep him from coming back.

Nobody knew the circuitous route that finally saw this primitive child graduate from law school, as editor-in-chief of the UCLA Law Review, no less. But everyone was pretty certain he'd never finished high school.

"Jimmy." Jennifer was hesitant. "You never talk about how you got to be a lawyer. What led you into it?"

His eyes clouded. "There's a reason. I don't think there's anything worth telling."

That surprised her. "But your associates miss out that way! You've got so much to teach us. And it isn't just motions and trials. We all want to know more . . . about . . . you."

"I'll tell you one story, Jennifer, and maybe it'll show you why you don't want to ask." His rasp was unexpectedly harsh. "I was maybe twelve or thirteen when I had, you might say, my epiphany. Like St. Paul on the road to Damascus, only more convincing. The Deacons' territory butted up against ours. Five of them took me to the sixth floor of the empty cotton warehouse. And pushed me off."

It took a minute for Jennifer to absorb it. "But . . . why?"

"To kill me, of course. But it didn't. I hit the concrete standing up, and it broke both my legs. But that didn't satisfy those vicious little bastards, the Deacons. Two minutes later, they're escorting me up the stairs to push me off again. This time, from the top of the building. And that's when the cops finally got there."

Jennifer held her breath. She knew what both of them were thinking. Her background wouldn't ever let her understand where Jimmy had come from.

He looked out the window at the cars swarming by. When he finally spoke, he had dismissed the subject from his mind completely, and once again, he was the friendly teacher.

He looked at Jennifer and grinned with his uneven teeth. "Conflict of interest!" And he wheezed as he laughed at his own joke. "But still," he added, more cautiously, "Robert Herrick is a dangerous opponent. He's interested in his clients and justice, not just the money. So that's why we've got to have our judge as an ace in the hole.

"And I'll take that and run with it," he exulted. "Because in this trial, we're gonna have my friend, Dexter Medaxas, helpin' us beat Mister Herrick!"

He pumped his stubby fist.

Robert Herrick was occupied with his own problems—such as Esparza, and Squint, and the "sHYsTer" letter. Not to mention Judge Dexter Medaxas, who had been assigned to the propane truck disaster and was a disaster himself, as far as Robert was concerned. And things just seemed to be getting worse.

It was noontime. Robert gazed out of his window, five blocks from the courthouse. He felt less and less secure, even with two DPS officers just outside the door. He didn't like what he was hearing from the policeman in charge of his case.

"I'm sorry, Mister Herrick," said Derrigan Slaughter. There was disappointment in the homicide detective's voice as it came through the speakerphone. "I'm sorry, but we didn't find no fingerprint match for Squint in the NCIC."

"No match for Squint's fingerprints? What does that mean?"

"It means that there ain't no fingerprints of our murder suspeck, Mister Squint, in the en-tire National Crime Information Computer. He ain't never been handled before."

"He's never been arrested?"

"That's right." Detective Slaughter hesitated. "But then, there's one other possibility."

"What's that?"

"It's possible it ain't Squint's fingerprints. Maybe it wasn't Squint who delivered that cut-up-newspaper letter."

Robert was puzzled. "That's—possible, I guess."

"It might even be, that whoever's prints are on that letter has no connection to Squint. We may have an independent suspeck sendin this 'sHYsTer' letter on a frolic of his own. And that person ain't in the NCIC."

"Oh, great," Robert thought to himself. "First there was Esparza. Next there was Squint. Now, there's a third suspect standing in line to assassinate me."

"Well, we still got that composite drawin' you did with the artist." Slaughter's voice was a little more cheerful. "It was a good picture of Squint on TV, so maybe somebody will give us a call."

After the detective hung up, Robert stared out the window. And he thought about Squint, and Esparza, and now, this third would-be killer; whoever left the fingerprints on the "sHYsTer" letter.

Not to mention his problems in the propane truck case. On top of everything else, it was just his luck to have drawn that crooked dunce of a judge, Dexter Medaxas! The propane truck trial would be like a battle in enemy territory. Medaxas hated Herrick, and Herrick hated Medaxas. Two years ago, Robert had tried a case in front of Medaxas, and he had had to fight throughout the whole ordeal to protect his client's most basic rights against the judge's rulings—which were made because the judge was lazy, and because it was obvious that he wanted the other side to win. In fact, Medaxas had been furious when Robert's client, who was badly injured, won the verdict.

Now, Robert felt the same kind of disgust for Medaxas as he felt for Esparza the case runner and Squint the assassin. Medaxas was just a crook who wore a judicial robe. He was nothing but another kind of assassin, lined up with all the others.

Back in divorce court, the lunch break was almost over. Judge Trobelo called in the jury for a trial that had been going on for two weeks.

This case sounded like "Divorces of the Rich and Famous." The husband was claiming forty-eight bank accounts in Grand Cayman Bank as his separate property, worth two hundred million dollars. "This isn't really a divorce," Judge Trouble thought. "It's more like the dissolution of a corporation."

The husband was wearing a fifteen-hundred-dollar suit and a red, gold and blue tie. The wife had on a tan Dior dress and a costume-jewelry-size necklace that obviously was real gold instead. The man on the witness stand wore a dull gray suit and the square bifocals of an accountant.

"And what is your conclusion about these bank accounts?" the wife's lawyer asked.

"These bank accounts were community property," said the gray accountant. Barbara Trobelo's head started to hurt, because the husband's accountant had just finished testifying exactly the opposite.

Suddenly, the telephone under the bench went "ping!"

"It's Carmelita Bueno again," said the clerk.

Jurors are always surprised, Barbara Trobelo thought, when a judge answers the phone in the middle of a trial. Some judges do it routinely, and so the lawyers are used to it. But they don't like it, either. Still, with the governor's assistant calling me . . .

"Hello, Cappy!" Judge Trouble hunched down. "I've got to whisper, because I'm up to my tush in tarantulas."

"Never mind!" Carmelita Bueno's voice boomed confidently. "You're not going to believe this!"

She sounded excited. "Harmon Bilandic lives in Senator Bonham Butler's district. They're the worst of enemies. And Senator Butler took the opportunity to blackball Bilandic. Senatorial privilege.

"So anyway, Harmon Bilandic's judgeship is dead. And you, Judge Trouble, are next on the list." Carmelita was exultant. "You're going to the civil court after all. You're going to Medaxas's court!"

"I'm taking over Medaxas's court?" Barbara Trobelo looked over toward the accountant, who was still droning on. "Thanks, Cappy," she stammered. "Holy shit!"

The accountant stared at her. So did the jury. They were uncertain that they had heard the judge correctly. Several awkward seconds passed before the witness finally picked up his pointer and started to explain the next entry in the bank records.

It gradually dawned on Judge Trouble that in taking over Medaxas's court, she had inherited the highest-profile case in the city.

Across town, Jimmy Coleman sat in front of the flowered chest. But this time he wasn't smiling, because he had just learned about Judge Medaxas's retirement. "What the hell got into him? Holy shit! Why would he resign all of a sudden like that?"

"The announcement said something about his recent heart bypass," Jennifer answered. "And also about financial sacrifices. You know, 'I've been here twenty years and I've got three kids in college.' Medaxas wants to take it a little easier and make some money."

"And we've got Barbara Trobelo instead! I've barely heard of her. She's a *divorce* judge. And now, she's got that propane truck case instead of my buddy Medaxas!"

"After all that effort with our guy in the clerk's office," Jennifer wailed. "Just so we could get the case into Medaxas's court. And now, he's not even there any more."

"Shit, shit, shit!" said Jimmy Coleman. "We've got a tiger by the tail. We've got Robert Herrick going after our client, Maxxco, as the main target. And right at the beginning, we've got trouble." He waved his chubby arms. "We've got *Judge* Trouble!"

When Robert heard the news, he broke out a bottle of Talisker Scotch.

Twenty-five years old, bottled on the Isle of Skye. Tom Kennedy lifted his glass: "Here's to Dexter Medaxas's retirement."

"Right." Robert felt more relaxed than he'd been in weeks. "And here's to our new judge. I don't know much about her, but I expect she'll give us a fair trial."

"And that's all we really need."

"So, here's to good old Judge Trouble!"

At this same moment, sixty miles to the north, Maria Melendes wasn't thinking about Judge Trouble. Or about Judge Medaxas.

She was concentrating on completely different business as she drove toward one of Texas' meanest prisons.

Maria was on her way to death row. There, she would be the assistant D.A. responsible for representing the State of Texas in the final hours before the execution of a death sentence. She was on her way to do her job as the district attorney's official killer.

14
A HARD DAY AT THE OFFICE

For Maria Melendes, this was going to be a hard day at the office.

It was just after four o'clock in the afternoon when she arrived at the Walls Unit of the Texas Department of Corrections. She always tried to get to death row early on the eve of an execution.

In law school, Maria hadn't been in favor of the death penalty. She probably would have said she was against it, if anyone had asked. And she still wasn't "in favor" of it, but today, her attitude was different, because she'd seen the kinds of cases that qualified for capital punishment. These weren't the genteel murders that graced Agatha Christie novels. And so Maria saw her job as necessary, even though the responsibility was superhuman.

Sometimes she had to fight against the defense lawyers with all of her energy, brandishing crime scene photographs so gut-wrenching that it was painful to look at them. Sometimes she had to admit that the defendant was entitled to a new trial. And always, it was her job to know the difference.

She read the warning signs for the hundredth time. The message was, "If you are taken hostage inside this prison, the State of Texas will not bargain for your release." Maria shuddered as she thought, "That applies to me, too." The Walls Unit was where Texas' most dangerous prisoners were located, including hundreds of murderers on death row, just warehoused for extermination.

A wiry little man in a double-breasted suit was waiting at the interior gate. Maria smiled. "Hi, Buzzy!"

"Hi, Maria." His tie had splashes of red in a blue field that matched his suit. Buzzy Barron was a sharp dresser, however improbable that seemed for the warden of death row—where the steel was painted with multiple, flaking coats of a terminally dull pinkish-brown color.

"You'll be happy to know that Johnny Ray Garrison hasn't gone anywhere," Buzzy said, with a trace of irony in his voice.

"Johnny Ray Garrison. The man the other prisoners call the Duke of Death Row." He was the reason Maria was here. She had come to argue for the execution of Johnny Ray Garrison's sentence. "I'll tell you what, Buzzy. I'm going to try to do my job, and at least we'll find out what's going to happen sometime tomorrow morning."

"Yeah. Well, let's hope it turns out better than your last visit. How many stays of execution? Six? Last one came about two a.m. and shut us down?"

"That's right. That was Gilberto Vargas."

"What was it he did? I mean, who'd he kill?"

Gilberto Vargas's case stuck in her mind because the autopsy was the strangest one she'd ever read. Chunks of the skeleton were missing. The heat had crumbled the bones.

"He killed his eighty-year-old landlady," she said finally. "First he kidnapped her and raped her and beat her up, and then—that fine humanitarian, Gilberto Vargas—he put this eighty-year-old victim on a stack of automobile tires and set them on fire."

She still wasn't used to the evidence she saw every day. "But the court of appeals decided that Vargas's lawyers could have developed some mitigating evidence, because he claims he was emotionally mistreated as a child. The court still hasn't decided, but the stay will put the execution off for years."

"Guess it's Gilberto's rights that count, not the victim's. She's dead."

"That's just the way it is. Maybe that's the way it has to be, because the courts have to take their time with these cases."

Then Maria brightened. "Say, Buzzy, this might perk up your afternoon. We just got three new prosecutors. And they'd be perfect if Texas still had an electric chair, because their names are Watts, Sparks, and Burnham."

Warden Buzzy laughed: "A-HA-HA-HA!" then added, unnecessarily: "Gallows humor."

"Literally."

They walked into the bowels of the Walls Unit. Without warning, Maria's thoughts shifted and focused on Robert. She always was able to soften tense situations by making him laugh, just as she had done with Buzzy just now. "If Robert were here," she thought, "he'd be even more uptight than I am, but he'd have laughed harder than Buzzy.

"I wish he were here." The thought came in a rush, before she could dismiss it. "I really do wish Robert could be here, right now, in this dismal situation."

The passageway to death row was like a journey to the center of the earth, a sequence of iron barriers connected by a maze of corridors. The dapper warden was her guide, just as the poet Virgil had escorted Danté into the Inferno.

"Well, here you are, Maria." Buzzy stopped at a tiny guard station. The glass was thick, and colored everything a hellish green. "I got the stuff you asked for. Two telephones, clear outside lines, and a fax."

"Thanks." She dropped her burgundy briefcase on the dented desk. "This is such a strange way to practice law," she mused, as much to herself as to Buzzy.

"Why? What do you mean?"

"Well, all these overlapping layers. You've got the state trial court, and then you've got the state court of criminal appeals. Those two have already turned down Johnny Ray Garrison's stay. But then there's the governor's office, which can order a stay any time."

"You're right." Buzzy replied. "Seems to me the procedure ought to be a little more straightforward. But then, I just work here."

"Plus, there's the federal district court," Maria went on. "And the federal court of appeals, and the United States Supreme Court. And any one of *them* can issue a stay. But the federal judges don't follow any predictable rules. You take a federal appeals judge. Say he was appointed by President Carter. He might go off on a tangent and decide the indictment's not detailed enough. It doesn't say what time of day the victim died, or something like that, something nobody'd ever include in an indictment. But this guy practiced municipal bond law, maybe, and now he's a judge, and he's unfamiliar with criminal law, and he decides it violates due process. And bingo, the execution gets stayed."

She shook her head and smiled. "You never know what to expect."

"Well, from what I hear, you're the best there is at this crazy job." Buzzy backed out of the door.

She smiled. "Thanks."

After he left, Maria called all of the state and federal courts to give them her two telephone numbers. Then she dialed Tom Holloway's office and left the same information. Holloway was the defense lawyer for Johnny Ray Garrison.

And then she thumbed through a *McCall's* magazine, looking for the story she'd started yesterday. It was about how Sophia Loren had raised her children during a show-business career. This was going to be a long night, and although it might seem strange, Maria needed some easy reading. Her mind couldn't stay at full tension for the next twelve hours.

But she couldn't concentrate on the *McCall's* article. Johnny Ray Garrison filled her mind. She studied the file until it sickened her. Then, involuntarily, she daydreamed about Robert and wished again that he could be here.

Sixty miles to the south, back in the city, the shadows lengthened. At last, it was six forty-five. Time for the weekly soccer game at the West Side YMCA.

Robbie Herrick was a member of the Cats. He was out on the soccer field, with his shin guards, his absurdly expensive shoes, and his red CATS! jersey.

Robert was also there, to watch Robbie play. It all started with the Cat Cheer: "Go, Cats, go! MeeeowwrrrrRRRRR!" After which, the Cats broke their huddle, yelling and running in every direction. Robert found himself yelling the Cat Cheer louder than anyone else. "Judge Trobelo has the propane truck case," he smiled to himself. It even made the soccer game more fun.

The Cats lined up at midfield. Across the semicircle, the golden-amber jerseys of the Yellowjackets were as still as the summer air. A little boy named Tommy wiped his nose one more time on his red CATS! shirt, then vaguely nudged the ball. Immediately there was a dusty tangle of seven-year-old athletes kicking wildly in different directions.

Robert Herrick smiled when he saw his son abandon his post at right wing and rush to join the battle for the ball. Robbie was completely out of position, but still, it was exactly what Robert had hoped he would do.

Meanwhile, back at the Walls Unit, Maria continued her death watch. She had set aside her magazine, unread, hours ago. She'd studied and re-studied the file on Johnny Ray Garrison. And then, absent-mindedly, she dialed Robert's number, only to be disappointed when she couldn't reach him. Finally, she remembered about Robbie's soccer game.

That was when the fax machine beeped. It was an order from the federal district court, denying the stay of execution. A seventeen-page opinion by the district judge would follow. But this was only the beginning, because Tom Holloway had the duty to appeal all the way to the Supreme Court. Maria found she couldn't concentrate on the seventeen-page opinion, either.

Without wanting to, she found herself fantasizing—daydreaming, again, about Robert. Of all things to think about on death row, this was the weirdest! But her mind stubbornly kept returning to that one image, the way he had looked the first time they were lovers. It had been amazing, fulfilling, and scary, all at the same time. His body, cool and hard, was like ice against her nipples, and his arm had held her like a vise while her emotions climbed and climbed and both of them were sweating . . . .

The climax had been an explosion. She had first suppressed her cries and then let them loose. The shadows on his face were beautiful, and she had felt herself becoming giddy, as though she might do something reckless, like fall in love with him, even though it wasn't supposed to happen this way, the very first time.

The ringing telephone startled her. She realized that she had drifted off for an instant. It was a little more than four-and-a-half hours to midnight, and midnight marked the time for the court's order of execution. She desperately needed to recover her concentration and to banish these erotic thoughts that were so misplaced here.

The telephone rang a second time; a throaty, grating sound. She lifted it mechanically.

"Hello. This is Maria Melendes."

"Hi. Whatcha doin'? Thinking dirty thoughts, I bet."

Maria smiled. "Wendy, you always know just what to say. But since you ask, the answer is . . . yes, I was. What's up?"

"Well, it may not be as exciting as mind sex with Robert, but all hell's broken loose here. The federal court of appeals is calling for you. I gave them your number. Do you need anything?"

"Yes. Somebody else to do this job."

"Can't help you, there. But I do have one suggestion. We can still tell the court of appeals how Johnny Ray's lawyers at the trial fucked up some of their objections. If that worked, it would just about shut down Johnny Ray's best arguments in this appeal."

"You already tried to get me to do that." Maria didn't have to weigh the idea for very long. "I appreciate it, but I still wouldn't feel comfortable using that kind of argument to a federal court in a death penalty case."

"Suit yourself. I just think Johnny Ray deserves it, that's all."

"I know." Maria hesitated. "Anyway, Wendy, there's one thing I do need your help with."

"Sure. What?"

"See if you can locate Robert. I hate to admit it, but it would really lift my spirits if I could talk to the big jerk."

"Lift your skirts, you mean." Wendy always sounded cynical, even though she wasn't. "But, sure. Anything that helps you get the job done on that charming Mister Garrison."

Suddenly, Maria's other telephone started ringing. "Thanks, Wendy, and good-bye." She grabbed the other line. "Hello. This is Maria Melendes."

"This is Francis Broussard, law clerk to Judge Harold Devereaux, United States Court of Appeals. I need to talk to the assistant D.A. in the Johnny Ray Garrison case."

"Speaking. It's me, Maria Melendes."

"Ms. Melendes, Judge Devereaux has asked me to set up a conference call. It will include Tom Holloway, the lawyer for Johnny Ray Garrison. It will also include Judges Spaeth and McDonald, who are the other two judges on this appeal."

"I'll stand by."

"It'll be a couple of hours. We're still trying to get the judges ready, you know. They've got to read everything first. But yes, you'd better stand by."

Maria's mind swam. She envied lawyers who became accustomed to the pressure. She was always nervous when she stood up to say anything in a courtroom. And this strange process that was about to happen on the telephone, now, was so very different from what she prepared for in law school!

A panel of three judges. Not sitting in front of her, but listening silently at distant telephones. Her opponent, Garrison's lawyer, wouldn't be like the real Tom Holloway, because she would hear only his disembodied voice, battling against her with words before three invisible judges for Johnny Ray Garrison's life or death.

She wondered, again, where Robert was and what he was doing.

15
JOHNNY RAY GARRISON

Back on the west side of the city, the sky was dusky. The soccer game was almost through half time, and Robert was hoarse from cheering.

On the patchy field at the West Side YMCA, the Cats and the Yellowjackets lined up for the second-half kickoff. During these few seconds, all of the seven-year-olds were close to their correct positions.

The Yellowjacket center pushed the ball. Immediately, there was the inevitable tangle of dusty children. The ball emerged and rolled slowly out of bounds near Robbie's position. "Reds' ball!" shouted the referee.

Miraculously, Robbie managed to follow the rules—to use both hands to throw the ball in, and to keep both feet on the ground. Robert barely dared to look.

The little boy named Tommy trapped the ball smoothly under his foot, like a grownup. He seemed surprised, as if the maneuver was an accident, and then he kicked as hard as he could. The ball sailed toward Robbie, who by now had run halfway toward the Yellowjacket goal. It was the perfect seven-year-old version of the old "give-and-go." Robert started yelling and jumping up and down in his glen plaid business suit.

With the Yellowjacket defenseman behind him, Robbie positioned himself to cross the ball to Tommy, whose red shirt was alone in front of the goal. But the sand and patchy grass confused Robbie, and his foot sideswiped the ball, which went spinning toward the boundary. Robbie sprawled on his back. But, then, as only a kid can do, he was up and running again. Just before the ball went out of bounds, he dove and tackled it. The referee whistled. "Hands! Yellowjackets' Ball!"

But at this point, the game was interrupted, because Robert was on the field. He was yelling as he lifted his son up on his shoulders. While all the moms and dads watched with wonder, the lawyer in the expensive business suit danced a little dance with the red-shirted boy on his shoulders. And when he got over being startled, Robbie was smiling and yelling, too. The Cats' coach, a gentle black-bearded giant who was a plumbing contractor in real life, roared his approval: "A-HA-HA-HAAA!" And then he had the presence of mind to yell, "Time out, ref!"

Robert found himself shouting, "What a play! What a play! What a PLAY!"

You can't use your hands on a soccer ball, of course. But that was what Robert liked best about what Robbie had done. The boy had done something instinctive and unorthodox, something out of the ordinary, when the ball seemed lost. Instead of giving up.

All the parents were cheering, and even the two DPS officers in the baggy suits started smiling and clapping. But Robert didn't notice. "Attaboy, Robbie!" he roared, and he lifted his son from his shoulders and hugged him.

Finally, the soccer game was over. The Cats lost. Robbie was dejected—not just sad, but dejected—as only a seven-year-old can be when his team has lost.

In Robert's car, on the way home, the telephone beeped. He had been the last lawyer he'd known of to install a car phone, and he still resisted the intrusions it made. But it was a practical necessity.

And anyway, this turned out to be a call he needed to take. "Hello, Robert baby." Her voice came slowly through the earpiece. "I'm here at the Walls, just waiting."

He turned to his son. "Robbie, I'm sorry, but I've got to take this." Then: "Maria, you've got a little less bounce to your voice than usual."

"Yes. Because I feel—well, I feel . . . so . . . small and insignificant. I'm wondering if I'm up to the job. Robert, tell me how to handle it, because you're always so self-assured and poised in court. You handle cases that you believe in—big cases, important ones."

At that, he laughed. "When I'm in court, Maria, my calm exterior is only a front. It hides the jelly underneath." Suddenly, he was more serious: "Listen. You're tougher than I'll ever be. You're as tough as they come."

She knew why he was saying these things, but still, it seemed to work. "I only wish it were true."

"And besides," he went on, "you've already told me all about this case. Somebody's got to do something about a crime like that, and Maria, you've got a job that you can believe in. I know the death penalty's hard, but that's why it matters. In your work, you wrestle with the hardest questions there are. It's a lot more significant than my cases. They're all civil ones, about money."

"How come I don't get a one-third contingency fee, then?" The mischief was back in her voice again.

She always made him laugh, even now, when the tension was hers. "Gallows humor," he said, just as Buzzy had.

"Yes. And obviously, I don't want one third."

She still sounded uncertain. But he sensed that she was as ready as she'd ever be to do the best that she humanly could. And he realized that his love for her—was it love? well, whatever it was—had grown so that even during this trying time, she seemed comfortable letting herself depend on him. And what was more amazing, he felt right about it, too.

"Thanks for listening." Her voice was soft, but more even.

They said good-bye.

He looked over at Robbie, crumpled unhappily in the seat. He tousled the boy's hair and smiled at him. "That's okay, big guy. You played like a tiger, and the Cats still have a chance to win the championship."

❖ ❖ ❖

The minutes passed slowly as Maria waited on death row. Even more slowly, the minutes became hours, until finally, finally, the telephone rang. "Ms. Melendes? Can you hold for a conference call?"

And then, a moment later: "Judge Devereaux?"

"Here."

"Judge Spaeth?"

"Yes, ma'am."

"Judge Constance McDonald?"

"Present."

"Mister Holloway?"

"Present," said Tom Holloway. "I represent Johnny Ray Garrison."

"Thank you. Ms. Melendes?"

"Also present." Maria kept her voice steady. "I represent the People of Texas."

"Go ahead, please."

"Good evening, lady and gentlemen. I'm Judge Devereaux." The gravelly voice was Cajun-accented. "This court must immediately decide whether to grant Mister Holloway's motion for a stay of execution for Johnny Ray Garrison, who is under a sentence of death."

The judge cleared his throat. "We will issue an order before midnight. And so, Mister Holloway, I would advise you to take your best shot first."

"Well, your honor, asking for my 'best shot' in a state that does lethal injections—it sort of makes my hair stand on edge!" In such a tense situation, even weak humor works, and the joke focused attention away from the facts of this brutal murder. Holloway was unorthodox, but Maria knew he also was effective. The judges laughed politely.

"Our first ground is simple," Tom Holloway began. "Johnny Ray Garrison is innocent." He paused, because that was a jarring statement. "I don't mean he's completely innocent. He's guilty of murder. What I'm saying is, he's not eligible for the death penalty."

Again a dramatic pause. "That's because, our habeas corpus petition contains twelve different affidavits showing that Johnny Ray Garrison has given his life to Christ." There was not a trace of insincerity in Holloway's voice. "His conversion is genuine. Johnny Ray is a member of the prison lay ministry. He's gotten other inmates to give their lives to Christ. He's away from the drugs, and now he's a different person.

"If the jury had seen this Johnny Ray, they'd never have imposed a sentence of death. And here's the key thing." Holloway's voice rose. "The Texas statutory law provides absolutely no way, in any court, to take Johnny Ray's present life into account." The defense lawyer spat out the words in disgust. "In fact, that's our second argument for the stay: Texas statutory law doesn't even let us tell a court about this religious awakening that ought to save Johnny Ray from the death penalty."

"All right," said Judge Devereaux. "Let's hear from Ms. Melendes."

Maria spread out her notes. "I'd like to tell the court the evidence that the jury had when it sentenced Johnny Ray Garrison to death."

Her voice was steady, now. "This is Johnny Ray Garrison's fourth time to have his case considered by this court. The judges of this court wrote an opinion when they denied his first habeas corpus petition. That opinion is at 18 Federal Reporter Third, page 1216. It tells how Johnny Ray Garrison robbed a Go-'N-Tote supermarket, how he made four customers lie on the floor, and how he shot each of them in the back of the head."

Now it was time for Maria's voice to rise. "The clerk's name was Patsy LoSoya. Johnny Ray Garrison forced this young girl to commit oral sex on him, on her knees on the bare concrete floor. With the bodies lying around her, and with blood splattered all over her, mixed with human brains. And when he was finished with that, Johnny Ray Garrison inserted the barrel of a shotgun into Patsy LoSoya's vagina and pulled the trigger. His confession tells how he watched her squirm around on the floor until he finally shot her again. All of these facts are in the court's earlier opinion."

There was silence as Maria paused for an instant. "Your honors, I agree with Mister Holloway that evidence of innocence ought to be considered, even after conviction. Even if it's the 'I'm-guilty-of-murder-but-I-shouldn't-get-the-death-penalty' type of innocence. The Supreme Court covered this issue in a case called *Sawyer v. Whitley*."

"Yes," said Judge Devereaux quietly. "My law clerk, Mister Broussard, pulled that case for me."

"Then your honor knows what the Supreme Court said. The petitioner has to produce evidence so convincing that no reasonable juror could possibly have given this defendant the death penalty. And frankly, when you look at the evidence of the crime, I don't think Johnny Ray Garrison even comes close."

"What about Mister Holloway's second argument, Ms. Melendes?" asked Judge Spaeth. "He says Texas doesn't have any procedure for considering late-breaking evidence."

"Well, Mister Holloway chose his words. He didn't say there's no procedure. He just said there wasn't a statute that made the Texas *courts* do it. The governor always considers claims of innocence. Occasionally, they raise enough doubts so that Texas governors have commuted death sentences."

Maria paused before making her next point. "And there's another case, called *Herrera v. Collins*. There, the Supreme Court said that the trial is the time for deciding guilt or innocence. *Herrera v. Collins* approves the Texas procedure. The same procedure used in this case. And besides, the Texas courts do consider late claims of innocence, even if there isn't a statute that makes them, because they've followed what the Supreme Court said in these two cases."

Judge Devereaux interrupted. The clock was moving. "Well, we'll remember all of that. What's your next argument, Mister Holloway?"

Maria no longer was nervous. She and Tom Holloway battled toe-to-toe as the defense lawyer told the court about his next argument, which was based upon a Supreme Court case called *Penry v. Lynaugh*. He said the Texas courts hadn't followed the Supreme Court's requirements for telling the jury about mitigating evidence—the facts helpful to the defendant. Maria disagreed. By now, she was functioning on pure adrenalin.

At the end, she added, "Even if Mister Holloway's argument under *Penry v. Lynaugh* were correct—and it isn't—it wouldn't matter in this case, because the whole theory depends on mitigating evidence, and there wasn't any mitigating evidence in this case that was kept from the jury. Texas has complied with the full requirements of the *Penry* case."

It was ten forty-eight. Just over an hour until midnight.

"Judges, please stay on the line," said Judge Devereaux. "We will either grant or deny the stay before midnight."

Maria's telephone clicked off.

Suddenly, she felt alone, frighteningly alone. Thinking about Johnny Ray Garrison's crimes, and the job she had to do, brought on a cold, unmanageable dread, like the desperation she'd felt when they marched her father off to Castro's prisons. Or the fear of the unknown when she floated ashore south of Miami a lifetime ago, before the comfort of relatives in Little Havana, before her parents had found their bungalow in Hialeah. "My God," she thought suddenly, "it's scary how much I wish Robert were here. Talking to him earlier just wasn't enough."

She thought about the way he listened to her and the way he liked to argue about the way the law should be, always with a smile of amusement. Not like this telephonic street fight she'd just participated in. And she thought about the way he knew when to stop the verbal sparring and just hold her, whenever he sensed she was vulnerable—and suddenly her eyes welled up, and there was another thought, outside this high-pressure case, that worried her.

Because suddenly she knew, better than ever before, how intertwined she had become with him.

Back in the city, it was just before midnight at the Herrick household, too. Robert was reading the *Houston Chronicle*. Sitting in the family room in his River Oaks home, he slowly folded the paper and put it away. Then he remembered the soccer game today. And he smiled.

"What a fine little man Robbie is," Robert said to Rosalie Herrick.

Grandma Rosalie smiled too. "Yes, he is."

"He acted funny when I put him to bed. I told him I was proud of him, but he was about to cry. I said, 'Robbie, what's the matter?,' and then it all came out. 'Daddy, they cheated! The Yellowjackets, they were always offside!'"

"Seven years old," said Rosalie contentedly.

"He doesn't give up, Robbie doesn't."

"Why do you like that? It's hard on the child."

"Because that's what life's all about." His answer was immediate. "I never want Robbie to give up that spark."

Rosalie laughed. "It wouldn't hurt Robbie to accept the fact that his team lost the soccer game by the score of one to nothing."

"No. And I realize that Robbie gets it from me. Maybe I try a little too hard at everything. But I'm a firm believer that when you give up, you lose out on what life is about. When you give up, you die."

Meanwhile, at the Walls Unit, the minutes crawled by. Maria had never gotten accustomed to the tension during the time that the judges took to decide on a stay of execution.

Finally, the telephone rang, and the clerk of the court read the one-sentence order. "It is ordered that the stay of execution is hereby"—Maria held her breath—"denied."

Maria had won.

Except that it didn't feel very much like a victory.

And she knew that she was still on call, because the Supreme Court hadn't spoken yet. Tom Holloway, of course, was in constant communication with other lawyers in Washington, and they would have a request for stay already drafted. In fact, it probably had been filed with the high court by now.

It was just after one in the morning when the Supreme Court's order came. One short sentence: "Petitioner's motion for a stay of execution is denied." And so it was that Maria learned, unless the governor was heard from again, or one of the courts, that the execution was going to proceed.

Buzzy Barron was at the door. "I never say 'congratulations' in these kinds of cases."

Maria nodded. "No. I don't feel as though I've won when it's a death sentence. It feels like winning a bankruptcy case. Poor Patsy LoSoya."

"Well, you do a necessary job, and you do it very well for your clients. Including Patsy LoSoya and all the people of Texas."

"Thank you." She thought, "But—I am so very drained!"

"You wanted to witness the execution?"

"'Want' is the wrong word, but yes."

It surprised Maria when she saw Johnny Ray Garrison, even though she had seen the same prison pallor before. Absence from sunlight gives Caucasian convicts a color that is almost translucent. It looked even more odd on this particular occasion, because Johnny Ray Garrison was lying on his back, strapped to a gurney.

But the convict's eyes were alive in that chalk-white face, burning as bright as two diamonds. They sought out a man who stood behind the glass, the man in the Highway Patrol uniform. Maria recognized him. This was Armando LoSoya, the victim's brother.

Officer Armando LoSoya had worked tirelessly toward this night. He had led victims' rights groups that marched on the capitol. He had written Op-Ed pieces. He wanted justice for his sister. And now, when the two men's eyes met, the born-again convict mouthed the words: "I'm sorry." The man in the uniform nodded once. Then Johnny Ray Garrison turned away.

The prison physician stood by as the needle went in. The first of three drugs began to flow into Johnny Ray Garrison's arm. This was not the poison, but a painkiller, and as the second valve opened, Maria looked up. It was one-seventeen in the morning. She had felt she ought to be here, but now she couldn't make herself watch.

Finally, the third valve opened. The doctor still stood by while the mixture of sodium thiopental, pancuronium bromide and potassium chloride did its work.

At one twenty-nine, it was over, and the corpse that once had been Johnny Ray Garrison had been wheeled out by another door.

At one thirty-six, Maria realized that she had been sitting for several minutes in the guard room that Buzzy had let her use. Just sitting. And staring at the desk. She reached for the telephone and dialed the number like a sleepwalker.

"Hello?" said Robert Herrick at the other end of the line.

"Hello, sweetheart."

"Hi," he said. "Maria, you sound terrible."

He wanted to run to her through the telephone wire. He knew he would never understand the pressures she felt, the uncertainty, the guilt—and the paradoxical feeling of helplessness that comes from using the state's awesome power over questions that human beings can never understand. Questions like the life-or-death choices in Maria's job. But he also knew that she was afraid and doubtful and insecure, and he felt her fear even more than he would feel it in himself, as he waited and listened for her to speak.

"Oh, I think I'm okay. But look: Do you suppose there's any way you could, maybe, come over to my place tonight? It's just—well, I'm still here at work. Just sitting here. But I'm—I'm done. It's time to leave."

She paused. "And I don't know exactly how to put it, except to say I need for you to hold me. Because . . . you see . . . this has been a hard day at the office."

16
THE BOMB SQUAD

Friday evening. Maria still was stunned by the responsibility she had shouldered several days earlier at the Walls Unit. Robert knew he needed to pamper her. And so tonight was a night to recuperate. First, the symphony. For two and a half hours, they sat still and let the music wash over them. Now, he was taking her to dinner.

Robert steered the Duesenberg down Smith Street toward the freeway. "After Squint shot the car up, I had to put it in the shop. I decided to get the exhausts chromed at the same time."

The twelve cylinders emptied into an elaborate system of pipes that stuck out from the hood and trailed along the sides. "Those guys at the body shop love this baby, and they polished the pipes so you can see your reflection. Like a trauma-unit operation with cosmetic surgery thrown in at the same time."

Maria had to laugh. "It's beautiful. But speaking of Squint, it sure is weird having those two DPS guys follow us everywhere." She looked back at the ugly green Plymouth.

"Well, be glad they're there. You told me that yourself." Robert maneuvered the Duesenberg onto the freeway. They both tried not to think about the Plymouth, or about the one-eyed assassin who was the reason it was following them.

"Anyway, the music was just what I needed." Maria leaned back in the huge leather seats. "Thanks for taking me." She laughed her little-girl laugh. She sometimes laughed at odd times, Robert thought. "I liked the way they did the first movement of the Haffner Symphony. When they do that part right, it's really almost erotic."

"Keep that thought." He was trying to keep her mind away from business and away from Squint.

They both were laughing at that when the Duesenberg crested an overpass, rising like a hill at the edge of a long valley. The freeway undulated over a series of smaller overpasses and then, in the distance, threaded under the four-level spaghetti bowl at Interstate 610.

"What's all that stuff they have tied around the propane truck overpass?" Maria asked. There was a multicolored streamer looping over one of the ramps.

"The National Transportation Safety Board." Robert nudged the Duesenberg rightward. "The same people who investigate train wrecks. This accident triggers their jurisdiction, the NTSB, because it's a hazardous cargo on the Interstate. I'm afraid they're going to mishandle the case."

"How do you mean?"

"The NTSB will usually pick out the simplest target and say that's the only one who did it." His voice was heavy with disgust. "They might pick out the truck driver and make a finding of fact saying it was his negligence alone. The NTSB is clumsy. It's part of the federal government."

Off to the right, the Transco Tower rose up through the mist, dark against the gray clouds of the sky. "If Darth Vader were a building," Maria thought, "he'd be the Transco Tower." It made her shiver, almost as though the Tower was a sinister force that had something to do with making the propane truck blow up, a force that threatened disaster in the future.

"I sure do wish, Robert baby, that you weren't involved in that awful case," she murmured.

But Robert was thinking about the federal government, and he didn't hear her. He frowned. "The NTSB already has rented a warehouse and assembled all the debris, like putting together dinosaur bones to make a skeleton. Huge expenses, but poor investigation. And they've sent out these amateur FBI agents who've overlooked the obvious witnesses. And it really matters, because I'm worried they're going to hurt my clients' case."

"Oh, well. Now I'm beginning to understand," said Maria. "That's what's wrong with the federal government. It hasn't gotten on board with Robert Herrick's trial strategy."

Robert had to laugh at that. Whenever he got on his high horse, whenever he sounded just a little too pompous, she had a way of puncturing his balloon. But she always did it in a way that made him laugh.

"Anyway," he continued, "the NTSB will write a report with a big gold seal. And eagles. And red, white and blue ribbons. And with my luck, that report will only mention the Louisiana Trucking Company as a possible suspect. I'm afraid they'll leave out the people who built the road and the guardrail, such as Maxxco Construction Corporation, even though there's plenty of evidence that Maxxco was negligent. And even though those are exactly the kinds of dangerous highway conditions that you'd want a safety board looking into."

Now the Duesenberg was rounding the ramp that connected the Southwest Freeway to Loop 610. The guardrail was a twisted confusion of metal tinker toys.

"And of course there are very skillful defense lawyers in my case," Robert went on. "From Booker & Bayne. If the NTSB leaves the construction companies out, the defense lawyers will show the report to the jury, so they can tell them that the truck driver is the only one at fault."

"Let me see if I have it figured correctly," Maria said. "You've got a good lawsuit against the Louisiana Trucking Company, except you're *worried* that the NTSB is going to blame the trucking company."

"Well, not exactly, Maria."

"Which leads me to conclude, Mister Herrick, that the Louisiana Trucking Company must be pretty near bankrupt, and that's why you don't want it to be the only one blamed. You want to sue somebody else. Somebody with real deep pockets."

"Well, not exactly. There's also lots of evidence that Maxxco was negligent.

And the trucking company isn't entirely bankrupt. It's just that it only has five million dollars worth of insurance."

"Oh. Just five million dollars? My condolences." Then, after shooting off her mouth, she thought for an instant and she understood the problem. "It sounds like a lot, but I guess you're right. It won't even begin to compensate all the hundreds of survivors of the disaster. And that's why the simplistic conclusion, to blame only the most obvious defendant, is wrong. And so your job is to be more thorough than the federal government, and you have to look into those bad guys who built the road.

"And let me guess," she went on. "Those guys have a whole lot more financial stability than the trucking company."

"Yes," he agreed. "The Maxxco Construction Corporation is one of the biggest industrial companies in the world. With a net worth of several billion. And they have the ability to build safe roads, but in this case they didn't, because they wanted to cut corners. Maxxco's own files are full of incriminating memos. I just hope the NTSB considers all of the evidence, because otherwise there'll be another accident like this in the future."

"Gee, I guess that's the reason they're bad guys. They've got a bottom line in the billion dollar range, and that's what makes them evil."

Robert steered the Duesenberg under the awning at Valerio's Restaurant. "You're right. I want to sue defendants who can pay the judgment. But only if there's evidence I can believe in. That's the only way I can do my job—and help my clients."

"I hope you get 'em all, sweetheart," Maria said with mock seriousness. "All those guilty construction companies. I'd rather you weren't in the case in the first place, but long as you are, I want you to have lots of money so you can keep taking me to expensive places like this. The doctor says it's good for my complexion, and he doesn't like the NTSB, either."

He stared at her, so caught up in his thoughts that it took a minute for him to realize she was teasing him. The case was getting to him. "A trial lawyer's eleventh commandment," he thought, "ought to be, 'Do not take thyself too darn seriously.'" If you became too sanctimonious, you turned into a loose cannon, and it was easy to hurt people by accident. Maybe Maria was just administering a necessary correction to his self-importance.

And then, finally, he laughed at himself. And with that, they walked into Valerio's.

But Maria was thinking, "I wonder if the Louisiana Trucking Company is a 'good' guy, since it's too poor to pay a judgment? Does being broke make it a good guy, even though it's the most obviously guilty defendant?" And then, immediately, she knew the answer.

Yes, the trucking company would turn out to be a "good" guy. It would admit fault, settle, and become a source of witnesses against Maxxco. And Robert's job—his real job—would be to pursue the other defendants, such as Maxxco. Ironically, Robert's duty to his clients would be to fight Maxxco's exaggerated claims that the accident was all the truck driver's fault, and so he would act at times almost like a defense lawyer for the trucking company, to counter the misrepresentations that were sure to be made by the other defendants.

It certainly was a complicated world. And Maria was superstitious. She thought back to her days in Miami, where Santerians foretold the future by sifting the blood and entrails of sacrificial goats or the beaks of battered chickens—the tarot cards of a new and more bizarre revelation. From where she stood, she couldn't see the Transco Tower, but she knew its Darth Vader face was looking down at them. For an instant, she felt a powerful premonition for what this sinister force might do in the future. And once again, for the umpteenth time, she wished she'd never heard of the propane truck case.

A few minutes later, they were seated inside Valerio's at Robert's customary table, and the conversation turned to a different subject.

"Well, I really didn't know what I was supposed to do," Maria said. "And I don't think I've ever felt so . . . well . . . so naked, in all my life. And that was my first time," she concluded. "What about yours?"

"More or less the same," said Robert. "I didn't know what to do, either. But it's a rite of passage, you know? And so you can't let it be obvious that you don't know how to do it. I fumbled around a lot."

"That's exactly the way it feels. Even if you're a complete bumblepuppy, you can't admit you don't know how."

"That's right," said Robert. "My first time, I was shaking so much I couldn't have found my rear end with both hands. I just didn't have the right techniques. You know?"

They had not noticed that their voices were rising until Eugenio, the waiter, broke in. "Mister Herrick!" His usually unflappable face was an embarrassed red above his starched wing collar. "The folks at the next table can hear you, and . . . on this subject of conversation, they . . . wanted you to know that they can hear you!"

"What subject?" asked Robert with surprise. Then he remembered their words. "Naked" . . . "rite of passage" . . . "fumbling around." And he smiled.

"It's all right, Eugenio. We were just talking about the first time each of us tried a jury trial." He started laughing. "And that's the way you feel when you try your first jury trial. More naked than you've ever felt in your life."

"But I guess our language was a little colorful," Maria said. "We'll try to hold it down. And in the meantime, Eugenio, would you tell those nice people what the real subject of our conversation was, so they won't be worried about us talking in a lewd manner any more?"

Maria was enjoying herself, finally. Robert was embarrassed, but he was glad to see her gradually returning to her old personality. And when he asked for the check, he saw that Eugenio the waiter was still laughing, because he had a story that he could tell from now until doomsday.

Robert was wearing a dark gray suit with a subtle blue stripe that sometimes you could see and sometimes you couldn't, together with a solid blue tie that was the same color as his eyes in this light. With the white shirt it was simple but elegant, and it all combined in a way that made her want to keep looking at him.

"Let's go to my place, Robert sweetheart," Maria said suddenly. Fortunately, she was whispering this time. "All of this conversation about jury trials has gotten me into a romantic mood, and I just can't wait to be alone with you."

He looked at her, again. She was kidding about the mood created by the jury trial talk, but she wasn't kidding him about the rest of what she had said.

Maria's townhouse had a high entry hall with a crystal chandelier. They went into the living room, and Maria sat them down on a billowing white couch. "Yes, kiss me like that," Maria said to Robert. "And put your hand on me, here. I like that."

Robert did what she told him. And then he thought about the two DPS officers standing just outside. The bodyguards the governor had sent. But then, almost immediately, he put the bodyguards out of his mind. He discovered that with Maria next to him, he could forget about them effortlessly.

Her hand reached over to him and touched him. "That's very nice," she said as she felt his response. "Come on." She got up from the couch. Obediently, he followed her.

In the bedroom, Maria quickly unfastened the buttons on her silk blouse, one-two-three. Her skin was incredibly pale and clear. As she turned her shoulders to let the blouse slip off, and bent over with one more fluid motion and unsnapped her bra, Robert watched and fumbled with his own buttons. "Sort of like my first jury trial!" he thought.

Her breasts stood out, arching away from her chest and swaying slightly, with pink aureolas and large hard nipples under her sweet, cameo face. Quickly, she unzipped the short gray wool skirt and slipped it off, then peeled back the black patterned pantyhose with pretty little bows. The triangle of glistening dark hair was held up by two long, smooth legs.

From nowhere, Maria had a plastic package in her hand. She stroked Robert's chest, with the brown hairs folding inward, and she helped his fumbling hands to loosen his cuff buttons. "Whatever a guy like you might think, 'safe sex' doesn't mean that you do it in the bank vault," she said, and laughed for the hundredth time. She showed him the little plastic package. Then, she pulled him close and felt how firm he was.

And then, she nudged him toward the bed.

Now, Maria was slitting the package with her teeth and touching Robert with her other hand. She was beautiful, she was smart, she was nice, and she was a wonderful lover, and he was overwhelmed by it all.

Suddenly she shifted her position, and he felt her breasts touching the insides of his thighs. "I hope you don't mind having a woman who's aggressive." She looked up at him. "Because I couldn't change it even if I wanted to." She was suddenly quieter and more serious. Behind the curtain of her hair, he saw her dark red lips poised over him. Her tongue skipped around the top, the ridge, and then settled into flicking up and down over the sensitive seam on the underside, away from him. Her nails ran up and down the insides of his legs. Then she took him in her hand and rubbed him slowly all over her breasts, and between them, and up and down on her nipples.

At last, she lifted her face and looked at him while she engulfed him completely, running her hand through the curtain of her hair. And with that, he felt as big as the Transco Tower, and full of reckless confidence.

He pulled her up to kiss her. And in what seemed like one movement, she opened the package, slipped the covering over him, and used her hand to put him inside her. Straddling him, she pushed up and down, faster, faster. More slowly, she took her breasts in her hands, and put first one, then the other, into his mouth. Then she saw the look in his eyes, and she said, "Oh, Honey, just go for it!" And so he reached for her shoulders and pushed her on her back, and then he was on top of her, between her legs, thick and hard, feeling for the entry. He heard her inrush of breath.

Soon, she began to give herself up to him, and she felt him giving to her. Alternately she felt a warm nothingness and an aching urgency, but without anxiety, only desire. Gradually, the walls that separated her from him, her from the room, her from the rest of the universe, all dissolved. Her back arched and her eyes glittered, and then she shut them while the pounding compulsion to go as high as she could swept her upward through the alternating floods of excitement and calm. He was beautiful. The sharp lines around the muscles in his chest, the dark brown hair, and the deep blue eyes, dark as midnight, looking not at her but into her. He was very strong, and it drove her irrationally higher to fantasize that, as much as she had been in control a few minutes ago, now she couldn't escape. She usually was more cautious than this. But it was exactly that, the recklessness of it all, that increased the erotic drive and chased away the last ghost of inhibition, so that finally it was her body that was in control.

By now, her neck was thrust off the side of the bed, and she was letting out a stream of little rhythmical cries. Then, suddenly, the boundaries were gone and she was screaming. She tensed, tensed, tensed—he could feel her muscles clamp down on him—and her legs wrapped around him. And then she was quieter.

"Come on, baby," she said so urgently that it surprised him. "I want you to feel good, too." And with that encouragement, he felt himself shudder and begin to lose control, with all his own inhibitions long since gone.

Then, both of them were silent, and alone with their thoughts.

"I've fallen in love with this woman," he said to himself. "And it wasn't supposed to happen. She loves to get mushy cards, and I always forget Valentine's Day."

He looked around Maria's bedroom, which was littered with stuffed animals. And he thought: "She's messy and I'm neat. The biggest problem is, she wants to get married and have children, and I've already got two.

"Anyway, would I really be able to get along with her? Whenever she's dissatisfied, she stamps her foot and yells, and so far, it works, because I haven't learned how to deal with it. But she's pretty self-disciplined, and she always does what's right. And she acts like she's invulnerable, but she's afraid of heights, and she couldn't balance her checkbook if her life depended on it. And everybody's her friend, including the derelicts."

He lay still and was silent.

She rested, her face at his neck. And then she laughed. "That was wonderful, sweetheart." She turned to face him. "You see what you can do when you put your mind to it?"

"I have to get up early in the morning," she explained to him.

And he said gently, "I have to go home, anyway." He got up slowly and dressed.

As he drove toward Interstate 610, with the two DPS officers in the Plymouth following him, he thought about Maria's family. Seven children, with her in the middle, but with her being the oldest girl. "Maybe that's why she's such an overachiever," he thought. "Fighting the boys."

As he exited Interstate 610 and steered toward River Oaks, Robert's mind wandered back to an evening two months ago. Maria had bamboozled him into taking her to a dive called Marty's Mardi Gras Bar, because she knew one of the band members. A guy named Eric, in a band called KBN. Then it turned out Eric was in a gangsta rap group, and KBN stood for Killa Blak Niggaz. These guys sang the most disgustingly violent, anti-female stuff:

"Gonna dog 'er in da tree-tops

"Dog 'er in da woods

"Dog 'er in da boss's bed

"Dog 'er in da 'hood.

"Help you cure yo' white-girl pussy

"Outta them nigga fears

"Shoot yo' ass all inside-out,

"And up and thru yo' ears."

He had been amazed that she would bring him here, to listen to this kind of trash. "Relax, Robert!" she had said. "They don't mean it, they're just rapping. Don't you think you ought to get out more, beyond the Rotary Club?"

And so he had asked her, "Well, then is it okay if I call you a bitch, just like they talk about in their rap?"

And she just laughed, and said, "No, because you and me isn't a rap song. It's real life."

She always surprised him.

His mind was churning as he turned the car onto River Oaks Boulevard. "She and I are so different! Maria loves those slice-'em-and-dice-'em horror movies, and I think they ought to be shut down. But I like the way she always looks elegant, even in her work clothes, and sexy at the same time."

It wasn't supposed to happen. But he had to admit that it felt good, even as scared as he was.

It was just after midnight, with these jumbled thoughts in his mind, when Robert pulled through the long circular drive in front of the colonial home he shared with Rosalie and his two children.

He knew immediately that something was wrong. There was a box sitting at an odd angle by the side door, and he sensed that it might be dangerous.

"Hey, come here quick!" he stage-whispered toward the green Plymouth. Across the street, the two DPS officers were settling in for the rest of the graveyard shift.

Suddenly Robert had sweat all over his back, and all of it felt ice cold. It pasted his shirt down against his skin. In his mind's eye, he saw the image of Squint with that cruel, misshapen socket. His vision flipped over to a larger-than-life Esparza, then back to Squint again. It would be so easy for the one-eyed assassin to put a bomb here and then wait for time, or pressure, or movement to set it off. Or was Squint watching from a position close by, with an electronic detonator in his hand? As the two DPS officers hustled over, the thought made Robert's stomach turn. His hand shook when he pointed.

"The screen door's unlocked. And look at that box. Why's a breakfast cereal box sitting on the kitchen steps? I don't like it!"

The box of Froot Loops looked innocuous enough, by the kitchen door. It had a torn flap. And cellophane sticking out. But they could tell that something was terribly wrong.

"I can't see inside," said the first DPS officer to reach the Froot Loops. "The lining's too messed up."

"Don't touch it!" said his partner. "I'm going back to the car to call the bomb guys."

"All I can tell is, there's something metal inside," said the first officer. "Looks like a little copper plate, about the size of a penny."

"And look here!" Robert ran up to the door and stuck his key in the lock. "There's a piece of broken glass in the door, and it wasn't that way when I left."

What if Squint or his pals had gotten to the children? What if someone was inside there now? He looked up and saw the upstairs hall light, and then he saw something move, like a shadow. Was it a reflection of the trees in the wind?

"How could I have done this?" Robert's voice broke in anguish. "How could I have brought this kind of danger down on my family?" It was his own fault, for paying attention to nothing but his business problems. "Pepper! Robbie! My babies! I'm so selfish that I've always got to be pushing the edge, and now I've gambled with the lives of my own kids, my own mother!"

He panicked as he grabbed for the door.

"Don't you go inside!" Officer number one shouted. "Let us do that!"

"The bomb guys say they can't X-ray it without moving it, and they can't move it because it might be triggered by a motion sensor!" Officer number two was back from the car. "They're going to put a steel plate over the door and blow up the Froot Loops. But right now, everybody's got to get the hell out of the way!"

Two flashlights marked the officers' progress through the house. The children were evacuated first, still in their pajamas, then Grandma Rosalie in her nightgown, and then the officers began to search all the closets. Suddenly the street was a convention of blinking gumball machines, and everyone watched, in mesmerized awe, as the bomb truck floated majestically through Herrick's circular drive toward the Froot Loops.

Pepper stumbled sleepily along in her flannel pajamas, protesting the whole way. "But Daddy . . . Daddy, it's . . . all okay . . . ."

Her nonchalance pushed him over the edge, and he shouted at her. "Shut up, Pepper! There comes a time when we can't have all this back talk. Move it! You just shut up and *move*!"

Robbie and Rosalie hustled along behind them. Pepper looked as though she wanted to say something else, but then she thought better of it. And everyone looked back at the bomb squad. Robert was already anticipating the noise and the fireball, because in his mind, this hellish thing had already exploded a dozen times.

The cannon that they unloaded was specially designed for bomb detonation. Its trigger was a remote hand-held radio, and its ammunition would fragment to set off the bomb on contact. First, it took time for setup. It was only a few minutes, but it seemed like forever. Then there was a deafening sound as the gun went off.

The Froot Loops box puffed into chunks of paper and dust. But there was no explosion, yet.

The captain of the bomb squad wore an asbestos bodysuit as he approached the scene. A five-dollar bill wafted down through the air and settled gently on the concrete steps. Pennies, dimes, and quarters were scattered around it. The captain finally counted forty-seven dollars and fifty-three cents.

"You mean that Froot Loops box was nothing but a substitute for your piggy bank?" Robert stood behind the huge oak tree on his back lawn, fifty yards from the combat scene. Pepper and Robbie waited beside him, while the two DPS officers stood guard. As for Rosalie, she was still shaking, even though she was trying to look calm, and at the same time, she was gradually letting her fear give way to irritation at her granddaughter for this false alarm.

"That's what I've been trying to tell you!" wailed Pepper. "I kept my allowance and my babysitting money in there."

Robert's voice strained with incredulity. "But why on earth . . . did you use . . . a Froot Loops box?"

"Well, why not?"

"And anyway, what about that hole in the glass door?"

"The glass broke 'cause I accidentally hit it with my rollerblades, carrying 'em inside. That's all!" Pepper was plaintively defiant. "And that's why I put my money down on the steps, inside the Froot Loops box! And I just *forgot* about it! So sue me!"

"Well, in calling us, you did the right thing," said the asbestos-draped bomb squad captain. "If a package arouses a reasonable suspicion, you shouldn't approach it. We always neutralize it, first. We err on the side of caution."

He grinned. "But I gotta admit, this Froot Loops box—this is a first for us!"

"Can I have my money back now?" Pepper wanted to know.

Slowly, Robert let out a long, deep breath. It was over.

Or rather, it had never really happened. There had never been any danger.

"My God," he thought to himself. "Squint the assassin and Esparza the case runner—they don't need to worry about me. They don't need to kill me. They've already succeeded. They've already made me into a candidate for the nut house."

Five miles away, in her bedroom, Maria was occupied by problems of her own. "I've got to get to sleep," she thought. "I've got complaint desk duty, starting at seven."

Every assistant D.A. hated the complaint desk. Maria would confront sixty or seventy irate citizens tomorrow, all with reports of alleged crimes that the police had rejected. Out of that sixty, one or two would qualify for filing. The other fifty-eight citizens would end up yelling, "You mean to tell me **this** isn't a crime?" or "I don't believe you! Where's your boss?"

It dawned on her that, here and now, in the middle of the night, she really missed Robert. There had been a new tenderness in their lovemaking. A new and more intense passion, a feeling that didn't end with the moment. She turned off the TV set. Then she turned it back on.

It was two-thirty in the morning, and she was wide awake.

"I'm falling for Robert Herrick," she thought. "And it scares me. Or rather, I've already fallen in love with him, and it scares the hell out of me."

She turned on her side. "He's always telling me what to do. He's uptight and I'm not. He's a member of both the ACLU and the National Rifle Association and gives tons of money to Right to Life, and even though I don't have enough money to give it to anybody, I'd give it to the abortion rights people if I did. He's not as brutally honest as I am, and he thinks I'm too blunt.

"We're so damn different!"

And yet, the way he made her feel—it reminded her of the simple, pure happiness she had known, the childish excitement, when she had shared the beach at Miramar with her family and let the salt breeze from the north flow all around her. Long before the confining suspicion of the Cuban state had spoiled it all, there was that pristine and unforgettable time, the time before struggle. The time before America. She felt the same contentment with Robert.

"But I've got to get to sleep so I can make it through the day on the complaint desk!"

17
THE COVENANT

Robert was handing the keys to the Deusenberg to one of the DPS bodyguards when Tom Kennedy walked into the office.

"Tom, this is Harley Andrews. He's one of the DPS officers the governor sent to look out for me."

Outside Robert's floor-to-ceiling window, the mist was beginning to turn into rain, and as it struck the glass, the water drops beaded and branched. Tom Kennedy thought to himself, "This guy's got his work cut out for him, being Robert Herrick's bodyguard." Kennedy had heard about last night's incident with the bomb squad and the Froot Loops. By now, almost every officer in the entire Department of Public Safety was laughing about the Froot Loops caper, not to mention half the lawyers in town.

"Anyway," Robert went on, "turns out this guy here, Harley the Bodyguard, is from Rhode Island. My old home."

"Well, I'm from Texas myself, and I don't know that I really want to meet another guy from Rhode Island." Tom Kennedy grinned and shook the DPS officer's hand. "You know, Robert, you two even look alike! But I guess that happens, what with all the inbreeding in that little bitty state!"

"You can insult me as much as you want," laughed Harley the Bodyguard, "as long as I get to drive that Duesenberg." He rattled the keys.

"He's going to take the car over to the shop," Robert explained. "They usually come pick it up, but Harley's been bugging me for the last two weeks to let him drive it. He's an old-car nut, same as me."

Suddenly, the intercom buzzed, and Donna de Carlo's voice came over the speaker. "Robert, the lawyer for the Louisiana Trucking Company is here. Mister Francel Williams. The insurance company sent him, and he says you have a meeting scheduled with him right now."

"See you later," Robert said to Harley the Bodyguard. "This is a meeting Tom and I have been looking forward to for a long time. We're going to try to settle the case with this propane truck insurance lawyer, and maybe then we'll do a better job of going after the real bad guys. Such as Maxxco."

"I represent the insurance company," said Francel Williams. "The one that insures the Louisiana Trucking firm, that is."

As he said it, Francel Williams grinned, or rather, he beamed. Robert Herrick liked Francel, even though he always was on the other side and always was a skillful opponent. "My client regrets this accident, of course. But nevertheless—"

Francel's smile got bigger—"I'm so-o-o-o pleased to be involved in this case against you, Robert!"

Francel stretched the word "s-o-o-o-o" to about five seconds long, and he made it descend all the way from treble to bass in pitch. Then he added, "Because if I should happen to lose, at least I'll know the finest lawyer in the whole wide world was on the other side."

Robert Herrick smiled in spite of himself. Francel Williams was six-foot-three, balding on top, and full of power and confidence. He was the best known African-American lawyer in town, by far, and he was a leader not only in the black community, but in the city as a whole. In fact, Francel had once been a judge. He was one of the first black lawyers appointed to the bench in modern Texas. He had resigned, though, because he enjoyed practicing law too much. He just couldn't make himself sit quietly during a trial, the way a judge had to do.

Francel always wore a dark pinstriped suit and a silver tie, almost like a trademark. His real trademark, though, was his optimism. He always saw the bright side of anything that went wrong, from petty annoyances to major disasters, and he always was happy, jolly, and cheerful, no matter what happened.

"This is a won-der-ful-l-l-l case!" Francel boomed, as he dropped his Redrope file folder on Robert's conference table. "The trucking company has been just wonderful to work with. And my other client, the insurance company, they've been the greatest!"

Thinking back, Robert Herrick remembered the trial of another lawsuit, which had been interrupted in mid-testimony so the bailiff could tell Francel Williams his uncle had died. "Uncle George was the one who raised me after my daddy passed away," Francel had said, with a stricken look on his face. "How did it happen?" The bailiff quietly answered, "Your uncle had a heart attack while he was teaching his class at Huston-Tillotson College." And that explanation had made Francel grin as wide as the courtroom. "What a wonderful thing to happen to Uncle George!" he had said, in that rich, booming voice. "He always said he wanted to go that way."

That was Francel Williams. And now, Robert realized, this same Francel Williams was going to use his trademark optimism, as well as his other lawyering skills, to try to walk his client, the insurance company for the world's most guilty trucking firm, right out of the courtroom scot-free, if he could.

"I'm sure we can work this out and settle this case!" Francel smiled, and he waved a hand as big as the hood of the Duesenberg. "With fine lawyers like you, Robert, and you, Tom, I know we can! After all, you don't want the jury to pin the blame on the Louisiana Trucking Company, what with it having nothing but this piddling little five million in insurance coverage."

Francel showed two perfectly parallel rows of clean white teeth. "And after all, Maxxco's an American Stock Exchange company with a net worth of ten billion, just waiting for you to collect it. So Robert, I'm sure you'll want to go after Maxxco—instead of my client."

"Well, you're right, of course. Our obligation is to do what we can to get our clients compensated." Robert was trying not to smile. This was serious. "But Francel, you know that the trucking company was negligent, too."

"Well, I'd have to agree. So let's settle it! My insurance company will pay you, o-h-h-h-h, say, a million dollars." Francel's "o-h-h-h-h" was dragged out for ten seconds, and it went from fortissimo to pianissimo. After which, he beamed, and added, "And then, Robert, we'll supply whatever information we have to help you and all your nice plaintiffs to prove your case against Maxxco in front of the jury!"

"Well . . . a million isn't quite what I had in mind."

"Okay! We'll compromise. Two million! And I've got to congratulate you, Robert, because you're fighting to get every last penny for your clients!"

Robert smiled again, in spite of himself. "Thanks. But I've got a different settlement in mind. And in the first place, it's got to involve the whole five million, Francel, and you know that. My clients would think I'd let them down if I didn't at least collect your full insurance coverage in a case as bad as this."

Again, Francel responded with his usual optimism. "Well, the trucking company's my client, too. And if we settle for the insurance policy, that will mean that my client, the trucking company, won't owe anything. And that will at least make my other client, the trucking company, very, very happy!"

"But we can't settle it," Robert went on. "Not completely. Not yet. I need to keep you in the case, Francel, because I want you to argue to the jury right along with me."

"We can't settle it? Not even for the whole insurance policy?" Francel looked surprised. But then he brightened. "Well, Robert, I'm sure you've got a reason. And I'm sure, knowing you, that it's a very good reason!"

Robert laughed at that. "I'll agree to limit the trucking company's share of the damages to no more than the insurance coverage. Five million—that's the maximum we get from you. And that'll be a good deal for both of your clients, because if the jury puts all the damages on Maxxco, the insurance company can leave the courtroom along with the trucking company. It won't owe anything, either."

Francel looked like he was thinking it through. "And that way, I would have to stay in the case, representing the Louisiana Trucking Company. And we'd have every motivation to do what we would do anyway. That is, to show the jury that Maxxco was negligent. I've always said, the real cause of this accident was bad construction."

"Of course, we'll have to disclose this settlement to the court right away. The rules say so." Robert was beginning to get the idea that he'd been snookered, but somehow he didn't mind. The real issue wasn't the five million in insurance; any competent lawyer for the insurance company would cheerfully pay that. The trucking company also had several million in assets, and the real issue was whether Robert was going to go after those, too—and try to get the trucks, or whatever they could be sold for, in addition to the insurance. "Oh, well," Robert thought, "it's always a pleasure to deal with Francel, even if you don't get everything you want."

"I knew we could work it out." Francel's grin was as bright as a floodlight. "We just needed to reason together. You see what I mean, Robert? This is a won-der-ful-l-l-l case!"

As Francel put it, "When an agreement is this good, it's always best to paper it up right away."

And so, after Francel had left, Robert sat in his office—studying a twenty-page document that Francel had given him, called "Trial Agreement and Covenant Not To Execute." Its basic message was simple, even with all the "ifs," "buts," and "provided thats." Robert agreed not to go after any recovery from the Louisiana Trucking Company directly. The plaintiffs would be limited to whatever they could get from the five-million-dollar insurance policy. And of course, they would get whatever they could win from the other defendants, including Maxxco. Francel would stay in the case, but he and Robert would have the same interests. They both would be trying the case against Maxxco. The judge would disclose the settlement terms, so that everything would be known to the jury. Everything would be open and above board.

Robert smiled to himself. Francel Williams had whipped this document out of his file as soon as they shook hands on the covenant. "I just happen to have it all written up. You won't have to do any more work on this deal at all, Robert." It was disconcerting, after what you thought were skillful negotiations, to find out that your opponent had written up the result beforehand, and Robert realized that he had agreed to exactly what Francel had wanted. But it wasn't so bad, because Francel was so entertaining that he took almost all of the sting out of it.

Robert gazed out the window, and his mind began to wander.

For a long time, he had wondered about Francel. Was his niceness for real? It was almost too much to believe. Maybe it was all an act. Maybe it was Francel's way of manipulating people, like his negotiations with Robert just now. Or maybe Francel was boiling with rage inside. Maybe he was a black man who wanted to be successful in the white world, and he would pay whatever it cost in self-esteem to achieve that goal. It was hard to tell. Then, too, maybe Francel's optimism was genuine. Maybe he simply was one of the truly nice people in this world.

Two years ago, Robert had won a hard-fought jury trial against Francel. It lasted two weeks, and in that environment, you really get to know your adversary. A couple of times, Robert thought he was going to see a crack in the armor when Francel got irritable or impatient for a moment, but every time, Francel recovered the smile, usually with a joke about himself, and always with a display of courtesy. And when Robert had won the verdict, when the jury had given him everything he'd asked for, Francel had shaken his hand enthusiastically, with the same bright smile, and had bantered with Robert as though he, himself, had won. Robert couldn't have done that. His teeth always clenched when he congratulated a winning adversary.

Evidently, Francel just had tremendous inner strength, and he genuinely felt the same attitude when he lost as when he won. And so, was it all an act? Maybe it didn't make any difference. "If Francel's an actor," Robert thought, "then let the world be filled with actors."

So now, with Francel gone, Robert sat in his office, musing and looking out the window. And smiling, because Francel always made him smile. But then his thoughts were interrupted.

Suddenly, he heard a strange commotion just outside his office. He put down the wad of paper on which Francel's agreement was written, and he hurried to Donna de Carlo's desk. She and five other secretaries were crowded around the window.

"There's been some kind of accident," Donna blurted out. "And Robert, it looks like it involves your car!"

He strained to look out the window, but he couldn't see anything except the burgundy Duesenberg, pressed against a pole on the plaza in front of the building, with a crowd of ant-sized people milling around it in the swirling rain.

As Herrick and Kennedy took the elevator down, they cursed every second they had to wait, until finally, they ran out onto the plaza. The DPS bodyguard ran to keep up with them. The rain drenched them, but nobody noticed.

There was Harley Andrews, the other DPS officer, sitting behind the wheel of the Duesenberg. But he wasn't exactly behind it. His torso sagged to the right, against the passenger's seat. The blood made him look as if he had spilled something red all over the front of his white shirt.

With Harley the Bodyguard driving Robert's car, and with both of them being about the same height and build, the killer, it seemed, had made a mistake.

"Somebody shot him!" said a bystander. "But I was across the street, and with all of this rain coming down, I only got a glimpse of the guy. All I remember is, one of his eyes was really ugly. Really nasty looking. It was messed up and folded, if you know what I mean."

"Yes," said Robert slowly. "I know exactly what you mean."

18
STATE'S WITNESS

At the same moment, in the gritty atmosphere of the central police station, Maria Melendes was doing her job as Assistant District Attorney in charge of the complaint desk.

Earlier that morning, by nine-thirty, in fact, Maria already had heard nine citizen complaints. And she had turned down all nine. Every one of them had been considered and rejected by the police, and then rejected again by police supervisors, and so it wasn't too surprising.

The complaint division occupied two hole-in-the-wall rooms. The floor was a checkerboard of green linoleum, the walls were quarter-inch paneling printed to look like wood, and the desks had frayed Formica tops. Outside the inner sanctum of the prosecutor-in-charge, a secretary with a huge pile of orange hair manipulated an automatic typewriter that could produce the words of any Penal Code offense in the form of an indictment.

The assistant D.A.'s all hated the complaint desk. There were many reasons, but the most important one was that you had to explain to each irate victim why you were turning him down. That was what Maria was doing now.

"Mister Hatch," she said to a grizzled citizen wearing a John Deere cap, "How can we prove that this suspect, Danny Kowalski, is the same person who did this damage to your rental house? The police couldn't find any evidence of who did it."

"Look at them pictures," Citizen Hatch answered confidently. "See how all that sheetrock's been knocked out? See the broken glass? And that's part of the commode, there. He pulverized it with a hammer."

"I can see the damage. But I've got to have evidence that Danny Kowalski was the one who did it, before I can charge him."

"Ain't these pictures enough evidence?" Mr. Hatch sounded frustrated. He held two handfuls of photographs up like a deck of cards.

"But you see, Mister Hatch, if I were to take these charges I'd have to prove he did it. Danny Kowalski. And I'd have to prove it"—Maria emphasized each syllable—"beyond . . . a . . . reasonable . . . doubt. That means, I've got to prove it couldn't possibly have been anybody else, like vandals. Or kids. Or whoever."

"Listen." The man was turning a dark red color. "Kowalski called me. Didn't have the rent. Would I take half?" Hatch shook his head, hard. "He already owed me two hundred dollars, and folks was always complaining about him getting stoned at four in the morning. So I told him, no. After that, I don't hear nothin', so I go over there—and bingo." He slapped the pictures. "This is what I see! Now you tell me, who the hell else could it be?"

"I can see how you suspect Mister Kowalski, but—"

"Suspect, hell! He's moved out and he's laughing at me! You file these charges! God damn it, I don't suspect, I know!"

Maria listened as Citizen Hatch vented, and then she gently interrupted. "Mister Hatch, I'm not unsympathetic. I'm deeply disappointed to tell you what I have to tell you. But here it is. It would be illegal for me to accept these charges, because I don't have any evidence at all to show this suspect did it, much less any evidence that would prove it beyond . . . a . . . reasonable . . . doubt."

The man looked at the floor for what seemed like an eternity. Maria was wary, because every now and then a complaint desk prosecutor would find it necessary to call an officer to prevent an assault by an enraged citizen.

Finally, the man named Hatch stood like an automaton and stalked out of the room.

"Next! Number Eleven!" The red-haired secretary shouted it in an indiscriminate voice, in the general direction of the crowd sitting on benches outside.

As Citizen Number Eleven walked in, looking hopeful, Maria realized ruefully that she still had a perfect record. Ten cases down, and none accepted.

Suddenly, around eleven o'clock, Maria looked up and saw two familiar faces in the doorway. Officers Slaughter and Cashdollar, from the Homicide Division.

"Miss Melendes," said Derrigan Slaughter, "we got a real weird one for you."

"Well, don't just stand there! Come on in. My two favorite homicide cops! What kind of trouble are you guys in this time?"

Slaughter wore a sharp blue suit that shimmered beneath his full black beard. He seemed nervous. His partner, Donnie Cashdollar, had on a tweed jacket, a flower-print tie, a maroon striped shirt—and this time, his polyester pants were bluish-gray. His beard wasn't really a beard but only a byproduct of the fact that Cashdollar shaved once every sixty days or so.

"This case is kind of disgusting," Slaughter announced.

"That's okay. It's my job." Maria reached for the police report. She noticed that the officers were unsure even what crime was involved, because the box marked "OFFENSE" was filled in with the words, "Unknown agg assault." Apparently, it was something that resembled an aggravated assault, according to the best guess these two detectives had been able to make.

Maria shuffled the pages, which were in rainbow colors because they came from several different agencies. "Can you give me the *Reader's Digest* version?"

"Okay." Slaughter cleared his throat. "The victim decides to order a pizza. He calls Primavera's and orders a DeLuxe. Guy delivers it. Victim eats the pizza." Slaughter was speaking slowly, with a puzzled look on his face, the kind of look that meant he was coming to the disgusting part and was trying to think of the best way to tell it to this pretty redheaded prosecutor.

"Anyway, he's eaten all of the pizza except for two slices when the phone rings. Delivery guy from Primavera's asks if the complainant liked the pizza. Victim answers, yes, he did.

"Now, here comes the meat of the coconut." Detective Slaughter looked at the floor. "Delivery guy says, 'Good, I'm glad you like
all over that pizza. And you're gonna *die*, 'cause I have AIDS!'"

Maria waited, with revulsion and curiosity rising inside her.

"Anyway, victim immediately goes over to the emergency room at Ben Taub. Turns out that, yes indeed, there is semen smeared on the remains of the pizza. Then—get this—it turns out that the delivery guy, whose name is Kim Garrisch, does in fact have AIDS. The Doctor has the semen tested, and bingo! The pizza is HIV-positive."

"Was it him? Garrisch, I mean, who—smeared the pizza?"

"Yes."

"What I'm asking is, can we prove it was him?" Maria was still thinking about the Citizen Hatch type of case. Or here, the unidentifiable pizza assassin.

"Yes. We can indeed put it on him. First, he's the guy who delivered the pizza. Plus, victim recognized his voice. Also, victim says he made change out of a twenty. Caller on the phone mentioned the twenty in the same conversation where he talked about—well, about jacking off and so forth. And if that's not enough, the owner at Primavera's was the only other one there, and he's the one told Garrisch to call the victim. Yes, we can put Mister Garrisch behind the smoking weapon. Or, in this case, the dripping pizza."

"Why'd he do it? I mean, why do you think he did it?" The prosecution wasn't legally required to prove a motive, but she knew the jury would want one, anyway.

"Near as we can tell, he's mad at Primavera's. He never even saw this victim before. But then, Mister Garrisch ain't talkin' to us, so we really can't say what was on his mind."

Maria flopped her head forward. "Damn."

"We got enough of the semen to do a DNA, we think," said Cashdollar helpfully.

"You're getting way ahead of me," said Maria. "You know what I was thinking? I was thinking, I wonder what kind of offense category there is in the Penal Code that might cover this sort of escapade."

"Well, we booked him for assault."

"I see that. And I guess it fits. But it's sure a strange assault. I'm thinking about a completely different kind of crime." She riffled through a paperback copy of the Texas Penal Code. "Here it is: Section 32.42, Deceptive business practices." Maria read from the Code: "'A person commits an offense if he commits one of the following deceptive business practices.' And then there's a long list of prohibited acts."

"I see," said Detective Cashdollar. "And here it says that 'selling an adulterated or mislabeled commodity' is one of the prohibited acts. That's subsection (4)."

"Yup," said Detective Slaughter. "And in this case, the 'adulterated or misbranded commodity' would be this semen-smeared pizza that our suspeck jacked off on."

"Right," said Maria. "Only I'll tell you what's the problem with this deceptive business practices statute, and the assault statute, too."

"Okay, what?" asked Detective Cashdollar.

"Assault is a Class C misdemeanor when there's no actual bodily injury. Because even assuming we can make it an assault, the only section that fits is subsection (3), which is 'offensive or provocative contact.' And that's only a Class C misdemeanor, which is the same as a traffic offense. Maximum penalty's a small fine."

"What about this other thing, the business practices stuff?" Slaughter wanted to know.

"Deceptive business practices is a Class A misdemeanor. Standard bond is four hundred bucks. This guy will be out on his own recognizance right after we charge him."

Everybody looked at the ceiling.

"Well, maybe that's all we can do." Detective Cashdollar sounded philosophical, almost professorial. "Maybe the majesty of the law has a light touch when it comes to pizzas garnished with HIV spermatozoa."

"I sure don't like putting him right back out," said Maria. "What's he going to do next? Have sex with his girlfriend? Or boyfriend? Sell his blood to a blood bank? Go onto the schoolyards with a razor blade?"

"Any way you can make it an aggravated assault?" Slaughter asked hopefully. "That's what we booked him for." He sounded like he thought the officers' own designation ought to be sufficient evidence. Sort of like, "We thought that might be the right crime, so isn't that enough?"

"No," said Maria. "No way. For agg assault, it has to be serious bodily injury. If your complainant dies, or if he gets real sick, maybe then we can make an aggravated assault."

She tapped a pencil on her teeth. "Tell you what I'm thinking. He didn't cause bodily injury, at least not yet. And he didn't kill the complainant, yet. But he tried. He *attempted* to kill him, maybe. Or at least, that's what he said: 'You're gonna die.'"

"The semen-stained pizza is the murder weapon," Detective Slaughter said matter-of-factly.

"The *attempted* murder weapon," Maria corrected.

Suddenly her mind was crowded with a dozen cases from law school. Can you be guilty of attempted murder if you try to kill somebody with pins in a voodoo doll? What if you believe in voodoo and you intend to kill him? Or what if you try to blow up the victim with talcum powder? She also remembered a case where a man had sex with a woman who was unconscious—but it wasn't rape, because the woman actually was dead from alcohol poisoning. And yet, that court had affirmed the conviction for *attempted* rape, because the defendant had *tried* to do it.

"I don't know if Mister Garrisch could have killed your guy with this pizza,"

Maria said. "Frankly, from what I know about AIDS, I doubt it. But I do know this. He darn sure could have attempted to kill him, and he even said so."

For the first time, the detectives smiled.

Two minutes later, the automatic typewriter was spitting out the words that would make it official. "In the name and by the authority of the State of Texas, the Grand Jury of Harris County, Texas, duly organized at the April 1997 Term of the 208th District Court of Harris County, Texas, do present: that on or about March 28, 1997, in said County, in said State, one KIM GARRISCH, hereinafter styled the Defendant, did unlawfully, intentionally and knowingly attempt to cause the death of an individual, Augustus M. Wylie, hereinafter styled the complainant, by causing the complainant to eat pizza which included semen carrying the human immunodeficiency virus. Against the peace and dignity of the State."

"Who on earth is this, Augustus M. Wylie?" Maria was struggling to proofread the indictment.

"Why, that's the complainant. Good old Gus Wylie. He's the victim," said Detective Cashdollar. "He's the guy that made all of this possible. The guy that was attempted to be killed in the Semen-Stained Pizza Caper."

"Oh!" Maria laughed at herself, with embarrassment. "The victim. I forgot all about him." That was terrible to admit, but it happened sometimes. A lawyer's job, at times, requires strictly logical analysis, stripped of all emotion. Maria had found that to be one of the hardest things to learn in law school.

"I guess that's why the victim usually has the least desirable role in the entire criminal justice system," she added.

At three o'clock, Maria took a break. In addition to the pizza case, she already had seen fifty-three citizens but had accepted the charges from only one, for "terroristic threat," against a young man who had repeatedly threatened to blow up his ex-girlfriend's home. It was the only one where there was evidence to prove a crime.

And now, Maria was taking ten minutes just to look at the ceiling and breathe slowly. This was the worst time of the entire day on complaint desk duty, because you'd been there long enough to be dead-dog-tired but not long enough to coast to quitting time.

Moments later, there was a loud rap on the door. Maria's ten minutes were up.

Detectives Slaughter and Cashdollar entered for the second time that day. They had a suspect with them. The prisoner grimaced when he sat down with the cuffs on, and he showed an odd-shaped gold tooth. He also had a spidery tattoo that seemed to reach out of his shirt collar and onto his neck. Maria hid her distaste as she stared at the man and then tried to look away.

"This here is Mister Esparza," said Slaughter. "He's gone by nothin' but 'Esparza' for so long, it's become his first and last name, both." The name sounded vaguely familiar to Maria, like the identity of a suspect who'd never been successfully tied to an obscure but nasty crime sometime in the distant past.

Detective Cashdollar took over the narrative. "Anyway, old Esparza's in big-time trouble. We got him on a real good heroin buy. Arrested at the scene holding the money, and we got movies and everything. But it's worse than that. We also got him for murder."

Slaughter pointed at Esparza as he picked up the story. "We been 'splainin the law to Mister Esparza. Turns out, he knows it better'n we do. He was in the course of committing a felony, the drug sale. One a his sidekicks gets carried away with a machine gun, and a stray bullet kills an innocent bystander. Nineteen-year-old girl who ain't involved."

"It's a felony murder," added Cashdollar.

"Kill somebody in the course of committing a felony, it's murder whether you meant to do it or not," Slaughter agreed.

"Sounds right to me so far," said Maria. She was trying her best to follow the story, because the two cops sounded like Tweedledum and Tweedledee, the way they were bouncing back and forth.

"In fact, it sounds right to Mister Esparza, too," said Slaughter. "We been visiting with him, and we suggested that it might be a good idea if he helped us. You know, he wants to turn state's wit-a-niss." Slaughter said this last phrase, "state's witness," with exaggerated dignity and drama, as if he were an actor on *Murder She Wrote*, or maybe, *Perry Mason*.

"Actually, Mister Esparza wanted to talk to you, Ms. Melendes," said Detective Cashdollar to Maria. "He asked for you, by name."

"To me?" Maria stared at the man again. "Why?"

"Seems that old Esparza is substantially empty-handed," Slaughter said. "He ain't got nothing much to give us. His seller was a mule from south of the border, and all he knows her by is Luisa, which may have nothin' to do with her real name. Frankly, I doubt it does. Anyway, old Luisa's on a plane back to Ecuador before the deal even goes down. Now, Esparza's tryin' hard, and he's even tryin' to give us the guy he bought the stuff from in Ecuador. Guy's supposedly a real big dealer. He's known only as El Perro."

"That means 'The Dog,'" Cashdollar added helpfully. "In Español."

"It means a whole lot of nothin', is what it means," Slaughter said flatly.

"So where do I fit into all this?" Maria wanted to know. She was puzzled, frankly. But of course it was common for defendants to talk to each other about the prosecutors, and Maria had a high visibility, so it really wasn't surprising that Esparza knew her name beforehand.

Esparza spoke up for the first time. "Ms. Melendes, I was a case runner. I ran cases and sold 'em to lawyers. I know all about it. The other case runners who're doing it, the lawyers who use 'em, the whole works."

"He figures lawyers are safer to turn in than dope dealers," said Cashdollar. "That's smart, at least."

"Well," said Maria dubiously, "I don't know. Give me some names."

Esparza settled in his chair. "Well, the one I did the biggest piece of business with," he said proudly, "was a lawyer named Robert Herrick. And I can give you Robert Herrick on a silver platter."

There was a strange kind of croaking sound from Maria, partly a laugh and partly a gasp. Cashdollar and Slaughter both stared at her. She had put down her Mont Blanc pen and was looking at Esparza with the most unusual expression they had ever seen her wear.

19
THE EXPERT

Y ou know, Wendy, I just can't get this stuff with Esparza out of my mind." Maria shook her head. "You know, back when I was on the complaint desk. It was pretty scary, but when we got to the end of his story, there wasn't anything to it."

"Are you sure?" Wendy looked up. "It's always a problem when some turd makes accusations like that. It's always somebody like Esparza, somebody who's got nothing to lose."

"Well, the good thing about it was that Esparza's story was so wild, everybody ignored it. Esparza even said Robert was the one who proposed the deal. He claimed Robert called him and asked him to run the propane truck case. Made it sound like Robert used runners all the time. It all collapsed, because Esparza got caught in a bunch of lies."

Wendy nodded. "I bet the cops didn't pay any attention to that asshole in the first place. Probably just brought him there because he asked for you."

"Probably." Maria pursed her lips. "Anyway, I didn't even bother Robert about it, because he and I have bigger problems. Esparza's just a little bitty piece of it."

Wendy looked up again. "Yeah? What kind of problems do you and Robert have that are bigger than that?"

"I've been watching Robert fall apart." Maria's eyes watered. "That DPS officer who was guarding him got killed by a bullet that was meant for Robert. And now, Robert feels guilty for being alive, and disgusted by the murder, and ashamed of giving the car to the bodyguard so that the killer confused them. He's got all these emotions at once. It's survivor's guilt, and this may sound crazy, but it's literally got him paralyzed."

Wendy thought it over. "Shit. It's understandable."

"And he's frightened, too. Even though he won't say so, of course. Robert's still got to worry about getting shot again, himself."

"Sure. That guy Squint is still out there."

"And there's more. Robert doesn't talk about it, but I know he's obsessed with his losing streak in the courtroom. He's asking himself, 'Do I still have it? Am I finished as a trial lawyer?' And he's wondering, 'Am I going to lose the propane truck case too?'"

Wendy was staring at her. "So what are you thinking, Maria?"

"His depression's lasted a long time." Maria shook her head again. "It's turned into days on end, and the days have turned into weeks. He gets drunk way too much, and he's not working at all. I'm not worried about that piss-ant Esparza. I'm worried about Robert, and I've got to do something."

"Maria, you need to mind your own business. You're likely to fuck things up if you try to play psychiatrist for him."

"Oh, I'm not going to push. I just need to change my approach. I've got to find something to jolt Robert out of this do-nothing, stare-at-the-walls mood. Otherwise, he's going to go crazy and take me with him."

Wendy didn't say anything. She just looked up and frowned.

"*Que pasa*, Robert? What's the matter? Are you having your period or something?" The bouncy voice made fun of him, but deep down, she was sympathetic.

"I . . . I . . ." He stared at the telephone. Sometimes the things Maria said were so outrageous, they stopped him cold.

"Look. You didn't go to the office for more than a week. You just moped around your house. And now you go to the office, but you don't do anything. You've got all your friends worried. Except me, because I know better."

He laughed in spite of himself, then swallowed fast, to quiet his raging stomach. "I just can't concentrate on anything."

"Listen to me. Do you think this is how Harley the Bodyguard would have wanted you to act? The whole reason he was watching out for you was so you could do your job. If you just sit around doing nothing, it's like he died for nothing. You don't want that, do you?"

"Well . . . you're right, of course."

"Baby, you know I love you, and I can understand you being depressed for a while, but Jimmy Coleman's working this whole time. He's not sitting around like you are. You think maybe you ought to refer that propane truck case to somebody else? Some other law firm that can handle it like it ought to be handled?"

"Heck, no! Are you crazy?" And he realized, once again, how easily she could get under his skin.

"Well, all right! Then you need to show a little self-discipline. Start taking some positive steps, even some little ones."

He was silent. Then: "Okay. Okay!" She was one of the few people in the world who could lecture him about self-discipline. That dangerous passage from Cuba had left her with an unstoppable drive.

After they said good-bye, he looked out the window at the stone-gray sky that signaled winter in Houston. The black spire of the Transco Tower stuck out just past the tree skeletons in Memorial Park. Maria had succeeded in touching a nerve. Robert's depression was quickly replaced by anger. Anger about what had happened to Harley, and anger about the propane truck disaster. And then the anger was replaced by determination.

But then . . . the depression took over once again and overwhelmed him. His mind reproduced a snapshot of the blood on Harley's body, and then he thought of Squint, and then Esparza, and then Jimmy Coleman exulting over winning that medical malpractice case. If only he could summon the will and start working again, he might break this cycle, but he knew he couldn't do it, because the depression paralyzed him.

He tried hard to concentrate, and again he felt the anger, and then the determination. And then, for the hundredth time, the determination weakened into depression. "That Froot Loops episode was a wake-up call. Why didn't I get out of this propane truck case to protect my family?" That was when he hobbled over to the bar hidden in the wall of his office and poured four fingers of scotch over one ice cube.

Maria wouldn't understand why he was going to get drunk again in the middle of the afternoon. But at least another day would be gone soon. In his mind's eye, he pictured Harley bantering in the office while he twirled the keys to the Duesenberg. Then he saw Harley slumped behind the wheel with the blood bubbling out. And that image was replaced by the twisted face of the assassin he knew as Squint.

The next day looked even worse, with biting winds and cloud cover without a flicker of life in it. Robert dragged into the office at eleven-thirty. He lumbered past secretaries who fell silent and then whispered to each other about how hungover he looked. He sat at the big mahogany desk and stared out the window toward the propane truck intersection. Once more, he felt the anger-weakness-depression cycle. And he walked to the bar.

Aimlessly, he set the glass on the desk and dialed "1-0" on the intercom.

"Yeah," answered Tom Kennedy through the speakerphone.

Robert stared for a long moment at the phone and then at the clouds. He considered his alcohol-wounded head for several seconds, wondering idly when Kennedy would speak again to break the silence. Then, he barked, "Tom! You've got to get moving on those discovery requests to Maxxco. Get your ass in here."

"Yes, sir, Cap'n, sir! You want me to finish cleaning all the ashtrays before I hustle on down there?"

"Suddenly I'm surrounded by comedians. You and Maria, both. Seems everybody's turned into a damn comedian. Why don't you just get off your ass and haul it in here, like I just told you to do, and forget about clowning around? Damn!"

He realized that he sounded too vehement. Irritable, out of proportion to any imagined irritation. Depressed, indifferent, hoarse, and annoyed.

Kennedy was subdued. "Okay. Okay. I'm on the way."

Two hours later, Herrick and Kennedy had somehow managed to slog through a list of the documents produced from Maxxco's files. Robert's head hurt, and he didn't remember any of the specifics in the papers he'd looked at.

But there was good news. Kennedy's document requests had been effective, and Maxxco's memos had lots of discussion of guardrails and road widths. And plenty of descriptions of safety problems. Robert's normal coloring was gradually returning, off and on. "During the depositions, we'll cram all of this down Maxxco's throat and make 'em eat it."

He usually didn't talk about his lawsuits in such hostile terms, but today it felt good. It helped overcome the depression. Besides, it was easy to justify a certain amount of aggression against Jimmy Coleman and Maxxco. He winced as his headache spun back into focus.

"Speaking of depositions," Kennedy handed him the list of potential witnesses submitted by Maxxco, "which of these people do you want to take depositions of?"

Robert quickly crossed off a dozen names and wrote in several new ones by hand. That way, he produced a list of sixty-six witnesses, all of whom he wanted to examine in front of a court reporter. "That's a lot of depositions for one case, but after all, this is a big case." Robert was starting to feel like a lawyer again, even if he was only doing all of this to keep from drowning. "You know, this might even turn out to have been a productive two hours."

"Well, don't get too excited. We still have to go over the written interrogatories."

Robert groaned. Like every lawyer, he hated written questions. But he was back in the harness again, and he reached for Kennedy's draft of questions to send to Maxxco. He scanned quickly, then stopped when he got to interrogatory number 10. "Who-a-a-a! I don't know about this one."

The interrogatory looked innocuous enough:

```
"Interrogatory Number 10 to Maxxco: State the
maximum load, in pounds, that could be supported
by each column under any ramp or road in the Route
59-Interstate 610 interchange, as of the date of
the accident."
```

"Well now, Tom." Robert held his head in both hands, hoping that he could keep it from hurting. "I realize a good lawyer can draft interrogatories in an hour that will cost the other side fifty thousand dollars to answer, but I've never used that kind of tactic. So, before we send this one to Jimmy Coleman, just how much money do you think it's going to cost Maxxco to answer that one?"

"I talked to Professor Cziplacki, our concrete expert. He figures it'll take an engineer about a week, assuming he pounds away at his calculator for eight hours a day. And so, yes, it'll cost Maxxco several thousand dollars to answer this little one-sentence interrogatory."

"Well, discovery is certainly a way that some lawyers use to bankrupt their enemies, but don't you think this one's a little too much?" Robert had worked hard on bar association committees to stop abuse of lawsuit procedures by Rambo-minded litigators. His associates knew he wouldn't put up with dirty tricks from his own office. Even if Jimmy Coleman was on the other side.

But Kennedy stood his ground. "Cziplacki says he needs this information if he's going to figure out the sway in the road. You know, he's an expert on concrete structures, and he can tell us how much the propane truck would make the road wobble."

Robert thought for a minute. One of the interesting issues in the case was the sway caused by a passing vehicle. Just how stable was this overpass? If a big vehicle made it shudder and shake, the road might be difficult to negotiate during a rainstorm. Maxxco might have been negligent by building the columns too small.

And so maybe this question was necessary in spite of the expense. Both sides would spend hundreds of thousands of dollars getting ready for the trial of this case. The Herrick firm had to advance those kinds of expenses without knowing whether they would ever be repaid because it was one of the hazards of contingent-fee work. If you couldn't ante up, you couldn't fight in this arena. Maybe that made the cost of this interrogatory seem a little more reasonable.

"So the road sways less if it's a compact car than it does if an eighteen-wheeler goes across?" Robert asked.

"Yes. Exactly. Or imagine, maybe, a fully-loaded propane truck goes across. Then, the ramp wiggles a whole lot more. Cziplacki says it's like a guy on real tall stilts. If it's a little bitty guy, the stilts will be pretty firm, but put a 300-pound guy on a skinny pair of stilts—"

"Like, maybe, one of those big sumo wrestlers?" asked Robert. His eyes started throbbing in time with the pulsations in his brain.

"Exactly. It's like sumo wrestlers on stilts." Kennedy liked the idea. "Picture those stilts, swaying like crazy, just like the columns under the propane truck."

"The jury's going to love that," Herrick said. "When Cziplacki's on the witness stand, we'll get him to figure out the sway. 'Professor Cziplacki, how many inches is that road moving around?' And then, at the end, we'll get Cziplacki to spend about five minutes giving the jurors a visual image: 'These concrete columns are exactly like one of those humongous sumo wrestlers perched way up on a set of long, skinny stilts. And that's why they're defective.'"

"That sumo's gonna tump over on his butt any minute, just like the propane truck!" Kennedy said, and they both laughed.

"You know what, Tom? This is one of the reasons I went to law school. Of course, we're all primarily concerned about people's rights. We all care about justice. But there's more to it. When you're on the right side and you believe in what you're doing, practicing law is just plain exciting. It's a real mental challenge." Robert had almost forgotten about Squint, and Esparza, and the sHYsTer letter. Then a painful red slash tore through his plane of vision to remind him about his hangover.

Robert and Tom worked for most of the day, while Robert silently nursed his nausea. They prepared for depositions, so they could question Maxxco's corporate officers from the president on down. And they drafted subpoenas and document requests. In a case like this, it wouldn't be unusual for the documents to number in the millions, so they could search for the one smoking-gun memo that would win the case. And they wrote and rewrote written interrogatories to Maxxco, like the one about the columns, that would cost Maxxco thousands of dollars to answer. Robert changed them several times, trying to get the necessary information with the least expense.

"Discovery is a marvelous thing," said Robert. "At least, it's marvelous so long as the we're the ones asking the questions. But it'll be a whole lot less fun when Jimmy Coleman's asking us questions. I want us to keep from asking expensive interrogatories any more than is absolutely necessary, and then, maybe, we can persuade the judge not to let Maxxco be abusive toward us."

He was holding his head in his hands by the time he finished. It hurt, but the work made him feel good.

The telephone rang. Herrick and Kennedy were concentrating on the interrogatories, and it startled them both.

"Hello?" said Robert into the speakerphone.

"It's Professor Singh," Donna de Carlo announced. "He's from Stanford Research Institute in California. Says he's returning your call."

"Ah. Great. I'm glad you're here, Tom, because this is our metallurgist. He's going to be an expert witness about the guardrails, about why they didn't stop the propane truck." Herrick looked at the telephone. "Okay, Donna, put him on."

There was a pause. Then, a very British-sounding voice wafted from the speaker. "Hello? This is Singh."

"Hello, Professor Singh!" said Robert Herrick. "You already know a little bit about our lawsuit from my earlier call. So, do you think you can help the jury understand our case?"

"Certainly!" said Professor Singh warmly. He sounded as though he was thinking about his fee. He'd already explained that his "standard charges" were three hundred dollars an hour. Robert remembered thinking that lawyers had a bad image even though most of them charged less than that, but Dr. Singh hadn't batted an eyelash when he specified the three hundred. Maybe that meant that he really was an expert? Robert's brain was hurting again.

"Good," he said to the metallurgist. If he was going to get soaked for this kind of fee, the guy better be worth it. "Now, start by telling us who you are. Your background, qualifications and so forth. I have your resumé, but I want it in your own words."

Dr. Oberoi Singh had graduated first in his class in mechanical engineering from the University of New Delhi. He went to CalTech for graduate school, and then he had switched to metallurgy and earned a Ph.D. His doctoral thesis proposed a new theory about the effect of small quantities of iridium in steel alloys. The title used the word "ion" four times, all crammed inside a mass of scientific terminology that Herrick and Kennedy did not understand.

"That's a pretty complicated name for a thesis," said Herrick, dubiously. He was wondering whether the jurors would be impressed, or whether they'd just think this expert was too pointy-headed.

Dr. Singh did postgraduate work at Stanford on the crystalline structure of aluminum. And while he was there, he'd won the Chemical Industry Association prize for an article about the prevention of aluminum stress fractures. Today, he consulted for Alcoa, Exxon Chemical, Boeing, NASA, and the CIA. "But I'm not sure I'm supposed to tell you about the CIA," he added.

"Okay. I promise we won't tell anyone else about the CIA." Robert found himself speaking in a conspiratorial tone of voice. He was beginning to enjoy Dr. Singh. "But now, what about these guardrails? They're supported by these skinny little posts made out of real thin steel. And from our earlier conversation, Dr. Singh, I understood that you think they're likely to break if a vehicle hits them. What's your opinion?"

Oberoi Singh cleared his throat. This was his cue, and when he started speaking again, his voice no longer was hesitant. He became the learned professor.

Unfortunately, he also became terminally dense and confusing.

"For homogenous material configured cylindrically," Professor Singh began, "the tensile strength function is a quadratic one. That contrasts to the cylindrical height, which is linear." The thin voice became jolly and excited. "Actually, tensile strength in such a configuration follows the inverse square rule in relation to height. But that is only the beginning, because the tensile strength of a homogeneous structure of this kind is subject to more precise calculation through an elliptical integral of the third type . . ."

Professor Singh's first language was Hindi, and his British accent was softened by the singsong quality that affects the speech of natives of India. He went on to name the two physicists who had first applied this "elliptical integral of the third type" to shapes like the guardrails. Dr. Singh's voice was so soothing that Robert's mind began to wander.

Next, the professor explained in excruciating detail how the electron clouds of the zinc atom interacted with those of the iron atom in this particular alloy to produce "a different kind of crystalline structure. It inhibits longitudinal stress fissures but is susceptible to horizontal ones, and so the inverse square formula dictates a greater difference in the concentric diameters."

Dr. Singh paused. And for a few seconds, so did Robert Herrick and Tom Kennedy. Both with their mouths open.

"Doctor, that is wonderful," Herrick gushed. "I'm so glad you know how to do an analysis like that, right down to describing the electron shells of the ferrous ion. But there is just one problem. I didn't understand any of it. Neither did Mister Kennedy. And neither will a jury."

Robert's voice sounded like honey, or like someone training a beagle puppy. "And so, Dr. Singh, I'm going to ask you to start over, and give me the simple version."

Dr. Singh was silent for a moment.

"Very well," he began. "The posts are tall, and the material is thin. The longer you make a homogeneous rod, the thicker you must make it to maintain its integrity, because tensile strength against deformity is a quadratic function instead of a linear one."

Again there was a pause.

"Doctor Singh," said Robert, "there won't be any metallurgists on this jury. There almost certainly will not be any mathematicians. Instead of mathematicians, there probably will be beauticians."

Robert's head was pounding. "So, do you think you can put it in words that a beautician can understand?"

"What is a beautician?" Oberoi Singh singsonged politely.

Herrick stuck both hands in the air. Tom Kennedy laughed silently. This expert could reel off the electron shells in the iron atom, but he had never heard of a beautician?

"It doesn't matter," Herrick said finally, in a voice thick with honeyed frustration. "Let me just put it this way. Ordinary people will need for you to leave out the mathematics. If you talk that way, the jury will not understand it."

"Very well," said Dr. Singh brightly. "How about if I just explain about the tensile strength being a quadratic or inverse square function? Surely the jury will know what that means."

"Professor Singh," said Robert with determination, "what kind of car do you drive?"

"A Mercedes."

"If you crashed your car head-on into a guardrail made of materials like these, do you think it would restrain your Mercedes?"

"Of course not! The posts are too skinny for how long they are, and they would deform."

"Bingo," said Tom Kennedy.

"Wonderful, Professor Singh." Herrick smiled. "That is marvelous. Of course, I want you to give the technical explanation to the jury too, but we'll give them this simple one first. 'Too skinny for how long they are!' But there's just one more problem. You said the metal would 'deform'?"

"That is correct."

"'Deform' means it would bend, or it would break? Is that right?"

"Well, . . . more or less. Bend or break. I guess so."

"Would it be accurate to say 'bend,' then, instead of 'deform'? I think the jury would understand it better. But I only want you to say it if it's true."

"I suppose so," said the metallurgist. He hesitated, and then he blurted it out. "Trial lawyers! I work with trial lawyers sometimes, and always I find it uncongenial. You always are so very . . . well, so very . . . difficult! You are difficult even when you represent injured, deserving citizens, like this case."

The metallurgist paused again. "But the worst part of it is, lawyers always make everything way . . . too . . . complicated!"

Fifteen minutes after they ended their conversation with the metallurgist from New Delhi, Herrick and Kennedy were still laughing.

"I sure do like our new friend, Professor Singh," said Kennedy with a big smile.

"Yeah. And so will the jury. Once they peel themselves off the ceiling after hearing about those elliptical integrals, they'll realize he knows his stuff. And he's telling them the truth." Herrick was smiling too, in spite of his headache. "Dr. Singh's a true expert, all right."

20
SAN FRANCISCO

The Gulfstream II broke the clouds at ten thousand feet, just north-northeast of San Francisco Bay.

"Wow," said Maria. She had asked Robert whether she could sit in the cockpit. And now, here she was.

They were on the way to San Francisco because that was where the lawyers in the propane truck case were going to take the depositions of the expert witnesses. The depositions didn't have to be taken in the courtroom, or even in the same city where the case was filed. They could be taken anywhere that the lawyers agreed. The experts, as it happened, were all in California, and none of the lawyers objected to this beautiful city as a place for this series of boring depositions.

It had been three weeks since Maria had met the horrible prisoner with the wild charges—that dope-dealing murderer named Esparza. There had never been any credibility in his accusations against Herrick. The detectives had figured that Esparza was nothing but human wreckage anyway, bargaining for his own worthless skin. And it would have been hard to give him much of a break, since he was under indictment for a slam-dunk heroin sale and a triple felony-murder.

Still, Maria hadn't felt very confident when, at last, she warned Robert about Esparza. True, Robert had explained about Icky Snopes's role in all of it, and she didn't believe any of what Esparza said. But she also wondered whether this slimy character's lies could bring down Robert's career like a house of cards. What if he ever managed to sell his falsehoods to Robert's enemies? She didn't want to think about that.

Anyway, she had been ecstatic when Robert had asked her to come along to San Francisco. The Gulfstream II could easily hold one more passenger. And so, in this beautiful moment, all of the things that bothered Maria seemed a million miles away as Robert pointed out the landmarks and explained why he had gone to so much trouble to see that they approached the Bay Area from the northeast instead of from the south.

"The pilots filed a flight plan for the Napa City Airport, then changed it in the air. It's perfectly okay if you do it right. Just a little more complicated. Otherwise, the air traffic control system would have made us come in from the south. You can see the whole San Francisco Bay so much better from the north, and I thought to myself, for Maria to see this, it's worth it."

The altimeter spun and the airspeed indicator slowed. Robert pointed out these gauges to Maria. She was like an excited child, and he wondered why he'd never thought of taking her on the plane before. Off to the right was the Napa Valley. The Mondavi Winery was at the south end, Sterling to the north, and there were wineries with names such as Beringer, Christian Brothers, Far Niente, and Stag's Leap in between.

"It's like a fairyland." Maria marveled at the neat separation of green fields, white city, and blue water.

"Chuck's about to put the flaps down," said Robert. Chuck was the co-pilot. "Watch the altimeter. Then look straight ahead."

And there, in front of them, was the city. The aircraft swooped between the Golden Gate on the right and the Bay Bridge on the left. "And with the sun on the other side, it really is golden!" she said with the amazement of a first-time tourist.

As they approached Treasure Island, he pointed out Fisherman's Wharf, the Presidio, and Golden Gate Park. "There's Coit Tower, and that pyramid is the Transamerica Building. And way over there is Sausalito, where we're going after we land." There were a hundred other points of interest, and Robert wanted to identify every one.

They skimmed south, down the bay. Robert named all of the little cities below San Francisco, with pretty names like Sunnyvale and San Mateo. Then Chuck banked the plane hard to the right and made a U-turn. A moment later, the wheels of the Gulfstream II glided onto the runway at San Francisco airport.

Two hours later, Robert and Maria were sitting on the wooden outdoor deck at the Alta Mira Inn in Sausalito.

"I'll get us the point position on the deck, so you can see everything," he had promised. Sure enough, the huge wooden deck halfway up the hill had one table at its outermost corner, and it was reserved for them. Across the bay, behind the green-gray hump of Alcatraz Island, was the city. Everything else was blue sky, blue sea, and green hills dotted with villas.

Maria thought it must be the most beautiful place on earth, outside of Cuba. "But that's because ever since you've been outside of Cuba, you've spent most of your time in Miami and Las Vegas," Robert teased her. Way down below, the sailing yacht named the Tobias II came about and turned to starboard, and its wake curved behind the church steeple in front of them. It was near where it had docked on their short sail to Sausalito from San Francisco.

"Robert, when I wanted to go sailing, I didn't expect you to charter a fifty-foot yacht with a crew of three," said Maria with mock disappointment. The Tobias II tacked away, into the wind.

"She's a beautiful one, isn't she?" said Robert. "One reason I asked for the Tobias II was because of the crew. Those guys love it so much, they can't stop sailing even after they've dropped us off."

They were silent for a moment as they looked at the postcard view.

"Listen, Robert." He had known it was coming. Her voice had changed. "I wish you would take this problem about Esparza a little more seriously."

"I do take it seriously." His voice was ernest. "What good do you think it will do if I take it even more seriously? I'd just wind up in the loony bin if I let it consume me."

"I don't know. Maybe you should get somebody else to handle this propane truck case so he can't hurt you. Plus, there's Squint."

"There isn't any 'somebody else' who I want to give the propane truck case to. And besides, Esparza would still run around, peddling the same bullshit story."

"Maybe it would do some good if you at least got away from that case. I'm telling you, Esparza could ruin you. The officers saw that he wasn't telling the truth, and they figured he had nothing worth trading on a heroin sale and a felony murder." She shook her head. "But Esparza hates you, and he'll keep telling his stories until, maybe, somebody listens. Just like Squint will keep trying to kill you."

She fiddled with her sunglasses and turned to face him. "Why on earth would you deal with somebody like Esparza? And why would you do something illegal, like pay a fee to a case runner?"

"I told you how it happened. If I hadn't stepped in to save Icky Snopes, they'd have had to fish him out of Galveston Bay. And they'd've had to take his shoes off with a jackhammer. You've got to remember, I didn't even know there was a case runner involved when Icky referred the case to me, and then it was too late."

Maria felt physically ill whenever she thought about Esparza. Even though she knew that Robert had done the only thing he could possibly have done. "Can't you step aside, just this once, and let some other law firm handle the propane truck case?"

"Maria . . . Maria. You just don't understand." By now, the case was woven into the stuff of his life. He had fought too hard for the plaintiffs, seen too many autopsy pictures, and listened too much to Jimmy Coleman's threats to give up now.

"I understand one thing, Robert. You're always pushing yourself too hard. In fact, you sometimes go past pushing yourself, and you push beyond the edge. You sometimes lean over the edge, to see how far you can push yourself without falling off."

"And just what do you mean by that?"

"You take on more cases than anybody could handle. When you're in trial, you stay awake all night and day. You mortgage your reputation to this piece of human garbage named Esparza, just so you can save your friend Icky from his own mess. And Icky's not much better than Esparza! And also, Robert—you've got a reputation for trying to make it with every skirt that walks by."

That last one surprised him. "Excuse me?"

"You know what I mean. Why do you do it? You don't need more money. You don't need more of a reputation. You don't need to prove anything to all the women in the world. You especially don't need to prove anything"—she hesitated—"to me."

So that was what it was all about. It was just her clumsy way of saying that she cared about him.

He took a deep breath. "I don't know, Maria. There come times, you crawl up inside yourself, sitting in the corner. I've had some cases that were real disasters—like ten years ago, when I lost that Westhaven Bank Case. I personally had a million-two in expenses already sunk into it, and the jury awarded my client only fifty thousand dollars. Times like that, I ask the same question: Why do I take risks? Why do I push the edge?"

He looked out at the Tobias II, which was tacking toward San Francisco.

"By the way, I didn't have a million-two at the time I lost the Westhaven Bank case. Technically, I was bankrupt. In the hole for that entire million-two. You see, I'm an entrepreneur, because trial lawyers like me are the last of the old-style entrepreneurs. We make money out of nothing, the way the railroad barons made it from carving up the wilderness. And it's hard. As an entrepreneur, you lose big sometimes, and when you do, you remember it forever. Because you don't ever want it to happen again."

She wasn't buying it. "Sure, but there are lots of fine trial lawyers who don't bungee-jump over every cliff the way you do."

"Okay, so maybe that's not it," he admitted. "Of course, right now, there's Squint the assassin, and Esparza the state's witness, and other nice people who'd like to kill me. And I've lost my last three jury trials. And frankly, I don't know why I'm the way I am, at least not well enough to explain it."

"Try me," she prompted.

"Anyway, I'm not trying to chase any 'skirts,' as you put it, except yours. There was a time when I did. But not now."

"Okay, okay. I'm just the jealous type. I didn't have any reason for saying that. But you know what I'm asking."

He hesitated. He wasn't sure whether to trust her with the answer.

"I went to see a shrink when my wife Patricia died," he said slowly. "Actually, I went to see a whole series of them. Usually, I think psychiatrists are nothing but charlatans and snake oil salesmen. But I came across this one psychologist, and she turned the question around. Instead of how was I going to live without Patricia, how was I going to live alone?"

"Well, that sounds profound, but not in a way that I can get hold of."

"It came down to this," Robert answered. "She wanted me to get to know Me. She wanted me to explore what my childhood was like, and I decided I'd better try."

He shaded his eyes with his hand and stared toward the setting sun. "My real daddy died when I was four. My mother—Rosalie, you know—she wore something black every day for more than a year, but finally, like anyone else, she found out that it was more fulfilling to have someone to care for who was alive." He shifted in his chair. "She really had just one of them, after trying out several. A year later she married him. I called him 'Pop,' and I guess my mother named him that for me. A different name from what I called my daddy. He was 'Pop,' instead.

"Well, anyway, they got divorced all of a sudden, when I was six. The divorce decree let Pop take me every other weekend and every Wednesday—you know, the usual divorce schedule. But Pop never did take me anywhere. Not ever. Instead, what he did was—well—he'd visit me . . . in the driveway."

"What?" asked Maria. This conversation wasn't going anywhere close to where she had expected it to.

He knew she couldn't guess what he was going to say next. But she had asked, and he was trying to answer her, to explain why he was the way he was.

"That's right. Pop never took me anywhere. Never showed up twice at the same time, or even on the same day of the week. I was crazy about him, but he'd never stay more than ten minutes. Ever. I remember Pop showing me how to dribble a basketball. He could do it so fast it was like magic. Another time he brought me a G.I. Joe action figure because I'd seen one on TV. But every time, Pop would stay for just a few minutes, there at the driveway, like he was on a hot griddle or something and had to get off it real quick. I would grab his hand. I would cry. He always left, anyway."

"My God," said Maria. "I'm sorry. You really don't have to tell me this."

"Yes, I do. And you've got to understand, I'm about to tell you something I've never told anybody except the psychotherapist. At first, I couldn't remember even the ten-minute visits or the G.I. Joe figure. It took about eight months while that lady helped me remember about Pop. I don't know why I was persistent enough to get there, but I did."

"I think I know. Always the overachiever, even at being psychoanalyzed."

He laughed. "I guess so. Anyway, this psychologist kept after it. There was still more that I needed to remember, she told me. Something important, still buried. I don't know how, but she knew. Months on end, we talked about my wife, my law practice, what I did in college. Everything except what mattered.

"Then one day, the ceiling fan made an unusual whirling shadow in the psychotherapist's office because the overhead light was burned out. There was a knock on the door. Somebody bringing coffee. But suddenly I remembered something, and it wasn't coffee. It was my mother knocking on the door and yelling at Pop to unlock it. And the ceiling fan looked exactly the same, thirty-five years earlier. I was five years old. My mother finally got the door open, and she hit him, because there was Pop . . . with . . . an erection, and . . . me—"

"Robert," said Maria, and stopped.

"Anyway, Pop was gone that same day. Rosalie, my Mama, she made sure of it. And I'm told I was lucky because it got stopped. All too often the mother participates by keeping quiet. I've studied the personality disorders that get produced by that sort of childhood experience. Lack of self-worth. Denial. Inability to trust anybody. Promiscuity. Some people are more prone to alcoholism or drug abuse. And the fact is, we don't know enough about the long-term effects of child abuse. And whether that's what makes me push past the edge, I don't know."

Maria was stunned. "And so that was the reason for the sudden divorce." She looked at the floor. "And the ten-minute visits in the driveway."

They both looked at the Tobias II, running with the wind back toward them. Then she looked at him, not knowing what to say. There was nothing she could say, not on this subject, anyway. She had only meant to ask what made him push so hard. But she had asked, and he had told her the answer. It was a deeper, harsher answer than she had dreamed she would hear.

Anyway, she knew, now, that there wasn't anything more she could say about Esparza or the propane truck case. She knew she'd have a hard time even mentioning her fears of the case ever again. But she still was petrified of what Esparza might do if Robert stayed on the case, because she'd seen the blind, reckless hate that had yellowed Esparza's eyes. That sinister force was still there. But how could she ever persuade Robert to give the case up if he wouldn't even listen to her about it?

"It's time to walk down the hill," he said. "By the time we get there, the Tobias II will be waiting for us at the dock."

The next day, in San Francisco, Robert went back to work. It was time for the depositions of the expert witnesses. In an ornate conference room high over the Embarcadero, with a view of both the Golden Gate and the Bay Bridge, Robert scribbled furious notes. But after the first hour, he slowed. Then he spent a lot of time staring out the window.

Because the deposition of the metallurgist, Dr. Oberoi Singh, took two unnecessary, excruciating days to complete.

Booker & Bayne had sent a five-year associate named Jeffrey Tait to take the deposition. This Jeffrey Tait worked for Jimmy Coleman, and he had a degree in mechanical engineering. Evidently, Booker & Bayne had decided that Tait would be better at questioning the expert witness because of his technical background.

But Jeffrey Tait had an annoying habit. First, he'd ask the witness what factors were behind his conclusions. He was exhaustive about this. Which was fine. When a lawyer takes the deposition of an expert witness, he's entitled to find out the expert's opinion in detail.

But Jeffrey Tait never stopped there. He would take each one of these "factors" and argue with the witness about it. Several times, he asked Oberoi Singh to explain "the factors that are behind this particular factor." Dr. Singh successfully avoided answering those questions, simply by not understanding them. Then, too, Tait would ask questions beginning, "Would you agree with me that . . . ," and then he would follow that phrase with a lengthy speech, which he evidently expected the witness to agree with.

"I object," said Herrick promptly, the first time it happened. "This witness is willing to answer your questions, but he isn't required to tell you whether he agrees or disagrees with your speeches. He might not want to put it exactly that way."

Dr. Singh understood what was going on. Every time Tait asked a question that started out, "Would you agree with me that . . . ," Dr. Singh would answer,

"I would not want exactly to put it that way," in his Hindi-British accent. Jeffrey Tait then would follow up with *another* question that started out, "Well, then, would you agree with me on this? . . ."

Finally, Jeffrey Tait would get frustrated: "Well, how would you put it, then?" and Robert would object that "The witness is not required to answer your speeches by telling you how he would put them."

Maria listened for about two hours. Then she excused herself and went back to the hotel, and she changed into something suitable for riding cable cars and having a good time in San Francisco.

In the end, it wasn't that Jeffrey Tait took a bad deposition, because he did manage to get the witness's opinions on record. It was just that he could have done it in one-tenth the time, Robert thought. And, of course, the deposition was tactically clumsy, because Robert had taken notes of Jeffrey Tait's questions. These long speeches showed Robert the kinds of attacks that Booker & Bayne planned to make against Dr. Singh's testimony. Robert knew them, now. His metallurgist would be prepared to answer them.

As for Booker & Bayne's expert, it took Robert one hour and fifteen minutes to complete his deposition. He was an Assistant Professor of Materials Science from CalTech, employed to testify in defense of Maxxco. The man was obviously just a hired gun. He claimed to believe that the guardrail was similar to others in widespread use, and perfectly safe. Robert's questions all were variations of three themes: "What opinions do you have about this guardrail?"; "What do you base those opinions on?"; and "Have you told me everything that was a factor in forming your opinions?" At trial, Booker & Bayne would learn for the first time how Robert would attack their expert witness. Since they couldn't anticipate the cross-examination, they wouldn't be able to shade his testimony. They wouldn't be able to "woodshed" their expert, to use the term that lawyers use for opponents who skirt the truth when they coach a witness.

But then, Robert Herrick could afford to take the simple approach. He didn't have to impress Jimmy Coleman, unlike the young associate from Booker & Bayne.

21
THE MOTION TO DISMISS

J udge Barbara Trobelo's courtroom was small and dilapidated. That was because she was the newest civil judge and had the lowest seniority. But she had inherited the biggest case, the propane truck case. And that case was on the docket today for its first public hearing.

Jimmy Coleman's army of assistants had dredged up an obscure law called the "Statute of Repose." It was a law that created a loophole for engineering companies like Maxxco. And based on this dusty old statute of repose, Jimmy had filed a paper called "Motion To Dismiss or For Summary Judgment." He was asking the judge to throw out the entire case.

Sitting in the crowded courtroom, Robert Herrick was worried. The statute of repose! He had never actually sat down and read the statute of repose before this case. The worst-case scenario was that the judge might agree with Jimmy. And if she did, she might dismiss his entire case against Maxxco, based on this musty old law.

"*Gutierrez versus Maxxco Construction Corporation and the Louisiana Trucking Company!*" Judge Trobelo announced, and she set the docket sheet down.

With a spring to his step, Jimmy Coleman answered immediately. "That's our Motion to Dismiss, your honor. I represent Maxxco, and I'm ready to proceed."

"I'm here for the plaintiffs, your honor." Robert Herrick's voice was equally confident. "There are many, many reasons why this motion should be denied. I don't think that this hearing should last more than fifteen minutes."

Francel Williams stood up. "I represent the trucking company, your honor. And there's no merit to this motion to dismiss, none at all." With that, Francel smiled, or rather, he beamed. "But your honor, that means you can deny the motion and get on to the other important matters on your docket."

Judge Trouble laughed. "Thank you—I think. But Mister Coleman may disagree about how long it's going to take."

"I do, your honor." Jimmy was enjoying this. "Respectfully, I'd suggest that you should go ahead and hear the other cases on this morning's docket and then devote this afternoon to our motion to dismiss."

The courtroom was full of news reporters. They had heard rumors that something big might happen. A buzzing sound went through the audience as the reporters realized, from Jimmy Coleman's confident attitude, that the judge might actually throw out the case against everybody but the trucking company. And she might even announce a ruling right after this hearing. That would make front-page news.

"Not the whole afternoon!" Judge Trouble groaned good-naturedly. "I'm going to set this hearing on the motion to dismiss for three o'clock. Gentlemen, you'll have two hours to argue about the statute of repose."

The reporters mobbed Jimmy Coleman. He luxuriated in their attention because it signaled that he had the momentum, like a steamroller. The reporters were puzzled about the statute of repose. "It says that ten years after something's built, you can't sue the engineer who designed it," Jimmy exulted.

"But isn't it just a technicality?" asked a reporter from Channel 3. "Why do we have a law like that?"

"Because after ten years, everything needs maintenance. Every road, every overpass, every building. There comes a time when the engineer shouldn't be responsible for the design because it's been too long since the structure was built."

What Jimmy didn't say was that he wanted to win above all else, and he'd like it even better if he won on a technicality. That would increase his reputation, and also, it would humiliate Herrick.

A smaller gaggle of reporters surrounded Robert Herrick. He was philosophical. "The reason we got saddled with this unfair law was because the engineers made lots of political contributions. The legislature caved in to their lobby. And so this statute of repose was a special favor to big engineering companies."

But unfair or not, the statute of repose existed. And so did the motion to dismiss. If they lost this way, the plaintiffs would get nothing from Maxxco, even if it was a technicality.

"I've got to admit, I'm worried about Jimmy Coleman's motion," said Herrick to Tom Kennedy as they walked back to the office.

"I can see why," Kennedy agreed. "But still, we ought to be able to keep Jimmy or anybody else from getting a dismissal or a summary judgment in a case like this."

"Right. Because if Jimmy's going to win, the rules say he's got to prove without any question that he's right. He's got to show that the facts about his defendant can't even be disputed."

"Everybody learned that in the first year of law school," Kennedy agreed. "But don't forget to remind the judge about it. Emphasize to her, if she grants a dismissal or a summary judgment, the plaintiffs don't even get a jury trial. And so the rules say Jimmy has to prove the evidence is all one-sided. He has to show that there wouldn't even be anything for the jury to decide."

Robert nodded. "I remember when Jimmy first filed this motion. I remember we had to go look up the statute of repose. And even then, we couldn't quite believe what it says."

"I know. It might be a good idea to read it one more time before the argument this afternoon."

And so Tom Kennedy thumbed through the briefs until he found it. He read the words of the statute aloud:

A person must bring suit for damages for a claim against a licensed architect or engineer in this state, who designs the construction of an improvement to real property, not later than 10 years after the substantial completion of the improvement.

"Okay," said Robert. "Now, let's do the job that lawyers do. We've already done this so many times we're tired of it, but let's do it one last time so I'll know I'm ready for any question the judge might throw at me. Let's analyze this law again, step by step."

The "job that lawyers do" was well known to both Herrick and Kennedy. It was a job they did often, and they had done it to the statute of repose before writing the brief for this hearing. The first step was to separate the law into a kind of list. The list divided the law into its most understandable parts, so it wouldn't be just a turgid string of legalese. Then, the second step was to argue both sides for each of the little parts. The assumption wasn't that the law fit the case, or that it didn't fit. Instead, the assumption was that you didn't *know* yet whether it fit. If you started out that way, and you tried hard, you could usually come up with your best arguments. The object was to represent your client in the most effective way possible.

"Well," said Robert, "the first words of the statute say that if the Maxxco Construction Corporation is going to use this law, they've got to be a licensed architect or engineer."

"And it's perfectly reasonable for us to argue that they're not." Kennedy settled into his role. "We've sued the Maxxco Construction Corporation. It's a corporation, not an individual. And only an individual, a human being, can be a licensed engineer. Besides, Maxxco has thousands of employees, and only a few of them are engineers. They've got secretaries, janitors, accountants. They've got a motion picture division, a sales department, a PR department. Maxxco, itself, isn't a licensed engineer."

"Good," said Robert. "Next, let's go on to the second phrase in the statute of repose. It says that what Maxxco did on this highway overpass has got to be 'architectural and engineering services' if they want to come under the statute."

"They miss on that one, too," said Kennedy. "They didn't just limit themselves to architectural or engineering drawings. They also did the construction of the overpass. They sent out the first bulldozers, and they were even there to cut the ribbon."

"And so our position is, they weren't only architects or engineers," Robert echoed. "Good. Now, the third piece of this repose law is that it's got to be an improvement to real estate. That sounds like a building, or something like that."

"And our position is that this overpass isn't an improvement to real estate,"

Kennedy agreed, "because it isn't a building. Most of the work consisted just of moving around the dirt. The concrete is just a thin layer on the top. It isn't an improvement, it's just the same real estate."

"Okay," said Robert. "And then fourth, it's got to be ten years since it was completed. Ten years and they're home free. This overpass was built more than thirty years ago. I remember, we thought they had us on that one at first. But we have evidence that it was still being worked on during the last ten years."

"That's right," said the resourceful Kennedy. "It might seem that it was built more than thirty years ago, but Jimmy can't prove it. You need to remind the judge—Jimmy's got to prove everything beyond dispute if he's hoping to win without a trial. And he can't. Because actually, what the law says, is it's got to have been *completed* more than ten years ago. 'Completed,' not 'built.' And anybody who's ever driven on an interstate highway knows it's never completed."

"They keep working on it. And re-designing it."

"Forever."

"And so Jimmy's got the burden of proof, and he can't prove when the ten years started to run. In fact, it never started to run, not even today, thirty-some-odd years after the ribbon was cut, because they're still changing it."

"I bet if you go out there today, you'd find crews working on it."

"Right." Robert suddenly laughed, self-consciously. "You know, this kind of legal analysis is so rigid that it seems strange, doesn't it?"

"Maybe so, but we're following the words of the statute. And it's very logical. I've always found it interesting to play this lawyer's game."

"It's interesting when it works, you mean," said Robert. He was the one who would have to stand up in the courtroom at three o'clock this afternoon and do the same analysis in front of the judge and Jimmy Coleman. Jimmy, of course, would try to interpret the statute differently. The people on the other side of the courtroom always did. That was what kept it from being just gamesmanship. There always were two sides.

The tiny courtroom was mobbed. Every reporter in town was there, and half the city's lawyers had come to watch this battle of the titans.

"I'm glad Mister Herrick is going to let me talk about whether my client, Maxxco, is an engineering firm!" said Jimmy Coleman. He was accompanied by four other Booker & Bayne lawyers at a total of more than fifteen hundred dollars an hour. The meter was running. Jimmy showed his teeth, as well as a half-dozen chins.

At that, the news reporters smiled, too. So did Judge Barbara Trobelo. Herrick had started his argument against Jimmy's motion for summary judgment by repeating the first one of the arguments that he and Kennedy had developed: Maxxco wasn't a licensed engineer, and its services in building the overpass weren't engineering services.

Now, it was Jimmy's turn. "Of course, my client does sell its services. It doesn't work for free, at least not always. I mean, the evidence shows that it does a lot of free charitable designs, like for the Boy Scouts and the Red Cross this year." Jimmy's brown teeth showed again. "But most of the time, it charges for its services, and that means it has to have salesmen, and being the biggest engineering company in the world, it just about has to have PR people, too."

Jimmy held up his index finger and widened his smile. "You know, I heard Robert Herrick has a PR department, too," he said. "But that doesn't mean Mister Herrick isn't a lawyer!"

Judge Barbara Trobelo laughed.

Jimmy looked straight at the judge. "Mister Herrick is a fine lawyer, in fact. He is such a fine lawyer that he has made just about all the right arguments. And luckily for Maxxco, there are lots of cases where other fine lawyers have made all the same arguments—and lost." Jimmy got ready to administer the *coup de grace*. "We cited the cases in our brief. For example, in *Suburban Homes v. Austin-Northwest Development Company*, the court of appeals said that a corporation can use the statute of repose. In fact, it is perfectly proper for a corporation to use the statute just as an individual would. All it has to do is have licensed engineers do the work. And the courts of appeals, plus the Texas Supreme Court, have all said that multi-purpose businesses can use the statute of repose. The cases are at pages five and six of our brief."

Jimmy took his glasses off while Judge Trobelo leafed through the briefs to find the cases.

"And Judge, I have to brag on Mister Herrick for his thinking up this argument that Maxxco isn't an engineer because it has a PR department to sell its services. It's a good argument for him to make." As Jimmy stretched his hand toward his adversary, Robert realized that he was getting beaten like a drum. "It's such a good argument that another fine law firm made it once before," Jimmy continued. "And thank goodness they did, because the court of appeals in that case said, of course engineers sell their services, and they're still engineers. That's the case of *McCulloch v. Fox & Jacobs, Inc.*, on page seven of our brief."

More than thirty-three people were dead, and the lawsuit was about Maxxco's negligence. But by now, Jimmy had diverted the issue completely. The case had become a game—a contest about the statute of repose, to find out which side would be best at manipulating its technical language.

At last, Robert stood up.

"If I get any more of these kinds of compliments from Mister Coleman, I think the bar association might try to take my license away." He had to strain a little bit, but still he managed to smile, too.

"All I can say, judge," Robert went on, "is that Maxxco Construction Corporation is more diverse, more commercially sophisticated, and more full of people who aren't engineers than any company that's ever used the statute of repose before. We think that Mister Coleman's cases just are—well—different from this case. No other case involves a company that's had an in-house PR department, for instance. And in one case, which was called *Kazmir v. Suburban Homes*, the court of appeals reversed a dismissal because the engineering company did other services besides just engineering."

Herrick and Kennedy didn't have the army of associates that Jimmy could command. They had done the research themselves, and Kennedy was proud of having found the case of *Kazmir v. Suburban Homes*. It was a recent precedent, very close to this case. And it said the statute of repose didn't apply.

"All right," said Judge Trobelo. "I think I understand both of your positions about that issue."

This was Robert's cue to move on to his next line of attack. "We also think that this overpass hasn't been proved to be an improvement to real property. That's the next issue."

"Well, fortunately, I think I understand that issue completely, too," said Judge Trobelo. "I've read your briefs, and it's pretty clear to me that Mister Coleman is right. A highway overpass is an improvement to the raw land. Makes it more valuable."

When the judge tells you she's decided against you, the best thing to do is to move on.

"Well, judge," Robert said, "we've saved our best argument for last. The statute of repose runs ten years. It runs from the time that the improvements were completed. 'Completed.' That's what the statute says. 'Completed.' And this overpass hasn't been proven to have been *completed* more than ten years ago."

Judge Trobelo stared at him. "The affidavits say it was put in service more than thirty years ago. There's even a photograph of Maxxco's ribbon-cutting ceremony that Mister Coleman put into the record."

"Yes, your honor. And Mister Coleman even has pictures of cars driving over it." Robert held up his hand. "But you see, your honor, that isn't the issue."

"What is the issue, then?"

"When the overpass was completed."

"Didn't it have to be completed for these cars to drive over it?"

"No, your honor." Now it was Robert's index finger that was in the air. "We've got affidavits, too, from our side. And we've got depositions of Jimmy Coleman's witnesses. And what these show is, the dismissal can't be granted. It would be illegal." Robert had everyone's attention now. He sensed the momentum changing.

"One hundred and fourteen times in the first year, the builders made changes in this overpass," Robert continued. "And in the second year, they made fifty-seven more changes."

"I'm starting to see your point," said Judge Trobelo. "I don't know whether I agree with it. But . . . anyway, go on."

"Every single year, there have been changes in this overpass," Robert almost shouted. "Our lawsuit is about the guardrail. Well, the guardrail's been changed more than two dozen times over the years!"

"I see where you're going," said Judge Trobelo, with an amused look on her face. She was familiar with the kind of analysis lawyers did. But a judge could play, too. And when the lawyers were good at it, that was when it was pleasant to be a judge. Barbara Trobelo was enjoying herself in this high-stakes banter.

But Robert had his clients to think about, and he was running scared. More than thirty-three dead people, killed by Maxxco's negligence, and it was all going to come down to a question of who was best at playing with words. This kind of gamesmanship was going to determine whether the plaintiffs got thrown out without a jury trial. It was the best legal system in the world, but sometimes this process seemed no better than the toss of a coin. Robert reminded himself that perfect justice exists only in heaven, and he felt his determination rise—his determination to fight the best fight he could for his clients.

"The fact is, this overpass has never been completed!" he thundered. "It hasn't been ten years. It hasn't even been one year! During the last calendar year, the construction companies have changed the design fourteen more times."

Jimmy waved his arms. "Judge, there's an old proverb: 'Putting a saddle on a duck doesn't change it into a horse.' And Mister Herrick is trying to stretch this case beyond recognition. He's trying to make a duck into a horse without even adding the saddle!"

Judge Trouble couldn't help but laugh at that one.

But Robert had the answer. "Your honor, I don't have the burden of proof here. It's not my motion to dismiss, not my motion for summary judgment." His voice rose again. "It's Maxxco's motion for summary judgment. They have to prove it's been more than ten years. And they have to prove it so clearly that there's no room for dispute, because they're trying to cut off all the plaintiffs without a jury trial. Maxxco shouldn't win on a technicality, especially when they're not even technically correct!"

The reporters loved that. They all wrote it down in their notes.

"Anything else?" asked Judge Trobelo politely.

"Yes, your honor. I represent the families of more than thirty human beings who are dead. Incinerated. Asphyxiated and burned alive, because of the defective design of this freeway overpass. A design that Maxxco knew was defective, and they covered it up. My clients want a trial by jury. They deserve a trial by jury."

Judge Trobelo sighed. "Unfortunately, none of that has anything to do with the statute of repose."

Robert knew it, too, but he also knew that it was important to keep the real case in focus. To remind the judge what was at stake.

"And I congratulate counsel for the plaintiffs on the ingenuity of his argument," Judge Trobelo went on. "It's true, no doubt, that this overpass is still being worked on and repaired. But that can't be what makes the difference, under the law. If it did, the statute of repose never could apply, because every engineering project has to be repaired eventually."

Robert had a sense of impending doom. His hands were clammy, and his stomach felt like it was in his shoes. He was going to lose again to Jimmy Coleman. This time, without even getting to try his case.

Jimmy smiled. "Judge, if you grant the motion for summary judgment, it will be good for Mister Herrick, because then he will be free to pursue his claims against the trucking company. And they, of course, are the ones who really are responsible."

"Maxxco is responsible." Robert's response was immediate. "The evidence against Maxxco is simply overwhelming." In a fight about the statute of repose, that wasn't the issue, but Jimmy had injected it, and so Robert had to answer.

"Here's what I'm going to do," said Judge Trobelo crisply. "I'm going to dismiss the engineering division of Maxxco, and also all the other architectural and design firms. And I'm going to dismiss every claim about engineering services. Now, nobody's left but the trucking people and Maxxco's construction division. But I'm not going to dismiss Maxxco entirely. If Mister Herrick can prove to the jury that Maxxco was negligent in some way that doesn't involve engineering designs, such as in constructing the overpass, that's the only way he can win."

She turned to Jimmy Coleman. "To that extent, your motion is granted. Draft me an order that says so, and I'll sign it."

Jimmy was exultant. But still he wasn't satisfied. He wanted more. "Judge, that's not fair! Maxxco shouldn't have been dragged into this case in the first place. You ought to just grant the motion and dismiss Maxxco completely."

"That reminds me of another ancient proverb, Mister Coleman." Judge Trouble smiled back. "'When a pig becomes a hog, it gets slaughtered.' Don't press your luck."

Jimmy laughed. He could afford to, since he had won.

Suddenly, the courtroom erupted with excited conversations. "I can see the headline," said one of the reporters to another. "'PROPANE TRUCK DISMISSAL CALLED ILLEGAL!' And then, in smaller letters, 'But Judge Frees Engineering Firms on Technicalities—Case Will Proceed Against Other Companies.'" The reporters hurried from the courtroom so that they could get it all on the air by six o'clock.

The reporters surrounded Robert as he left the courtroom. "What does this mean to your case?"

"I'm not sure it makes much difference." He was still shell-shocked, still trying to figure it out. "I hope there'll be no damage to our case at all. We can still sue Maxxco for negligence in constructing the overpass."

And they surrounded Jimmy Coleman, too. He had a different opinion. "It means Mister Herrick can't win just by proving that the engineering of the overpass was negligent. This cuts the heart out of their case."

Jimmy sounded like a heavyweight champion explaining how stupid his opponent had been in letting himself get knocked out. He went on and on, about how carefully he had planned for this hearing and how "sloppy" the performance of "my un-learned adversary, Mister Herrick" had been.

"I wonder," Robert thought to himself, "whether there's any difference between engineering and construction. Can't I really go right ahead and prove my case the very same way I would have before?" Because everything Maxxco had "engineered," it also had "constructed."

Would it really be that simple to prove his case after this hearing, he wondered? "What on earth does the judge's decision today really mean?"

But Jimmy Coleman had the last word, a parting shot below the belt as the two groups of lawyers left the courthouse. "You sure as hell got another crappy, dog-ass piece-of-shit case here, don't you, Herrick?"

22
THE PROM

The Booker & Bayne Spring Prom is always a lavish affair. Black tie. Beaded gowns in silver, gold and red. Canapés with glistening designs. Roast duck and chunks of jalapeño-barbecued venison. All at the Tanglewilde Country Club, which is Houston's most opulent setting. The Prom is the most formal occasion of the year, and this blue-blooded law firm goes all out.

It isn't really called the "Prom," of course. Not officially. The correct title is "The Celebration Ball." It celebrates the founding of Booker & Bayne a century ago. And now that the speeches have been abolished, everyone who is invited usually accepts—all the partners and associates, with their glittering wives, tuxedoed boyfriends, or strapless girlfriends; presidents of client corporations; friends; and plenty of opposing counsel. Because after all, it's a good party. Unofficially, everybody calls it "The Prom," even members of Booker & Bayne's Executive Committee, because that's what it most reminds them of.

And even at the Prom, Booker & Bayne lawyers talk shop. This year, everybody wanted to congratulate Jimmy Coleman. Today, Jimmy had done the impossible in the propane truck case by getting his motion to dismiss partially granted. It showed, once again, that this was the finest law firm in the world, and Booker & Bayne still could beat the crap out of everybody else. Better yet, if Booker & Bayne's client was guilty as sin, these lawyers could still find a technicality to whip the asses of the lesser people on the other side. Jimmy accepted his partners' accolades with the attitude of a Roman general after a victory against the Gauls.

Jennifer Lowenstein sounded like a cheerleader. "After that hearing today, we've just about won the case. Jimmy, you wiped Robert Herrick all over the courtroom floor."

"Unfortunately, I don't think so at all." Jimmy's corroded forehead looked as though a hurricane was kicking around in the middle of it. "Let me tell you a story, Jennifer. When I was a young lawyer in this firm, you could always walk by the library, any time of the night or day, and you'd hear a book slam shut. And some young lawyer would yell, 'We've got those dirty bastards now!'"

Jimmy pulled at his tuxedo tie, which was like a tourniquet on the ample folds of his neck. "At Booker & Bayne, we always want to believe we've got those dirty bastards on the other side. Trouble is, sometimes you find you haven't really got 'em. In the end, Herrick may turn out to be the real winner of that hearing today."

Jennifer was disappointed. She loved the idea of winning in a way that had nothing to do with justice. "But Jimmy, the judge granted your motion. Herrick can't win by proving that the design of the overpass was defective."

"Yes, but on the other hand, Herrick can still prove that Maxxco was negligent in constructing the overpass. And everything Maxxco was negligent in designing, it also was negligent in constructing."

Jennifer toyed with the pearl choker above her beaded silver dress while she thought about that for a minute.

"The judge's decision today might be a little bit helpful," Jimmy went on. "We might get the judge to tell the jury they can't consider the engineering designs when they decide whether Maxxco was negligent. We'll try to get the jury confused. You know, try to box 'em in and play word games. But Herrick can probably get them to focus on the real issues, and it will be hard to fool all of 'em. He'll just tell the jury, 'You don't have to consider the blueprints, because Maxxco built the overpass, and it's a dangerous overpass.' Which, of course, it is."

Jennifer still wasn't used to the concept that you could win a technicality in a hard-fought hearing and then still lose the jury trial. In law school, the most interesting court decisions had always sounded like they depended on technicalities. "Oh, well. I guess we haven't got those dirty bastards, at least not yet."

She got up to walk across the ballroom. Maybe seeing her co-worker on the propane truck case, Jeff Tait, would make her feel better.

A moment later, Jimmy Coleman's arm was around his wife's waist, which was covered with tiny beads in shiny silver and black. The beads were arranged in a design that branched and feathered under her breasts. At five-feet-eleven, Barbara Coleman towered over Jimmy like a blonde Valkyrie. That was one of the things Jimmy liked best in a woman.

He had met Barbara Coleman because she was the president of a small oil and gas company with a little bit of west Texas production, which he had represented in a lawsuit against the giant Sabio Pipeline. The company was worth less than a hundred thousand, but Jimmy used inflated reserve figures to win an astounding eight million dollar windfall. It wasn't long after the money was in the bank that Jimmy and Barbara told everyone they were getting married. "He took the money away from Sabio Pipeline like he was a bandit," Barbara said proudly.

"He always does," said Martha Peters, the oil and gas lawyer. "Jimmy's just a bandit at heart."

"Thank you!" Jimmy lifted a glass of Crystál Champagne. "Well, anyway, we got through the year."

"Yes," agreed Barbara. "And without any kind of sex scandal or criminal investigation over the firm's finances."

"Don't remind me," said Jimmy.

It was hard to run a law firm these days, Jimmy thought to himself. In a firm with five hundred lawyers, some of them could be expected to make a mess out of their private lives. And occasionally, they hurt other people. The law firm couldn't be constantly sticking its nose into their business or invading their privacy, but then again, neither could it ignore the problems. The trouble was, it was sometimes hard to find out about an emerging scandal in time to prevent the damage.

"Where was that sleazy party that happened with the insurance clients last year?" Barbara Coleman wanted to know. "Wasn't it Pierre's Ritz? In the party loft? You know, the party with the insurance people that turned into the Booker & Bayne sex scandal of the year?"

The Booker & Bayne insurance section dinner last year had been a nice gathering at first, but it went terribly wrong. It was sprinkled with top officials from big insurance companies. For some reason, there were very few women lawyers or clients in attendance, and all of the women who were there left early. That was when the partners who were left, all of whom were men, had suggested adjourning to the Play Mate Club. For a nightcap. Or something.

But Pierre, the owner, had implored them not to leave. He wanted to sell some more two-hundred-dollar bottles of wine. "You don't have to go to the Play Mate Club. Just go upstairs. Right here!"

As it happened, the Sausage Girls were entertaining in Pierre's party loft. It was a bachelor party, and Tanya and Tina, the Sausage Girls, were delighted to get paid for two shows instead of one. Their act featured intimate performances with various kinds of vegetables and bananas. And, of course, sausages. And one of the best-known features of the Sausage Girls' act was that they generally succeeded in involving the audience. This time, four drunk Booker & Bayne partners participated, or rather, Tanya and Tina participated on them. Right there at Pierre's Ritz! Right there, in the party loft.

The problem was, one insurance company president didn't like it. He happened to be a devout Southern Baptist, and he pulled all of his business from Booker & Bayne the next morning. But that was not all he did. The Baptist insurance president also did the unthinkable, but perfectly logical next step. He went to the police. It seems the whole thing just happened so fast that— goodness!—the partners in charge didn't think to ask whether any of the clients might be offended, or might consider the entertainment to be a crime. And so the story was front page news for months while the vice division conducted a thorough investigation. This included interviews of Tanya and Tina, who liked the whole affair because they got their pictures in the paper. But Booker & Bayne didn't.

"It killed our recruiting of new lawyers," said Jimmy. "No one signed up for a job interview with us because whenever we would arrive at a law school campus, the Women's Law Association would be picketing."

"Good," said Barbara. "And knowing your firm, I imagine everybody slapped the four partners on the back, the ones who 'participated.' And I bet you guys gave them a raise."

"No. They all got lifestyle-type pay cuts, over a hundred thousand each. Also, two of them were married, and those guys got cleaned out in their divorces."

"Good," said Barbara again.

What Jimmy didn't mention to his wife was that he himself had set up exactly the same kind of party for his own best clients about a week before. The difference was, Jimmy hadn't gotten caught. Even if he had, none of his partners would have dared to cross him. Still, Jimmy's escapade hadn't stopped him from making a sanctimonious speech when he voted to punish the four guilty partners in the Sausage Girls caper. "Outrageous! . . . We can't be respected as lawyers if we violate the law ourselves. . . ."

"Well, maybe it's time to forgive and forget," said Martha Peters. "Especially since all of the participants got caught, all of them got punished, and all of them got royally screwed to the wall."

Meanwhile, across the huge ballroom, Jeff Tait was whispering to Jennifer Lowenstein. They were the two main associates working on the propane truck case, and right now, they were trying not to be seen by Jimmy Coleman. Jimmy hadn't figured out yet that they were romantically involved, and they wanted to keep it that way. Jeff had on a tuxedo, in which he thought he looked awkward, but to Jennifer he looked cute. Jennifer had on a beaded sheath, in which Jeff thought she looked dynamite, with a push-up bra that made her breasts look as though there was a cantilevered shelf underneath them.

"I want to get out of here right now," Jeff whispered.

"Me, too," Jennifer answered. "I'm tired of being discreet."

"Well, we'd better keep on being at least a little bit discreet. If we start acting like dogs in heat—well, you know. That just wouldn't set too well with those tight-ass partners."

"So what do we do?"

"Keep on being discreet. But maybe we can find an empty room, or a closet. Or a pantry. Or something."

From across the room, Jimmy Coleman wasn't paying close attention to Jeff and Jennifer as they edged out of the ballroom. He lifted his glass again. He wanted to tell some more stories about the legalized banditry he performed for his clients.

Robert Herrick and Maria Melendes arrived at the Booker & Bayne Prom about an hour after it really moved into high gear. They were accompanied by retired justice Stone Taylor, formerly of the Texas Supreme Court, and his wife—who still, even in her sixty-seventh year, called herself "Bunny" Taylor.

Once inside the gold-encrusted ballroom, Robert tugged at his shirt just above the knot of his black silk tie. It wasn't that his collar was too tight, because it fit perfectly. The problem, of course, was that Robert didn't like Booker & Bayne, and he felt silly at formal parties. But the Celebration Ball honored a law firm that was a part of the state's history, for better or for worse. Besides, Justice Taylor had insisted. "Robert, my boy, it's the kind of clambake no politician ever wants to miss!" Stone Taylor still hadn't stopped acting as though he was running for re-election to the supreme court, even though he had retired five years ago.

Tediously, Robert worked his way through the receiving line. But all the while, he was thinking about how he could keep the evening from becoming a total loss. "Hello, there!" He smiled. "So nice to see you." It always was useful to watch your opponents in a social setting, outside the courthouse, where their guard was down. It provided insights into how they thought, how they reacted. "Hi. Great party! Thanks for inviting me." Sometimes, a well-oiled adversary would let slip important confidences. His estimate of a witness, or even his client's bottom-line settlement figure. You could do a lot of informal discovery of your case that way, not by the bar in the courtroom, but by the bar at the party.

Near the end of the receiving line, Robert saw Jimmy Coleman standing nearby. He hesitated an instant before reaching to shake Jimmy's hand. Jimmy responded by stumbling slightly, and he bared his teeth in a discolored parody of graciousness. "Well, Herrick! Surprised to see you here, after that symbolic beatin' you took today! Are you lookin' forward to the trial, when you're gonna really get your ass pounded?"

Robert stared at him in disbelief. Jimmy wasn't kidding. His tone of voice was crude enough to signal that he meant it. Jimmy was actually gloating.

But Robert's smile, by now, was on automatic pilot. "Great party, Jimmy! Thanks for asking me! It looks even better than last year." He had been practicing his pleasantries through more than a dozen handshakes, and with that, he moved down the receiving line. Jimmy's bland, alcohol-glazed look told him that by letting the insult roll off his back, he instinctively had given back the perfect response.

And once he was through marveling at the man's boorishness, Robert paused to digest the actual words that Jimmy had spoken: ". . . after that *symbolic* beating you took today . . ." Jimmy's victory, in his own words, wasn't total. It wasn't even meaningful. It was only symbolic. "Jimmy secretly shares my evaluation of today's hearing," Robert thought with satisfaction. "Otherwise, he wouldn't have used that word to belittle his win. And so, if I concentrate on Maxxco's negligence in constructing the overpass, I can prove my case in almost the same way I had planned earlier. Jimmy knows it."

Already, it was clear that the evening wasn't a total loss. Robert had learned enough from one word to make this whole stuffy affair worth suffering through.

Finally, when he stepped away from the receiving line, Robert heard a welcome sound. Stone Taylor's deep baritone voice was holding forth to Bunny and Maria on his favorite topic, judicial politics. "The REE-pubs are on the march in east Texas with that old-fashioned Republican message against frivolous lawsuits. And they're scarin' hell out of the Democrat judges who have to run for re-election!"

Robert thought, again, about Jimmy's slip of the tongue, and he felt an extra spring to his step as he smiled inwardly and walked over to join his distinguished friends. Justice Taylor always was interesting to talk to. And maybe this overdressed, overly extravagant, tasteless Prom would even turn out to be fun after all.

A good while later, after wandering all over the Tanglewilde Country Club, Jeff Tait was becoming frustrated. He and Jennifer Lowenstein had left the Booker & Bayne Prom. Good. So that they could have a private party of their own. Fine and dandy. She wanted him, and he certainly wanted her. Wonderful. All they had to do was find a suitable location. Great. Outstanding. But there was one major obstacle. They had looked at a dozen closed-off dining rooms, storage areas, and broom closets, and Jennifer hadn't liked any of them. None of them suited her taste as places for romance. Not even for quick romance, of the kind that Jeff and Jennifer had in mind.

"No," she pronounced. "Not this one, either. Just doesn't look like it would put me in the mood." And with that, she shut the door to a closet holding hundreds of stacked white linens. Jeff was thinking, "If a closet full of bed sheets won't do it, what on earth will?" But he managed to choke it back. "After this," he said to himself, "she'd better be sensational."

Jennifer's ample chest, meanwhile, squirmed and heaved so much that it reminded Jeff, with his brain fogged by lust, of two piglets fighting beneath a blanket. The view was enough to make him force at least a mesmerized brand of patience.

They wandered to the end of the corridor, took a left, and went up a small flight of stairs. Jeff was starting to wonder whether they'd even be able to find their way back to the ballroom after all these twists and turns.

But Jennifer wasn't paying attention to that problem, because she had discovered a mysterious paneled door cut into the hallway. Seeing her interest, Jeff started to become hopeful again.

The door was stuck, but it opened when both of them pulled. "A good omen," Jeff thought. "Great. Super."

Evidently, this promising little door was the entrance to a crawl space over some room on the floor below. But it was huge. In fact, it was stand-up crawl space. It was crisscrossed with raw wooden beams. About half of it was floored with cheap pine boards. And the floored area was littered here and there with an awning, a half dozen obsolete exercise bicycles, a mountain of china plates, and a pile of half-empty storage boxes.

Jennifer stripped off her pantyhose. Then she put her heels back on. Jeff Tait thought, "*This* is the kind of room that puts her in the mood?" But he didn't think for very long; he just was grateful that she finally had found a place she liked. He loosened his belt and dropped his boxer shorts. Fine and dandy! We're here!

Two naked light bulbs illuminated a forest of upright wooden studs. Jennifer grabbed hold of one of them and perched on her heels as she bent over and hiked her beaded gown over her pale, slender thighs and buttocks. She was sweating and breathing in heavy, sobbing gulps. Her eyes glittered as she looked back over her shoulder at him, and then, together, their bodies began to move.

Back in the main ballroom, down below, Jimmy Coleman pulled again on his bow tie as he told Barbara and Martha about the partner who got indicted for taking commercial bribes. "He came back and said, 'The jury acquitted me, so that proves I didn't do it.' He wanted his old job back. Personally, I tried to re-hire him, because he was a real rainmaker. Had a hundred-million-dollar book of business from his clients. But nobody else thought the presumption of innocence could stretch quite that far."

Suddenly, all of the partygoers heard a strange sound, a cross between a crunch and a rip. It came from up above, up in the ceiling. Involuntarily, Jimmy and Barbara and Martha looked upward. And eventually, everyone else in the room did, too. It took a few seconds, because of the loud volume of the band combined with several hundred people's conversation, but finally everyone was looking up toward the huge gold-and-crystal chandelier in the middle of the ceiling. What they saw, first, was a dangling pair of black shoes and tuxedo pants. Above them, a hairy pair of male legs stuck out of the pants. The legs disappeared into the ceiling.

In front of the male shoes and legs, also hanging from the ceiling, there was a second pair of shoes. These were women's shoes, with three inch heels. Above them, there was a pair of feminine calves that protruded from the burst ceiling just at mid-thigh. Right in front of the legs attached to the tuxedo pants.

Jimmy Coleman's face already had an even bumpier, more reptilian look than usual. He had guessed that there might be something between these two, because he made it his business to know. Out of the corner of his eye, he had glimpsed them when they had left the room, and so he already knew who it was, this couple that was stuck in the ceiling, even before he heard the startled cries of anguish and embarrassment that emanated from his two most trusted associates.

But there wasn't much that Jimmy could do about it on short notice. There were eight hundred people in the room. Maybe, with luck, this episode wouldn't run for a week on the front page of the newspaper, like last year's scandal with the Sausage Girls. Still, this was going to be news. Everybody in town would know the story by tomorrow. Red-hot sweaty sex on the ceiling! The scandal of this year was . . . Jennifer and Jeff.

Jimmy heard himself deliver several well-placed expletives under his breath as he joined the search party that spontaneously set off to rescue the two associates impaled in the ceiling. "You'd better not have gotten yourselves fired, you over-sexed little bastards," he muttered under his breath.

He needed them. These were his foot soldiers. "And that," Jimmy thought, "is the best job security these two hot-blooded kids have got at this moment. That, plus the fact that the trial of the propane truck case is only ten days away."

Robert and Maria were like all the other guests in the room. For several long moments, they stared at the ceiling, with their eyes wide and their jaws slack. Then the crowd started snickering. It grew into a roar of laughter that alternated with moans of horror and shrieks of concern.

Robert winced. "Ouch! I sure hope those two kids didn't hurt themselves."

"Yes." Maria was worried, too. "Especially considering the body parts that would be involved if they did hurt themselves."

Nobody could have wished this catastrophe on his own worst enemy. But there was at least one good thing that would come from it, Robert thought to himself. His loss to Jimmy earlier today on the motion to dismiss was only a distant memory by now. Because when you've seen your adversary scurrying to help two assistants hanging half-naked from the ceiling, you have the luxury of feeling sympathy rather than fear.

Suddenly, that powerful team of lawyers that Maxxco had assembled sure looked a lot less intimidating.

23
SHADOW JURY

A thick manila envelope had arrived from the NTSB. The National Transportation Safety Board. Robert stared at it for a moment before he began to open it.

He had had bad experiences with the NTSB. He remembered predicting to Maria, that the safety board would fulfill its federal mission by spending excessive chunks of money and hurting his case by an incomplete investigation. The NTSB report was dripping with eagles and banners that trumpeted self-importance. Robert feared the worst, but still, until he read it, he could hope for the best. He could hope that the NTSB would try to find out whether the overpass construction was dangerous, instead of just blaming the easiest target, the Louisiana Trucking Company. And in that frame of mind, Robert started thumbing through the report.

And he became increasingly disappointed. The federal government's investigation of this mass death case was superficial. It was less thorough than the one done privately by the firm of Robert Herrick and Associates. Worse yet, the NTSB report was going to help Maxxco Construction Corporation, simply because it didn't even consider whether the roadway was defective.

The report was divided into "Findings of Fact," "Conclusions," "Recommendations," and "Attachments." There were almost sixty attachments, containing statements, diagrams, weather reports, even data about the soil conditions under the freeway. But the Findings and Conclusions were the key parts. Robert read a few choice samples:

> "The accident was caused by the subject driver's failure to keep a proper interval."

The NTSB couldn't use normal English. Instead of talking about following too closely, they had to say it in fancy language about not keeping a proper interval. Also, in federalese, the man in the truck wasn't just the driver, but the "subject driver." Presumably, that was better because it sounded bureaucratic and confusing. Robert read on:

> "Also causally related was the subject driver's failure to maintain prudent operation and control of his motor vehicle."

That was federalese for "The truck driver was careless." And then, Robert found this strange sentence in the "Findings:"

> "Further causal relationship was found in subject driver's violation of hazardous cargo prohibited zones and maintenance of speed greater than was prudent under all the circumstances."

At that point, Robert gave up and buzzed for Tom Kennedy. "Tom, will you please come get this report and analyze it before I burst a blood vessel? The NTSB's a threat to western civilization, as far as I'm concerned."

It really was a serious problem. There was no mention at all of the design or construction of the overpass in the report, which was incredible. The jury might assume that it had been thoroughly researched, and that it meant that Maxxco had a clean bill of health, even though Maxxco's safety engineers had generated a hundred memos that charged their own company with negligence. But Booker & Bayne, of course, was going to love it. Robert could picture Jimmy Coleman arguing to the jury, "Even the federal government is telling you that Robert Herrick doesn't have a case!"

Across town at Booker & Bayne, the propane truck case was the focus of everyone's attention. In the white birch corridors, hundreds of lawyers traded bets on the outcome. There were only eight days to go.

In Jimmy Coleman's office, all the lawyers' eyes were glued to the TV screen. It was show-and-tell time for Dr. Randolph Murphy, the psychologist from Litigation Consultants, Inc.

This is the age of consultants. Everyone appreciated that. Almost like sorcerers, good consultants could tell you whether left-handed Lutherans would be biased against your airline when it was accused of negligence in a plane crash. Or whether Republican lesbians would acquit a serial killer. Dr. Murphy was one of the best, and he could tell you not only these things, but much more.

Booker & Bayne usually hired Dr. Murphy whenever a big case was about to be tried by a jury. His firm, Litigation Consultants, specialized in using "focus groups" to predict what a jury would do, forecasting how the jurors might react to a given witness, figuring out the most devastating cross-examination of that witness, or guessing what arguments to use at the end of the case. A focus group could function as a kind of substitute jury, or test jury. In fact, these groups sometimes were called "shadow juries." Right now, most of the lawyers defending Maxxco Construction were clustered around the priceless Italian furniture in Jimmy's office to hear how the focus groups had reacted to the evidence in the propane truck case.

Dr. Murphy started the meeting by explaining that he had assembled a typical focus group and had taken them to the scene of the disaster. The purpose was to help Jimmy decide whether to take the real jury to the actual scene during the trial and let them inspect it in person. This particular focus group, Dr. Murphy explained, included people from a cross section of occupations, ranging from a longshoreman to a retired geologist. That way, the group functioned as a good predictor of the jury.

The screen flickered on, and it focused into a picture. It showed the overpass at Route 59 and Interstate 610, the scene of the propane truck disaster.

Dr. Murphy had coke-bottle glasses and a head as bald as a frankfurter. He looked like a jolly genie standing there beside the TV screen with a collapsible metal pointer in his hand. He was wearing a red and green plaid jacket over his chubby frame, together with gray flannel slacks and Hush-Puppy-style shoes. "Dr. Murphy could benefit from consulting a psychologist to tone down his wardrobe a little bit," Jennifer Lowenstein thought to herself. But there was no question in anyone's mind about this man's professional knowledge. He was extraordinarily effective at what he did.

Jennifer paid attention, now, as the camera zoomed in on a burly young man with long matted hair who was a member of the focus group. "That's the longshoreman," Dr. Murphy explained, "and he's visiting the accident scene with the other members." All of the lawyers leaned forward. They watched the longshoreman bend down to pick up something, a small metal object, from the freeway shoulder, and then show it to the retired geologist, who came over to look. All the while, the rising and falling noise of nearby vehicles reminded everyone that cars were going by at sixty miles an hour.

"Now, watch what happens next," said Dr. Murphy. Jimmy Coleman shifted in his desk chair. Jennifer Lowenstein sat up straight. Jeff Tait slouched lower. But they all paid attention as Dr. Murphy aimed the pointer at the longshoreman's hands.

The man turned the metal object over and over. "This bolt I found on the ground looks like it's maybe three inches or so." He sounded knowledgeable. And authoritative.

The retired geologist responded with a muffled "Huh." And then both of them looked up at the curving ramp, the entrance ramp from Highway 59 onto Interstate 610. The place where the propane truck had fallen through the guardrail.

"See up there," said the longshoreman. "Hex bolts. Just like this one. Are they the same? Do you suppose maybe the truck fell because these bolts are too short?"

"Huh," responded the retired geologist, who evidently had a one-word vocabulary.

The longshoreman pointed up at the overpass. And Dr. Murphy's telescoping pointer pointed at the pointing longshoreman. Almost immediately, the screen showed the rest of the focus group congregating around the longshoreman. They included an aerobics instructor, a housewife, and a divinity student.

The longshoreman repeated: "What do you folks think? Are those hex bolts up there the same as this one I found beside the road? Does it maybe explain how the accident happened?"

"I don't know. Do you think they're the same?" asked the housewife.

"Huh," said the retired geologist. The lawyers watching the screen started laughing as they saw the other "jurors," particularly the longshoreman, casting annoyed looks in the direction of the inarticulate geologist.

The psychologist put the screen on "pause." He looked at the lawyers. "I could play all of it for you," he said, "but you get the idea."

He spread his hands in a matter-of-fact gesture. "This bolt was the third piece of scrap metal they found on the ground. All told, this focus group picked up seventeen pieces of steel, aluminum, galvanized strip, you name it. All under where the truck went off the ramp."

"Don't tell me," said Jeff Tait. "And all seventeen times, they huddled up. And they tried to figure out how the particular piece of metal could have fallen off the guardrail built by our client."

Dr. Murphy smiled and bobbed his shiny head. "Right."

There was a silence.

Then, Jimmy Coleman asked: "Dr. Murphy, do you think this is typical of what a real jury would do if we took them to the accident scene during the trial?"

"We recruited this focus group the same way we always do." Dr. Murphy shrugged. "A cross section of occupations, races, ethnic groups. Men and women. These five people are a good simulation of what a jury would be like. It's a true shadow jury."

Dr. Murphy waved his pointer. "And we didn't tell them which side hired us. They didn't know that it's Maxxco that paid their hundred-dollar-a-day fee. We showed them a short video about the case, so they'd know what the issues were."

He shook his bald head and laughed. "We had them do a straw vote before going out to the scene. Actually, it wasn't a vote, it was a questionnaire. And it was very striking," he held up the pointer, "very interesting from a professional point of view, because we had them do another copy of the same questionnaire after they visited the scene. And this visit to the scene made a dramatic change in their answers."

"And—?"

"And the second questionnaire showed that the focus group members were more than twice as likely to think that Maxxco was negligent after they visited the scene."

"Why?"

"Well, we can't be absolutely sure," said Dr. Murphy in a professional tone of voice. "At the scene, the members of the focus group spent all their time collecting debris and discussing it. And speculating about whether these pieces of metal could have fallen off the guardrail, and about how that could explain the accident."

He held up the pointer again. "But then, when we got them back to the office and taped what they talked about behind the one-way mirror, they didn't even mention the debris. They just talked about how important a guardrail was and how careful a construction company has to be in building something like this. It was as if the visit to the scene gave them a heightened sense of danger, or at least an increased expectation that a construction company should be held to a very high standard of safety."

"But it's crazy!" Jennifer Lowenstein was indignant. "Jimmy, you know that bolt didn't come from the guardrail. They used rivets on the metal. Concrete-imbedded rods at the bottom. The jury won't be fooled by that."

"There's no indication that the focus group thought the bolt really did come from the guardrail," Dr. Murphy agreed. "But that's not the way cognition works. It starts with attitudes and assumptions. What these pieces of scrap metal did, is they made the jury—I mean, the focus group—start asking questions about what happens if the rail is too flimsy. If it rusts, or cracks, or separates, or falls apart."

Jimmy intervened. "Dr. Murphy is trying to tell us something. Who cares what the so-called ultimate truth is? I don't want to search for the truth. I want to win. I want to win . . . this . . . case!"

"Thanks." The psychologist smiled. "Since you represent the defendant, Jennifer, there are attitudes that come along with that, such as, you take it for granted that your client wasn't at fault. That's your job in defending Maxxco. But the point is, the jury won't come at it from that direction."

He waved the pointer toward the TV screen. "The jury will be more like this focus group."

Jimmy cleared his throat. "The purpose of this exercise was to see whether or not we wanted to ask the judge to let us take the jury out to the scene of the accident. And after what Dr. Murphy has shown us, I'm satisfied that we don't want to. Telling too much of the truth can be a bad thing, I always say."

"You can show blowup photos of the guardrails," the bald-headed psychologist suggested. "They look sturdier when you see them in a picture, up close. And in a picture, there aren't loose pieces of metal for the jury to pick up."

"Right." Jimmy sat back. "The pictures make 'em look thicker than they are in real life. That's what I want. And thank you, Dr. Murphy. Your research has helped us decide on our trial strategy. Now, what else do you have to show us?"

The psychologist slid another cassette into the VCR. "Focus group number seventeen," he said. "Cross-examination of the plaintiffs' concrete expert. This one, I hope, will show you what works and what doesn't. So when you cross-examine the real concrete expert, you'll know what the focus group thought the best points of attack were."

And with that, the TV screen flashed into a picture. Dr. Murphy readied his pointer.

But the defendant's lawyers weren't the only ones who used jury consultants. So did the plaintiffs' lawyers. Right now, in fact, at the top of the Texas Commerce Tower, the lawyers for the propane truck plaintiffs were doing exactly that.

Robert Herrick had just received a report from a consulting firm named Calkins Jurimetrics. Professor Alistair Calkins was a member of the Department of Sociology at Rice University, but he made most of his income preparing reports like this one. It was called, "Jury Selection for the Trial of the Propane Truck Disaster: A Survey and Analysis."

"But it's crazy!" Tom Kennedy blurted out. "This 'Survey and Analysis' is crazy."

"Careful, Tom." Robert smiled. "I've generally found Professor Calkins to be pretty reliable."

"Well, but it doesn't make any sense," Kennedy insisted. "For instance, what Calkins is saying here, is that black jurors are good for us. For the plaintiff. And so are white jurors, at least Anglo ones. Anglos are about the same as blacks, favoring the plaintiff. But Mexican-Americans and Hispanics, he says, are 'much worse for the plaintiff.'" Kennedy read from Professor Calkins' report. "'And other recent-immigrant ethnic groups, such as Asian-Americans, favored the Maxxco Construction Company by a substantial margin.'"

"Of course, it's against the law to pick a jury by racial factors," said Robert. "And we won't do it on a racial basis. But you can bet that Jimmy Coleman will. For instance, he'll strike all the black jurors, I would predict. And if he does, this report from Professor Calkins will help us to fight back."

"But we've got a real sympathetic plaintiff, that little ten-year-old girl, Angela Gutierrez. She's Mexican-American. You know that Hispanics on the jury would identify with her."

"I suppose. But still, that doesn't mean Professor Calkins is wrong. He did over five hundred telephone interviews, he and his employees. He gave them all a scenario, then asked them questions."

"Which didn't show pictures of the victims, like we will. And it didn't include expert witnesses."

"No. All it does is measure people's initial attitudes." Robert smiled at his younger associate. "But I'll tell you this much for sure. If you give Jimmy Coleman a jury that has twelve people with the initial attitudes he wants—well, that's an advantage he'd win the case with, just about every time."

Kennedy read from another part of the report. "'The major religious groups differed in preference, also. Catholics and fundamentalist Protestants were less favorable to the plaintiff than Baptists, Methodists, Jews and Presbyterians.'"

"'And there is a strong gender bias,'" Robert read on. "'Men favor the plaintiff by fifty-seven percent to forty percent, which is a seventeen percent difference. But women favor the plaintiff by a much bigger margin, sixty-three percent to twenty-four percent, which is a thirty-nine percent difference.'" Robert held up an index finger. "And listen to this: 'The most important predictor of male preferences was whether the men had children, which made them heavily favor the plaintiffs.'"

"Robert, this stuff is pure voodoo," said Kennedy in frustration. "Look here. 'Occupational data show that groups like medical personnel and college professors are very good for the plaintiffs. So are traditionally female occupations such as secretaries, clerks and beauticians. Teachers and ministers are about average. Retired persons and middle managers are much worse and tend to favor the construction company. The worst group are white-collar types such as loan officers, geologists and upper managers.'"

"Well, I'll promise you this," Robert answered. "I'll take it all with a grain of salt when we actually pick the jury. We'll also consider what the people do and say when we question them, of course. But this research"—he patted the Calkins Jurimetrics report—"this is a real good starting point for keeping Jimmy Coleman honest."

"Great." Kennedy shook his head. "So the profile of our ideal juror would be that it's a woman, either African-American or white but not Hispanic or Asian, uneducated and not very smart, middle-aged or young, but not elderly, who is working as a secretary."

"Well, according to Professor Calkins, that's right."

"Robert, if we're going to pay attention to that kind of nonsense, why don't we just throw out the jury and use an opinion poll for the whole trial?"

Robert laughed. "Don't worry. We'll eyeball these jurors, and question them, and get the feel of it. If there's one thing I've learned, it's that a lawyer can pick a jury better than a sociologist."

He suddenly became serious. "And there are a couple of other things that this report tells us. First of all, the highly educated people tend to be the leaders of the jury. They have more influence. They're not our best group, because they tend to identify more with big companies like Maxxco, and so they tend to be biased against us. But we can't get them all off the jury."

"And so we want bankers with the souls of poets," said Tom Kennedy.

"More like, we want geophysicists with the hearts of beauticians," Robert corrected. "Oh, and Tom," he added, "there's one other thing about these highly educated people. It's true, maybe, that wealthy people do tend to favor the big construction company. They tend to say that Maxxco's not negligent, more so than the uneducated ones. But page twenty-five of Professor Calkins' report says the well-educated jurors have at least one characteristic that we want."

"What's that?"

"Reasonable amounts of damages. You see, when educated people get persuaded that the plaintiffs are right, they award damages that really can begin to compensate the plaintiffs."

"Oh. Yes. Makes sense," said Kennedy. "And yes, that certainly is a characteristic we want in our jurors."

24
TRIAL PREPARATION

J ust two more days until the propane truck trial. Jimmy Coleman was ready. At ten o'clock at night, after spending sixteen hours at the office, he was doing what he usually did to prepare himself mentally for a heavy-duty trial.

People are strange in their ways of handling stress, and lawyers are stranger than most. But this particular high-powered lawyer, from the blue-blooded old-line firm of Booker & Bayne, used a method that was much more bizarre than the average lawyer's. At this moment, Jimmy was sitting in the middle of his living room on top of an oriental rug, with his legs bent into the yoga position. The bottoms of his flat, chubby feet pointed straight up. He had on a huge silk robe with contrasting lapels, the kind that a champion boxer might wear as he zigzags through the crowd on his way to the ring. But the robe was off Jimmy's shoulders, revealing a paunchy abdomen that disappeared into a pair of boxer shorts.

Behind him, his blonde wife bent her almost six-foot frame over, so she could rub coconut oil into Jimmy's back. Barbara Coleman had on a black T-shirt that said, "Soldier of Fortune: The Magazine of Professional Adventurers," which was printed underneath an orange sunburst and a mean-looking picture of a helicopter. With her wide gold choker-type necklace, she looked like a Norse goddess preparing for modern jungle warfare. Or maybe, a figure from a Wagnerian opera getting ready for the beach.

As Barbara Coleman squeezed the heavy liquid into his skin, she chanted: "Next week is going to be a great week for Jimmy. Next week is going to be a great week for Jimmy."

And this was how Jimmy Coleman, for years, had always gotten ready to steamroll his opponents in court. It usually worked, and being a pragmatist, he kept using the method that had worked in the past.

He kept his eyes shut. He cleared his mind and tried to absorb it all. The oil, his Norse goddess wife, and the power he hoped to get from Barbara's magical incantations. "Next week is going to be a great week for Jimmy. Next week is going to be a great week for Jimmy! . . . ."

Finally, Jimmy Coleman stirred and opened his eyes. "Now would you please do it the other way—the 'bad week for Robert Herrick' mantra?"

His Viking wife poured on more coconut oil, and then started the new chant. "Next week is going to be a bad week for Herrick. Next week is going to be a bad week for Herrick. He's going to get stomped . . . . Chopped up in little pieces . . . . Next week is going to be a terrible week for Herrick."

With his street fighter's mentality, Jimmy had found that it was more useful to run down the guy on the other side than even to believe in his own case. He liked to picture his opponent as unworthy, barely human, no better than a criminal. That was how Jimmy had always prepared for trial. For him, it worked.

"... A bad week for Herrick. ... Stomped. ... Murdered. ... Humiliated. Next week is going to be a miserable week for Herrick."

Just two more days until the trial. Jimmy felt his attitude shaping up. Robert Herrick wasn't a "learned adversary." Instead, he was the enemy—or better yet, he was a despised, incompetent, slimy insect, who didn't have a right to be in the same courtroom. A worm, a slug, or less. It wasn't necessary to be fair to Herrick or his clients.

And with that, Jimmy Coleman knew that he was ready.

Robert Herrick had worked sixteen hours that day, too. He wasn't sure whether he was exhausted or whether he was about to feel his second wind. Maybe Maria could help him to put it all in perspective. She was good at that.

"Just two more days to go!" she said to him cheerfully. "Do you feel ready?"

"No." He smiled. "But maybe that's because I never feel ready. I have a huge responsibility to my clients, and I don't ever want to become complacent."

"But you're as ready as you possibly can be."

"I think so. Yes."

"Well, in that case," she murmured, "there's another level of trial preparation I'd like you to do. With me. Come here." She slipped off her wrap skirt.

"Oh, Maria, knock it off. I can't even get interested. I'm too wound up."

"I wouldn't have even suggested it, except for the fact that you're as ready as you'll ever be. And I think you're especially cute when you're worn out from grueling days on end of getting ready for trial. So—come on."

He complied because he was too tired to argue.

"Just what part of the trial should we work on first?" she teased. "Should it be the direct examination? Followed by opening, closing, the charge—and maybe a little *voir dire*?"

"Also, a request for production." He was too exhausted to do anything but play along. "After we depose each other."

She peeled off her T-shirt. "I like that part called the oral argument, or whatever you call it, the best."

"That follows right after the offer of proof, I guess."

"You know, I've heard of people playing doctor," said Maria. "Too bad! I guess this shows that playing lawyer is more fun." She dropped her black lace undergarments on the floor.

"No objection," he answered.

"You'd better win this trial." Her voice suddenly was fierce and insistent, the stereotype of the fiery Cuban. "I didn't want you even to take the case, but since you did, you'd better win it. And if you don't, I'm going to call all the associates in your office together and tell them this is the way you prepare for trial."

"Oh, no! Anything but that!"

"Oh, don't worry," she reassured him. "We're only doing this because you're ready. Besides, they'd never believe it, knowing what a boy-scout type you are!"

Just two more days until the trial. It was true, Robert Herrick thought. He was as ready as he ever would be.

On the last day, he spent the evening at home. Again trying to unwind after another sixteen hours at the office.

But the problem was, Pepper Herrick sat in the den with her friend Roxella Martin. They were talking about sex, and they were doing it just loud enough so that Pepper could be sure her father could hear.

"I wonder what it'd be like to do it with Jonathan Morse," Pepper breathed. "Awesome, I bet."

"He's awesome," Roxella Martin agreed from under her bright-orange, one-side-chopped hairdo.

"I see him in gym class, and his legs just turn me on. I walk by the field after three. He plays linebacker." She pretended to fan herself with the patchwork vest that flopped over the long flannel plaid shirt that flopped over her black skin-tight leggings. "And Jonathan Morse, he's got on those sausage-type football pants. They really show what he's got. And big shoulders. He's so hot!"

"Awesome!"

"Tubular!"

"Co-o-o-l!"

"Jonathan Morse! He's a fox, and I want him!"

Robert Herrick, sitting in the living room with Grandma Rosalie and Robbie, couldn't stand it any longer. "Cynthia!" he yelled. "Cynthia, come here!"

Silence.

He waited. "Cynthia! Get your tail in here right now or you'll be grounded so long they'll have to pipe sunlight to you!"

She was there in a moment. A very long moment. With an expression of disgust so complete it could have intimidated a twelfth-grade algebra teacher. It was one of the few things at which Pepper-Cynthia truly excelled. She could look more disgusted than just about anyone else on earth.

"My name is Pepper," she said. "It's what everybody calls me. You are the only one who calls me Cynthia, and I don't appreciate it."

"Cynthia, it is time for your friend to go home for the evening," Robert said with studied calm, "and for you to go to your room and get ready for bed."

"It figures."

Pepper-Cynthia turned deliberately on her heel and walked away. She even managed to look disgusted while walking away. The stereo played some kind of undecipherable rap music, undecipherable at least to Robert Herrick. The artist, if you could call him that, called himself Ice-T or Vanilla Ice or something. A few moments later, the noise clicked off. And then the front door slammed. Roxella Martin was taking her chopped orange hair home.

"She needs to see more of you," said Rosalie. "What with this trial coming up, she hasn't seen you, and she feels neglected."

"Funny," Robert answered. "I got the distinct message she'd like to see less of me."

"She's a teenager. She doesn't know which end is up. She needs you."

Rosalie's advice on these matters was usually counter-intuitive. Sometimes it sounded wrong. But Robert knew that his mother usually was right, sort of like what he'd been telling Tom about Professor Calkins.

"Okay," he said gently. "I'll try to spend some more time with Pepper."

It instantly occurred to him that it was going to be hard to think up an activity that he could share with a sullen child whose means of projecting disgust for her father included verbalizing sexual fantasies in front of him. But he left it unsaid.

Instantly, Rosalie read his thoughts. "Robert, you know that Pepper goes to St. Martin's for church at eleven o'clock every Sunday. You could start by taking her. And of course, you know she plays on the Lamar High School basketball team. Next game, the Lamar Lady Redskins play against the Bellaire High School Lady Cardinals. It's on Thursday. At eight o'clock. In the Lamar gym. You know where that is."

"Okay. I'll try." But, he thought to himself, how could he? That's right in the middle of the first week of the propane truck trial.

"Goodnight, Daddy," said Pepper-Cynthia. She gave him a halfhearted hug and then said, "Goodnight, Grandma" to Rosalie.

There was a silence, filled by the episode of *Men Behaving Badly* that Robbie was watching on television.

"Time for bed, Robbie," said Robert. "And turn off that trash. You know you aren't supposed to be watching that show."

After he said it once more, Robbie clicked it off.

"Come here, big guy," said Robert. He hugged his son. "Should we sing our favorite song one time tonight?"

"Yeah! Yeah!" said Robbie, and he bounced up and down. In a year or two, Robert thought with regret, his son would begin the long slide into teenage cynicism that already had captured Pepper. But for now, Robbie was still enthusiastic about father-son ceremonies.

They went through this ritual before Robbie's bedtime every night when Robert was at home. Their "favorite song." Like most family rituals, it was silly. He couldn't say exactly when they had started doing it, or what the song meant.

Robert sang the song loud and clear, with Robbie's much smaller voice stumbling along with him:

"Do ye ken John Peel? Do ye ken John Peel?

"Do ye ken John Peel? Do ye ken John Peel?

"With a loud Haloo-oo-oo-oo—"

They both howled this part. This was the best part, and they howled it for as long as they could both hold their breath. Howling was a customary part of the ritual. And then they both cracked up laughing before they went on, because laughing was also part of the ritual. Finally, they finished:

"With a loud Haloo-oo-oo-oo,

"He would wa-a-ake the dead

"And the fox from his lair in the morning."

Robert didn't know where the song came from, except that it was an old folk song. But his father had sung it to him when he was less than four years old. And his father's father had sung it to him, with the same ritual. It was a song that fathers and sons were supposed to sing together because it just felt right.

"Especially," he thought to himself, "fathers who struggle and fail and try again and never feel they're doing it quite right, because they're single parents. Like me."

As he hugged his son, it occurred to Robert, "The trial is tomorrow. I'm as ready as I'm going to be. This is the kind of thing that I feel like doing now, only a few hours before it starts. Being with my family. This feels more important than using all the focus groups in the world. Or all the jury studies that we pay for."

But it also occurred to him that if he convened the lawyers in his office and told them that this was part of the way he prepared for trial—hard-charging, hard-driving, hard-nosed Robert Herrick, spending time at home with his family right before picking the jury—they wouldn't have believed it.

The sun set, and the moonless night was deep and black, but Robert bucked and twisted across the bed and slept only fitfully. And when the rose-colored day finally touched the edges of his plantation shutters, he was wide awake and pacing his bedroom.

Today was the day. The lawyers all would crowd together in the Twelfth District courtroom, together with the army of reporters, jurors, victims' families, and spectators. Because today was the day—the big day, when the propane truck trial would actually begin.

Already, he was frightened. Frightened of losing, afraid of doing something dumb, fearful of Jimmy Coleman, and terrified of putting the biggest case of his life into the hands of twelve strangers. He picked out a solid navy suit, and he chose an expensive, custom-tailored shirt. He didn't usually wear such costly clothes, but for this trial, he wanted to look and feel right. As soon as he slipped his arm into the sleeve, he could feel his sweat seeping out through the shirt.

25
THE JURY PANEL

Robert thought to himself. You could play a pretty good game of touch football in here if you cleared away all the furniture.

The ceiling towered more than twenty-five feet high, with intricately carved white wooden squares that alternately held light fixtures, air ducts or ornate circular decorations, all in brass. From there, the eye ran down through solid wooden paneling, again with rows and rows of squares, all stained in a dark walnut color. Behind the judge's bench, the downward-moving eye abruptly stopped at the focal point of this imperial room; two hundred square feet of dark green marble, as solid and polished as the counters in a Wall Street bank. All shining like a monument to the authority of the man or woman who represented the judicial branch of the Great State of Texas in this regal courtroom.

But the jury box was best of all. The bar in front of it was topped with brass. The rest was made of wood that resembled the walls and the judge's bench, with the same kind of walnut panels. A series of brass stars was embedded in the panels. The seats were modern, made of imitation leather that looked like the real thing until you were very close. The original ones actually had been made of wood, with beautiful curved wooden backs. Their replacements were a necessary concession to the comfort of today's jurors, who often heard cases that lasted weeks or months.

When seated in this jury box, the twelve chosen citizens would face three rows of oil paintings, each in a huge gold frame. These were portraits of the two dozen judges that had presided over the Twelfth District Court since it first was established in the days when Texas still was an independent nation, a country complete unto itself, the Sovereign Republic of Texas. The Executive who had signed the law creating this court was none other than General (then President) Sam Houston, the man who had won independence for Texas in the Battle of San Jacinto.

Needless to say, this was not the usual courtroom for Judge Barbara Trobelo. The Chief Judge of the District had assigned Judge Trouble a small, cramped courtroom in one of the nearby buildings outside the courthouse itself, into which the growing number of courtrooms had overflowed.

But then Barbara Trobelo had inherited the propane truck case. The tiny courtroom assigned to her would not comfortably hold even the panel of citizens from which the jury would be selected, much less the army of attorneys, the battalion of reporters, the legion of family members, and the crowds of spectators who would descend on the courthouse for this landmark trial. And so, it was going to be necessary to reassign Judge Barbara Trobelo to a much bigger courtroom.

At about that time, the Chief Judge had succumbed to a debilitating battle with lymphoma that left him unable to fulfill his duties. The Acting Chief had inherited the job of assigning a courtroom for the propane truck case. And there had been only one realistic solution. The Chief Judge's resplendent courtroom lay vacant, and it was the only one that was both large enough and available to be used without uprooting other senior judges. The Acting Chief made the assignment cautiously, only for this trial, so as to avoid any implication that the Chief Judge was unlikely to return to active service.

And so it was that the most prestigious courtroom in the district was assigned to the most junior judge, Barbara Trobelo, for the propane truck trial.

Robert Herrick had been relieved—overjoyed, in fact—when the propane truck case had been assigned to the Twelfth District courtroom. It would have been difficult to try the case in that other tiny place where Judge Trouble usually held court. Its wheezing window air conditioner periodically switched on and off. It would have distracted jurors and drowned out timid witnesses. And as Robert knew from bitter experience, the biggest problem with trying a serious case in Judge Trouble's courtroom would have been that it was dingy, sloppy-looking and just plain seedy. An odd quirk of trial psychology made it harder for juries to award damages in a big case when they were in a cheap-looking courtroom. And so, in a very real way, Robert felt that the move to this monumental courtroom—the Twelfth District courtroom—was a pre-trial victory, because it would make it less uncomfortable for the jurors to assess realistic damages against Maxxco Construction.

Right now, the judge, the lawyers, and the spectators all sat quietly in the huge Twelfth District courtroom. Waiting. The judge had called for a jury panel to be sent in.

Suddenly, a pair of deputy sheriffs known as "jury shepherds" noisily opened the heavy swinging doors and announced the arrival of the jury panel. Everyone strained to see. Robert Herrick, Jimmy Coleman, Francel Williams, and their retinues; the bereaved families, the press, and the court personnel; the law students in the galleries, the curious citizens, and Judge Trouble herself—all of them lifted slightly from their chairs and arched their necks to get their first look at the sixty randomly-chosen citizens from which the twelve to decide this case would eventually be selected.

And then, Robert scrambled to his feet, with his shirt already damp. Jimmy Coleman also stood, across the courtroom. And they searched every face as the sixty citizens silently filed in.

In some places, the jury panel is known to both sides' lawyers ahead of time. Actually, in smaller Texas counties the list is public, and lawyers can expect that

they will personally know most members of the panel. It will include the local
barkeep, grocer, doctor, butcher, baker, and candlestick-maker. Not so in the big
city, where a computer cranks out more than a thousand summonses each week,
and panels are peeled off from a central jury room to service scores of district
courts. "Thirty-six jurors to the 106th!" a jury shepherd might call, and then he
would lead the thirty-six to that courtroom to decide an aggravated robbery case,
in which each side would strike ten citizens. "A panel of twenty-eight to hear a
slip-and-fall case in the 73rd!" And so on.

In each instance, the panels were led from the central jury room by these jury
shepherds, whose job was to single-file the citizens and keep them in the correct
order. To a jury shepherd, it made no difference whether the individuals would
make good, bad or average jurors. What mattered was that the one with the
lowest computer number was first, the next lowest was second, the highest was
last, and the ones in between were in exact order, like sheep. The name "jury
shepherds" was appropriate.

Judge Trobelo had ordered an extra-large panel for this case after consulting
the lawyers and considering the publicity. Many of the potential jurors were
likely to disqualify themselves. And so the propane truck panel shuffled in one
by one and assumed the sixty audience seats that were at front and center. Their
footsteps were the only noise that anyone could hear in the strained silence that
descended on the courtroom during this tense moment. Then, at last, one of the
jury shepherds silently walked to the counsel tables. Moving with excruciating
deliberateness, he handed first Jimmy Coleman, then Francel Williams, and then
Robert Herrick photocopies of the "juror information forms" for the panel.

These forms contained a storehouse of information about each potential
juror: occupation, family, previous injuries, previous lawsuits, length of residence
in the county, and more, all crammed into a three-inch-by-eight-inch card crisscrossed with boxes and blanks. A careful lawyer could figure out even more
information by studying subtle cues, such as the juror's spelling, handwriting and
zip code, because these were indicators of intelligence levels, education and
economic status. And a more experienced lawyer could read still more by
considering what was left out or stated obliquely. For example, a man with five
children, who put "None" in the blank that asked for "serious injuries to family
members," presumably wouldn't have much sympathy for somebody else's
problems. He would regard only a few horrible kinds of injuries as bad enough
to be called "serious." He would make a good defense juror and a bad plaintiff's
one. Both sides knew that the ability to read indirect clues in this manner would
be crucial to a lawyer in the propane truck trial, because it might mean the
difference between a friendly jury and a hostile one.

And so the lawyers began scanning the juror information forms. They tried
to look dignified. They tried not to seem too eager to pry into the jurors' secrets,
while the same jurors who would decide the case looked on. But dignified or not,
the lawyers felt the adrenalin rush, and they turned the pages with fingers that
were clumsy from the pressure of the moment.

Judge Trouble smiled. "Good morning, ladies and gentlemen. The case on trial is one that the public sometimes calls 'the propane truck case.' The formal name that the lawyers use is *Gutierrez versus Maxxco Construction Corporation and Louisiana Trucking Company*, but I'll explain what all of that means later. In addition to Pedro Gutierrez, there are two hundred and sixty other plaintiffs whose names will be read to you shortly." The judge cleared her throat and got ready to read the standard introduction. "This is a civil case, and it will be tried before a jury."

The words that Judge Trouble was speaking were formula words, or what lawyers call "boilerplate." The Rules of Civil Procedure actually set out this introduction, word for word, for the judge to read. But in this setting, Judge Barbara Trobelo seemed larger than life, and the boilerplate sounded profound, almost historic. Every eye in the jury panel was riveted to the judge by the green marble monument behind her.

Robert Herrick felt his shirt sticking to his back as he studied the juror information forms.

"It's a horrible panel," said Tom Kennedy under his breath. "These jurors look tough enough to tear the cigar out of Clint Eastwood's mouth."

Robert flipped through the juror information forms at the rate of one each five seconds or so. "It's really an awful panel," Kennedy repeated, over Robert's shoulder. "These people look mean enough to rassle the tablecloth off of Yassir Arafat's head." Robert just ignored him and kept plowing through the juror forms.

The judge continued to read the instructions. "Do not mingle with or talk to the lawyers." Since these words came straight from Rule 226a of the Rules of Civil Procedure, it was hard to read them without adopting a singsong voice. The lawyers concentrated on the forms and ignored the boilerplate.

The number one juror was named Hartley Rehm. He was an accountant, employed as an office manager for an independent geologist. This occupation fit neatly into the category of "other white-collar workers," which the jury research had shown was the worst possible group for the plaintiff. Right now, Hartley Rehm sat ramrod straight in the first pew, with his legs crossed and his hands folded in his lap. His suit was gray. His shirt was gray. Even his tie was gray, with a small black stripe. You could tell just from one look that he wouldn't be a good plaintiff's juror.

Next to Hartley Rehm was Johnnie L. Webber, juror number two. An African-American, sixty-two years old, living in an integrated neighborhood. Grizzled, with close white hair, and wearing starched khaki pants. This man might be expected to be a good plaintiff's juror if you just looked at him superficially, but Johnnie Webber had put in thirty-seven years as a letter carrier for the post office, and these workers often were surprisingly good defense jurors for large corporations. They usually had what the psychologists called "trust in institutions"—a great deal of faith in large bureaucracies. Also, Johnnie Webber had seven children, but he had written the words "no injuries" in the box that asked about family members. He probably had an unusually high threshold for pain.

Judge Trouble was continuing to read the instructions to the jury panel. "Do not discuss anything about this case, or even mention it to anyone whomsoever, including your wife or husband." This was an absurdly difficult instruction, which the jurors routinely violated. But it was standard.

Juror number three, Lydia Blanco, gave her birthplace as "Baranquilla, Colombia," and her occupation as "secretary." She worked at Exxon Chemical Corporation. Secretarial work was a "good" occupation for the plaintiffs, according to the jury research, but if Lydia Blanco liked working at Exxon, and if she liked her employer, she might identify with the Maxxco Construction Corporation and resent loose allegations that a large employer was at fault for somebody else's mishap. And although it was illegal to consider her ethnicity, the jury study said that Hispanics, like Lydia Blanco, were unfavorable to the plaintiff.

Judge Trouble's voice droned on. "The attorneys have the right to direct questions to each of you concerning your qualifications, background, experiences and attitudes," she continued. "They are not meddling in your personal affairs, but are trying to select fair and impartial jurors who are free from any bias in this particular case."

That instruction, usually, was flatly untrue. Adversary lawyers didn't want "fair" jurors. Robert knew, for instance, that Jimmy Coleman would have loved to have a biased jury, provided of course it was biased in his favor. Robert continued to concentrate on the forms and to listen to the judge's instructions with only half his attention.

Juror number four, whose name was Herlinda Strock, was a welfare mother. Even if she turned out to be favorable, she wouldn't influence anyone on the jury. A pure "follower," who made no difference either way. Number five, Elaine Chao, was an accounting clerk for the City of Hunter's Creek. Bad. Then there was number six, Edgar Owens. Produce manager for a grocery store. Bad.

The bottom line was, Robert didn't see much in this panel to be happy about.

"Do not conceal information or give answers which are not true," the judge instructed. "Listen to the questions and give full and complete answers."

Robert stared at the sixty citizens. Usually, to see a jury panel is to be encouraged, even uplifted, about diversity and tolerance in this great democracy. All races, all classes, all creeds are interspersed, in a true version of the rainbow that is America. This panel was no different as far as the rainbow was concerned, and yet, Robert Herrick and Tom Kennedy both knew, it *was* subtly different.

The luck of the draw had sprinkled in a larger-than-normal share of doctors, company presidents and small-business owners. There were fewer cab drivers, ministers, shoe clerks and stenographers than a plaintiff's lawyer usually could hope for, and the ones that were present all seemed to have something else about them that was unfavorable. There were twelve Hispanics, which was a large number, and seven Asian-Americans, which was a very large number. Unfortunately, the jury study said that these two groups were the least favorable ethnic minorities for the plaintiff. The study also said that having children was the "best predictor" of favorable jurors among older men. Unfortunately, most of the men were either unmarried or childless. That was very bad.

"It's a horrible panel!" Tom Kennedy wailed for the third time. "They look cold enough to kidnap Michael Jackson and turn him over to the Bloods and the Crips!"

"Stop it, you stupid idiot!" Robert finally snapped. His nerves were whipsawing him even without Kennedy's remarks. But instantly, he regretted it. His whisper had been sharp enough to be heard everywhere in the courtroom in one of the gaps of silence that punctuated the mechanical instructions that the judge was reading. The sixty citizens turned to look at the plaintiffs' lawyers. Judge Trouble stopped for an instant.

"This is not a very dignified beginning," Robert thought. He tried to look inconspicuous.

After what seemed like a very long silence, the judge resumed reading. "Do you understand these instructions? If not, please let me know now." Naturally, none of the sixty citizens volunteered anything in response to that. They didn't understand a great deal of what was going on, of course, but jurors at the beginning of a case never say anything to "let the judge know" they don't understand.

A few seconds later, the judge's monologue ended. That was when Jimmy Coleman stood. "Your Honor! Before we start the trial, I have a motion to make on behalf of my client, Maxxco Construction Corporation!"

What happened next was a blur, from Robert Herrick's perspective. The only thing that was clear when it was over was that Jimmy's motion wasn't a "motion" at all. It was a jury speech that hammered home his version of the case. It started with a request to "realign the parties" and ended with Jimmy shouting that the truck driver was the only person responsible for the tragedy. But Robert sat powerless, unable to anticipate Jimmy's tactic, unable to control his own movements, almost like a drowsy man watching a movie of himself in a darkened room. When he finally realized what was happening, it was too late.

By now, his sweat was even heavier and colder than before. Jimmy had gotten away with it, and Robert had only himself to blame because he hadn't stopped it.

It was ten o'clock when Judge Trouble finished the prepared text that the rules required her to read. She had overruled Jimmy Coleman's "motion to realign," but the damage already was done.

Next, the judge started speaking on her own, because she needed to cover some of the issues in this particular case. And with that, the lawyers started to listen carefully, because this was the real beginning of the trial. There had been "a great deal of pre-trial publicity," Judge Trouble told the members of the panel. It would be necessary to ask them about what they had read, or heard, or seen on television.

"This is one of the biggest cases ever to be tried in this city," she added.

Instantly, Jimmy Coleman was on his feet. "Objection, your honor. May we approach the bench?"

The lawyers—all nine of them, including the associates—trooped up to the judge's bench and huddled there. Jimmy made his objection immediately. "Your honor's remark about 'the biggest case' violates the court's neutrality," he said, in a voice like honey but with steel inside it. "The court's remark suggests to the jury that this is the biggest case in terms of damages. I am sure the court meant no harm. I know the remark was inadvertent."

"This guy is as smooth as his reputation," Robert thought with grudging respect. "Even if he's usually nasty to his opponents. Such as me."

"Nevertheless," Jimmy went on, "despite the court's good intentions, Maxxco must ask for a mistrial. Actually, we do not want a mistrial, because we are satisfied with this jury panel, but still I must move for a mistrial to protect my client."

"I'll bet you're satisfied," Herrick thought. It was obviously true that Jimmy didn't really want the mistrial he was asking for, to "protect" his client. This panel was a defense lawyer's dream.

But Jimmy continued to maneuver. He didn't want the mistrial, but he wanted something else. "If the court denies our motion for mistrial, it is important that you instruct the jury to disregard the 'biggest case' remark that your honor just made. And there is nothing that really can cure the error, but the best you can do is to tell the jurors that this may be a case with zero damages, because the defendant, Maxxco, denies liability. *Zero* damages!"

Jimmy wore a light blue suit with narrow stripes and a dark blue tie with small red dots. Conservative and proper, but projecting friendliness and approachability instead of power. No dark pinstripes for the defense. This way, Jimmy overcame the big-firm, big-corporation image and made himself seem soft and cuddly. But the suit was perfectly cut, and Jimmy could take command. His speech to the court was perfectly cut, too. It was calibrated to avoid a mistrial, keep this pro-defendant panel, and yet make the judge fearful of unfairness so serious that it might cause a reversal in the court of appeals. In fact, that was the reason Jimmy stressed that "the court's error couldn't be cured." This was a veiled reference to the possibility that the court of appeals might slap Judge Trouble down by reversing the case at the end.

All of the lawyers marched back to their seats. Judge Trouble faced the jurors, who did not know what had just taken place. But the lawyers all knew. Jimmy was angling for a retraction from the court, one that would emphasize the defense position.

He got it. In fact, he got exactly what he wanted. "Ladies and gentlemen, it is not necessarily the biggest case," Judge Trouble backtracked cheerfully. "Mister Jimmy Coleman has reminded me that the defendants are not liable for anything until it's proven by *evidence* that they're liable. And unless that happens, it's a zero-damages case."

The sixty citizens nodded at that. Innocent until proven guilty. It's a zero damages case. The judge had said so. Zero damages. "We've got our work cut out for us with this defense lawyer," Herrick thought. "Like him or not, Jimmy Coleman is good. That's how he got where he is."

His mind was racing as he tried to figure out whether he should object, now, for the plaintiffs. The pendulum had swung too far. The judge's attempt to "cure" the biggest-case remark had overemphasized the defense version of the case. Right at the beginning of the trial, when the jury was most impressionable, she had all but instructed the jury to return a verdict of zero! But then, painfully, Robert decided to hold back.

He knew that it was a delicate art to represent his client in trial without seeming too pushy. The judge wasn't likely to make another correction, and so she probably would overrule it if he made an objection. And if he acted like a bull in a china shop, he would lose with both the judge and the jury. Often the harder choice, but the wiser one, was to let it go. And so, with conscious effort, Robert did just that.

It was harder because he knew that Jimmy had walked the tightrope perfectly. Not too pushy, not too agreeable. And the court's zero-damages remark gave the defense the advantage. Robert was behind. That was dangerous in this part of the trial. First impressions not only counted, in this trial they might be what counted the most.

The judge's examination of the panel about pre-trial publicity went on for hour after hour. There were a dozen skirmishes among counsel, all huddled at the bench. Finally, the first day ended. The questioning by the lawyers had not even begun. But Robert felt that awful feeling just the same.

He was losing.

26
THE FIRST WITNESS

I t had been only seven hours since the first day of jury selection had ended. But to Robert, it seemed like a lifetime. The jury panel had been so bad, and he'd had such bad luck with the judge, that he almost wished he could forget the whole thing. Instead, of course, he had returned to the office with his tail between his legs, hoping it wasn't too obvious to all the other lawyers. He would work most of the night, so that maybe with luck he could do a better job tomorrow.

Shortly after one o'clock, Maria showed up and tried to rescue him. "Donna told me you still were here. I think that's crazy! You need to get back home and get some sleep." But after half an hour of fruitless argument, she gave up and just stayed to watch and listen.

"It probably isn't as big a disaster as it looks like," Robert said finally, in a thin, tired voice. "The jury panel, I mean. I think I can weed out the worst ones."

That intrigued Maria. "How are you going to do that—weed them out?"

By now, it was almost two o'clock in the morning. Herrick's office had settled into trial mentality, which was to say, war mentality, in a case against Jimmy Coleman. Three lawyers and a paralegal would spend the day at the courthouse. They'd rush back to the office when the judge ended the day. Number two pencils, and more number two pencils, worn to a stub on yellow legal pads. Support staff were expected to work all night, and everyone got by on a diet of pizza, Chinese food or spaghetti, all washed down with coffee, juice, and a few carefully spaced Lone Star longnecks.

"For weeding out the bad jurors," Robert continued, "our plan is to quietly repeat, over and over, that we think it's going to be a six-month trial."

Maria had never tried anything but criminal cases. "Why? Don't you think everybody would want a six-month vacation?"

"Not everybody, but the people we want on the jury—the good plaintiff's jurors, I mean—they work for other people," Robert explained. "Usually, for big companies. What they like best is to get time away from work. They won't mind being away from the office for six months, the ordinary working people and the clerks and secretaries. Not nearly as much as the ones we don't want."

"Of course." She smiled and shook her head.

"Take a small business owner. He or she can't close up the shop for six months. A middle-level manager, it's hard for him to do it. A doctor? Forget it."

"And so—"

"And so, the ones we want off will be fighting to get off, all by themselves," he said. "They'll claim that six months of solid jury service will be a terrible hardship. Which is true. The judge won't want to let them get off, of course, and she'll try to hold the line. She won't excuse them just because they say the word 'hardship.' She'll make them show her why it's a bigger hardship than the average person would have. But unless she's really ruthless, the judge is going to have to let a lot of them go. Unless she tells that general surgeon, 'Doctor, I don't care about your operating schedule, and this trial comes before the lives of your patients'—unless she does that, the ones that are biased against us will take themselves off the jury. The worst ones, at least."

"But can you really talk about the trial lasting six months?"

"It really will take that long," he answered. Now, at two o'clock, he seemed a little more cheerful and optimistic. Maybe he was getting his second wind. "In fact, it will. We have two hundred and sixty-one plaintiffs. One poor girl who was killed, for instance, has ten brothers and sisters. What if all of them testify?"

"Most of them won't be on the stand for very long."

"But it could easily be six months."

"Sounds devious to me," she said with mock indignation.

"No, unfortunately it's entirely true." He blinked his eyes at the ceiling. "This is going to be a long, hard case. It's the biggest case I've ever handled."

She thought it was too late at night to be concentrating this hard. She was worried. He needed to loosen up. "Music to my ears. That's exactly the way I like to handle you," she said, playfully.

He laughed, but with a touch of exasperation. "Maria, I'm too busy. Plus, I'm too tired. You're just clowning around because you can afford to go home to sleep."

"I'll even take you with me."

"I've got to work on what I'm going to say to the jurors tomorrow." He said it in a voice that ended the argument.

And then he added, "I'm hoping I can avoid getting beat up tomorrow as bad as I did today." She was glad to see that he said it with a little bit of a smile.

"Good," said Maria. "After all, today was only the first day. And besides, a trial lawyer can be his own worst enemy. Especially when he gets past thinking and starts worrying too much."

That was a perfect description of Robert Herrick. She was right, and he knew it. But he laughed.

Jimmy Coleman was working late, too.

At just about the same time of night, in the white birch offices of Booker & Bayne, Jimmy's eyes were fixed on a television monitor. A picture of a highway appeared on the screen. Suddenly, a truck moved into the forefront. There was lettering on the screen that identified the videotape as, "PLAINTIFFS' RE-ENACTMENT: PROPANE TRUCK DISASTER." The letters faded.

"This is Robert Herrick's videotaped reconstruction of the accident," said the defense psychologist, Dr. Murphy, holding up his metal pointer. The recessed lights gleamed from his bald, genie-from-the-bottle head, and his clothes were the usual mix of colors. "The video is done by computer animation," Dr. Murphy went on, "and I've picked up something. I think it might be important. Watch, and see whether you see anything unusual."

The plaintiffs' re-creation of the accident looked like an animated cartoon which, in fact, was exactly what it was. The images were computer-generated. With enough hard work, it was amazing what you could do with today's technology. The Herrick firm had prepared a video, all in this same cartoon, of the propane truck entering the ramp, colliding with the silver Toyota, splintering the rail, and spinning as it fell. The fourteen cars below crashed and rolled, and at the end, the fireball lit up the darkened sky, just as the witnesses had described it.

Booker & Bayne had gotten this copy of Herrick's videotape by requesting it during discovery. The computer images were realistic, and the whole thing was carefully produced. At trial, Jimmy knew, Herrick would have all the necessary expert witnesses to explain the cartoon images fully to the jury—a physicist, an accident reconstruction expert, and a computer animator. All of them would testify.

The psychologist stopped the video. "Did you notice anything unusual?"

Jimmy thought for a minute. "No," he answered, slowly.

"Not anything that we haven't already seen," Jeff Tait and Jennifer Lowenstein echoed in unison. By now, they had all looked at the videotape so many times they had it memorized.

"Look again." Dr. Murphy replayed the critical few seconds before the collision and tapped the screen with his collapsible metal pointer. "Right there."

When they still didn't see it, he explained. "Right at that point, the video switches over from actual speed to slow motion."

"Well, I'll be damned," said Jimmy.

"Right here." Dr. Murphy replayed it. And pointed again. "Just after it's entered the ramp." This time, the switch to slow motion was obvious to everybody.

"Does that make a difference?" asked Jennifer.

"You bet it does!" Dr. Murphy answered. "We already had a focus group watch this video, you remember. They were impressed by it. They thought the plaintiff had a very strong case against Maxxco. What impressed them was that the guardrail comes apart like a bunch of match sticks, while the truck seems to be moving so slowly."

"And—?"

"And so, we did a remake of the accident reconstruction. Only difference is, our remake goes at actual speed all the way through. Mister Herrick was honest, and he gave us both the slow-motion and the regular version. We spliced in the regular speed one."

Jimmy, Jennifer and Jeff looked at each other. They knew Dr. Murphy was expensive. They also knew he was worth it. This sort of thing, what they were hearing right now, was the reason why.

"We then showed our version of the re-creation to a different, fresh focus group," the psychologist went on. "And guess what happened?"

"What happened?" Jimmy demanded. Jennifer had never seen Jimmy Coleman get excited this way. His eyes were as wide as a child's. "Just tell us, damn it!"

"I'll let you see the video of the focus group yourself, in a minute," Dr. Murphy answered, calmly. "But the long and short of it is this. When you speed it up, the truck goes faster. And it's not as easy to see that the guardrail was defective."

"And so the actual-speed video makes it look more like the accident was the truck driver's fault," said Jimmy. "It hides Maxxco's negligence."

"Yes. That's the way it comes across when you run the cartoon truck at actual speed. Of course, the focus group still argued about how much Maxxco was to blame, but not as much as the group that saw the slow-mo."

"That sorry son of a bitch," said Jeffrey Tait. "That sorry, sleazy Robert Herrick. He figured all this out, and that's why he put it in slow motion. It's just plain crooked."

"Not crooked at all." Jimmy showed his teeth in a huge, crinkly smile. "I doubt Herrick really intended to misrepresent anything. That's not his style. He probably was trying to show it more clearly, and remember, he gave us both versions. Including the actual-speed one. He gave us that one, too."

Jimmy thought for a minute, and then he spoke up again. "And so I'm sure it wasn't crooked," he repeated, "for Herrick to use slow motion. But now we can set a trap for him. I'm sure he's squeaky clean, and I know from experience that he's not dishonest. But he's gonna look dishonest to the jury when I get through with this movie. It'll look crooked."

"Yes, now you can object to the slow-motion video," said Dr. Murphy. "It seems possible that the judge will sustain your objection, and you might have a chance to keep it out of the evidence. To hide it from the jury."

"Object? Keep it out? Heck, no! I wouldn't dream of it." Jimmy Coleman could barely control his excitement. Jennifer could almost see the street fighter inside him, coming alive. "This is great! It's like the old days, when we really screwed our opponents. I love a trial by ambush."

By now, it was almost two in the morning, but Jimmy didn't seem tired at all. He always believed that luck was a big part of any lawyer's skill. And now, he was proven right. He was one lucky lawyer! He was going to convince the jury that his honest opponent was dishonest, and the fact that that wasn't true—well, it just meant that it would be a bigger accomplishment to tar Herrick with undeserved sleaze. Jimmy stuck a fist up in the air, and then he said what everyone in the room was thinking.

"We've got those dirty bastards now!" he shouted.

The next morning, at nine o'clock sharp, Judge Trouble announced: "The attorneys will now begin their examinations of the jury panel. By custom, the plaintiffs go first. Mister Herrick?"

Robert stood up and faced the sixty citizens who had ultimate power over his case. "Good morning, ladies and gentlemen," he said, and smiled with genuine confidence. The jade-blue eyes made contact with them. He was sincere, he was honest, and he could sense that at that crucial moment, the jurors began to trust him. With his cheerful energy, he looked friendly as well as competent, because in spite of the late hours last night, he was casual—yet precise. Robert's stamina and poise were part of his gift as a trial lawyer.

The jurors felt the connection. In chorus, they said "Good Morning!" back to Robert. And with that, Robert got right to the point.

"We will prove three major facts to you in this trial. And you will see that all three of them are supported by overwhelming evidence." Robert was a careful student of the science of persuasion, and he knew that modern jury psychology stresses simplicity. Only one or two themes in the opening, or three at the most. And all of them should blend into a simple scenario, familiar to the jurors, one that the evidence will clearly prove, and one that the lawyer himself believes in.

Robert held up his index finger. "First, we will show you that the highway overpass was extremely dangerous. Maxxco Construction built it so cheaply and carelessly that this kind of disaster was just an accident waiting to happen."

He added a second finger to signify his second point. "Then, number two, we will show you that Maxxco knew about the danger. In fact, they went to a lot of trouble to cover it up. They covered up this problem and hid it from the public."

With that, Robert waited an instant. To let the explosive cover-up accusation settle in with the sixty citizens. Then, crisply, he held up three fingers.

"And third," he said, "we will show you that it will take more than two hundred and fifty million dollars to compensate the families of the more than three dozen people who died in the accident. As damages for the lives of these innocent people who were killed, incinerated, by Maxxco Construction Corporation's gross negligence."

The jury panel was silent. "Good," Robert thought. "They didn't flinch at the two hundred and fifty million." That didn't count the punitive damages and pre-trial interest, which would boost the damages to the billion mark.

His strategy was clear, and his words were carefully chosen. They also were short. Words of one, two or three syllables. Robert wanted to emphasize that he was trying the case only against one main defendant. Maxxco. And he wanted to emphasize the two hundred and fifty million dollars. To put it at the beginning.

"How do you feel about it? Does two hundred and fifty million dollars sound like too much to anybody?"

No response.

"I take it from your silence that no one would have trouble awarding two hundred and fifty million dollars if that's what the damages are proved to be. And that's good, because it makes sense. More than three dozen human beings. Burned alive. There's no amount of money that can make up for their deaths."

He had a consensus. The group had tacitly accepted his numbers. Still, he wanted to drive the point home.

He looked straight at Hartley Rehm, the gray-suited geologist's office manager. Juror number one. "Mister Rehm, how do you feel about the two hundred and fifty million dollar figure? Does it sound like an astronomical amount?"

"Sure," said Hartley Rehm, "but I understand why. You've got all these families of the victims. If my son or daughter was one of them, I'd want a jury who could see that millions of dollars wouldn't be enough to make up for the loss."

Perfect.

"Thank you, Mister Rehm. Now, let me ask all of you on the first row. Do you all feel the same as Mister Rehm?" They nodded. "The second row?" The heads bobbed. "Third? Fourth? Fifth? Sixth?" All sixty heads were bobbing.

"Thank you. Because at the end of the trial, I will be asking you to do just that. To fulfill this promise. It's not a promise to me. It's to this man. Stand up, Mister Gutierrez, please." Robert pointed at Pedro, who stood quietly with his hands folded.

"I take it by your silence that you promise to my friend, Pedro Gutierrez, and all the other families, that if we prove our case, you'll write that figure of two hundred and fifty million as actual damages in your verdict."

Silence. He now had a contract with them. Not an enforceable contract, of course. But at the end of the case, in final argument, he would be able to remind the jurors of this moment. It usually worked, because they would want to keep the promise.

"Now, let me ask you something else." Robert slowly walked to the other end of the row, to reinforce the change of subjects. "How many of you are familiar with the overpass at the Southwest Freeway and Interstate 610? Next to the Galleria?"

Every hand in the panel shot up. There was a chorus of nervous laughter.

"Whoa! Not everybody at once!" said Robert. Not funny. But everybody in the panel laughed harder.

"Does anybody have an opinion about the dangerousness of the ramp that's involved in this case?" Robert asked innocently.

Several hands. Surprisingly, one of them was Hartley Rehm. The "white-collar" guy, who the jury study said wasn't very desirable! Robert had been worrying about Mr. Rehm, but now, he was starting to like him. Jury studies were just generalizations, after all, and they couldn't categorize everybody. There was always that possibility of a banker with the soul of a poet. Was it Hartley Rehm?

"Mister Rehm, you're turning out to be the one who answers all the questions!" said Robert enthusiastically. "What's your opinion about this overpass?"

Hartley Rehm didn't hesitate. "It's a death trap. It's way too narrow. It leans to the outside. And the guardrail is just plain flimsy, like it's made out of tinker toys. If you had to dodge out of the way—"

"Your HONOR!" Jimmy Coleman had been on his feet and waving his arms for several seconds, before he managed to stop Hartley Rehm. "Your honor, may we hear this outside the presence of the other jurors?"

All nine lawyers trooped up to the bench. Plus Hartley Rehm. In response to questions, the number one juror explained that he had decided to investigate the accident scene, personally, last night. "I drove over the ramp so I could see for myself," he said proudly. "And Mister Herrick is absolutely right. It's dangerous!"

The other jurors couldn't hear what he was saying, now. But, of course, they had heard Hartley Rehm's earlier "death trap" speech. Everyone in the courtroom had heard it. The only way you could have missed it was if you were wearing earplugs. Jimmy made the usual motion for a mistrial, and Judge Trouble made the usual ruling. She denied it.

"Thank you, Mister Rehm, for your diligence. And your candor." Judge Trouble smiled, because after all, jurors were voters. "You are a good citizen."

And then, of course, she disqualified Hartley Rehm on the spot.

"What we want are bankers with the souls of poets," Robert thought. "Or, in this case, a geologists' office manager with the heart of a beautician." Hartley Rehm didn't fit the statistical profile, but Robert was mighty sorry to see him go.

"That man was our first witness," Robert whispered to Tom Kennedy, "before we even started the testimony." And it was true. The jurors had heard what Hartley Rehm had said, just as if it had been witness testimony. And they couldn't help believing it, because it came from juror number one, who was one of their own.

They battled back and forth for the rest of the day. Jimmy objected numerous times to Herrick's tactics, and most of his objections were sustained. Occasionally, Judge Trouble went even farther and ordered the jury to disregard what the plaintiffs' lawyer had said. To Robert, that kind of instruction felt like a knife in the back. But even if Jimmy won most of the battles, Robert felt, at the end of the day, that he had won the war.

He had started with a panel that was stacked with unfavorable jurors. And he had managed, by the end of the day, to thin the ranks of the "worst" ones. Which meant, of course, that he removed most of the jurors that Jimmy thought were the "best" ones. He had done it as he had planned, by emphasizing that the trial might last six months. Most of the citizens in the panel flinched when they heard that. But just as Robert had hoped, the ones who flinched the most were the professional, managerial and "other white-collar" types.

Robert built up the tension in these undesirable jurors by using a few carefully chosen questions and comments. "If the trial lasts for six months, can each one of you give it your full attention? Without being distracted by worries about what's happening back at work? The judge might need to sequester this jury. Sequester means that you would stay in a hotel, rather than going home. Is there anyone who would be distracted from the evidence if you were sequestered in a hotel for the length of this trial?" And, more simply: "Is there anyone who feels that he or she would suffer an unfair hardship by serving on this jury if the trial lasted up to six months?" Almost half the panel held up their hands in response to that last question.

The judge and the lawyers then had to interview each one of these "hardship excuses." It was repetitious and boring. But this also was one of the most important events in the whole trial.

Jimmy Coleman recognized what was happening to him, of course. He fought to keep the professional and managerial jurors, because he knew, just as Herrick did, that they were more likely to be biased in favor of Maxxco than the blue-collar working people. Time and again, the lawyers trooped up to the bench accompanied by a juror who owned a small business. Or who maintained a professional practice. Or who was a key supervisor of hundreds of employees in a large corporation. Just as Robert had predicted, Judge Trobelo tried to hold the line. "You realize, Mister Cronin, that jury service is a duty of citizenship?" she asked the first hardship case. And she asked the same question of every one after that.

But there was a flood of excuses that she had to give in to. For instance, the first juror excused on hardship grounds was a fifty-one-year-old physician who ran his own solo practice. He had six other employees, all dependent upon this man's efforts. There was no way that Judge Trobelo could justify destroying the doctor's entire medical practice and throwing all seven people out of work just so she could keep him here. Robert Herrick tallied that ruling as a victory. One solidly unfavorable juror gone.

Then, the judge interviewed the manager of a country club, forty-five years old and a widower. Irreplaceable at his job. Excused. Next, a bicycle shop owner. Thirty-seven and highly unfavorable. Excused. In the end, when the dust had cleared, fourteen members of the panel had been eliminated this way. All were white-collar, professional or managerial. None was a union member, none was a day laborer, and none was a professor, nurse or shoe salesman. And that was why Robert felt that, even if he had lost some of the battles, he still had won the war.

The afternoon's most exciting moment came later, around three o'clock, when Robert had moved on to other issues. He told the panel that he admired the jury system, primarily because "it doesn't depend on a single man adjusting cases all by himself and sitting in a tall building in Omaha, Nebraska or in Hartford, Connecticut."

At that, Jimmy instantly bounced to his feet, and his face was crimson as he angrily objected. But before he even got the objection out, Judge Trobelo shouted, in a voice of thunder, "Counsel, approach the bench!" When Robert complied, the judge reminded him that it was improper to suggest anything about insurance to the jury. "Why, then, would you mention Omaha? Or Hartford?" she asked. Robert looked like a choirboy, but Judge Trouble was not mollified. "That's your bite at the apple. And if you do anything like that again, you'll be checking in at the county jail."

"When you're trying a case against Jimmy Coleman," Robert told himself, "you can't pull your punches any more than you can wish away the trees during jungle warfare. I've got to be fair, but I've got to fight hard."

Jimmy asked for a mistrial again, of course. The judge denied the request for the umpteenth time, but then she proceeded to instruct the jury panel to "disregard those highly improper remarks by the plaintiffs' attorney." And with that, Robert changed the subject, but he took pains to look upbeat. The jurors had heard the Omaha-Hartford remark. The smart ones understood what it meant. And probably, all the fuss had only succeeded in reinforcing it. Jimmy Coleman was getting a dose of his own medicine.

Anyway, after the hardship excuses, Robert had the satisfaction of knowing that the jury panel was better. Much better. The end of the day was approaching, and today was far more pleasant than yesterday had been.

After Robert had questioned the jurors for almost a full day, it was Francel Williams' turn. Francel was faster. In fact, he took less than five minutes with the jury panel, right at five o'clock. But he did his job effectively, as it turned out. "I represent the Louisiana Trucking Company," he said happily, and spread his arms wide. "And we agree with Mister Herrick on just about everything!

"The truck driver was just unlucky," Francel went on. "He was in the wrong place at the wrong time. After all, with the bad weather and with the poor arrangement of signs at this interchange, the driver might have just been confused. It wasn't his fault. And it certainly isn't the fault of the Louisiana Trucking Company. Is there anyone in the jury panel who couldn't accept that fact, if the evidence proved it?" The silence showed that all of them could accept it.

"But," Francel hastened to add, "that doesn't mean this horrible disaster was nobody's fault. Certainly not! Just as Mister Herrick said, this intersection was dangerous. Maxxco built the ramp so that it is unstable. Too narrow. Too slippery. And protected by a too-flimsy guardrail. Maxxco is at fault. In fact, Maxxco knew the interchange was dangerous, and so Maxxco was grossly, inexcusably and criminally negligent." Francel beamed. He looked like he was trying to show all thirty-two teeth at the same time. "Is there anyone who couldn't step up to the line and say Maxxco was grossly negligent, if the evidence proves it?" Again, the same silence showed that they could accept it.

"And," Francel went on, "I'm not here to quarrel with the plaintiffs' right to collect damages. For that, no amount of money is enough. Billions wouldn't be enough. The damages are enormous. Astronomical. And the Louisiana Trucking Company agrees with the plaintiffs about that. Is there anyone who would hold it against the Louisiana Trucking Company, just because its lawyer agrees with the plaintiffs that their losses are astronomical?"

He took it by their silence that no one would hold it against the trucking company just because its lawyer was honest.

With that, Francel Williams turned a dazzling smile toward the jury and sat down. But his five minutes were surprisingly influential. Later that evening, when Herrick's people interviewed the shadow jurors that they had hired to sit in the audience, it turned out that they were very impressed with Francel. "I liked the way he smiled," said one of them. "He was honest."

"Francel can beat me at smiling any day of the week," Herrick laughed, when he heard about it. There was no way to predict how jurors would react to the lawyers' personalities. If they liked Francel, that was fine. So did Robert.

27
AUTOPSY DAY

The morning of the third day of trial dawned clear and bright. The sunlight shone in dappled patterns on the lawn in front of the courthouse, and even the lawyers had an extra bounce in their feet as they opened the heavy brass doors of the gingerbread building with the odd little cupola. In the Twelfth District courtroom, Judge Trobelo seemed unusually cheerful, and the effects of the weather trickled down to the bailiff and the court personnel, the court reporter and the lawyers, and even the spectators and the prospective jurors. All of them greeted each other with renewed enthusiasm for the start of day three of the propane truck trial.

It was Jimmy's turn to address the jury panel. And so the judge announced, "Mister Coleman, you may question the panel on behalf of Maxxco Construction Company."

Jimmy's expression was stern. He was going to throw cold water on the springtime cheer that had blossomed both outside and inside the courtroom. His first words were designed for shock value: "Ladies and gentlemen, the only reason my client Maxxco is in this lawsuit is because of greed."

With that, he had everyone's attention. "Take the amount of money Mister Herrick claims," he went on. "It amounts to almost ten million dollars per family. Let's say you invested that money in high-grade, blue chip bonds. Every year, just the interest on ten million dollars in bonds would be around a million dollars. Per year. Every year. It would earn each of the plaintiffs more money in a year than most people ever see in a lifetime. Every single year! These people would get rich from this tragedy."

Jimmy's aggressive strategy might have seemed risky, but it wasn't, because it wasn't done at random. The jury consultants had tried out this "blue-chip bonds" argument on two different focus groups. The results showed that it was the best argument for defusing the plaintiffs' case. Both focus groups agreed, and so did Jimmy's psychologists.

It was unfair, Robert thought to himself. All the law provides for is money damages. That's all that can be used to stop Maxxco, tomorrow, from snuffing out another three dozen lives. And "per family" wasn't the way the damages would be awarded, since some had as many as a dozen plaintiffs. But fair or not, the defense was entitled to have its say.

"That's why I use the word greed," Jimmy went on. "Everything in the plaintiffs' case is exaggerated and untrue, just like the damage claim. By bringing Maxxco in, these lawyers are just trying to profit from a tragedy. It's nothing but an effort by them to get money out of the bodies of people who are dead. Because this accident was simply not Maxxco's fault."

Jimmy had read some of the same psychological studies as the plaintiffs' lawyer. And so he said, "I have three main points to make. Just like Mister Herrick. Except that I don't agree with any of his three points. My first point is, Maxxco built this overpass properly and safely. Maxxco is a fine company, and it did the job right."

It wasn't true, but if he looked the jurors in the eye and seemed sincere, maybe they would swallow it.

"My second point is, this tragedy didn't happen because of Maxxco. Instead, it happened because the truck driver was going way too fast. And he committed a crime by taking his hazardous cargo where the law told him he couldn't. In other words, the conduct of this driver for the Louisiana Trucking Company was more than enough to cause this accident. That's my second point."

Jimmy pointed over toward the plaintiffs' lawyers before continuing. "And my third point is that these lawyers haven't sued Maxxco because they think Maxxco's guilty. They couldn't have. Because Maxxco isn't guilty! Instead, they've sued Maxxco because it's the deepest pocket. In other words, it's just because of greed."

Robert Herrick always hated to sit and listen. Usually, when he was listening, it was because the other side was talking, and that usually meant they were trashing Robert's case. As a young lawyer, Robert had had to learn to restrain himself, to keep from objecting to everything. That was unwise. It would have made him look ungentlemanly. It also would have made jurors think he was trying to hide something, and it sometimes reinforced all the bad things the other side was saying. Right now, it was possible that some of Jimmy's comments were objectionable, but the judge might not think so, and anyway, an after-the-fact objection wouldn't cure the problem. Robert forced himself to sit quietly and listen.

Jimmy was telling the panel that anyone could file a suit. Just by paying a two-hundred-dollar fee. Without checking with the judge. Or anyone else. "In fact, anyone can file suit against any of you jurors, tomorrow, even if there's no merit to the suit. Does everyone on the jury panel understand that? If there's no merit to the claim against Maxxco, can all of you say so?" And so forth. It was standard stuff, and Robert knew to expect it, but still, it hurt to sit still and listen to it when he wanted to shout, "We can't bring back the people who were killed. All we can do is award damages because that's all our legal system allows for!"

Jimmy shifted into asking whether everyone could be fair to Maxxco, knowing it was a large corporation. Knowing that it had built the interchange where the propane disaster happened. "Is there anyone who'd judge Maxxco more harshly than a business owned by an individual shopkeeper, just because it's big and it was involved in constructing this overpass?" Robert sat powerlessly and cringed as he saw the hands go up. The hands of his best jurors.

Jimmy used this question, first, to disqualify a college student. In front of the bench, the young man said he couldn't be fair to Maxxco. Then, a secretary for a tool and die company. Disqualified. A cosmetics saleslady. Disqualified. A cab driver. Disqualified. All told, Jimmy removed seven potential jurors with that can-you-be-fair-to-great-big-Maxxco question, and Robert had wanted to keep every one. He was particularly disappointed about losing the cab driver from the jury, because if anyone would have sympathized with Louie Boudreau's shortcut, it would have been the cab driver.

It was a long morning for Robert. And it merged into an even longer afternoon.

Each side gets six free challenges when picking a jury in Texas. Six strikes. Six people who can be removed for any reason, or for no reason. Judge Trobelo lumped the trucking company together with the plaintiffs. They would share six strikes. Robert, of course, would make the strikes. He and Tom Kennedy went into the jury room to make the marks on their list that would strike the worst six.

Most of it was easy. The plaintiffs' first strike was a bank president. Then, a grocery store manager. Third, a woman who identified herself as an "independent investor." The fourth strike was a bricklayer who had kept asking Robert, why was Maxxco still in the suit, if the truck driver was at fault? And then, fifth, a woman who managed a credit reporting service. Finally, the plaintiffs' sixth strike fell into place when Robert and Tom agreed that the civil engineer was more dangerous than the respiratory therapist.

"He does the same kind of work that Maxxco does," said Robert, as he drew his sixth line through the civil engineer's name. "We can't afford to take the risk."

They both knew that Jimmy Coleman was doing the same thing nearby in the attorneys' conference room. Actually, nobody would get to "pick" the jury. It was a process of elimination. Each side removed the six that it liked the least, who were probably the same six that the other side liked the most. The jury would be the first twelve whom nobody disliked enough to strike. That meant that nobody would like them too much, either.

The clerk read the final twelve names, slowly. Mrs. Patterson, an elementary school teacher. Mr. Chavez, a tree trimmer. Ms. LaGarde, a homemaker. Mr. Stein, a die stamper. Mr. Fries, an architect—and, Robert thought, this architect probably would be the foreman of the jury. Ms. Ezrailson, a bookkeeper. And so forth.

The lawyers all noticed that the anxiety level was suddenly lower. Picking a jury pumps up the adrenalin. The excitement peaks when the clerk reads the names. Then, there is a letdown when the jury is in the box. Because usually, neither side really likes the chosen twelve as much as they did those that the other side discarded. But then, neither do they dislike them as much as the ones they themselves struck. And so it was with this group of twelve.

They were mostly blue-collar, but with a sprinkling of professionals. Seven women and five men. There were two Latinos and three black jurors. Robert noted with satisfaction that the architect and the letter carrier were the only two who wore ties. He preferred the loose, free-spirited types, with open-necked shirts.

"Well, we've got our jury," said Robert. "For better or for worse."

With the jury finally in the box, Robert Herrick called his first witness. "Mister Hartley Rehm." Everybody in the courtroom thought that name sounded vaguely familiar, but they couldn't quite place it, and they wondered who Hartley Rehm was.

Jimmy Coleman wondered too, for a few seconds. But then, suddenly, he realized that Hartley Rehm was the same person who had been a member of the jury panel and had been disqualified because he thought the overpass was a "death trap." Jimmy was on his feet immediately. He almost shouted his objection. "Your honor, the rules prohibit a juror from being a witness!"

"That's exactly right, your honor," Robert replied calmly. "A juror can't be a witness. That's what the rule says. A juror. But Mister Rehm isn't a juror. He never was a juror. And he isn't a juror now."

"That's a hypertechnical distinction!" Jimmy retorted. He made it sound as though Booker & Bayne never used technicalities. "Mister Rehm was a member of the jury panel. Besides, we didn't get his name during discovery. He's not on the witness list!"

"Of course it's a technical distinction, but that's only because the law makes lots of technical distinctions." Robert's voice was calm. "He isn't a juror, so the rule doesn't apply. He's not going to have to decide anything about the case, so it shouldn't apply." Robert turned and addressed the judge directly. "And as for giving Mister Coleman this witness's name, your honor, we supplemented our discovery responses yesterday. To add the name of Hartley Rehm. I personally gave it to Maxxco's lawyers just a few minutes after we met Mister Rehm, in fact."

The Booker & Bayne lawyers were in complete consternation. "Your honor, we also object under Rule 403. This testimony would be prejudicial and misleading to a degree that would substantially outweigh its value!" Jimmy's voice sounded angry, confused, and anguished, all at the same time.

Judge Trouble had the rule book out and open. "I can't see how the testimony is improper," she said finally. "The witness, Hartley Rehm, isn't a juror, and the plaintiffs' lawyers couldn't have disclosed his name any earlier than they did because both parties found out about him at the same time yesterday. The objection is overruled."

And so Hartley Rehm raised his right hand and swore to tell the truth. And then, he told the jury about the overpass. About how he had driven on it after the first day of jury selection, just to see if he agreed with the plaintiffs that it was dangerous. About how his car had pulled to the outside, how narrow the ramp had been, how spindly the guardrails were, and how the overpass still "seemed like a death trap" to him. Then, Robert said, "Pass the witness."

"You aren't a safety engineer, are you?" Jimmy Coleman asked. He said it as though nobody should be allowed to testify about anything unless he had an advanced degree in the subject.

"That's true," the witness admitted. "But so what?" Robert was thinking.

"And if the truck driver hadn't been violating the law," Jimmy went on, "he wouldn't have been on this overpass at all?" True. "And the accident wouldn't have happened, then?"

"Yes," Robert thought to himself, "and if your grandmother had wheels, maybe she'd be a wagon." Anyway, it wasn't very good cross-examination; but it was the best that Jimmy could do under the circumstances.

The jury loved Hartley Rehm's testimony. Robert could tell. They had listened to Jimmy's objections, and they were offended. Again, Robert could tell. As far as the jurors were concerned, this witness was one of them. Jimmy's attempt to silence him wasn't just an effort to keep the jurors from hearing something, it was an attack on a member of their own ranks. Besides, Hartley Rehm was a neutral witness. He was chosen by chance, not by Herrick, and so he was the most effective kind of witness anyone could imagine.

"Just one question on redirect examination," Robert was saying to Hartley Rehm. "Let's assume that, at some time or another, there's going to be a traffic law violation and a truck driver will get onto this overpass because he cuts corners with the law. Just as Mister Coleman has suggested happened here. Is the overpass safe, given the fact that this is bound to happen?"

Hartley Rehm's answer was perfect, because it so obviously came from the heart. "No. This overpass was nothing but an accident waiting to happen."

And with that, Hartley Rehm's testimony ended, and the first witness stepped down from the stand.

The rest of the day was an anticlimax. It was consumed mostly by testimony from two eyewitnesses. They described the fireball and the flipping, spinning cars that sped into it. They described their own efforts to escape, which were barely successful. Then, Robert put on his concrete expert. "The modern type of guardrail is made of reinforced concrete, from two to four feet wide at the base and tapered at the top." That kind of guardrail would have prevented this accident from happening, in this expert's opinion. All of the testimony was dramatic enough to keep the jurors interested.

But the witness everyone remembered at the end of the day was Hartley Rehm. Everyone. The shadow jury even said that it was sneaky of Jimmy Coleman to try to censor such an important witness. As for Jimmy, he kept repeating his own opinion, which was that the judge's ruling was "reversible error."

At that, Tom Kennedy just smiled and shook his head. He figured that only Robert Herrick would have been creative enough to think of calling a jury panel member to the witness stand. Only Herrick would have the perceptiveness to do it, the clout to get away with it, and the squeaky clean reputation that made the judge allow it.

Trial or no trial, Robert had agreed to be at the Lamar High School Gym that night to watch Pepper play basketball. It was the Lamar High School Lady Redskins against the Bellaire High School Lady Cardinals. Pepper was five-foot-nine-inches tall and played strong forward.

Pepper had a pretty good hook and a deadly jump shot. She was good enough, in fact, so that Robert's reaction, the first time he had seen her play in junior high school competition, had been, "Hey! You don't shoot like a girl at all!" To which Pepper had responded with the most disgusted expression Robert had ever had targeted at him. Remembering that experience now, he wondered where teenage girls learned that skill—making faces that simultaneously conveyed utter contempt and utter indifference, both so effectively.

Lamar High School was an unusual place. In the fifties and early sixties, it had been an enclave for the city's most wealthy residents. It was located at the intersection of Westheimer Road and River Oaks Boulevard, and so the typical high school senior back in the fifties lived in a three-story, ten-thousand-square-foot River Oaks swankienda with a domestic staff of three or four full-time servants. When Bellaire High School had been built just a few miles south, the two became arch rivals. Bellaire's student body was slightly less rich, and so Bellaire students looked down on the white-glove sissies who went to Lamar. The white-glove sissies at Lamar reciprocated, of course, by thumbing their noses at the low-class dorks at Bellaire. Robert's late wife, Patricia, had gone to Lamar back in the sixties, and she had reminisced about it often.

All that was long since over, of course. After years of desegregation decrees, Lamar was now a magnet school. So was Bellaire. Each was roughly one-third black, one-third Anglo, and one-third Hispanic. But there were a few things that had remained the same. Lamar still had a manicured lawn dotted with oaks and carefully trimmed crepe myrtles. It still had a few students drawn from the River Oaks neighborhood, who were used to old-style southern homes with huge Ionic columns. Like Pepper Herrick. The difference was, even if they entered the school unsure about the black kids, the rich white kids quickly learned how to sass them back, and they even learned—miraculously, to their parents—how to be real friends with them. And Lamar and Bellaire still kept the tradition of looking down on each other, and each school wanted to win their games against each other more than winning the state championship.

Now, it was the fourth quarter in the Lamar-Bellaire basketball game, and the Lamar Lady Redskins were behind by six points. They had been down by ten earlier, but late in the third period, they had scored eight unanswered points. Suddenly, down on the court, the point guard found Pepper just outside the foul line. Pepper turned and passed off to the Redskins' six-foot center, Candace

Gonzales. Pepper stood perfectly still, while Candace moved behind her, bouncing the ball twice. The Lady Cardinal guarding Candace got neatly picked off by Pepper. The Cardinal's teammate was five inches shorter than the Redskin center and lost almost a second before switching, because of the pick. Candace Gonzales put up a six-foot jump shot, and banked it in. The swish of the draperies was drowned out by the roar from the crowd of Lamar parents. With that, Robert almost forgot about the propane truck case. He stood up and cheered. Pepper had done the pick perfectly, and the Redskins were only four points down!

The Lady Redskins went into a full-court press. The red-shirted Cardinal guard couldn't find anyone at first. Finally, she bounce-passed the ball in to the Cardinal center. She was tall, but awkward, and her first efforts to dribble the ball almost seemed to invite a steal. Suddenly, a blue shirt worn by a tiny Lamar guard seemed to flash beneath the Cardinal center's hips. The ball reversed course, dribbled by a small African-American girl in a Lamar uniform. The little guard passed off to Pepper, who immediately passed back. The guard had an easy lay-up. And as the ball went in, to make it only two points down, the referee's whistle sounded. "Foul! Red number twenty-three!"

But the Lamar guard, whose name on Robert's program was given as Viviana Zuckerman, got flustered at the foul line. "Miss it! Miss it! Miss it!" the Bellaire crowd chanted. And she did.

The score was forty-two to forty as the clock ran down to five seconds, then four, then three. From midcourt, the tiny point guard heaved a Hail Mary that flew fifty feet through the air, slammed against the backboard and bounced harmlessly off the hoop. The Lady Redskins had lost by one basket.

Robert Herrick went down to the court to meet his daughter. He expected to have to console her, because like her father, Pepper usually was a poor loser. Robert thought, suddenly, "I hope this game isn't a metaphor for how the propane truck case is going to end." But to his surprise, he found Pepper in pretty good spirits. And no, she told him, she wasn't planning to drive home with her father. "I'm going to go with my friend, Jonathan," she told him breathlessly. Robert couldn't tell whether she was out of breath because of the game, which he doubted, or because she thought this boy named Jonathan, as she put it, was "way awesome."

"Daddy, this is Jonathan Morse," said Pepper. Robert turned, extended his hand, and paused with his mouth open. Jonathan had an earring with a cross at the bottom, hanging from a half-moon chain, a three-day growth of beard, and a flannel plaid shirt with the sleeves cut off to show tattoos of dragons and daggers on his biceps. His hair was long on top and shaved around the ears. Black jeans and muddy black boots. And Robert had to look up as Jonathan grinned and took his hand, because Jonathan was about six-feet-five-inches tall.

"Nice to meet you," said Jonathan politely.

Jonathan Morse? Jonathan Morse? Robert strained to remember where he had heard that name before. And then he knew. Pepper's sexual fantasies, verbalized to her teenage friend within her father's earshot. The boy who wore the skin-tight football pants. "Awesome." "Tubular." "I want him!" This guy was her heartthrob? This guy was Jonathan Morse?

Evidently, he was.

Pepper took Jonathan's arm and innocently said, "We might be out real late, Daddy. Don't worry about me." Robert thought, "You're too late. I already am worried!"

Earlier in his experience as a father, he had tried to act on his worries. But it had dawned on him that it didn't do much good to try to choose his daughter's friends. And it was next to impossible—or, at least, something to be done only in rare cases—to tell a teenager that she couldn't hang out with a boy she liked.

So with that, it was back to the office to work on the next day's testimony in the propane truck case. All he could think of as he drove downtown was, "I sure hope Jonathan Morse turns out to be the biggest surprise I'm going to have this week."

Down at the courthouse, the next day of testimony also dawned bright and clear. It was just as pretty as the day before. A thousand robins stopped by on their way north, and the lawyers slowed down for a moment to watch them strut through the bright green grass with their red bellies swelling under the blue sky. Again, the mood in the courtroom was cheerful, and again, it was about to be set aside by serious business. But this time, it was Robert, not Jimmy, who was going to be responsible for breaking the spell. He was going to present the medical examiner as a witness, to testify about the dead bodies. Today was autopsy day.

Doctor Bill Brczykowski was the Chief Medical Examiner in Houston. He was a colorful sight on the witness stand. He sported a blue and white seersucker jacket with a wide awning stripe, a yellow button-down shirt, and a red bow tie with bright blue dots. His powder-blue trousers ended in white socks—and unbelievably, in white patent shoes. The only way he looked like an expert witness was by wearing coke-bottle glasses. And maybe he looked "expert" because of the white hair that he parted in the middle and his short white beard. The jurors almost had to shield their eyes from all the bright colors as the medical examiner swore to tell the truth, the whole truth, and nothing but the truth.

His name was easy, Dr. Brczykowski explained. "BAR-chee-KOW-ski. Nothing to it." Still, everybody called him "Doctor Bill." The tall, gaunt pathologist with the narrow face and the jolly disposition always feigned astonishment at the way people froze when they saw the string of consonants that traced his Polish heritage.

Robert started with the basics. "Doctor BAR-chee-KOW-ski, your field is forensic pathology. Will you tell us, please, what that means?"

"It's the study of diagnosing disease or injury. Or determining the cause of death. And that's what I do, as the Chief Medical Examiner for this county." Dr. Bill smiled a big, toothy smile. He made it sound as though determining the cause of death was a delightful job. "The medical examiner, here, is like what they call the coroner in other places."

"Thank you, Doctor. Now, will you tell us your qualifications, please?"

Every lawyer in Houston enjoyed asking that question of Doctor Bill Brczykowski. It was like turning loose the key to a wind-up toy. He was an experienced courtroom witness, and so Doctor Bill turned and faced the jury before beginning his answer. His career had started when he studied chemistry at Texas A & M. Then came Harvard Medical School. Internships at Johns Hopkins and Berkeley, residencies at Baylor in Houston and at the University of Texas Southwestern Medical Center in Dallas. Then, with that testimony behind him, Dr. Bill sailed through his association memberships, board certifications, and public offices, all without any prompting from Robert. Next—without false modesty, and in the same rapid-fire rhythm—he described the thousands of autopsies he had performed, his publications in scholarly journals, and the techniques that he had pioneered. Almost as an afterthought, he added that he was an ordained deacon in the church. Oh, and he also had a J.D., a law degree, in addition to his medical degree.

When the jurors blinked, Robert couldn't tell whether they were impressed by Dr. Bill's credentials or merely protecting their eyes from his clothes.

The qualifications were finished. It was time to get down to business, and the business was gruesome. Robert approached the court reporter carrying a blowup photograph with styrofoam backing. "Will you mark this, please, with the plaintiffs' next exhibit number?" The huge photograph was marked as Plaintiff's Exhibit 23.

"Doctor BAR-chee-KOW-ski," said Robert carefully, "can you identify Plaintiffs' Exhibit 23?"

"It's a photograph of the body of Marian Cortelli, immediately before the autopsy," the witness answered. "She is one of the deceased persons in this case."

"Does Plaintiffs' Exhibit 23 truly and accurately depict the appearance of the body of Marian Cortelli immediately before the autopsy?"

"Yes. That's her, after the accident."

With that, Robert walked to Jimmy Coleman and let him inspect the exhibit. It had been seen by both counsel earlier, during the pre-trial discovery, but the rules required it to be shown to him again, now, so that Jimmy could object if he wanted to.

And Jimmy did want to object. He drew himself up to his full height and put on a stern expression. "Your honor, the misleading nature of this photograph is so prejudicial that it substantially outweighs any relevance it might have, and therefore, under Rule 403, it should be excluded." It was as if Jimmy was accusing Robert of doctoring up the photograph, and saying that that was why it was gruesome.

"That's overruled." The judge's response was prompt. Even gruesome pictures were routinely admissible under the rules of evidence, if they showed the injuries traceable to the incident in the lawsuit. In fact, Jimmy didn't expect to keep this exhibit from being admitted. He had made his objection and adopted his disapproving look because he wanted to try to divert the jury's attention away from the consequences of the accident.

"Your honor, the plaintiffs offer Exhibit 23," said Robert.

"It is admitted," said Judge Trouble.

"Doctor Brczykowski," said Robert slowly, "would you kindly reveal the exhibit and explain it to the jury?"

Jimmy Coleman had painstakingly prepared the jury panel for the autopsy pictures before jury selection. In an effort to desensitize them, he had even shown them some of the photographs that he had expected Herrick to use. It was good strategy to confront the potential jurors with your opponent's strongest evidence, and in fact to get them used to it, while extracting their commitment to treat the defendant fairly in spite of it. Even so, the jurors gasped as the medical examiner flipped the blowup to let them see what was left of Marian Cortelli.

It was more like a lump of coal than a human body. The face was missing, and the scorched bones were easily visible underneath. The hands were skeletal claws. The jurors were vaguely aware of Dr. Brczykowski's cheerful voice, explaining that this claw-like closure of the bones in the fingers was the typical result when the flesh of the hands was, as the jolly doctor put it, "oxidized into elemental carbon, water, and carbon oxides."

The jurors looked at Jimmy Coleman with a newfound skepticism about both him and his client.

Herrick and Kennedy had carefully chosen the order of questioning about the autopsy photographs. They had decided it would be advantageous to begin with the picture of Marian Cortelli because it was typical of the more severely burned victims, and because the twenty-three-year-old college student's photographs during lifetime created such a sharp contrast. And they had decided to end with an autopsy photo of another victim that showed a mixture of third-degree burns and second-degree ones, because those were typical of other victims. In some ways, the second-degree burns seemed even more gruesome.

After a suitable interval, Robert went on. "Doctor, please describe the autopsy that you conducted on the body of Marian Cortelli," he said.

With that, the jurors heard about "the usual Y-shaped incision" that the medical examiner had used to open the dead woman's chest and abdomen. The autopsy photograph sat on an easel, and it still faced the jurors, as they learned about the removal of Marian Cortelli's heart, lungs, liver and kidneys, to be weighed and sectioned for inspection. In fact, Dr. Bill added as an afterthought, the lungs were thoroughly burned on the inside, too.

"After which, the head was reflected in the usual manner," the medical examiner continued, brightly.

"So that the jury can know, Doctor, what does it mean to reflect the head?"

What that meant, as it turned out, was that Dr. Brczykowski had cut the crown off Marian Cortelli's skull with a small circular saw. He had removed the brain. And he had weighed, sectioned, and examined it. Just to be sure that the brain was normal. It was a routine part of a complete autopsy.

"Doctor, what is your opinion of the cause of death?"

"Asphyxiation and cardiac arrest," answered Dr. Brczykowski.

"Are these the kinds of injuries that would cause severe pain and suffering to Marian Cortelli, from their onset until the time of death?"

"Obviously. Of course!" The doctor looked at the jury and smiled as if he were wishing all twelve of them to have a nice day.

It took over four hours to take Dr. Bill through all of the autopsies. Robert spent most of that time, though, on just three of the victims. One was Marian Cortelli, the one he started with. One was a victim named Brian Wisenbaker, the one he ended with, because the second-degree burns were so vivid. And the third one was little ten-year-old Angela Gutierrez, who died in the Andrews Burn Center of massive pneumonococcal infection and cardiac arrest. Robert and Tom had decided to emphasize Angela because her innocence would make such a strong theme during final argument.

Some of the bodies could be identified only by dental records, and there were a few that couldn't even be identified that way, because it wasn't possible to locate their dental records. In that case, the identification was made by the general characteristics of the body, such as height and weight, plus the location of broken bones, which could be seen even if they had healed. The truck driver was one of these. The body they suspected was his had been found near the cab of the truck. By stripping the flesh from the right forearm, Dr. Bill had found a fracture of the bone known as the ulna, and it matched a break that Louie Boudreau had sustained two years earlier. "As far as we know, Mister Boudreau may never even have consulted a dentist in his entire lifetime," explained the medical examiner.

"Pass the witness," said Robert finally. It was now just past noon. It had happened by chance, but Robert's direct examination had ended at a time when it was impractical for Judge Trouble to allow Jimmy Coleman any cross-examination before the jury went to lunch. "Sometimes," he thought, "you have to settle for the little victories, the ones that come by accident."

Suddenly, Tom Kennedy came running up. He was holding a pink telephone slip. And he was excited.

"Call Detective Derrigan Slaughter right away! They've caught Squint!"

Robert just stared at him. The words took a long time to sink in. "Squint," Kennedy repeated. "You know, Squint! Robert, they've just caught the guy who tried to kill you!"

It was almost seven o'clock when they held the lineup at the police station.

"No," said Robert Herrick. "That's not him."

The first stand-in ambled slowly across the stage. The man was about Squint's height and had a strange defect in one eye. But it wasn't Squint.

"Just wait until they all get lined up." Detective Slaughter was patient. "We got five folks who ain't the right guy, cause that's what a lineup's all about."

Robert felt a little foolish.

"Took us most of the day to find five other guys with squinty eyes." Detective Cashdollar sounded apologetic. "Supreme Court says we gotta try to make 'em all look alike. I guess they mean we gotta try to confuse you. Anyway, that's the reason we kept you waiting so long on this lineup, Mister Herrick."

Now, at last, there were six men on the little stage. As promised, all six had eye problems. They shuffled their feet and looked around under the harsh lights.

It was easy, even with five other squinting suspects. Robert felt cold when he saw the man who wanted so much to kill him. "Number four! That's Squint. He's number four."

Slaughter stared at him. "Let me tell you, it ain't no good to us at all 'less'n you say your I.D. is positive. So, I need to ask you: Are you sure?"

"I'm positive. And you don't need to coach me that way."

"Okay. Thanks. Sorry we took so much of your time."

"Wait just a minute!" Robert certainly wasn't ready to leave, not until he found out what was going on. "Who is this guy?"

"Oh. Sorry. I forgot. We couldn't tell you nothin' before the lineup."

"These detectives forget the strangest things," Robert thought.

Detective Slaughter turned to face him. "Guy's name is Herbert James Kronkeneck. And you done picked out the correct dude, all right, 'cause old Kronkeneck, which we call him—you been callin' him Squint—he just happens to be an out-of-work engineer. And it just so happens, he used to work for . . . guess who? . . . Maxxco Construction Corporation."

Robert's eyebrows arched. Actually, it felt like they shot up three or four inches.

"Old Kronkeneck, or Squint, he says he got fired," Slaughter went on. "They fired him the day after the propane truck went down. This Kronkeneck, he was an assistant to the president of Maxxco. Reason they fired him was, they said he was responsible for supervising maintenance of this overpass. But the way Kronkeneck sees it, he's a scapegoat. Of course, that would be the way he'd see it, right?"

"So anyway, that's why Squint—or Kronkeneck, whatever his name is— that's why he shot me?" Robert wanted to know.

"Yup. That, plus the fact that he's probably gonna diagnose out as somethin' close to a paranoid schizophrenic." Slaughter saw Robert's startled look, and he laughed. "No. Don't get the wrong idea. I don't mean he really is a loony. We'll get him shrunk, 'cause it's routine, and I 'speck he'll test out in the normal range. But Mister Kronkeneck does dislike you intensively, Mister Herrick, and he rants and raves a lot. He thinks you're the guy who pulls all the strings. He figures you got Maxxco's president runnin' scared, and he actually has concluded that you're the guy who caused all a his troubles."

Robert was silent for a minute. He was used to having people blame him for their troubles. It happened every time he sued somebody. But in this case? It was pretty extreme.

"Well," he said finally, "what about that threatening letter? The one that called me a 'sHYsTer' in cut-out newsprint? You know, the one that had somebody else's finger prints all over it."

"Funny thing." Slaughter had stopped laughing. "Old Squint—I mean Kronkeneck—he says he don't know nothin about that sHYsTer letter. We asked him over and over, and frankly we put the question ever which way we could think of. He insists he didn't send that letter, and he don't know who did. And I been startin' to believe him, 'specially seein' as how his prints don't match."

"So you mean there's another person out there who's still threatening me?" Robert didn't like this, at all.

Detective Cashdollar nodded. "And it's somebody who's never been arrested before. Somebody who never had to give any prints to the FBI."

"Yup." Detective Slaughter shook his head. "One down, but there's still one to go. And I'd suggest, for the time being, Mister Herrick, you oughta keep those two DPS officers who been bodyguardin' you, 'cause we still got another suspeck, one that's still runnin' round loose out there."

"I wonder," Robert thought. He was scared, but also, he was curious. "I wonder who on earth that other suspect could be?"

28
THE VIDEOTAPE

Barbara Coleman hated it when Jimmy was in a long trial. She especially hated the first part of a long trial if Jimmy was representing one of the defendants. That meant that Jimmy not only worked later than usual— he not only put in twenty-hour days and was more grumpy and stressed out than usual—the first part of the trial meant that Jimmy's client was getting attacked every day by an army of witnesses for the plaintiffs. And, like any trial lawyer, Jimmy was not able to avoid feeling attacked himself, personally, when his client was constantly being vilified by the other side.

All Jimmy did when he got home, nowadays, was lie in bed and stare at the ceiling. Or pace around like a hamster in a cage. Or rant and rave about how unfair the trial was and how much he wanted to beat that pip-squeak, Robert Herrick, into the ground. Actually, it was better when he griped and complained, because at least then he had something to say. What Barbara hated most were the hours when he lay in the bed and stared at the ceiling. Things would be much better when the plaintiffs rested their case, because then Jimmy would get a chance to call witnesses for the defense. He could start confusing the jury and putting on carefully coached witnesses, the things he was best at.

"The jury will find anybody guilty after all that autopsy stuff today," Jimmy groused.

He studied the ceiling for a few minutes before he said anything more. "After those autopsy pictures they saw today, that jury's probably in a mood to nail just about anybody," he went on at last. "I mean, just about anybody! How can I defend Maxxco against that? It wouldn't matter if it was Walt Disney. If Walt Disney got sued and the jury saw that autopsy stuff, they'd nail him, too!"

"I'm sure you must have done some good by cross-examining the medical examiner," Barbara soothed him. She had found from experience that it made him less gloomy if she focused attention on Jimmy's defense rather than on how badly the plaintiffs had beaten him up. Positive thinking.

"But what can you do to cross-examine an autopsy?" Jimmy griped. "Maybe I should ask, 'Are you sure they're all dead?' All I could think of to do is to bring out the fact that they all died quickly. There's less pain and suffering that way. But I'm not sure it even works to point that out to the jury, how quickly these people died. It just emphasizes that they got incinerated. And that way, it increases the horror factor."

"The what factor?"

"The horror factor. A psychologist might not understand my terminology, but any trial lawyer would. I call it the horror factor. It's not logical, and so you can't argue against the horror factor by the usual kind of rational arguments. You can't reason with it, by saying that there's less pain and suffering in an explosion. It just makes the whole thing worse, because of the horror factor."

"Well, what did you do during cross-examination that you think might have worked?" Barbara was still trying to accentuate the positive.

"I asked him, 'Well, Doctor BAR-chee-KOW-ski, your autopsy reports don't even mention the Maxxco Construction Company, right?' And he had to say, 'That's correct.' Then, I said, 'Your reports mention the Louisiana Trucking Company's truck, don't they?' And he said, 'Well, not by name, but they mention the truck. Yes. That's correct.' And I spent about fifteen minutes repeating that same idea. The autopsy reports trace the cause to the truck, but not to Maxxco. Maybe it will confuse the jury."

"That sounds good."

"I guess." Jimmy was gloomy. "The point is, the autopsy evidence shows what a big risk Maxxco took. It cut the budget on this intersection, and those burned-up people are the direct result. I tried my best to get their attention away from that, and maybe it'll work. But I doubt it, because of the horror factor."

He stared at the ceiling some more. "And the jury loved the witness right after the medical examiner, the guy who was Herrick's metallurgist," he went on finally. "Guy from India. Named Dr. Oberoi Singh. He gave it to them real simple: 'The guardrail is too thin to resist a collision with a large, fast-moving truck, and it would bend and break just the way it did here.' He also used this simple analogy about how the posts were like a sumo wrestler up on stilts that were too skinny. Jurors all nodded and smiled at that. And then, when it was my turn, I had a hundred good questions to ask, but when I cross-examined this Indian guy, he was ready for all the questions. I'm not sure how."

"That all sounds sort of silly, those sumo wrestler analogies," said Barbara. "If it was me on the jury, I'd want something more scientific."

"Oh, this guy did that, too." Jimmy studied the bumps on the ceiling. "He talked about the electrical charge of the ferrous ion. The inverse square rule. The hexagonal and octagonal structures in the crystalline matrix of this alloy. And he even talked about computing tensile strength by using an elliptical integral of the third kind, whatever that is. The jury didn't understand a word of it, but they loved it anyway."

"Well, you had something to say about that, I'm sure."

"At one point, I did ask this metallurgist whether it wasn't a close encounter of the third kind, instead of an elliptical integral. I was trying to get the jury to see the guy as a pointy-head. To ridicule him. This Doctor Singh, he was completely confused by my question. The jurors all giggled a little bit. But the problem is, they giggled like they liked Doctor Singh."

Jimmy inspected the little bumps on the ceiling some more. He sounded really unhappy when he finally spoke up again. "Herrick's got the horror factor going for him, plus the humor factor, too. And I sure hope something changes, because otherwise, that's going to be an unbeatable combination."

❖ ❖ ❖

Something did change, sooner than Jimmy expected. And it happened with one of Robert's best witnesses.

The next morning was uneventful. Robert presented testimony from what he called the family witnesses. These were the bereaved husbands, wives, children, parents, brothers and sisters of the victims. It would take weeks to hear from all of them. They would tell the life stories of the dead and injured, and they would explain how life was different without them. All ending with the phrase, "I love him. I miss him so much," or the rough equivalent. For most lawyers, it would have been difficult at times not to become cynical about the family witnesses, because the testimony always was so painful that it had to be carefully coached, and the questions followed a well-scripted formula. But usually, the cynicism dissolved the moment a family witness said something raw and unrehearsed, backed by emotion that obviously was genuine. Jimmy Coleman's cross-examination of these witnesses was short. Mostly, it was confined to showing that the witnesses had no personal knowledge about Maxxco.

By mid-afternoon, Robert had put on two widowers, several brothers and sisters, and an orphan, all of whom told about their dead relatives and emerged from cross-examination untouched. It was a Friday afternoon. Time for a change of pace. Robert was a firm believer in strong finishes. He always adjusted for weekends and holidays, so that the jury would hear memorable testimony right before the break points. That way, they would have something to think about during the off days. Now, it made sense to show his videotaped re-creation of the disaster. This evidence would follow naturally after the family witnesses, and the weekend would give the jurors time to absorb it.

And so, the next witness Robert called to the stand was Howard Listrom, the audio-visual director at the firm of Robert Herrick and Associates. Howard always was a wonderful witness. He loved his work, and he had plenty of experience at giving testimony, because every audiovisual exhibit had to be authenticated by a witness who could explain how it related to the case. Robert took Howard crisply through the testimony about the video, starting with a description of Howard's beloved domain, the audio-visual production facilities at the firm. Howard explained the firm's methods for preparing medical models, reconstructing deformed vehicles by computer technology, and, of course, simulating accidents by videotape. And he explained how a picture of a truck, for example, could be scanned and accurately reproduced in the memory of a computer and then turned, rotated and steered over an overpass that was computer-generated the same way.

"And does Plaintiffs' Exhibit 119, the video reconstruction, fairly and accurately represent the accident according to the eyewitness testimony?" Robert asked. That was the question that would authenticate the videotape.

Jimmy Coleman's objection lacked the usual fire. In fact, the objection was kind of—well, kind of—perfunctory. Maybe Jimmy was having an off day. Or maybe he knew the video was admissible, and he was just going through the motions without really hoping to get the objection sustained. Judge Trouble overruled Jimmy's half-hearted objection and admitted Exhibit 119, the accident reconstruction. The jurors stared at the television monitor as Howard Listrom popped in the tape and started it rolling.

In the dimmed light of the courtroom, the jury saw the four-level spaghetti-bowl interchange from a helicopter's vantage point. The picture looked just like the overpass in the propane truck disaster, except that it had a cartoon-like quality that was characteristic of computer animation. But as Howard Listrom had explained, it wasn't really like a cartoon, since it was more carefully proportioned and more—well, more accurate. The viewer's vantage point, like an imaginary helicopter, soared around the intersection, showing it from all three hundred and sixty degrees. It was an impressive demonstration of technology, and that point was not lost on the jury. This exhibit looked authoritative, scientific, and precise, just as Howard Listrom had testified it would be.

Suddenly, the propane truck approached from the west. The points of the compass were marked on the video. The jurors recognized the truck from photographs already in the record of evidence. It, too, was accurate. They could compare the video truck to the one in the still photographs, and they could see how careful the computer reconstruction really was. Near the interchange, the truck realistically slowed and gradually turned onto the exit ramp. At this point, there was a jump, as the videotape shifted to slow motion.

Next, the jurors saw the silver Toyota. In the flash of lightning, which also appeared on the video, they saw the Toyota begin to spin, saw the truck move slowly into it, and saw the tank hit the guardrail. The rail parted easily, the way a knife parts butter. And then, just as the eyewitnesses had described it, the jurors saw the truck twist once as it dropped, saw the fireball envelop the screen, and watched the careening cars shoot into it. The wreckage afterwards looked just like the still photographs that were already in evidence. So did the damage to the silver Toyota, and so did the twisted remains of the spidery, spindly guardrail that Maxxco had so negligently constructed. The whole videotape was accurate. The jurors could tell that from comparing it with other evidence that they already had.

The bright lights came back on. The jurors blinked. Robert asked, again, whether the videotape was a fair and accurate reconstruction. "Yes," Howard Listrom answered.

"Pass the witness," said Robert Herrick.

Jimmy Coleman was on the edge of his seat. He could barely control himself as he started his cross-examination. "Mister Listrom, how much money did Robert Herrick's law firm pay you last year?"

This was an unorthodox beginning for a cross-examination, and Jimmy Coleman intended for it to be. The conventional wisdom is, you don't attack the witness at the beginning of the cross-examination. There usually are points where the witness will agree with you. Get those facts out first, before you attack the witness' credibility. But Jimmy had thrown the conventional wisdom out the window. With this particular witness, he didn't plan to start out nice. Instead, he was going to attack, attack, attack.

He had everyone's attention, at least. And when it took three more questions to get out into the open the fact that Howard Listrom had gotten paid more than two hundred thousand dollars by the Herrick firm last year, Jimmy was way ahead in the game. The witness looked evasive and sleazy. He looked like a whore who was bought and paid for.

"That video isn't a fair and accurate reconstruction at all, is it, Mister Listrom?" Jimmy almost shouted.

"It is, to the best of my ability," said the witness confidently.

"Well, let's see about that. Did you have any outtakes?"

"Sure," Howard Listrom answered. "'Outtakes' just means film that you decide not to use. You always have that. By the way, we gave all the outtakes to you, Mister Coleman, before the trial."

"Were there any outtakes that you produced where the truck went over the side at actual speed?"

The witness paused. Frowned. And thought for a minute. "I think so."

"You think so? There were actual-speed versions, weren't there?"

"Not 'versions' plural," Howard Listrom corrected. "As I recollect it, there was only one like that."

"Which you decided not to use!"

"Well . . . that's correct." The witness didn't understand why Jimmy Coleman seemed so much like an avenging angel. "We provided you with a copy of the actual speed outtake. Didn't you get it?"

"Your honor, I object to that last unresponsive remark and ask that it be stricken." Jimmy wanted to keep the jury from focusing on the fact that he'd had the outtakes. That would defeat his plan for destroying this witness.

"Sustained," said Judge Trouble. "The jury will disregard the witness's unresponsive remark and consider it for no purpose whatsoever." The jurors didn't understand all that, but they figured the witness was out of line. Jimmy was ready to spring his trap.

"Why did you decide not to use the version that showed the actual speed and replace it with a slow-motion version?"

The instant he asked that question, Jimmy regretted it. He wanted to pull the words back in. You should never ask the witness to explain anything on cross-examination. Never. If you do, the witness will climb up on a soap box, face the jury, and give an explanation that puts the best light on it that he possibly can. It may be the God's honest truth or it may be an utter falsehood, but the jury knows that the lawyer has invited the witness to give it. And now the witness, Howard Listrom, proceeded to take advantage of Jimmy's blunder.

"Because we wanted to make this videotape accurate as well as understandable," he answered in a puzzled tone of voice. "And I might add, as I said before, we provided all of the outtakes to you, Mister Coleman. The outtake that we decided not to use, it goes by so fast that the viewer is likely to miss important details. The ones the jury really ought to see. We thought this videotape, where the truck speed is altered to slow motion, showed it so the jurors could inspect it more carefully."

"Damn!" Jimmy was thinking. "I screwed that one up royally."

But then he realized that Howard Listrom's answer had given him a new opening. The witness had said the truck speed was "altered." Jimmy could use the unintended implication of dishonesty in that word to twist the testimony back around and then spring his trap.

"And so you gave the jury this *altered* videotape, is that right?"

"Maybe 'altered' is a poor choice of words," the witness backtracked.

But Jimmy wasn't going to let him get away so easily again. "In fact, the speed of the truck is altered from actual speed on this video, isn't it?"

"Well, it's slower. That's what slow motion is."

"And by using this altered speed, you also slowed down the speed at which the truck hit the guardrail. That's obvious, right?"

The witness was thinking. "Yes."

"So the *altered* videotape changes the speed of impact with the guardrail, right?" Jimmy knew that cross-examination really works well when the lawyer manages to pick up an unguarded phrase used by the witness and then uses it in his own questions. The altered videotape. The word made it sound dishonest, even if it wasn't. Which might not be fair to the witness, but that wasn't Jimmy's concern.

"Yes. Of course," said Howard Listrom. "That's what slow motion is all about. So you can see it better."

"And in the altered video, it looks like the rail breaks with a slower impact than what actually happened," Jimmy almost shouted.

"It doesn't look that way to me."

"And, of course, the altered video was altered precisely because the jurors would have seen that a truck traveling at the real speed was fast enough to break through any guardrail. Even if it was as strong as Fort Knox."

"Absolutely not," the witness said firmly. "That wasn't what we had in mind at all. You're twisting it around, Mister Coleman."

"And you made the altered version because you intended for it to be misleading."

Robert objected. "Counsel is arguing with the witness because he doesn't like the answer." But Judge Trobelo was watching the witness just as intently as the jurors were. "That's overruled," she said immediately. "Answer the question."

Jimmy took the opportunity to repeat the question. "You made the altered version because you intended for it to be misleading, didn't you?"

"No," Howard Listrom thundered disgustedly.

"And that's why, as you put it, you decided not to use the version that wasn't altered. You wanted to mislead and fool everybody in this courtroom!" Jimmy thundered. It wasn't really a question.

"No," the witness repeated.

"Didn't you think you had a conflict of interest in deciding to alter the videotape? During all this time, you got paid more than two hundred thousand a year by this plaintiff's lawyer, Mister Herrick. You wanted to help him in this case, didn't you?"

"That's not why I did it."

Jimmy was ready, now, to close in for the kill. "In fact, this altered video and the actual-speed video that you 'decided not to use' are both part of a cover-up by the plaintiffs' lawyers in this case, aren't they?"

"No!" shouted the witness.

But the pained looks on the jurors' faces showed that they thought the answer was yes. Robert realized, too late, that Jimmy had succeeded in turning the truth upside down. He had made it seem that the video was a misrepresentation of the facts, engineered deliberately by the plaintiffs' lawyers with the assistance of the man who now was on the witness stand. The jurors' expressions didn't change when Robert pointed out, on redirect examination, that the outtakes had all been provided to Mr. Coleman before the trial, and so there couldn't have been any attempt to hide anything at all.

When the smoke cleared, Robert miserably surveyed the damage. Jimmy had managed to portray an act done with innocent intentions as an act of rampant dishonesty. He had converted a situation of full disclosure into a cover-up by Robert. And he had turned the testimony of Howard Listrom, one of the plaintiffs' best witnesses, into an unmitigated disaster.

Tonight it was Robert's turn to go through what Jimmy Coleman had been going through. He was lying on his back staring up at the ceiling. "I'm going to lose," he said tonelessly.

"Oh, come on, Robert!" Maria protested. "You know what trials are like. I've won cases I was sure I was going to lose. So have you. This trial isn't over yet."

"I'm also going to get sued. For malpractice. I'm going to lose this case! Just like I lost those other three cases, in fact. And then I'm going to get sued myself, by my own clients, for malpractice."

"Robert! Shut up! If my family had thought that way, we'd still be on the beach in Havana!"

He did. For a minute. And he stared up at the cornice boards.

"After we finally ended the testimony for the afternoon, I went into the bathroom," Robert said finally. "I said to Kennedy, 'You know, Tom, we just blew the whole thing with that video, and we're going to lose.' And he says to me, 'I know it. We didn't do anything dishonest, but the jury thinks we did.' He just kept saying the same thing: 'I know it.' I went into one of the stalls. I felt like I was going to throw up."

Robert's voice had no expression at all. Maria waited and held her breath. "I didn't throw up," he went on, "but it took a long time for me to be sure I wasn't going to. I was in there for what seemed like forever, literally getting ready to wipe the barf off my pants."

He obviously didn't want to tell her the rest of it. But he needed to tell it, and so he did. "When I finally got out of there, Kennedy told me that one of our jurors had been in another one of the stalls in the bathroom. A man named Arnold Fries. An architect. We figure he will be the leader of the jury. Probably the foreman. Had his badge on, with 'JUROR' in big black letters, so there was no mistake about it. And this juror, Mister Fries, obviously heard me tell Kennedy that we had blown the whole case with the video."

"Oh, no," was all Maria could say.

"The jury foreman. He heard us predict we were going to lose. He couldn't have helped hearing it. Damn! Any decent lawyer is always aware of the possibility of jurors being within earshot, especially in the bathroom, and it's the kind of dumb mistake my clients just can't afford."

She put her arms around him. He could feel her breasts against his back, soft but forceful. "What can you do about it?" she asked finally.

"Not much. I suppose we can have the judge ask Mister Fries whether he heard anything. And whether he can ignore it."

He shook his head. "And of course, we can move for a mistrial because of what Mister Fries heard me say in the bathroom. Just like Jimmy's been doing about twice a day. Except now, we'll be the ones asking for the mistrial. And then, of course, the judge will do just like what she's done for Jimmy. She'll deny it. And she'll be right, especially since I'll be moving for a mistrial because of something I said, myself!"

He looked at the cornices again. "I'm going to get my ass sued all over the place for malpractice," he repeated, in a voice as dead as ice. "Right after I lose this propane truck case."

Jimmy Coleman celebrated that evening by telling Jennifer Lowenstein and Jeff Tait what was going to happen to them on account of the ill-advised caper where they fell through the ceiling at the country club. The law firm of Booker & Bayne had decided, after due deliberation, not to punish them at all. Jennifer and Jeff were going to get off scot-free.

"There are a lot of misconceptions about big law firms," Jimmy explained. "Paradoxically, these mega-firms can tolerate an exuberant range of non-conformity, as long as it doesn't hurt the clients, the other employees, the money, or relations with the courts. A behemoth firm like Booker & Bayne," he added, "will actually bend over backward to seem magnanimous to its errant lawyers."

In fact, if either Jennifer or Jeff had been a solo practitioner, the repercussions probably would have been much more painful, and they would have lost clients from the embarrassment. "But no corporate client's going to stop doing business with a firm like Booker & Bayne just because the associates happen to include a few who are like scarlet threads woven into the gray fabric of the other five hundred lawyers. Even if they're so sex-starved that they jump each other in a country club attic and fall through the damn ceiling."

And Jimmy made several more carefully chosen points to Jennifer and Jeff. "Be grateful," he said. "Don't do anything like this again, especially not any time soon. And keep billing three thousand hours a year on my cases. Because another reason the firm didn't come down hard on you, Jennifer and Jeff, is this. I reminded them who you work for.

"Me. Jimmy Coleman. And that's why you didn't get fired."

Jennifer and Jeff were profusely appreciative. This good news made for a perfect day, especially when it was added to the fact that they were immensely enjoying the way the propane truck case was going. Because in spite of how hard they may try to affect sophistication and detachment, Booker & Bayne lawyers were just like children, and they tended to enjoy themselves whenever they thought they were winning.

The next day was Saturday. Robert hated even to get out of bed. But he had to get up, because he had an important appointment, one he had promised to keep, one that had nothing to do with the propane truck case.

Tomorrow was the season opener for the University of Houston Cougars, the baseball team. And a long time ago—a lifetime ago, it seemed, before he had started worrying about getting sued for malpractice, before the propane truck trial had even started—Robert had promised to be on the baseball field at eight o'clock this particular morning.

He didn't want to go. He should be going to the office instead, to try to repair the damage that the videotape disaster had done to his case. For the thousandth time, Robert reflected on the most fundamental conflict of his profession. It was much easier for a lawyer if he never tried to have any other life than his work and if he never promised to go anywhere.

29
THE INSIDER

Head Coach Corbin York stood in the first base coach's box during the intra-squad game. Suddenly, he touched the right side of his baseball uniform, then he touched the left side at the script that said "Cougars," and next, he touched his nose, right ear, and elbow.

Robert sat in the dugout and watched as Coach York gave his signals. Every instinct told him that he should be working all weekend, especially after the thrashing that Jimmy Coleman had administered to him yesterday. But tomorrow, the Cougars would play the University of Texas Longhorns in the first conference game of the season, and Robert was a major supporter. He had promised Corbin York he would be here today, and Coach York had told the players. So Robert was here to keep his promise.

Now Coach York was touching his index finger to the bill of his baseball cap. This signal was the "indicator." The next signal would be the real one. The earlier ones were only camouflage, to confuse an opposing team. This touch of the cap was an instruction that said, "Watch the next signal and do what it tells you to do."

The Coach touched the left side of his chest. The hit-and-run. Even though it was only an intra-squad game, Robert felt his pulse quicken with the memories of thirty years ago. When he had played the game back then, the hit-and-run was the most exciting play in all of baseball.

The pitcher looked over his shoulder at the runner on first base. Cautiously, the runner crow-hopped toward second base. The pitcher stepped toward the plate, and at that instant, the runner jumped. The pitch was a fast ball, low and six inches inside, but the hit-and-run meant that the batter's responsibility was to hit it no matter what, and so he swung, almost vertically. The bat nudged the top of the ball, and it dribbled on four bounces straight into the third baseman's glove.

By now, the runner was only a few steps from second base. The third baseman looked up just as he started to hit the dirt. There would be no double play, because the runner was already there, and so the third baseman instinctively did the only thing he could. He made the long, looping throw diagonally across the diamond. The ball barely slipped into the first baseman's glove in time to nip the batter. And with that, the batter was out, but still, the hit-and-run had worked. The runner dusted himself off at second base, in scoring position.

"Beautiful! Excellent!" Corbin York's fist pumped the air. He waved his hand to stop the intra-squad game, and he shouted, "Everybody huddle up! Everybody huddle up!"

His face split into a grin. "Now that's just good baseball, that last hit-and-run was, and it's a beautiful, excellent game, just beautiful, whenever you play good baseball like the kind of baseball you just played, with that last hit-and-run," Coach York circumlocuted. Like all baseball coaches, he was incapable of direct expression. Instead, he had mastered the style of wandering and redundant speech that is characteristic of the breed.

Coach York didn't even stop to catch his breath, then, as he reached over to put his hand on Robert's shoulder. "And I'm glad you Cougars played good baseball just now, and I'm glad because of this man being here. And this man's name is Robert Herrick, and he's here taking time out of his incredibly busy schedule. You know, he's been trying that lawsuit about the propane truck that killed all those people, which was just awful, but he's here with us anyway today."

The Coach shook his head to show he thought the propane truck disaster was just awful, but he didn't stop rambling or even take a breath. "And this man, he's an important member of our team, Mister Herrick is, and the day he came on the scene, the future of this here ball club immediately started looking up. Because he took on this here team of ours! And he adopted it as his own! It was this man, who gave us the furnishings for the entire dressing room we use, and the visitors' room too, and lots of other contributions. And all you men need to get to know this Mister Herrick. Because back when he was in college, he pitched at the College World Series in Omaha, which is right where we're aiming to go with this Cougar baseball club of ours!"

The players opened their eyes wide when they heard that. This guy actually pitched in the College World Series? A couple of them made spitting noises that showed they were impressed.

"Thanks, Coach," said Robert. But he felt embarrassed, because Corbin York was laying it on too thick.

"Now listen up, you Cougars." Coach York got ready for his next non-sequitur. "Tomorrow's the conference opener." He frowned. "You got to keep your life on a short rope, meaning good self-discipline. What I mean is, you might have a girlfriend, and you might even love that girlfriend, but you got to love baseball more. Ten o'clock, that girlfriend's got to be out of your place. You can't have a long rope. You got to have discipline!"

Coach York touched his cap, like the indicator signal, before he charged into the next unrelated subject. "The conference opener. Tomorrow. And so what's important for you to think about? I'll tell you what it is. It's—attitude!" The Coach was shouting, now. "Even if you get ahead, you can still lose it, because of your attitude. If you tell yourself to let it go, you will lose it!"

Again, Coach York touched his cap. Robert was fascinated. "And also, to the converse, you can be behind and you can still win it, if you got the right attitude. You can come from behind to win the game, the whole game, provided you live your life clean and with a short rope, and if you got that come-from-behind attitude!"

Nobody cracked a smile. The whole team was listening. And Coach York couldn't have targeted his message any better as far as Robert was concerned.

"All right!" yelled a couple of players. The team crowded in a circle and stuck their hands together. They all shouted "Cougars!" before they broke the circle and ran to the locker room.

On Monday morning, just before he walked into the courtroom, Robert found out that the Cougars had won the season opener. Donna de Carlo relayed the message from Coach York. "The Texas Longhorns were winning by a score of three to two all the way from the second inning to the bottom of the eighth, and then the Cougars executed a perfect hit-and-run and scored a runner all the way from first base." After that, Donna said, "All hell broke loose, and Robert, coach says your adopted team finally buried the Longhorns by a score of eight to three."

At that, Robert's face split into a grin as wide as the courthouse doors, and he actually jumped up and down in the hallway. Tom Kennedy didn't quite understand, but he liked what he saw, because today, Herrick was enthusiastically saying to himself, "It's that attitude! That come-from-behind attitude!" Instead of trying to throw up in the bathroom.

Now, all that Robert had to do was to come from behind, himself. The videotape disaster was the last thing the jurors had heard on Friday, and now, on Monday morning, it was important to erase that memory. Herrick and Kennedy had rearranged their order of presentation so they could call one of their most impressive witnesses next.

"Your honor, the plaintiffs call William J. Winograd!" Robert told the judge. His voice had regained its confidence, and there was a smile behind each word. The bailiff brought the witness into the courtroom. Robert almost added: "This is our 'insider' witness!" but he stopped himself just in time.

William J. Winograd had on an expensive chalk-stripe suit, English shoes, and a solid gray tie. He looked like a million dollars, which in fact he was worth many times over. William J. Winograd had started his career as a civil engineer for Maxxco Construction when he was right out of college, and one of his first assignments had been to supervise the Maxxco concrete crews that were constructing the overpass at Interstate 610 and the Southwest Freeway. The propane truck overpass.

"I left Maxxco less than a year after I started," he told the jury, "and I went on to become the founder of the Winograd Engineering Group." With his meticulous gray hair and $600 suit, the witness didn't look like an engineer. He looked like an executive, which was understandable, since Winograd Engineering

Group, today, had ten billion in assets and operations in twenty-three different countries.

"Mister Winograd," said Robert Herrick, "when you worked for Maxxco Construction, you fought against the construction of this overpass because you thought it was dangerous. Is that right?"

"You're absolutely correct, Mister Herrick," said William J. Winograd firmly. "I certainly did oppose this overpass then, and I would oppose it if it came up today."

"Now, as an insider, can you explain the reasons you told Maxxco that the overpass was dangerous?"

Winograd answered crisply, and he pointed out all the problems on a blueprint. The first danger, he said, was that the passageway was too narrow. Also, the ramp lacked the proper banking to overcome the centrifugal force that might push a fast-moving vehicle outward and make it collide with the guardrail. And the rail itself wasn't substantial enough to hold a heavy object, such as a fully loaded tank truck, when it was pushed against it. The witness also explained why the ramp didn't measure up to the official standards of the American Society of Civil Engineers.

"Did you raise these concerns with the vice-president who supervised you?" Robert asked.

"Of course!" said the witness in a confident voice.

But when William J. Winograd had told his vice-president what was wrong with the overpass, the result had been puzzling. Immediately, Maxxco had transferred him to a job that involved supervising construction of a straight, flat highway in the Mojave Desert. But Winograd was persistent, and after he had sent four separate memos to the vice-president about this overpass, he finally got his answer.

The vice-president said there would be no change in the overpass. The soil embankments were in place and fully compacted, and the concrete pillars already had been poured. Any attempt to change the design at this late date would create a "ticklish situation." Those were the actual words the vice-president used in his return memo, "a ticklish situation!"

In every question after that, Robert referred to "The Ticklish Situation Memo." The Ticklish Situation Memo led Winograd to make a follow-up telephone call to the vice-president, but that didn't do any good either, because the vice-president just stuck to what he had said in The Ticklish Situation Memo, and finally, The Ticklish Situation Memo was one of the reasons William J. Winograd resigned. Out of the corner of his eye, Robert Herrick observed contentedly that every reference to The Ticklish Situation Memo made Jimmy Coleman react as though the present Situation was Ticklish, too.

"Pass the witness!" said Robert finally, in a tone of voice reminiscent of Coach York's come-from-behind philosophy.

"Mister Winograd," said Jimmy Coleman immediately, "wasn't the overpass perfectly proper under the standards of the American Society of Civil Engineers that were in existence when it was built?" His voice was pleasant and light. This was the conventional method of cross-examination. Get the witness to agree with you before you attack him.

"Yes, but I thought we ought to pay attention to the new, *proposed* standards that I learned about in college, especially since everybody thought they'd probably be adopted someday."

"Someday. And they weren't adopted until more than ten years after this overpass was built. Isn't that right?" Still the honeyed voice.

"That's right."

Jimmy shifted in his chair. "And the reason you resigned was that you were asked to resign, right?"

"It certainly was mutual, and the management at Maxxco didn't like me very much. I'll agree with that," admitted William J. Winograd.

"And one of the reasons you were fired was that you called your vice-president a quote, 'sorry, candy-ass son of a bitch,' unquote. Isn't that right?" Jimmy's voice had shifted too, and now it sounded like the kind of voice a person uses to talk to a dog after it has defecated on the carpet.

But William J. Winograd was unflustered. "Yes, I said that," he admitted. "But I only said it after my vice-president had addressed an even longer string of cuss words at me. Which I'd rather not repeat, because there's some chicks on this jury. And ladies—which—well, I respect all of 'em."

Mr. Winograd still had a lot of the salt of the earth in him. Robert cringed imperceptibly, until he cast a sidelong glance at the jury. The women were smiling and laughing. "Chicks," indeed! But they liked William J. Winograd, because he was such a familiar kind of character, and they weren't about to reject his awkward courtliness just because it came with a dose of political incorrectness.

"And all of this happened while you were less than a year out of college?" Jimmy asked.

"That's right."

"You sued Maxxco after you left, didn't you?"

"That's right."

"And you lost, didn't you?"

"That's right."

Jimmy Coleman stood up. "I have no more questions of this witness." He spat out the words.

Robert had anticipated all of this. "This forced resignation, did it have anything to do with whether you were a good engineer?"

The witness couldn't help smiling at that one. Neither could the jurors. "Heck, no! They told me that it was because of my being too obnoxious in complaining about this dangerous overpass. If I'd been a lousy engineer, I never could have gotten where I am today, president of a ten-billion-dollar company."

"And so," Robert asked, "would you say this forced resignation was just another part of Maxxco's cover-up?" It wasn't really a question.

"Objection, your honor, because this man can't possibly have personal knowledge of any such thing," said a disgusted Jimmy Coleman.

"Sus-TAINED!" said Barbara Trobelo. "The jury is instructed to disregard that question!"

But the witness did what he thought he was supposed to. He went ahead and answered the question, anyway. "Yes, it obviously was part of Maxxco's cover-up," said William J. Winograd pleasantly. The objection to the question had been sustained and the jury had been instructed to disregard it, but nobody had told the *witness* not to answer it!

"Objection!" said Jimmy again. "Sus-TAINED!" said Barbara Trobelo again. But it didn't do much good to instruct the jurors this time, because by now they were laughing too hard. William J. Winograd had gotten the last word.

In their private conversations, Kennedy and Herrick had always affectionately referred to this witness as "our insider." They hadn't been sure William J. Winograd would come across well in front of the jury. They had expected Jimmy Coleman to treat him like Benedict Arnold. Winograd had received a severance package of over thirty thousand dollars when he quit Maxxco, and during Winograd's deposition, Jimmy had sanctimoniously compared the thirty thousand to "Judas Iscariot's thirrrrty . . . pieces . . . of SILLLLL-ver." But here today, Jimmy's cross-examination hadn't even touched William Winograd. And his insider testimony had done a lot of damage to Maxxco.

In the crazy world of the courtroom, he'd even won points with the women jurors by referring to them as chicks. He was what he was, and nobody was going to shake him from the truth. Besides, some of the women seemed, secretly, to take it as a compliment.

Robert wanted to jump up and down and yell, "Hey, Coach York! How's that for the right attitude?"

But instead, all he did was smile and say, "Pass the witness."

The next six weeks of the trial were a blur while Robert called a steady stream of family members, psychologists, economists, and safety experts. The jurors got used to the rhythm. They went through three or four witnesses a day, mostly widows, widowers and orphans who wept for their lost relatives, punctuated by an occasional man or woman in a gray suit testifying on some technical subject. These witnesses got by with a little less bickering from the lawyers, because most of the dramatic testimony about Maxxco's negligence had already been heard. Jimmy handled the bereaved families with kid gloves, and there wasn't even very much that was fiery in the cross-examinations.

There still were a few minor skirmishes. Robert's clinical psychologist diagnosed some of the family witnesses as suffering from post-traumatic stress disorder, for instance, and Jimmy got mildly exercised about that. His cross-examination implied that Robert's "hired-gun psychologist" lacked the experience to recognize this "disorder," because after all, "the diagnosis of post-traumatic stress was first used to describe Vietnam veterans who suffered through constant battlefield carnage. Not civilians who learned of a relative's death by telephone!"

And Jimmy objected to the entire testimony of Robert's labor economist. But Judge Trouble overruled him, so the testimony came in, and Robert was able to show that the victims of the propane truck disaster would have earned a surprising amount of money if all of them had lived out their full life expectancies. It totaled in the scores of millions, in fact.

In the middle of a particularly dull week, Robert offered into evidence the report of the National Transportation Safety Board. He read a mild reference to the guardrail, in which the NTSB had concluded the obvious:

> "The subject guardrail, although constructed of standard kinds of ferrous materials, evidently was insufficient to withstand the force with which it ultimately was struck by the subject motor vehicle."

What this clumsy language meant was that the propane truck had crashed through the rail. Everybody already knew that, of course, but Robert read it in his best, most clear speaking voice, hoping that the jury would also understand that, in that strange tongue known as federalese, it meant the guardrail was too thin. It was "insufficient." Once more, he lamented the NTSB's inability to write a comprehensible English sentence.

It was a beautiful afternoon in late springtime when Robert finished his case by calling the last safety expert to the witness stand.

Aside from the technical jargon, there was nothing in this last witness's testimony that hadn't been said much more dramatically by the insider witness, William Winograd. Jimmy's cross-examination didn't seem to do much, and it didn't have any drama when it was compared to the cross-examination of the insider.

But now, the time was right, and Robert stood up at last to say, "The plaintiffs rest."

The "altered" videotape seemed like ancient history, and so did the disaster that it had produced. Robert felt good.

Miraculously, Pepper Herrick actually came to visit the courtroom on the last day of Robert's witnesses. What was more, Pepper didn't even act sullen. She even dressed appropriately and was polite. That was a major accomplishment for this particular teenager. Robert felt even better, at that.

And Grandma Rosalie Herrick helped by doing what she was best at, which was puncturing Robert's balloon when he needed to have it deflated. "Now don't you get cocky," she said to her son, "and don't you go getting a swelled head.

And don't you start thinking this run of good luck came along because you've led a Spartan clean life and you deserve it, or anything ridiculous like that."

Robert had learned from experience that he needed to listen to Rosalie when she talked this way. He struggled to make himself anticipate the darker days that might be lying ahead. Rosalie was reminding him that just because things looked good right now didn't mean they couldn't take a turn for the worse suddenly and without warning, and he knew that she was right.

30
ROLL CALL

The defense started its case the very next day. The Louisiana Trucking Company went first. And when the day was over, the news reporters rushed to get in on the six o'clock news, even though it was a confusing story.

At Channel 7, the six o'clock broadcast was known as "Action News." And it didn't matter that the story was hard to understand, because the reporters were grateful that the propane tank disaster still gave them such good material. The producer looked down from the control booth and cued the anchorman exactly as the music started to fade. At the front of camera one, the red light came on, and at the stroke of six o'clock, the anchor's head and shoulders filled a million television screens. "Good evening, friends," he said. "I'm John Moreno. And, This! . . . Is! . . . Ac-tion News!"

The anchorman favored his audience with a gleaming show-business smile. And then he followed up with the line that television journalists call a "tease." "Coming up next on Ac-tion News, the defense started calling witnesses today in the propane truck case. But the defense witnesses only seemed to help the plaintiffs!"

From the tease, you could tell that the propane truck case was going to be a big story. A minute is a long time in television journalism, and two-minute stories are reserved for truly cataclysmic events—such as the resignation of a president, the bombing of the World Trade Center, or opening day at the Livestock Show and Rodeo. Immediately after the tease, the screen filled with spectacular views of the city, followed by smiling portraits of the anchors, the sportscaster, and the weatherman, and all of these images were accompanied by the majestic kind of music that always fills the opening moments of a television newscast. But the audience could tell that the propane truck case would be the first story, and it obviously was going to be one of those sensational two-minute epics.

It was time, now, for the big story. And so the producer pushed a button, and a million TV screens immediately filled with file footage of the propane truck fireball. Through the magic of a television illusion known as chroma-key, John Moreno seemed to be sitting in front of the explosion, dramatically framed by the flames, almost close enough to be singed by the heat. "The Louisiana Trucking Company got its turn in the propane truck case today," John Moreno announced excitedly. "Afterward, each side claimed victory. But here's the big surprise: Courtroom observers think the trucking company's defense actually dug the hole deeper for the trucking company!"

The flames subsided, then grew again, and the Transco Tower glimmered behind the anchorman's shoulder. "Our Ginger Anderson is at the courthouse with this live report." And with that, John Moreno turned to watch the monitor.

Action News Reporter Ginger Anderson appeared on the screen, with the heavy doors of the Twelfth District courtroom behind her. "That's right, John." Her voice was breezy. "In a surprise move, the Louisiana Trucking Company called only one witness today before resting its case. That witness was the trucking company president, Phillipe LeClair. He testified that most trucking accidents are caused by improper construction of the roads, not by driver error, and he also said that this particular disaster happened because the overpass was too narrow and the guardrail was flimsy."

Ginger Anderson acted as though that testimony, in which the trucking company pointed the finger at Maxxco, was a wondrous development, and then she breathlessly turned to the meatiest part of her story. "But the trucking company president added that he had no quarrel with the astronomical damages claimed by the plaintiffs. This was a defendant, John, and he actually agreed with the plaintiffs' damages! And then the Louisiana Trucking Company surprised everyone and rested its case. Earlier this evening, I asked the trucking company's lawyer, Francel Williams, why he used this unexpected tactic."

Immediately, the screen showed Ginger's interview with Francel, who was saying: "Well, we rested our case after only one witness, because we're confident that the jury will see the truth, which is that Maxxco Construction is the guilty party, and our driver wasn't at fault." Francel beamed. "And this has been a fan-n-n-tastic trial, and the plaintiff's lawyers have done just a superb job!"

Then, the picture changed again, and the screen was filled with lettering that said, "ROBERT HERRICK, LAWYER FOR VICTIMS." It was superimposed upon an image of Robert speaking on film. "Well, it really isn't that surprising to see the defendants pointing the finger at each other, Watergate-style. And it's hard for anyone to say that the damages for two hundred and sixty-one plaintiffs are any smaller than that, and still be credible."

Robert had figured that a simple, straight answer was best.

Another scene shift. Here was Ginger Anderson, in front of the courtroom. "And with me here, live, is Jimmy Coleman," said the Action News Reporter. She turned toward him and asked, "Jimmy, how can you possibly defend Maxxco after the devastating events of today?"

"By pointing out what's already obvious to the jury," said Jimmy pleasantly. "Which is that Robert Herrick is a poor excuse for a lawyer, and his evidence is one hundred percent phony." He smiled his best thirty-two-teeth smile.

"Well, that's Maxxco's comment, and there you have it. This is Ginger Anderson, Action News, live from the courthouse! And it's back to you, John!"

With that, the two-minute epic was over. John Moreno went on to a story about local efforts to send a ship full of medical supplies to war-torn countries overseas.

❖ ❖ ❖

At the end of the two-minute epic, Robert and Francel stared at their television sets. They were in different homes, but each had the same look on his face. Both of the lawyers, as it happened, were watching the story that Action News had made of their trial, and each one shook his head.

Jimmy Coleman certainly represented his clients vigorously, but it was equally certain that he did it in a style that was all his own.

The next morning, it was Maxxco's turn. Jimmy started his case for the defense by calling the man in the silver Toyota to the witness stand.

The man's name was Clayton Wilchester. He was a stocky African-American wearing starched khaki work clothes and small gold-rimmed spectacles. He explained how the propane truck had slammed into him from behind.

"Man who was drivin 'at truck, he have a face white as a sheet. An' he have real big buggy-out eyes, like he's up on somethin," Clayton Wilchester testified. "Like he's up on somethin' like, maybe, speed or PCP. I don't know just what it was, but I guaran-tee, that truck driver looked like he was takin' some kind of off-brand medicine."

It was useless to object, so Robert just let it go. In his neat khakis, Clayton Wilchester made a good impression. He looked like a hard-working man who was precise and careful, and he had an interesting turn of phrase, too.

Jimmy asked the witness to describe how the propane truck went over the side.

"That truck driver was really haulin' it, time he whumped into me, an' he bounced slap-dash into that guardrail an' done broke it like it weren't even there," was Clayton Wilchester's answer.

"Then the truck wasn't going in slow motion, I guess?"

Clayton Wilchester did a double-take so big his neck should have snapped. "No, suh!" he said, and he made a noise that sounded more like a snort than a laugh.

Herrick objected a few times to some of the more far-out language that Clayton Wilchester used, such as "that truck looked like it was about to run off and leave behind all eighteen a them tires it had on, 'cause it was goin just about that quick!" But every time he objected, Judge Trouble just snapped, "That's overruled," and it wasn't long before Robert figured out that it was better just to shut up, hunker down, and hope for Jimmy to get finished with this witness. And Jimmy finally did finish, but only after Clayton Wilchester had the whole jury laughing and nodding their heads.

The next issue was the National Transportation Safety Board report. Jimmy wasn't content to let the report lie where Robert had left it, and so Maxxco's second witness was the bureau chief who edited the report. Jimmy got this witness to read out loud to the jury all of the conclusions that mentioned the truck driver. And he pointed out, over and over, "That conclusion doesn't mention Maxxco, right? In fact, the only person it says is at fault is the truck driver, right?" Jimmy milked it for everything it was worth. "And when all is said and done, there isn't a single accusation of negligence against Maxxco in the entire NTSB Report, isn't that right?"

And Jimmy concluded by reminding everybody that the National Transportation Safety Board wasn't a party to this case. The NTSB was completely neutral, and it was "a part of the Executive Branch of the Government of the United States of America. Isn't that right?"

Next, Jimmy put on three engineers from the Escher Engineering Corporation, who testified that the construction of the overpass had followed the engineering drawings to the letter, and that Maxxco hadn't done anything wrong. Robert felt like a punching bag during this entire testimony. And after that, it got even worse, because Dr. Randolph Murphy showed the jury how the accident reconstruction videotape looked when the truck was run at actual speed. The propane tank was a juggernaut on the television screen, and it sliced through the rail like a bull going through a picket fence. So much so, in fact, that it must have been painfully obvious to everyone on the jury that the rail didn't offer any resistance. It didn't prove anything, because Robert's experts had shown that a better guardrail could have made all the difference, but that wasn't the point, because Jimmy had turned the issue around. Never mind that it wasn't true, or fair. Never mind that Jimmy knew it wasn't done dishonestly. The question Jimmy was inviting the jurors to ask themselves was, "Why did that sleazy lawyer, Robert Herrick, doctor up the videotape?"

In all, Jimmy took two weeks for his defense. There were two safety experts who said there were four thousand trucking-related fatalities a year, mostly caused by the seventy percent of drivers who stay on the road longer hours than the law allows. And there was an ex-colleague of Louie Boudreau, who testified that the sawed-off Cajun always kept two sets of mileage records. One to show the government and one to collect his money, since he was paid by the mile. "But that's not unusual for us truck drivers," he added helpfully. Then the foreman, Pointevent, was questioned by Jimmy as a hostile witness, to show that the Louisiana Trucking Company pushed its drivers to break the law.

As his last witness, Jimmy called a white-haired, aristocratic man named Max Leitinger, who had founded the Maxxco Construction Company. When he vehemently denied that Maxxco had done anything wrong, even the walls seemed to shake, and Robert felt afterwards that he hadn't been able to touch Max Leitinger in cross-examination.

The defense rested, and later that evening, a shadow jury told Robert what he already knew. He had had a bad two weeks.

Two days passed. The lawyers fought over every word, every sentence and every comma in the instructions the judge would read to the jury. And at last, they were ready to give final arguments to the jurors. The shadow juries were consulted like modern-day oracles at Delphi.

Robert was exhausted as he turned on the TV set.

The six o'clock news. A million television sets were tuned in to hear about the end of the propane truck case, because the jury arguments finally were over. The anchorman favored viewers with his show-biz smile, and the swirling music, spectacular city views, and portraits of all the newscasters followed close behind. "Good evening, friends," said the image on the screen. "I'm John Moreno, and this . . . is . . . Action News!"

And then John Moreno was silhouetted in front of the fireball footage, with the flames curling artistically around his shoulders. "Lawyer Jimmy Coleman gave a final argument to the jury today in defense of Maxxco Construction Company. And he had almost as much fire in his speech as the fire in the propane truck disaster itself. In fact, the defense lawyer quoted more than a dozen philosophers, all the way from Socrates to Mark Twain, condemning what he called the greed and avarice in this case. And Mister Coleman told the jury that if the plaintiffs got the money they wanted, then every single plaintiff would collect a fortune just in tax-free interest every single year. He said that the plaintiffs were just trying to get rich out of blood money from this tragedy."

Next the screen showed the image of Jimmy arguing to the jury. "This accident happened for one reason, and one reason only," he was saying. "Because of the gross, criminal negligence of the truck driver. Louisiana Trucking let this man drive for forty hours with no sleep. And these lawyers"—he gestured over to Robert as he roared his condemnation—"these lawyers are so greedy that they made a doctored videotape, to try to hoodwink you twelve people into wrongly blaming it on Maxxco instead!"

With that, the anchorman, John Moreno, took over again. The fire was still exploding around him, as he said, "Robert Herrick shouted his summation for the plaintiffs. He blamed Maxxco Construction Corporation for a cover-up that he said was still continuing today. It was Jimmy Coleman who was trying to hoodwink this jury, he said.

"Mister Herrick reminded the jurors that engineer after engineer had criticized the guardrail. Maxxco's own engineer, William J. Winograd, said it was dangerous. And what did Maxxco do? They fired him. Then there was the number one jury panel member, Hartley Rehm. The plaintiff's lawyer said he was a man with no motive to do anything but tell you jurors the truth. Then, Robert Herrick told them why they should write a verdict for two hundred and fifty million dollars as damages, plus five hundred million in punitive damages."

The scene switched to a film of the courtroom, and the camera panned over the autopsy photos. "More than three dozen people were blown up, vaporized, and incinerated," Robert's voice was saying. "Maxxco caused an amount of suffering no one here can even imagine. Now their loved ones are going to have to live with that pain, day by day and year after year, for the rest of their lives.

Let's say you award only a small amount—say, a hundred dollars a day—to each relative. Three hundred and sixty-five days a year, day after day, year after year, it adds up to over a hundred million dollars! Add in the wages all of them would have earned if Maxxco hadn't killed them, and then you have more than 250 million dollars in mathematically proved damages."

The scene shifted back to John Moreno in the television studio. "Robert Herrick ended with a powerful plea that jolted everyone in the courtroom," said the anchorman. "We've got film, and we caution our more sensitive viewers that the autopsy pictures are graphic."

On the film, Robert was saying: "Let me do the roll call of the dead." He held a blowup of an attractive woman. "Marian Cortelli," he said. "That's name number one on the roll call." And with that, he exchanged Marian Cortelli's lifetime image for the lump-of-coal autopsy picture. A million television viewers gasped—just as the jurors had gasped, two hours ago in the courtroom.

Robert paused for a few seconds, then went on. "Bruce D'Arbeloff," he announced. "Number two on the roll call of the dead." A smiling young boy, whose picture was replaced by a hideous image from the autopsy. "Next, Felicia Vasquez." Robert held up the portrait of a white-haired woman, and then he exchanged it for a photograph of the same woman's charred flesh at the autopsy.

In every mass accident case he had ever tried, Robert had done this "roll call of the dead," and it always affected the jurors exactly as it was affecting these jurors now. Their eyes were shocked and wet, and their attention was riveted on the pictures. Robert ended with little Angela Gutierrez. First, a smiling lifetime photograph, with braces on her teeth and a velvet dress with a lace collar, and then, the gruesome image of Angela Gutierrez in death, with red blistered skin that alternated with coal-black burns. "Angela Gutierrez. On the roll call of the dead, she is the last." He paused, put the pictures down, and looked at the floor.

There was only one way, Robert said quietly, that he could describe his feelings about Maxxco Construction after looking at the pictures of little Angela Gutierrez. And that was by quoting a verse from the Holy Bible. The courtroom was hushed. The jurors waited. Finally, Robert said it, in a voice that choked and halted, a voice that went the range from a whisper to a shout and almost seemed to pin the back row of jurors against the courtroom wall, because there was not a trace of insincerity in these last, few simple words.

"For inasmuch as ye have done this unto the least of these, my children," Robert quoted, "ye have done it unto me."

31
KRONKENECK

The earnest young man on the left side of the television screen spoke first. "My name is Darrell Vaughan. I am an assistant district attorney. Do you understand that?"

"Of course I do." The man with the ugly eye almost was shouting, as if he'd been insulted. "I was the one that asked to talk to you, remember?"

The propane truck jury had gone home for the evening, but Robert hadn't. Instead, he had driven to the police station. The detectives had said they wanted to show him a videotaped statement from the man named Kronkeneck. A confession. They thought he'd better know about it.

So here he was, staring at the videotape, and wondering exactly what he ought to be watching for. Detective Slaughter sat beside him impassively.

"Mister Kronkeneck, you have the right to remain silent," Darrell Vaughan went on. "If you give up that right, anything you say can and will be used against you in a court of law."

"I know. And I've also got the right to an attorney, and I can have one appointed to represent me, and I can terminate this interview at any time."

"Correct. And if you can't afford one, an attorney will be appointed by the court for you, before any questioning. Understanding these rights, do you wish to give them up and make a statement about the charges against you?"

"That's why I asked to be brought here in the first place!"

Derrigan Slaughter reached for the VCR and pushed the fast-forward button. The split-screen images of the two parties to the interview jerked and blurred. "This assistant D.A.'s real, real thorough," the detective explained. "He done given the Miranda warnings about four different times. Drove old Squint crazy. Plus, he done tacked on an hour's worth a Squint's family history, plus his work experience, all a his engineering degrees, et cetera. None of which, do you need to see at all."

"I understand. I just want to see the part of the tape where he talks about me." Herrick was still puzzled about why this stranger had chosen him as the target of his assassination attempts.

"Okay. I think this'll be it." The detective moved his hand, and the tape clicked to a stop.

"—and that's how my daughter died." When the video picked up, again, in mid-sentence, the squinting man on the right side of the screen was battling to control his anger. "And I didn't have any health insurance, because I didn't have a job! And it's all because of what that lawyer did. That lawyer, Robert Herrick."

"What?" Herrick didn't understand. "Why's he saying all that?"

"Watch the tape." The detective shook his head. "Old Kronkeneck, he's about to tell you."

"I was a civil engineer for a different firm, then. Helvering & Coats." The man had an odd, fiery gleam in his good eye, and his squinting eye was completely closed. "We did contract work for the State. Along comes this Herrick, this lawyer, and files a–a–a lawsuit against Helvering & Coats! The lawsuit claimed somebody got killed on a job I was supervising."

Herrick recognized the case immediately. "My client was a state inspector who got disemboweled by Helvering & Coats' crane boom. Just standing there, and the thing absolutely tore his guts open. It's a miracle they managed to keep him alive. Turned out, Helvering's people had just left that crane running unattended, and they had even disconnected the safety catch."

"Yeah, but it don't matter to this loony tune. Listen."

"That lawsuit shut down our job site." The squinting man's voice rose. "It's a big outfit, Helvering is, but they laid me off, and all 'cause of this lawyer named Herrick." The word "lawyer" sounded like a dirty word, the way the man said it.

Detective Slaughter paused the VCR. "Now, a whole lot a what Squint says ain't true, but the point is, he imagines it's true. In real life, Helvering & Coats admitted fault and they paid up in your lawsuit, because its guys were negligent as all get out. And Helvering didn't 'shut down' the job. They finished it. As for Squint, he resigned—voluntarily quit—'stead a bein' laid off, like he said. Helvering & Coats even says he's eligible for rehire. The layoff was all in his head!"

The detective looked at Herrick before continuing. "But here's the deal. Kronkeneck figures that lawyers are responsible for just about ever' thing that's gone wrong in the mess he's made of his life. And one lawyer in particular. You. And problem is, he sure has got a great big imagination."

"So there was this earlier lawsuit." Robert was trying to sort it out. "My lawsuit against Helvering & Coats. And Kronkeneck thinks my lawsuit got him fired?"

"Not only that, but after he quit, he didn't have no health insurance, so he figures you killed his daughter. But actually, that don't make no sense either, since his daughter was killed in a car wreck. Guy has a real active fantasy life. Our shrink says Kronkeneck is what they call a narcissistic personality, which means he knows what he wants, what he feels, and what he imagines—but he don't care how much he hurts nobody else. Very intelligent. But unfortunately, Old Squint—he's narcissistic."

Detective Slaughter obviously liked that word. He said it again, and drew it out. "Squint is Nah-h-h-sis-SISSS-tick." It was a word shrinks used, and Slaughter, who had a taste for irony and redundancy and rolling rhetoric in the best Southern literary tradition, recognized it as a word worth savoring.

But Robert still was having trouble following it all. "And now, recently, I've sued Maxxco, and that case involves Kronkeneck, too. That's two lawsuits he's angry about."

"And this second lawsuit, the propane truck lawsuit, sorta made the guy snap. When he got fired—or rather, when he thinks he got fired—for the second time, outta lawsuits filed by that same Great Satan, namely you, Mister Herrick, that's when he sorta snapped."

"Well, I guess it's unusual that he'd be involved in two different lawsuits of mine."

"Maybe. Maybe not." The detective shrugged. "Kronkeneck's smart, but he's also kinda weird, and he didn't get along with *nobody*. And a lot a his business compatriots describe him as real accident prone. One guy said Kronkeneck was a walking negligence lawsuit, all by himself. Maybe that goes along with bein Nah-h-h-sis-SISSS-tick, I don't know."

Robert still didn't see why the man could be motivated to shoot him. He wondered aloud whether it would be worth meeting with Mister Kronkeneck and seeing whether he could talk this angry stranger out of his hard feelings. "Maybe he just doesn't understand what those lawsuits were about."

The detectives' eyes got big, and then an amused look spread over his face. "You'd sooner be able to talk Charles Manson outta doin' the criminal stuff he done. That Manson don't make sense to me, and same way, neither does this Kronkeneck. You got more faith than I do in reasonin' with people, Mister Herrick. More faith in human nature."

"That's the story of my life," Robert said. "And maybe I'll never change." He always hoped for—and believed—the best about people, even when it got him into trouble.

"You gotta remember, old Squint is locked up for capital murder." Detective Slaughter was calm and philosophical about it. "He's the one killed Harley Andrews. That DPS officer. And one a his miscellaneous crimes is, he shot you, too, Mister Herrick. He don't understand you, don't wanna understand you, and ain't gonna understand you."

"You're right, of course." The mention of Harley Andrews, once again, made Robert feel that old numbing mixture of depression, guilt, anger and fear.

Finally, he asked: "What did Kronkeneck say about the murder? Did he admit it?"

"Oh! Yeah. Real simple and clear, at the first part of the tape. He ain't insane, and he knows what he did. He just don't care much about his own crimes, 'cause he's narcissistic. I almost forgot to tell you about his confession to the murder, because ninety percent of the tape is about you, and about lawyers, and how much this guy hates all a you."

Derrigan Slaughter smiled. "And I'm glad we got him under wraps. I 'speck we'll keep him for a long time. Which is good for you, Mister Herrick, 'cause you're the one thing in his life that he really thinks about. You're the one constant thing, his pole star, the purpose of his life. To him, you're more important than a day's worth a fatback. And frankly, he thinks about you all a the time."

Robert left the police station feeling unhappy for Harley, unhappy for himself, and unhappy, even, for the squinting killer who'd ruined his own life. So that was all there was to it? Robert desperately wanted a world where things made sense. He needed for the murder of Harley Andrews not to be the random act of a demented failure. It ought to have some greater meaning. It frustrated him that he couldn't understand Kronkeneck's motives, or answer the one great question that drives all crime victims to unhappy frustration. "Why? Why is this nightmare happening to *me*?"

That thought gave way to a more chilling one. "This deranged man, this Kronkeneck-Squint, he's still deranged, and he still hates me. He'd like to crawl between the bars just so he could get out and shoot at me again. If he could, he'd like to find some way to take out his revenge even from inside those prison walls. He's that crazy.

"So I'm still not safe from this guy," he thought unhappily. "I never will be. He'll move heaven and earth to get at me, no matter how securely they've got him locked up. I just wish it made sense."

But important as it was, he couldn't afford to think about that now. The propane truck jury had just begun to deliberate. Robert was due at the courthouse early tomorrow morning.

32
THE WORST LAWYER

The first note from the jury was written in elegant capital letters, and it came after four hours and seventeen minutes of deliberation. It was in the handwriting of the juror named Arnold Fries, the architect, who had become the foreman of the jury, just as Herrick and Kennedy had expected. It said, "YOUR HONOR, WE NEED TO HAVE MORE INSTRUCTIONS ABOUT WHAT THE WORD 'NEGLIGENCE' MEANS." It was signed, also in neat, blocked capitals, by "A. FRIES, PRESIDING JUROR."

The note was straightforward and to the point, and it couldn't have sounded more innocuous. But immediately, both sides strained to guess at the motives of the jurors, as though the fourteen words in the note were an encyclopedia of their intentions, or at least a tarot card foretelling what they might do. Lawyers always know that this kind of crystal-ball gazing is foolish, but still, they can never avoid it. At the defense table, Jimmy Coleman tried hard to caution himself against optimism, and yet he knew that an analytical jury, determined to follow the judge's instructions and let the chips fall where they may, was Maxxco's safest refuge. This note was a good omen for the defense. The corners of Jimmy's mouth curled upward in a half-smile, half-sneer, and he settled back just the slightest amount in his chair at the counsel table.

As for Herrick, although he knew in the right side of his brain that the note was useless as an indicator, he read the tea leaves with his left brain just as Jimmy had. This was terrible. The jury wanted more instructions on negligence? These twelve people had lost sight of the big picture. This note was a sign that they were getting lost in the kind of technicalities that might let Maxxco squirm free.

Judge Trouble dealt with the jury's question in the usual way, by refusing to answer it. This was the time-honored method used by judges in Texas. "You are directed to carefully consider the court's charge to you, and the instructions," said the typewritten sheet of paper that the bailiff ferried in to the twelve citizens. The judge didn't want to flirt with danger by giving additional instructions, because the most likely result would be that whatever she said would give the court of appeals an excuse to embarrass her by reversing this important case.

At five o'clock, the jury was still working. In the courtroom nearby, the lawyers passed the time by talking about the Dallas Cowboys, the latest sex scandal in the legislature, and where it's best to shoot whitewings. And when they had exhausted those topics, they exaggerated at length, like fishermen, about the cases they had won, and they told equally mendacious but better stories about the ones they had lost.

At one point, Robert went over to Jimmy and shook his hand. It was a habit he had formed from the beginning of his practice. Even if you're angry, even if you don't like the opponent's tactics, force yourself to show the courtesy to approach him after the trial and shake his hand. But also, Robert took the opportunity to predict, "This jury's going to come out bragging on you, and saying that you're a much better lawyer than me. About how you're the best lawyer they've ever seen."

Jimmy frowned and vehemently denied it. "You're a much better lawyer, and the jury knows it because of that accident reconstruction videotape you put in evidence." And in spite of their battles, in spite of all the words in the courtroom, they both laughed.

These two adversaries knew that the lawyer who the jury thought was most clever, obnoxious and sneaky would lose, and yet, that lawyer would also be the one the jury would say was the best lawyer. To one side, the jury would award the verdict, which was the real trophy. To the other, the jurors would give the title of best lawyer as a consolation prize. No one knew, yet, which lawyer was which, but in the easing of tensions that occurs during long jury deliberations, even bitter rivals could forget the battle for just a moment—a moment that would pass like the eye of a hurricane. That was why Herrick and Coleman could banter, now, and kid each other almost like friends.

But both of them wanted the title of worst lawyer, to be labeled as the one that the jury thought was least cunning, least crafty. Because that lawyer, the "worst" lawyer, would be the one who would win.

The jury finally pushed the buzzer at 5:55 p.m. and asked to be let out. They went home at six, which was a more diligent work schedule than Robert was comfortable with. This jury was thinking too much, and that was dangerous, because the only way that Robert would win was if the jurors saw the case in terms of right and wrong. He dreamed that night about the jury's note asking for more instructions on negligence, but in his dream, the note was different. Instead, in nightmarish handwriting, he imagined that it asked, "Can we find Robert Herrick negligent, instead of the defendants?"

The next morning, the jurors started collecting in the jury room at 8:30. Judge Trouble had threatened them with contempt if they weren't there by nine o'clock, and all of the jurors were present at only ten minutes after the deadline. Again, Robert felt a twinge. This jury was too diligent for comfort. He didn't want a diligent jury, he wanted one that decided things in common-sense terms and that arrived at the courtroom just a little bit tardy. Human beings, instead of machines.

For twenty minutes the jurors met, and then, the bailiff brought in their second note. It was written in capitals again by the architect-foreman, Mr. Fries. "YOUR HONOR," the second note said, "WE WANT TO SEE THE ALTERED VIDEOTAPE. AND ALSO, WE WANT TO COMPARE IT TO THE UNALTERED ONE."

This was a bad sign for the plaintiffs. Robert's lungs started pounding when he saw it. But at the defense table, Jennifer Lowenstein and Jeff Tait hurried with footsteps as glad as the wind to retrieve both videotapes, and Jimmy Coleman even permitted himself to show his teeth. There was no question where the jury was headed with that comparison of the two sides' evidence. Robert could imagine the voices inside the jury room: "Why did that sleazy plaintiff's lawyer try to hoodwink us? What has he got to hide?"

It was Friday, and it made Robert even more unhappy when the jurors again were far too diligent. They stayed holed up in the jury deliberation room till 5:55 in the afternoon. But, mercifully, they didn't send out any more notes before the judge excused them for the weekend.

On Saturday morning, Robert did something he never did. He slept until noon.

Actually, it was not exactly true to say that he slept, because he woke up at six o'clock, seven o'clock, eight, nine, ten, and eleven, and he dozed for a few restless minutes in between. At noon, he decided to stay in bed and watch the tube. At first he tuned in to MTV and watched rock music videos. Then he switched to Yogi Bear cartoons.

At two o'clock that same Saturday afternoon, while Robert was watching Yogi Bear, Jimmy and Barbara Coleman sat in the bleachers at the Equestrian Center. Jimmy had wanted to do just what Robert was doing, sleep and watch cartoons. Or if he couldn't do that, he wanted to go to the office. But Barbara had vetoed both of those ideas, because, as she put it, "There's not a damn thing you can do any more to lie, cheat and steal your way into winning that case, you damn workaholic, and you've been ignoring me for just about long enough, and so you'd better take me to that damn polo match at the Equestrian Center."

And so here Jimmy was with Barbara, watching the River Oaks Charity Polo Match, not knowing the first thing about what was going on, because he didn't know a knock-in from a neckshot. He wondered whether he'd even know if either side scored a goal, and for that matter, whether a "goal" was even what it was called.

"That guy, there, is the prince," Barbara told him, and she pointed at one of the Oxford Knights. "They're the team with the funny purple helmets and the purple-and-white-checkered jerseys." The chestnut mare that the prince was riding flowed over the dark green grass while the prince's mallet swung invisibly in a semicircle to touch the ball and make it dart precisely across the field. Jimmy was vaguely aware that the prince moved to a position somewhere on the field that it seemed only he could know, to receive the pass back from his purple-and-checkered teammate.

Jimmy liked the bumps and hooks. "You're allowed to ride into the guy with the ball and ruin his shot," Barbara explained. "Sometimes these bumps are hard enough to knock the fillings out of the guy's teeth. You can also stick your mallet in the way." Jimmy was disappointed to learn that a cross-hook, where you reached up and hit across the guy's body, was a foul.

But it was the horses that were best of all, with their short manes bristling and their cloth-banded hooves sending divots at every step while the angular legs coordinated in ways that were impervious to the clumsy bridles of the mortals who rode them. The red jerseys of the American team, the Mavericks, moved with jerks and twists that were unknown to the English team, like cowboys at the Court of St. James. Finally, after what seemed to Jimmy like a couple of hours of confusion, the referee or umpire or whatever he was called blew the whistle and shouted, "Last chukker! It's over!"

The prince held his chestnut at mid-field while the Mavericks were still trying to line their red shirts up at the goal line. The score was eleven to two in favor of the Oxford Knights, and still the Englishmen were sullen as the Mavericks passed by. They had allowed these heathen to score an outrageous two goals.

"I love it," sighed Barbara Coleman, while her almost-six-foot frame drooped all over her smaller husband. "I love it, even if the prince is only a minor royal from Saudi Arabia who's studying at Oxford."

Jimmy reacted to the outcome of the game differently. He didn't like it when the English side won, especially when he was thinking about his own ongoing battle, with the propane truck jury still out. He wanted to be out somewhere in a hunting blind with his shotgun, killing unsuspecting birds or animals, preferably big ones. After he stopped thinking about that, he daydreamed about putting a polo mallet through a helmeted face that looked just like Robert Herrick's.

Monday morning. The weekend was over. The jury assembled at nine, and the lawyers settled in. To wait. And wait.

At ten forty-three in the morning, the jury sent out its third and final note. It was ominous for the plaintiffs. The note asked, "IF OUR ANSWER IS THAT MAXXCO CONSTRUCTION CORPORATION WAS NOT NEGLIGENT, DO WE EVEN NEED TO ANSWER THE QUESTIONS ABOUT HOW MUCH THE DAMAGES ARE?"

The lawyers had started a jury pool, which was just like a football pool except that it hinged on predicting the precise moment that the jury would pack it in for this Monday evening. The squares for the times between five-thirty and six in the evening were thickly populated. The squares before three o'clock and after eight were empty. When he saw this latest note from the jury, Robert swallowed and wrote his initials at the square for "4:55 p.m." Then he thought about those three painful cases, those devastating defeats, and went to the bathroom to nurse his stomach. More and more, the propane truck case was beginning to feel like the three he had lost.

To lawyers, there is no sound more raw and primeval than the noise of the buzzer that the jury foreman touches to signal that the jury has reached its verdict. The adrenalin rush, the dryness in the throat, and the hurrying heart all contradict the effort to avoid betraying the flood of self-doubt that the lawyer always feels. The sound makes even the most laconic attorney struggle to hide the anxious eyes that he turns toward the twelve strangers who are about to reveal how they have decided to use their awesome power over his case. It is an involuntary reaction, ingrained in trial lawyers the same way that Pavlov's dogs were taught to expect food at the sound of a bell.

Robert's stomach spun while the jurors filed silently to their seats. There were no smiles among the jurors, none at all. That was bad. What was more, they avoided making eye contact with the plaintiffs' lawyers while they stood at attention in front of their seats. That was even worse. And when the foreman handed the verdict sheet to the bailiff, he crossed his arms and looked at the ceiling. That, Robert knew, was terrible. And he also knew, with certainty, now, that he was going to get sued by his own clients for malpractice after this case— and he suddenly was sure that he would lose that suit, too, right after he lost this one.

Judge Trouble slowly adjusted her reading glasses. She counted the pages in the verdict form. She even looked at the edges of the paper, Robert noticed with dismay, before she started studying the verdict itself. It took her forever to read it, because the large number of plaintiffs meant that there were almost a hundred questions that the jury had answered. "Come on, your honor!" Robert whispered under his breath. "Tell us what it says before I have an accident in my trousers!"

Finally, Judge Trouble spoke. "The verdict is complete, and it is in order." And since the law required the judge to read the verdict aloud, she proceeded to do just that.

"The first question asks, 'Whose negligence, if any, proximately caused the incident in this case?'" Barbara Trobelo read. "And the jury's answer"—she paused to adjust her glasses before she went on, until Robert was about to yell, "Come on, Judge!"—"the jury's answer is . . . Louisiana Trucking Company . . . and . . . Maxxco Construction Corporation."

Robert's heart jumped, and he dared to hope. The jury had answered the first question the right way. Maxxco was at fault. But so was Louisiana Trucking. The plaintiffs weren't out of the woods, yet.

The second question asked the jury to assign a percentage of the blame to each defendant. This question was crucial, too. If the jury put only a small percentage of the fault on Maxxco, then Robert would lose the case. "And the jury's answer," Judge Trouble fiddled with the papers.

"Come on, Judge!" Robert thought. "They must have some kind of school where judges go, to learn how to drag it out when they read a verdict."

"The jury's answer is, ten percent of the fault is that of Louisiana Trucking, and ninety percent"—Judge Trobelo repeated it, because this was the key to the verdict—"Ninety percent. Ninety percent of the fault is Maxxco's."

Robert wanted to let out a whoop. He wanted to vault over the bench and give the judge a high five, or to jump the jury bar and hug all the twelve citizens at once. Surely the jurors knew what it meant, which was that the plaintiffs had won. Not quite a total victory, maybe, but close to it, because the jury had put ninety percent of the fault on Maxxco, the deep-pocket defendant, when they easily could have put ninety percent on Louisiana Trucking, and that would have meant that the plaintiffs would collect ten cents on the dollar. "God bless this careful, intelligent jury," Robert thought, because it seemed, now, that he had won the case.

But then, instantly, he realized that he hadn't won. Not yet. How much were the damages? The jury could still make him lose if it answered the questions about damages the wrong way. He had seen juries do that. One time, early in his career, a jury had awarded only nine thousand dollars in a wrongful death case, which had left his client's family without a father, husband or breadwinner.

Judge Trouble was looking at the edges of the verdict sheet again. It took her almost twenty minutes to read the damages that the jury had awarded. The answers came out in drips and drabs, some to this plaintiff and some to that one, and Robert wrote down the figures. At the end, he held his breath. The total was two hundred and fifty million dollars in actual damages, to compensate the plaintiffs, and five hundred million in punitive damages.

Robert stared in amazement. This jury had started with a terrible panel, and it had heard Jimmy's twisted argument about how the plaintiffs' lawyers wanted to fool everybody with a fake videotape. The jurors had been visibly disgusted, and they had been equally transparent in their distaste when they refused to even look at the plaintiffs' lawyers after delivering their verdict. It seemed like an awful jury.

But actually it was a wonderful jury. It had given Robert what he wanted; in fact, it had given him exactly what he had asked for, to the penny. He stood rooted to the floor, not daring to believe it, not daring even to move.

It wasn't time yet for the six o'clock news, but the propane truck verdict was such a big event that the Action News Anchor, John Moreno, interrupted a game show and broke into a million television screens. He was sitting at the anchor desk because there wasn't time to call up the file footage of the propane truck fireball. "This is an Action . . . News . . . BULLETIN!," he announced, and he got to the point without even giving his smile.

"Seven hundred and fifty million dollars!" John Moreno announced excitedly.

"That's how much the jury in the propane truck case says the defendants have to pay the families of the victims. That's a whopping three-quarters of a billion dollars, neighbors. And sources close to the case say that when you add in the interest from the time of the disaster until now, the final judgment will be well over a billion dollars. That's billion, with a 'B'!"

Now, at last, John Moreno's face formed the glittering smile. "Stay tuned for details from Action News at six," he enthused, "just twenty-three minutes from now!"

Four blocks away from the courthouse, in the county jail, a prisoner awaiting trial on murder and heroin charges flashed his gold tooth in a snarl. The tall, skinny inmate was only mildly annoyed when the game show got interrupted, but he went ballistic when he heard the jury's verdict. And then, this prisoner started yelling out loud when John Moreno had finished talking about the billion dollars.

But the prisoner only seemed to be hurling his words at the image on the television screen. In reality, the person Esparza had in mind was Robert Herrick, as he shouted his curses toward the flickering box. Finally, he quieted down, and he thought for a while, and then, at last, he said to the television image of Herrick, "That still ain't the end of it, you motherfucking son of a bitch!"

In the cell next to Esparza, there was another angry prisoner. This one had a folded, discolored, squinting eye, and he was charged with murder and attempted murder. This inmate hated Herrick even more than Esparza did, if that was possible. But he was much smarter than the case runner. Squint didn't scream. He contented himself with a blizzard of expletives.

But throughout his rage, Squint was thinking. It was an amazing stroke of luck, he said to himself, that the two of them were together in this jail. Esparza had the means by which to obtain revenge for them both, but Esparza was too stupid to see it. As for himself, Squint was powerless to act against Robert Herrick inside this jail, but he was smart enough to know what Esparza could do.

"All it will require, my friend, is a few words over the telephone to the right person," Squint explained. "And then, an army of lawyers will come to you, all eager to help you to ruin our mutual enemy."

And with that, Squint told Esparza where to place the call and how to seek revenge against Robert Herrick. The revenge of the assassins.

Back at the courthouse, the scene still was pandemonium. The lawyers hadn't left yet. Neither had the jurors. And the lawyers, as always, were curious.

In some places, lawyers are strictly forbidden to talk to the jurors after a trial. If an attorney even tries to talk to a juror without the permission of the court, the judge will all but hang him from the yardarm. Not so in Texas. If the jurors are willing, the lawyers can talk to them to their hearts' content, without checking with the judge, or the bailiff, or anyone else.

Tom Kennedy was chatting amiably with the architect-foreman, Mr. Fries, out in the hallway. The plaintiffs were grateful for the verdict, he told the foreman. "But why did you send out the three notes that you sent? Those questions made us think you were going to decide in favor of Maxxco."

"It was simple," said Mr. Fries, as Robert appeared beside Tom. "The notes didn't have anything to do with our decision. We knew what we were going to do after the first half hour we were in there. We just wanted to be sure we explored it from every angle."

"Great," thought Robert. "The only problem is, that method tends to inflict mental anguish and potential heart attacks on the lawyers who are trying to guess what the jury's doing." But still, he was grateful.

"Mister Fries, what was it that convinced you folks to decide in favor of the plaintiffs?" Robert wanted to know.

The foreman's face had been friendly, but now, suddenly, it turned red. "Do I really have to tell you that?" he asked nervously.

"No," Robert answered quietly. "You don't have to tell us, or anyone else." Sometimes it was tempting to stretch the truth so that you could get the information you wanted, but the last thing Robert would do, or even could do, was to misrepresent the law to a juror. "You're free under the rules to keep it a secret, Mister Fries, but you're also free to tell us if you're willing to. And it would help us a tremendous amount, because we'd know how to represent our clients better next time."

The man considered that. And he considered how he could say it. Finally, he just stammered it out. "Mister Herrick, everybody on the jury thought you were just too laid-back and lackadaisical in this case. Almost like you didn't care!"

He paused. Robert and Kennedy both froze. "Laid-back and lackadaisical?" When they'd been pulling all-nighters and fighting to keep their stomachs from exploding? "Didn't care?" After Robert's final speech, and the roll call of the dead, how could Mr. Fries possibly be saying these things?

"Mister Coleman was more skillful, and he was also more crooked," the architect-foreman continued. "It was obvious what he was trying to do with that videotape. He was trying to make it seem dishonest when it wasn't at all. And all the jurors were hoping you'd do something to defend yourself! We were pulling for you to do it. We waited. And you just didn't!"

Robert was dazed by what he was hearing from this juror. "Well, instead of defending myself, I tried to defend my *clients'* interests," he answered lamely.

"I understand that." Mr. Fries looked as though he was considering whether a lawyer ought to fight for his clients or fight for himself, even though to Robert, the choice was obvious. "But still," the juror's voice became plaintive, "we thought Jimmy Coleman was the best lawyer. He did more to represent his client. We finally saw the truth, but you didn't make us see it. We had to figure it out for ourselves."

"Well–but–that's why we have rules of evidence–and–well, that's what a jury is for!" Robert was dumbfounded.

Mr. Fries wagged his finger in Robert's face. "Here's what it came down to! Given the fact you did almost nothing to represent the plaintiffs, we had to do your job for you. In the end, we decided if we had any positive feelings about the plaintiffs' case, we'd better give the verdict to them, because it wouldn't be fair to decide the case by comparing the abilities of the lawyers."

Robert listened to this tirade with a stricken look. There was a silence when Mr. Fries was finished, and he tried to absorb it.

Finally, it dawned on Robert that the foreman's condemnation was actually the highest compliment the man could have paid him. Because one of the secrets of being a good trial lawyer, he thought to himself, is to do it so that the jury sees the truth, rather than admiring the lawyer's tactics.

It was the same, really, in any kind of craft. The poet works and reworks his lines until the taint of his own artistry is gone. He wants the words to sound natural and effortless, not stilted and forced. The painter seeks to capture the imagination, not show off his brushwork. Even the center fielder who makes a spectacular play earns a subdued admiration from his fans for making the tough ones look easy. And if it was true in other endeavors, how much more true it was of a trial lawyer like Robert Herrick. His performance was best when it didn't overpower the jurors. It was best when they said to themselves, "This lawyer's cause is just," instead of merely thinking, "My, isn't that a clever lawyer."

It was amazing that juries did what they did. They reached the truth, Robert believed, much more often than anyone who wasn't familiar with them would ever have guessed. It happened precisely because of the naïveté, the guilelessness of the citizens who made up the twelve. Together, they were more than the sum of all of them. And that, in a nutshell, was the genius of the civil jury.

"Thank you, Mister Fries." Robert shook the man's hand, and he meant every word as he looked him in the eye. "Thank you for helping me, once again, to understand what being a lawyer is all about."

And then he realized that Mr. Fries had called Jimmy Coleman "the best lawyer." He recalled his banter with his adversary, before the jury returned. "But the best lawyer may be the one that the jury thinks is the worst lawyer," he thought with humility. "The one who is patient, who helps the truth to come out, instead of the one who has all the tricks."

As Robert left the courtroom, he heard a loud commotion. Jimmy was talking, or rather, he was shouting, to a news camera. "Yes, we'll appeal. This is a horrendous injustice. We'll appeal to every court in the country. And believe me, we'll investigate every juror until we find some kind of jury misconduct, because I know there has to have been misconduct for it to turn out this way!"

He spluttered on in that vein, blaming the jury, the judge, and even his own junior associates, until Robert, mercifully, was out of earshot.

Maria Melendes heard about the verdict a few minutes after it was announced. She was there, just outside the courtroom, to congratulate Robert and give him a hug. Maria's sister, Elena, was with her, seeming even more bouncy and turned-on than Maria, and she gave him a hug, too. Elena always seemed unnaturally enthusiastic, Robert thought, but maybe this was the time for it. The two DPS officers, standing as bodyguards inside the courtroom, offered their congratulations. That was when Robert realized that the jury had returned its verdict at precisely four fifty-six. His guess had been four fifty-five—only one minute off. "I even won the football pool—I mean, the jury verdict pool, or whatever you call it," he said and blinked his eyes.

Finally, Robert Herrick, feeling like the world's greatest trial lawyer, broke away to call Rosalie. Excitedly, he told his mother that he had won the biggest verdict he had ever gotten. It probably was a record verdict for a case of this kind in this state, and maybe in the whole country. More importantly, it was right. It was just. It was fair to his clients. "And please pass the word on to Pepper and Robbie."

But to his surprise, Grandma Rosalie wasn't impressed.

In fact, there was something in her voice that said this victory was Robert's alone, not something to share, and certainly not something that was important in the grand scheme of things. "That's nice, I suppose," she said.

"And now," Rosalie added, "I have something that I need to tell you." Her tone was dead of any emotion as she said it, and it stopped Robert in his tracks. He had been shell-shocked by the verdict, but now, Rosalie had his full attention.

When she went on, Rosalie's voice was flat and even. "Pepper is pregnant," she said. "Robert, do you suppose maybe you can come down from Mount Olympus long enough to help us arrange for your daughter to have an abortion?"

33
MOTION FOR NEW TRIAL

Sitting there in the family room, he closed his eyes. For the thousandth time, he thought how sickening it was to see his daughter with a lifetime's worth of dreams lying wasted in her hands, when she was so beautiful, so smart, with so many advantages. This was a nightmare that only a parent could feel, in which all of the outcomes were too repulsive even to imagine without the most feral, most atavistic kind of dread. Flesh of his own, the intended object of all his toil, she had been defiled, desecrated, by this degrading union with a prurient, weird-looking jerk of a kid who had tattoos up and down his arms. And now, she had a life inside her, and that life, too, was flesh of his own, the child of his child.

But then, just as painfully, he opened his eyes. "Get it together," he told himself. "You can't begin to solve this problem by wishing it didn't exist." And at last he was able to force an uneven calm as he looked across the coffee table at Pepper and Rosalie.

"You should do the right thing," he said finally, "which is to have the baby and put it up for adoption."

"That's ridiculous," Rosalie retorted. "The only sensible thing to do is for her to get an abortion."

"Well," Pepper announced, "I want to thank both of you for your help and support. But what I want to do, actually, is to have my baby and keep it."

They stared at her. It had been almost a week since the propane truck verdict, but Robert hadn't had a chance to enjoy the victory. Pepper Herrick needed to decide, and decide quickly, on a different kind of verdict. What should she do about her pregnancy? Her family's disagreement was so profound that Rosalie referred to the growth inside Pepper's teenage womb as a "fetus," while Robert and Pepper both called it "the baby," and Pepper, meanwhile, glowed when she talked about setting up "the baby's room," which just about sent Robert and Rosalie into orbit.

Now, the sunlight slipped through the white plantation shutters in the family room of the huge pink brick River Oaks home, and it wrapped softly around Pepper's long auburn hair while her family stared as if she had just arrived from another planet. And yet, Robert and Rosalie were united only in disagreeing with Pepper. They disagreed with each other as much as each of them did with her.

"I'm not trying to force any philosophical views of mine on you," Robert said quietly. "This isn't about what the Supreme Court says. And it's not about the abortion debate. It's about you. Because the decision to have an abortion—well, it's so final. It can't be changed. And the memories would come back to haunt you if you lived a hundred years."

Grandma Rosalie frowned and shook her head. "You have no idea how terrible it would be if you tried to keep the baby, Pepper. Terrible for you. And terrible for this young man, this . . . this Jonathan Morse." Rosalie's arms were crossed, and she shook her head. "What kind of life can you build for a baby when you're in high school? With a young man you don't even know?" Rosalie was certain of the answer, and her voice was firm as she went on. "An abortion isn't just the only sensible decision. It's the only decision that's kind, and caring, and respects the rights of other people."

"Rosalie, that's just wrong," said Robert. "Pepper, if you have an abortion, for the rest of your life you'll wake up in the middle of the night screaming on the anniversary of the day you did it. It'll feel as though—well, you'll feel as though you've taken the life of your baby. You'll figure out when his birthday would have been. And every time you see a child, you'll die inside yourself, thinking about what might have been. This Jonathan Morse, I've met him, and he seems like a pleasant kid. I bet he'll cooperate with putting the baby up for adoption."

"Yeah," said Pepper. "But let me tell you this, Daddy. And Grandma, too. That's . . . just . . . not what I want to do."

This was the same sullen child, thought Robert, who was famous for her irresponsibility. How could Pepper possibly be a–a–parent? Last year, for instance, she had stolen her father's MasterCard and shared it with her friends. Nine different teenagers had used the purloined card to buy a small fortune's worth of sweaters, jeans and leggings from Neiman-Marcus. How could she possibly be a parent? She was still a child herself, and a difficult one at that.

If Pepper ever finished her homework, it was because either Robert or Rosalie stood over her like a policeman, and even then, half the time she got no credit for it, because she forgot to turn it in. This was the same child who wanted to set up "the baby's room." Even her classmates knew she couldn't be depended on. If you made plans to meet Pepper at the Galleria, you'd better be ready to hang around the mall all by yourself. After one of Pepper's no-show episodes, Robert had insisted that she start wearing a watch, but then he had had to buy her three different watches in a week. She kept the last one for ten days before losing it, too.

She was barely old enough to drive a car, but she was old enough to get pregnant. And to decide she wanted to keep the baby!

And yet, for a second, Robert listened to Pepper talking calmly about this impossible situation, and he thought to himself: "Well, maybe she's old enough." Pepper's usual response to polite requests from Robert or Rosalie was to ignore them, if that was possible, or if it wasn't, to deflect them with a loud stream of adolescent vituperation. But that wasn't what she was doing now. Strangely, here were the adults handling this debate clumsily—Robert and Rosalie had promised each other to disagree in private, and not to subject Pepper to their own anxieties and conflicts, but they both felt so strongly that it seemed they couldn't help arguing their cases against each other in front of Pepper. And yet, Pepper wasn't responding childishly. In fact, she listened quietly and stated her positions sensibly.

"It's been a couple of years that I've been absorbed in the propane truck case," he reminded himself. "She's not just fifteen any more."

She had acted maturely by telling her family immediately, and just as maturely, she had told Jonathan Morse. She had made detailed plans, she had gotten books from the library about childrearing, and she had been to the doctor a half-dozen times without being told. Maybe, . . . maybe it would turn out all right. . . .

But immediately, Robert knew it wasn't so. Calm responses didn't mean that Pepper had suddenly gained wisdom beyond her years. And her ability to engage in adult behavior, like getting pregnant and planning for a family, didn't change the fact that she was still a child. "The right thing to do is to place the baby for adoption, sweetheart," he told his daughter gently.

"Well, I still think that's like buying more trouble than you ever dreamed of," said Rosalie. Then she sat up straighter and changed her voice. "Your Daddy and I both love you and we'll be with you no matter what happens. I know it's hard for you to know what to do."

"That's right, sweetheart." Robert's voice, too, was quiet.

Pepper laughed a nervous little laugh, and then she said, "Well, I disagree about that. I'm sure it's going to be hard *doing* it. It's going to be a long, hard road, and I don't have any illusions about that."

She looked first at her father, then at her grandmother. "But even if I'd rather it happened a little later in life, I got myself into this mess. And I'll tell you this: As far as I'm concerned, it's not hard to know what to do. Because I know exactly what I plan to do about it." She paused, but it was a pause for emphasis. "I plan to keep my baby."

The next day was a Monday, and regardless whether the baby controversy was settled or not, it was time to go back to work.

Robert sat alone in his office, at the big mahogany desk. Summer was only a few days away, and the magnificent view out the west window shimmered with a blue sky and a broader expanse of vivid green than Robert could remember ever seeing before. The red and orange geraniums under the greenhouse-style glass were more brilliant than they had been a month ago. This morning, he had felt exhilarated by the shining earth and sky. Yet now, he felt an odd sense of foreboding as he pulled the document out of the envelope with Booker & Bayne's return address on it.

It was Jimmy Coleman's Motion for New Trial in the propane truck case. Robert had known it was coming, and now, here it was. The motion would accuse the judge and jury of all kinds of errors, and it would say that the verdict should be set aside and a new trial should be held.

It was just a motion for new trial. Nothing to worry too much about.

Filing a motion for new trial was standard procedure for a lawyer who'd lost a jury trial, Robert reminded himself. It was purely routine, and there shouldn't be any reason for the butterflies he already felt in his stomach before reading this document. The heading at the top of the document looked routine:

```
         IN THE TWELFTH DISTRICT COURT
             OF HARRIS COUNTY, TEXAS

PEDRO GUTIERREZ, et al.,          )
                                  )
         Plaintiffs,              )  NO. 93-185483
                                  )
    v.                            )  DEFENDANT MAXXCO
                                  )  CONSTRUCTION
LOUISIANA TRUCKING COMPANY        )  CORPORATION'S
and MAXXCO CONSTRUCTION           )  MOTION FOR NEW TRIAL
CORPORATION,                      )
                                  )
         Defendants.              )
```

There was nothing unusual about the appearance of the motion for new trial. It looked the same as hundreds of others that he had seen filed by losing lawyers in a hundred Texas courts.

The introductory paragraph also was standard, and it said the things Robert had expected it to say:

> "This Motion for New Trial is based upon the remarks and rulings of the court during jury selection; upon errors in the admission and exclusion of evidence, and in the court's instructions to the jury; and upon newly discovered evidence, jury misconduct, and the gross misconduct of the plaintiff's attorney, Robert Herrick."

In today's adversary system, it wasn't unusual for the losing lawyer to charge that the winning attorney was guilty of "gross misconduct," and so that didn't cause Robert any alarm. But he immediately flipped the pages to look for the allegations that supported Jimmy's accusation of misconduct. It was more curiosity than concern, Robert told himself, that made him search for these particular allegations first.

He finally found it on page thirty-one, and he began reading what Jimmy had to say. His stomach tightened and his breath quickened as his curiosity drove his eyes on. These allegations were so . . . so . . . crazy! And anyway, how on earth had Jimmy Coleman managed to find out about all these things? How had he managed to distort them so badly? This was what was written there, in paragraphs seventy-eight through eighty-two of the Motion for New Trial:

> "78.   Plaintiff Pedro Gutierrez hired his attorney, Robert Herrick, through the illegal services of a case runner, who was an individual named Esparza. Robert Herrick knew, then and there, that his deal with this case runner, Esparza, was illegal.

"79.   Knowing that it was illegal, the plaintiffs'
        attorney, Robert Herrick, illegally suppressed
        evidence of this nefarious arrangement with the
        said Esparza, because he wanted to cover up his
        violations of the disciplinary rules for
        attorneys. Under those rules, the aforesaid
        Robert Herrick was subject to disbarment, and
        therefore he unlawfully and wrongfully hid the
        truth about the arrangement with Esparza.

"80.   Because of this gross misconduct of Robert
        Herrick, Maxxco was unable to discover the
        evidence of the deceased ten-year-old child,
        Angela Gutierrez, who had witnessed the tank of
        the propane truck fly over the guardrail rather
        than through it. Specifically, the deceased
        child stated that she had seen the 'truck of
        fire' go 'over the rail,' before causing the
        accident.

"81.   This evidence from Angela Gutierrez would have
        shown the jury that the propane tank flew over
        the guardrail, not through it. Therefore, it
        would have shown that the guardrail could not
        possibly have prevented the propane truck
        disaster, since the guardrail could not have
        stopped an object that went over it.

"82.   This statement by Angela Gutierrez would have
        caused a different result at trial if it had
        been heard by the jury, because it showed that
        Maxxco's construction of the guardrail had
        nothing to do with the accident."

There even was a puzzling allegation that the death of Angela Gutierrez "was
caused not by the propane disaster, but instead, by an overdose of heroin."
"Bizarre!" thought Robert. But his curiosity had given way to anxiety, and then
to worry, and now it turned into panic as he read further:

"83.   Robert Herrick conspired with an Assistant
        District Attorney, whose name is Maria
        Melendes, to have her violate the public trust
        and ignore her oath of office, so that she
        would suppress and hide the evidence of the
        case runner, Esparza. Among other reasons, the
        said Maria Melendes performed these illegal
        acts because both she and the plaintiffs'
        attorney had a conflict of interest, which
        arose from the fact that these two attorneys,
        Robert Herrick and Maria Melendes, were
        conducting an illicit, meretricious and
        clandestine sexual affair.

"84.   It was because of this illicit, meretricious
        and clandestine sexual affair that Assistant
        District Attorney Maria Melendes illegally
        covered up the said evidence of the case
        runner, Esparza, in agreement with her sexual
        partner, Robert Herrick."

Robert felt his stomach rising. He got up from the mahogany desk and stared out
the south window. This was a twisted, malicious distortion! The true facts didn't
bear any resemblance to the awful conduct these accusing paragraphs described.
It had all been so much more innocuous than Jimmy made it sound. His motion

didn't even mention Icky Snopes, or the threat to Icky's life, or the fact that Robert had been compelled to help Icky, unless he wanted him to be killed. It was all the product of Esparza's lies. And as for Maria, she hadn't "conspired" with anyone. She just hadn't believed that murderous liar Esparza!

But then, he realized that he'd have a hard time clearing up the distortions just by blandly telling the truth. The truth was, he had paid Esparza, even if he did it from the purest and noblest of motives. And Maria had ended up protecting him, even if she did it because Esparza was a liar. The legalese in Jimmy's motion for new trial left no room for human understanding. It twisted everything! Robert stumbled toward the washroom at the corner of his office. The scope of the disaster became plainer and plainer to him with every second that he thought about it.

There would be a hearing, he knew. A hearing of this motion for new trial. And that hearing, he also knew, would be more dramatic, more sleazy, and more sensational than the trial had been. It also would be more public and more newsworthy. It would titillate people all across the country, because the story of intrigue, sex, drugs, murder, and misuse of public office would be the stuff of network television hype. All of the national networks would be there, ABC, CBS, NBC, Fox, and CNN, and also, there would be reporters from the *New York Times*, *Time*, and *Newsweek*. And for that matter, from the *National Enquirer*.

And, of course, an incidental result would be that Robert Herrick and his family would be destroyed. So would Maria Melendes. Robert made it to the washroom barely in time to aim in the general direction of the commode.

It wasn't easy to tell Maria. But he did tell her. About Pepper's pregnancy, and about Jimmy's motion for new trial.

Maria knew the answers. "Pepper's right," she said. "She should keep the baby. And Rosalie's right, too. Pepper should get an abortion. Those are two sensible solutions."

She wrinkled her nose. She sounded as disgusted as he had ever heard her sound. "The only one who's wrong, Robert, is you. You're just repeating what other people have told you, other people like the Rotary Club and the Catholic Church, because that's the kind of people who would happily say that Pepper ought to make herself into a pariah and torture her body pointlessly just so she can give her baby to somebody else. That's not the solution. All it is, is your own struggle to keep yourself politically correct." She looked as if the words were something rotten that she had to get out of her mouth.

"I guess I just don't agree with you," was all that Robert could say, miserably. Once again, he struggled against the vision of his daughter, his beautiful daughter, with a lifetime of dreams slipping through her hands, and with that fragile life inside her. Yet his own influence was fragile, too, like a clumsy gardener's attempts to water a desiccated orchid. The pain in realizing his powerlessness was overwhelming. Only a father could understand just how painful it was. For all of her life, his daughter had depended upon him to protect her and to fix whatever went wrong, and now he couldn't fix it. Also, for all of her life, she'd been the one thing that mattered most to him. Maybe Maria could afford the luxury of judgmental certainty. He couldn't.

Maria also knew exactly what he should do about the propane truck case. "Settle it," she said firmly. "For whatever you can get. And don't ever discuss the allegations in that motion for new trial with anybody. Not now, not ever."

He was aghast. "But all that Maxxco's willing to offer to settle the case is fifty million dollars. That's one-fifteenth of the judgment in a case my clients have already won! They'd never agree to it. And if I advised them to settle for fifty million, I'd be betraying them."

"I don't care if it's fifty million dollars." She sounded panicky. "I don't care if it's fifty cents! Because the other option is, all of those plaintiffs can wait until the judge wipes out that judgment, by *granting* this motion for new trial! Because Jimmy Coleman has got everybody trapped, and the judge is going to grant the motion, no question about it! And then, the judgment is going to be *zero!*"

Maria was firm and determined. She also was scared. "Get the plaintiffs to settle it! You can talk them into it. You know it's the right thing to do, to protect their own interests. If you don't, you're not going to believe the kind of disaster that's about to come down!"

But he couldn't settle it. The date for the hearing came closer and closer. Jimmy Coleman could smell the blood in the water. And finally the day came, and Esparza the case runner was there for the hearing on the motion for new trial, sitting in the walnut-paneled witness chair in the Twelfth District courtroom, wearing pajama-like prison clothes and jail-issued flipflops.

The word was that Esparza had made a deal to plead guilty in exchange for getting a thirty-five year sentence, which would probably see him paroled in eight to ten years. As for Booker & Bayne, it had spent almost twenty thousand dollars worth of attorneys' time to get Esparza here from the county jail by a special kind of subpoena. But it was worth it. Jimmy Coleman looked positively regal in his excitement. He expected to get his money's worth out of this witness.

The misshapen gold tooth flashed as Esparza told how he had signed up Pedro Gutierrez's case by telling Pedro that he was *un abogado,* a lawyer. Esparza also told the judge about his fake cards with the scales of justice and about the contract Pedro signed with the attorney's name left blank. And he explained how a junior high school dropout, "like me, Esparza," could make a killing as a case runner, even if he'd never spent a day in any kind of law class.

Esparza told how he'd peddled the case to Robert Herrick and about the twenty-five thousand dollars. And he told about the meeting with Tanya and Tina, the Sausage Girls, at the Play Mate Club.

"Mister Esparza." Jimmy Coleman made the witness's name sound like a title of excellence. "Mister Esparza, will you tell the judge, please, what Angela Gutierrez said, right before she died?"

This was the crucial moment. "Objection," said Robert Herrick. "Even assuming this poor child said anything to this Mister Esparza, this miserable piece of human wreckage, it would be improper for this court to hear it. It's covered by the attorney-client privilege."

Judge Trouble hesitated as though she thought she hadn't heard him correctly. Then she looked at Robert. "But it can't be covered by the attorney-client privilege, because Mister Esparza isn't an attorney. Everybody agrees on that."

"But your honor, all that's necessary for the privilege to exist is for the client to believe he's an attorney," Robert explained. "Rule 503 makes it clear that the focus is on the client's belief, not on whether the 'lawyer' is really what he seems to be. And so if Pedro Gutierrez believed Esparza was a lawyer, that's enough. It's covered by the privilege."

Judge Trouble still looked puzzled. "Look at it this way, your honor," Robert went on. "If the lawyer is an impostor, the client isn't to blame for that. And all of the evidence shows that Pedro Gutierrez believed Esparza was a lawyer. He genuinely believed it. And so it's covered by the attorney-client privilege. Rule 503 says so."

"Well, but that only counts if the client's belief is reasonable," Jimmy countered. "And no reasonable person would have believed that this Mister Esparza was a lawyer. For starters, Esparza didn't even have an office. And besides, the attorney-client privilege doesn't exist if it's used to perpetrate a fraud. Or a crime. And here, it was used to perpetrate both a crime and a fraud!"

Robert spoke up. "And judge, I also object on the ground that this evidence would be hearsay. The witness is being asked to repeat a statement that somebody else, namely Angela Gutierrez, said to him. Under Rules 801 and 802, it's a classic example of inadmissible hearsay."

"But judge, it fits the exception for a dying declaration under Rule 804," Jimmy shot back. "It's just like those old-time homicide cases where the victim identifies the murderer."

"But it doesn't qualify for that," Robert answered immediately, "because you can't prove that Angela Gutierrez was aware that her own death was imminent. And that's what's required for a dying declaration." Robert held up the rule book. "The statement has to have been made by a person who 'believed that his death was imminent.' Angela Gutierrez didn't know she was going to die, and so Rule 804 doesn't fit."

"Hold it. Hold it!" Judge Trobelo was waving her hands. "We're going to take a recess. Give me an hour to study your briefs, and if I see it's going to take me longer than that, I'll let you know."

Both lawyers had expected this battle. Both sides had written briefs for the judge to read, each of which was more than fifty pages long. Jimmy Coleman's brief gave a dozen reasons why the attorney-client privilege didn't apply, plus a dozen reasons why Angela Gutierrez's dying statement was admissible. And Robert Herrick's brief gave a dozen reasons why each of Jimmy's dozens of arguments was wrong.

Barbara Trobelo returned to the bench almost two hours later and looked just as puzzled as she had been before the recess. The only difference was that she now was ready to announce her ruling. "The rules of evidence weren't written with anything like this situation in mind," she said. "And I may be in for a hindsighter by the court of appeals. But here's my decision. The objection is overruled, and Mister Esparza will be permitted to testify about what Angela Gutierrez said."

Judge Trouble went on to explain her ruling. "This wasn't a conference with a client. Even if Pedro Gutierrez believed that Esparza was a lawyer, they were in the presence of a third-party witness, namely the child. And as for Angela Gutierrez, whatever her intention might have been at the time she spoke, it certainly wasn't for the purpose of getting legal advice. So my ruling is, the attorney-client privilege doesn't apply to the statement made by Angela Gutierrez."

Then, she turned to Robert's other objection. "The testimony technically is hearsay," Judge Trouble announced, "because Mister Esparza is being asked to repeat what he heard another witness say about how the accident happened. But I've concluded that it fits Rule 804, which says that a dying declaration is admissible in spite of the hearsay rule. Because the child did die within a short time, and there was a do-not-resuscitate instruction, and she could have been aware from her surroundings that she was going to die."

"That's the way the rules of evidence are," Robert thought miserably. "They have nothing to do with justice, and everything to do with technicalities. So what if there was a do-not-resuscitate? What did that have to do with trying to find out the truth?" But Judge Trobelo had decided, and that was that.

And so Esparza testified. The propane tank had gone over the rail, not through it, and so nothing that Maxxco had done in building the rail could have made any difference. That was the dying declaration of Angela Gutierrez. The court should grant Maxxco a new trial so that the jury could hear it.

"Pass the witness," said Jimmy Coleman finally.

Now, it was Robert Herrick's turn to cross-examine Esparza.

"You lied to Pedro Gutierrez when you said you were a lawyer, didn't you?"

"Yes."

"And are you being just as truthful to the court, today, as you were to Pedro Gutierrez?"

"No. I lied then. But what I've told the judge today is the truth."

"And you didn't mention Icky Snopes. The lawyer you actually peddled this case to, instead of me."

"Icky Snopes? Never heard of a lawyer named Icky Snopes. What kind of name is that for a lawyer?" Esparza was able to tell the lie with a straight face, because he had had plenty of time, in jail, to practice it.

"You telephoned Icky Snopes, and you had him call me. Instead of calling me yourself."

At that, the prisoner's eyes opened wide, and his sneer gleamed in derision. "Not just no, but *hell* no, Mister Herrick!" Esparza lied firmly. "You knew exactly what I was when you paid me the twenty-five grand. And there ain't no Icky Snopes involved in any of it!"

Esparza was a confessed liar, but he managed to sound truthful as he thundered this last accusation. The hatred boiled and burned in his eyes. Robert had underestimated the man's emotions. It was his hatred that made Esparza reckless enough to be convincing.

"It's fair to say that you dislike me, isn't it?" Robert went on.

"That's an understatement," said Esparza.

"And you came up with this concocted story just so you could besmirch me and save your own skin from charges of murder and selling heroin, didn't you?"

"No."

Robert nibbled at the edges of Esparza's testimony. Maybe he'd done enough to show that the man wasn't believable. But then again, maybe he hadn't, and anyway, the judge listened to his whole distorted story. Even down to the point that ten-year-old Angela Gutierrez hadn't died because of the propane truck disaster, the way Robert had proved to the jury that she had. Instead, everybody now had heard that little ten-year-old Angela allegedly had died from an overdose of heroin, administered by the same man who claimed he had sold the case to Robert Herrick for twenty-five grand.

It wasn't true. Or at least, it just wasn't an accurate description of the way Robert had gotten into the case. As he looked around the courtroom, Robert wondered what all these people believed, and he wondered whether even the truth could save him.

One thing was certain. The reporters loved the motion for new trial almost as much as Robert Herrick now hated it. The testimony from Esparza made lip-smacking prose on the six o'clock news.

"Good evening friends. I'm John Moreno, and . . . this . . . is . . . Action . . . News!" The inevitable file footage curled around his shoulders before John Moreno went on. "The hearing in the propane truck case keeps getting stranger and stranger, neighbors. Today, lawyer Jimmy Coleman called three surprise witnesses in his attempt to get a new trial for his client, Maxxco Construction.

The witnesses described how attorney Robert Herrick admitted paying a fee of twenty-five thousand dollars to a man he knew was a case runner."

There was a filmed interview with Esparza, conducted by Action News Reporter Ginger Anderson. And highlights of Esparza's testimony. Then, the screen shifted back to John Moreno, with the propane truck fireball behind him. "When the man named Esparza was finished, that wasn't all the defense had, because the other two surprise witnesses were topless dancers!" The anchorman enunciated these words with gusto.

The flames behind John Moreno burned higher, and the cyclopean eye of the Transco Tower winked. "These two topless dancer/witnesses were identified as Tanya and Tina McIngvale." The anchorman shook his head in disbelief, as he went on to the most salacious part of the newscast.

"These twin seventeen-year-old girls, Tanya and Tina, are exotic dancers, known as the . . . Sausage Girls, and they testified that Robert Herrick admitted making an illegal payment of twenty-five grand. According to the Sausage Girls, Herrick's admission took place at the topless bar called the Play Mate Club, while Tanya and Tina were dancing naked at his table at the very same moment!"

Again, there was no mention of how the case actually had been referred to Robert. The fact that he'd acted to save Icky Snopes' life was too complicated for sound bites.

It couldn't get any better than this, all the news reporters agreed. We are guardians of the First Amendment, servants of the freedom of speech, and preservers of American values. And it sure is great when we find ourselves forced, absolutely forced, to serve up a lip-smackin' story that combines hard news and soft core porn the way this one does.

The next day of the hearing started with a carnival atmosphere. The correspondents from ABC, NBC, CNN, *The New York Times*, and the *National Enquirer* all sat in the front row. Immediately behind them, in the heavy brown seats of the Twelfth District courtroom, were the reporters from CBS, Fox, AP, and the *Wall Street Journal*. The story was getting good. It was prurient enough now for daily network coverage. Especially when the next witness was called. "We call Assistant District Attorney Maria Melendes," Jimmy announced. "As an adverse witness."

Slowly and heavily, with her head down like a prisoner, Maria Melendes trudged up to the witness stand.

"State your name, please," said Jimmy Coleman.

"Maria Melendes." Robert couldn't look at her, but out of the corner of his eye, he saw that Maria looked ill as she was forced to testify in support of Jimmy Coleman's motion for new trial.

"Ms. Melendes, you are an assistant district attorney?" asked Jimmy.

"No. I was. But I've been suspended."

"While you were still an assistant district attorney, did you ever have occasion to meet a man who is a case runner, a man named Esparza?"

Maria breathed deeply and looked at the floor, and she paused for a long time before the words finally tumbled out. "Under the authority of the Fifth Amendment to the United States Constitution, I respectfully decline to answer that question on the grounds that it might tend to incriminate me."

The words were barely audible.

But Jimmy persisted. "And Ms. Melendes, did you take action to hide, conceal, and suppress the testimony of that same man, the case runner named Esparza?"

"Under the authority of the Fifth Amendment, I respectfully decline to answer," Maria repeated in the same miserable tone.

Jimmy had succeeded beyond his wildest expectations. He had made Maria look like the defendants she herself had prosecuted, as she participated, now, in destroying her own reputation. She belonged among those wrecks of humanity who stretched and squirmed like the cowards they were to avoid the consequences of their crimes. It was worse, though, because of the role reversal. Here was Maria in the dock, accused in the same way that she had accused others. It was the Constitution she was invoking, but her words sounded like the evasions of a criminal. She would have preferred to shout out the truth, but she couldn't, without risking the possibility that a grand jury might believe only part of what she said. It was cruel for Jimmy to continue, but it also was like him to want to continue, and so he did, with evident relish.

"And the reason you hid and concealed and suppressed Esparza's testimony," Jimmy thundered, "was because you were having a clandestine, illicit, and fornicatory sexual affair with Robert Herrick, the plaintiff's lawyer in this case. Isn't that right?"

Maria looked like she was about to suffocate as she took the Fifth Amendment again.

Mercifully, Judge Trouble stopped the proceedings. "It's improper to ask questions of a witness when we all know the witness has a valid claim of Fifth Amendment privilege," she said firmly. Maria's non-answers would mean nothing to the decision of the case, the judge added. "And everyone should respect the Constitution. This witness has a right to rely on it, just like anyone else."

With that, half of the reporters ran out of the courtroom. The other half clustered around Maria as she left, like scavengers covering a dead carcass. They wanted to badger and cajole her and to try to get her to answer the same questions she had just succeeded in avoiding by taking the Fifth Amendment.

34
WAKE THE DEAD

The room had been used at different times by Robert Herrick as a study and by Patricia, his late wife, as a sewing room. At this moment, it was cluttered with the debris of corrugated boxes and plastic sheeting which had held the baby furniture. There was a brass crib with moveable sides, a huge mobile with every character Disney ever invented, a swing, a changing table, and a comfortable chair for nursing. And there was a stack of raw tan packages sitting by the window still waiting to be opened.

This was the baby's room.

"What color would you like on the walls?" Grandma Rosalie asked.

"Blue, I think," Pepper Herrick said. "The walls ought to be blue, since the baby's going to be a boy."

Robert Herrick had arranged specially with the manufacturer for the mobile that would twirl over his grandson's head. When it had finally become clear that there would be a baby's room, Robert had firmly taken charge of this issue. There was only one tune that would do, only one song that he wanted for the boy, even if it meant that this would be the only five-thousand-dollar baby mobile in existence. For the third time this morning, Pepper wound it up.

"My silly Daddy," she murmured, and she and Rosalie dissolved in laughter while it played, "With a loud haloo, he would wa-a-a-ke the dead / And the fox from his lair in the mor-ning!"

"Be still, little one," Pepper said, and she ran her hand over her swollen belly. "He's going to be an athlete," she told her grandmother. "Just like his father. And his grandfather."

Downtown, at the courthouse, the hearing on Jimmy Coleman's motion for new trial was entering its third day. Jimmy had finished with Esparza and the Sausage Girls, and he had demolished Maria Melendes.

Finally, this morning, he presented an accident reconstruction expert who said it was "consistent with the physical evidence" for the propane tank to have gone over the rail. Just as little Angela Gutierrez had said. Then the cab would have crushed the guardrail from above and left it broken in exactly the way that the photographs showed.

And that, of course, meant that the guardrail didn't have anything to do with the accident. It was compelling testimony, and Jimmy had made a strong case for a new trial. With that, he rested his case for Maxxco.

The judge turned to the other side of the courtroom. "Mister Herrick," asked

Barbara Trobelo quietly, "do the plaintiffs wish to call any witnesses in opposition to the motion for new trial?"

"Yes indeed, your honor!" Robert answered. And he spoke confidently for the first time since this hearing had begun. "We have . . . a very important witness."

He expected to catch Jimmy Coleman flatfooted. There usually isn't much discovery before the hearing on a motion for new trial, and there hadn't been anything that would alert Jimmy to the next witness. For that matter, there was nothing that would make him suspect that Robert could even find this witness.

Judge Trouble glanced at the clock. "This is a good time to break for lunch. Everybody be back at one-thirty."

That meant Robert would have to wait before springing his trap. But he still felt confident, even if he looked a little disappointed.

Courtroom gadflies love surprises, but they don't like to be surprised. From top to bottom, the courthouse buzzed with rumors. Everybody, but everybody, wanted to be the first to figure out what Herrick had up his sleeve.

The cameraman from Channel 4 sounded excited. "Herrick's about to roll over. I could hear it in his voice. He's gonna give up and agree to a new trial!"

"A trial lawyer?" said the woman from NBC dismissively. "Nah! Not after winning the jury. I bet it's just another expert witness, a real boring one. And Herrick's trying to build it up."

"My guess, it's the doc who treated little Angela Gutierrez." This was the man from the *National Enquirer*. Then, somebody else said it might be a prisoner who'd heard Esparza tell a different story in jail. Or maybe it was the man in the silver Toyota. And on and on.

Jimmy Coleman had relaxed after he finished his witnesses, but now, at one o'clock, he paced in the hallway. Just thinking. And stewing. Robert noticed with satisfaction that Jimmy walked faster and faster as the clock approached one-thirty.

"What's this big surprise you've got?" asked the man from the *Houston Chronicle*.

"I'm sorry." Robert did his best to sound mysterious. "I can't tell you yet."

The propane truck survivors stared straight ahead with sunken eyes. The verdict had cheered them, this hearing had stung them, and now they just wondered what they'd have to put up with next. A gaggle of Maxxco employees jabbered away, like kids at McDonald's, about how Jimmy had "whupped up" on the plaintiffs.

But at one twenty-nine, as the lawyers tumbled into their seats and the reporters licked their pencils, the question still hung over the courtroom like smoke over a hickory hollow.

Who on earth was Herrick's secret witness?

It was one twenty-nine and fifty seconds when the clerk pounded on the chambers door. "Order in the court! Everyone rise!"

Judge Trobelo ascended imperially to the bench, with the light from the huge overhead lamps glinting from her little gold glasses and the green marble behind her.

"Be seated, please." She turned to the plaintiffs' table. "Mister Herrick?"

He stood and stretched his hand toward the entrance, slowly. With a stern look on his face and his back ramrod straight. He wanted to make the spell last as long as possible.

"Your honor," Robert announced dramatically, "the plaintiffs call . . . Louie Boudreau!"

The bailiff just stared at him instead of going out into the hall to get the witness.

Everyone else stared, too.

"That's correct." No one could blame him for savoring the moment. "The plaintiffs call Louie Boudreau to the witness stand. Louie Boudreau! The driver of the propane truck!"

Instantly, the courtroom was in an uproar. The bailiff shook his head as he stepped into the hall. Judge Trouble admonished everyone to remain silent, but it didn't do any good. It was a full five minutes after the bailiff had returned with the witness before Robert could ask him any questions.

The mystery man was five-foot-six, with the shoulders of a bear and the arms of a longshoreman. He had a bumpy face and Vaselined black hair, and an odd habit of lifting slightly from the chair every time he answered a question.

"State your name for the judge, please," said Robert.

Jimmy Coleman was pale, and his eyes were cloudy yellow. He looked like he wanted to get up, but he sat frozen in his chair.

"Louie Boudreau," was the answer.

"You are the man who drove the propane truck?"

"I am."

"And you are the man who was in the cab of the propane truck at the time it fell off the overpass?"

"I am," said Louie Boudreau. Again, the courtroom erupted, and Judge Trouble called for silence.

"Did the truck go over the rail?" Robert asked.

"Of co'se not!" the witness answered in a Cajun accent. He rose an inch or two out of his seat.

"Did any part of the rig, the cab or the tank or any other part, fly through the air and go over the rail?"

"No. It all done gone th'roo de guardrail."

Jimmy Coleman still looked as if he had seen a ghost. His face was white and his mouth was open. In a manner of speaking, that was exactly what he was looking at, the spectre of the dead driver.

"Describe for the judge, then, how the truck went over the side of the overpass," Robert said.

"It done gone crashin th'roo dat guardrail, like it wasn't dere at all." The witness bounced slightly. "I nev' gone forget dat sound, wif de steel rails breakin into all dose pieces! An' me knowin I was about to be daid."

"How can you be certain the tank didn't go over the guardrail?"

"I jus' know!" said Louie Boudreau firmly. "An' de raison I know is—well, I been dere!"

"What happened after the accident?"

"Door to dat cab, she fly open, an me, I fly raht th'roo dat door," the witness answered. "An' I guess I'm lucky, very lucky, and I'm protected by Saint Louis, because when I hit de groun', I done hit de groun' ronning. It just weren't my time of death."

"You hit the ground running." That wasn't too surprising, for the man who drove the propane truck. "And where did you go after that?"

"Back to Louisiana, raht away, to keep from gettin' arrested. When I figured out it wasn't safe dere either, I went to Canada. To Quebec. I knew all 'long, I'se in troble."

"You expected to get arrested if you stayed around?"

"You darn tootin'!" the witness answered. "I'se the driver of the in-fo-mous propane truck, and it's for sure, I didn't stick around!" For the third time, the spectators made too much noise for the hearing to continue.

When they settled down, Louie Boudreau said, "But by now, dat statute of limita-shon, she done run out, an' I can't no more be arrested today!" And that set off the spectators again. The courtroom went wild for a long two minutes.

"How'd you get caught, then?" Robert wondered.

"Comin back to America, the Immigra-shon asked me what citizenship, and I say U.S.A. But dey hear me talkin, an' dey get suspicious, 'cause dey never heard anyone talk Cajun. An' dey ask, what city you born in?, an' I say de firs' thing that popped in mah head, which is, 'I was born in Boo-falo, New York!'"

"'Boo-falo'?" Robert pretended to be puzzled. "Ah! You meant Buffalo, New York."

There was silence in the courtroom, then sniggers, and then wide-open laughter. "An' dey guessed it raht away," the witness explained unnecessarily, "that I was not born in Boo-falo."

"You got caught because of your Cajun accent, then?"

"That's raht," said Louie Boudreau. "And I tol' dem gentlemen from Immigra-shon, I plead guilty to mispronouncin' Boo-falo, but I don't have to plead guilty to no crime today." He grinned. "An' dat's when dey read up on dat short little old statute of limita-shon, and den dey let me go!" The courtroom buzzed.

"What about the body that they found near the cab of the truck and thought it was yours?"

"Dey need to go back to the drawin board on dat one," the witness answered. "'Cause de autopsy report on me, it'd be pretty much exaggerated."

Judge Trouble intervened for the umpteenth time. "I need to remind the spectators to keep silent." But the courtroom was in an uproar and stayed that way.

"Your honor," Robert explained when the noise level lowered, "I have informed the medical examiner's office that Mister Boudreau is alive. Obviously, they agree that the autopsy report is in error. A fracture of the ulna was the only identifying mark they had to go by. They're working around the clock to find the true identity of the body, a person who coincidentally had a broken bone in the same place this man does. And your honor, I'll be glad to call Dr. Bill back to the witness stand if you have any question about any of this."

"No!" The judge's answer was immediate. "No, that won't be necessary. And I assume this is the final witness."

She stared at Louie Boudreau, then blinked, then looked back at Robert before repeating it. "The final witness."

"Thank you, Mister Boudreau." Robert took the hint. "Pass the witness."

Jimmy Coleman talked to Louie Boudreau for two minutes or so about the guardrail and the propane tank. But he didn't really cross-examine him. Under the circumstances, that would have been well nigh impossible, because Jimmy wasn't prepared to cross-examine a dead man.

Back in River Oaks, the afternoon approached its end, and the shadows lengthened on the lawn in front of the pink Georgian house with the tall white columns. Inside the Herrick home, Pepper and Rosalie had finished planning the baby's room, at least for today. They were sitting in the family room. The television was on, but the sound was turned low so that they could talk over it.

"What are you and Jonathan Morse going to do?" Rosalie asked finally. It was a difficult question to ask.

"We still want to go out together, like, on dates." Pepper laughed. "Until I get too big to fit in a car, that is!"

"No," Grandma Rosalie said more seriously. "What I mean is, do you have any plans about what he's going to do to help with the baby, or anything like that, or maybe . . . about whether you might get married?"

"We haven't discussed that," Pepper said, and she laughed again. "Don't you think we're too young to be making plans for something that heavy, like getting married?"

And both of them laughed, until Pepper sat up with a start, and felt her stomach. But it was all right, and so they laughed some more.

"What did your father say when you got admitted to college at Rice?" Rosalie asked finally. "With early admission, yet?"

"His eyes kind of bulged out!" Pepper smiled. "He still thinks of me as a child. But then, he started jumping up and down and yelling, 'Great! That's marvelous! I'm so proud of you!' And then, after going on like that for about five minutes, he got this mischievous look and said, 'Of course, going to Rice, that isn't as good as going to the University of Houston, where I went.'"

Rosalie giggled. "He finally realizes how much you've grown up."

"Yes. But Grandma, I'm just so thankful that you can help me take care of the kid. Because, well, being pregnant and single while I'm starting college—it's not going to be easy."

They lost track of the time, Pepper and Rosalie, as they talked on, with Pepper noticing that Rosalie treated her with a new kind of respect, as though she were no longer a child, and Rosalie noticing that, miraculously, Pepper seemed to value her opinions, which was something she hadn't done in a long time. They talked seriously about what happens when a woman's water breaks at the onset of labor, and they laughed about how petrified Jonathan Morse had been when he was informed he was about to become a father.

Suddenly, this afternoon, Pepper and Rosalie Herrick were more than grandmother and granddaughter. Suddenly, they were just two women, talking. Two women, who were friends.

The television had been showing a late afternoon soap opera. With the sound turned down, Rosalie and Pepper barely heard the musical theme for Action News when it came on at six o'clock.

But suddenly, there was John Moreno, with the propane truck pictures behind him. "Good evening, friends," said the anchorman. "Just when it seemed that the propane truck case couldn't get any stranger, the hearings in the Twelfth District Court took a turn toward the bizarre."

Rosalie and Pepper were listening, now. Pepper fiddled with the remote control, and finally, the sound was blaring at them.

"Attorney Robert Herrick proved that he not only can win with juries," John Moreno went on. "He also can wake the dead. The truck driver, Louie Boudreau, was identified as having been killed in the accident, but when lawyer Herrick called him to the witness stand today, he was amazingly alive and well. And in his testimony, Louie Boudreau flatly contradicted the entire case that Maxxco's lawyer, Jimmy Coleman, had counted on to win him a new trial."

Behind the TV anchorman, the Transco Tower winked. Its dark windows shimmered in the distance past the fireball.

"In fact," said the anchorman slowly, "Judge Barbara Trobelo announced that the testimony from the truck driver was so clear that she was going to take the unusual step of deciding the case from the bench, right at the end of the hearing. She then said, 'The motion for new trial is denied.' And with that, the judge cleared the way for the plaintiffs to collect their billion-dollar judgment."

Pepper and Rosalie cheered. It was big news, and they were happy for Robert.

But for both of these women, it wasn't the most important thing that had happened that day.

Detective Derrigan Slaughter had called for Robert.

At six-thirty, when the news was over, Robert still hadn't left the courthouse. With a pink message slip in his hand, he stepped into a telephone booth and dialed the number for the Homicide Division.

"Detective Slaughter? I'm glad I caught you. It's Robert Herrick. What's up?"

There was a pause. Then, Detective Slaughter answered slowly. "We think we know who sent you the cut-up newspaper. The sHYsTer letter, I mean."

Robert held his breath. He sensed something he didn't like in the detective's hesitation.

Slaughter's voice was quiet and very serious. "Turns out the newsprint comes from a newspaper called the *Texas Lawyer*. They tell me it's kinda like a weekly report for the legal profession."

"The *Texas Lawyer*? Yes. It's kind of like a version of a major city paper, but for lawyers. Everybody reads it. I go through it every week, myself."

Silence.

"So tell me," Robert demanded. "Who was it that sent the sHYsTer letter?"

"You sitting down?"

It was incredible news. Robert told the detective, again and again, that there must be some mistake. How could he be so sure? But couldn't he be wrong? Wasn't it best to keep on looking?

When he hung up, Robert sat and stared at the receiver for a long, long time. He was as depressed as he'd ever been in his life.

35
CARELESS PEOPLE

Just coffee, please. I'm not hungry." But the real reason was, there was a knot in her stomach.

Something was wrong.

She looked out the curved glass wall, thirty stories up in the air. The service areas in the Spindletop Restaurant are stationary, in the center, but the restaurant itself rotates around them. It has a spectacular view, seen in one complete turn per hour. And that's slow enough, maybe, but Maria already felt dizzy.

She stared at him. "What is it, Robert?"

Outside the rounded windows and to the west, the flags on the city buildings flew in the wind of late August, and tiny cars crawled along the narrow freeways. The bayou meandered slowly toward the horizon, where the vivid green of West Memorial Drive faded to gray and merged with the blue and puffy white of the sky. Just short of that misty union, the rude spike of the Transco Tower stuck out of the green carpet, and the Galleria traffic swarmed over the Southwest Freeway interchange.

Robert stared at the clouds. He didn't answer her. He didn't say anything. Other people in the restaurant were beginning to steal glances in their direction, the way people always do when they wonder whether a couple is having a fight.

"Listen, honey. I know something's up." Her anxiety was turning into impatience. "Whatever it is, you're not making it any easier by not talking to me."

A shaft of the sun struck his face for an instant, like a spotlight. Robert usually loved the Spindletop, with the bright-and-dappled trees far below and the changing view of the whole city while the restaurant slowly rotated. But not this time. The sunbeam highlighted a curious mix of pain and anger in his eyes.

"Maria, I've got something . . . I . . . have to tell you."

He had trouble finding the words. "I . . . need to tell you . . . that we shouldn't . . . see each other any more."

This wasn't anything like what she'd expected him to say, and it took a minute for her to absorb it. More than a minute, actually, and she didn't absorb it.

"But why, Robert?" Her eyes were narrow, and her lips parted. "Why? You know I'm in love with you."

"Yes, and that's just one more thing we've messed up." His voice was firm, and this time it was his vehemence that surprised her.

He hesitated for an instant. And then, more softly, "I love you, too. But it doesn't matter, because this is just something we have to do."

"But why?" She knew she sounded foolish, repeating the same word over and over. But she couldn't help it. "Why? . . . Why?"

"Because it's the only solution." He shook his head in frustration. "If I want to keep from losing everything I care about, we're going to have to break it off. Like my family, for instance. I've fought for years to keep everything together for my kids without their mother."

"I–I don't understand."

"Then, there's me. Being a trial lawyer isn't just a job. It's not just what I do, it's what I am. And I can't afford to take these kinds of crazy risks, not to mention getting my stomach put through the wringer all the time. There's only one answer. It's unpleasant, and in fact I hate it, but we need to go our separate ways."

The waiter stopped by. He looked as if he wanted to ask them something, but then he looked at Robert and Maria and thought better of it. He fussed with an invisible blot on his jacket and wandered away.

Finally, the silence became so obnoxious that Robert had to say something. But he couldn't talk about the same painful problem any more. And so, at last, he changed the subject.

"Maria, what happened when you met with the district attorney?"

"Well," she answered, "the best news is, I won't have to go to jail. The district attorney sure was mad at me. What I did was improper, and I had a conflict of interest, and I should have gotten another assistant DA to interview Esparza. But I'm not going to get indicted."

"That's great." Robert exhaled a huge breath. "I'm relieved. But if he said it was improper, how do you know he won't prosecute you?"

"Well, the district attorney just sat there and twirled that handlebar mustache of his. And what he said was, 'I can't prove anything, Maria. It's theoretically possible that you committed a crime, but nobody can prove it.'"

She looked at Robert. "You see, under the Penal Code, I could only be guilty of criminal abuse of office if I intended to abuse it. If the reason I didn't listen to Esparza was that he was telling this wild story and I just didn't believe him, then I didn't abuse my authority."

"Oh," was all he said.

"And so I'm sitting there in that claustrophobic office, with my stomach going through the roof, and the D.A. says, 'Anyway, Maria, the public might think you're guilty of this crime, but if you are, you're the only one who knows it.'"

"So now, you can go back to work!" He was triumphant.

"No. Not yet."

"Why not?" This time, his voice was hushed.

"The D.A. went on to say, 'But what I can prove, Maria, is that your conduct was careless, unethical, and just plain stupid.' And he told me I still was suspended. You see, not prosecuting me is one thing. Letting me start back to work is another."

"Oh."

"It's my whole life, my job is." Maria shook her head. "I only got suspended, but if I got fired, it'd be like having my arms torn off. And who can I blame? Myself, that's who! I should have given this damn Esparza thing to somebody else."

"What's going to happen?" He held his breath.

"Well, the D.A. referred it to the disciplinary committee. And now, the disciplinary committee's voted to give me a one-month suspension." Maria sighed. "Frankly, I'm satisfied with that. When the dust cleared, everybody on the committee understood what happened. Esparza was nothing but a big, malicious liar. My actions created an appearance of impropriety, but it was only an appearance, and so they could afford to be lenient."

"Maria, it sounds like it's going to work out all right."

"I know."

They both looked out the window again. Off in the distance, the Transco Tower was there to remind them how careful you have to be when you move in the fast lane.

"But, Robert . . . what about you?"

"Oh, I'm fine." But the way he said it made it obvious he wasn't.

"Tell me! My God, Robert, I want to know!"

"Nothing's turned out simple." His face twisted. "My daughter is about to have my grandson, and she's not talking to me because of what I did. And the reason my daughter knows about what I did is, she read about it in all the newspapers and heard it on TV. The case runner, the twenty-five grand, the topless dancers, and the so-called conspiracy to cover it all up."

"Oh," Maria said quietly. "Well . . . I just hope and pray that Pepper won't stay angry."

"No. She'll come around. Maybe someday she'll even come to understand that I had to do it, to save Icky. Rosalie understands."

Robert looked out at the bright, beautiful view before he went on. "And then, too, the State Bar Association started investigating whether to disbar me."

"Oh, no." She stared down at the table. "Just what you needed. Disbarment proceedings by the State Bar."

"But you know what I did? I marched straight over to the State Bar's offices and talked to the investigator. How's that for a novel idea when a lawyer gets accused of something? I didn't try to take the Fifth. Didn't clam up. Just told the guy the whole blessed thing, exactly the way it happened."

"Wow."

"And you know what else? It worked. The State Bar understood it, the same way the disciplinary committee understood about you. They said, 'Mister Herrick, your payment to Esparza wasn't a violation of the rules, because you already had signed up the case. And it wasn't done with the kind of improper intent that would justify us yanking your license.' They knew I did it to keep Icky from getting killed."

"They looked into all of it?"

"Yes. The Bar Association had several interviews with Icky. He's marginal as a lawyer, but Icky's my friend, and he came clean." Robert shook his head. "Man! Thinking about getting my license pulled, it was . . . it was like looking down into an open grave."

"What will happen to Icky?" Her eyes were narrow.

"Hard to say. If he keeps on telling the truth, maybe they'll suspend him instead of disbarring him. I got Icky admitted to the Aurora Drug Abuse Program. He couldn't afford the cost, and he hasn't got any health insurance, so I paid the bill. I also hired Saw Mill Davis to defend Icky from the State Bar, and I paid Saw Mill's whopping legal fee because Icky couldn't."

She made a face. "Saw Mill Davis is a scum bag."

"A lot of people think that." Robert sighed. "But he fights hard for his clients. Icky's my friend, and if there's anyone who can get him a fair shake, it's that good old, alleged scum bag, Saw Mill Davis."

The waiter cleared his throat. "Your coffee, ma'am. Your coffee, sir."

And without any wasted motion, he was gone.

"But that's not all," Robert said finally. "There's also the propane truck case. And it's just amazing what's happened in the propane truck case."

He pushed the coffee aside. "Get this. Maxxco fired Jimmy Coleman after the verdict, and then–then–Maxxco pulled all of its business out of Booker & Bayne. That'll really hurt Jimmy inside his firm."

Her eyes got big. "Maxxco fired Jimmy? Yes, I'm sure that'll hurt Booker & Bayne. And they'll take it out on Jimmy. They'll . . . punish him for pulling all this crap. But why did Maxxco fire him?"

"Seems Maxxco's stock price took a nose dive, and they were desperate to settle the case." Robert pulled a page from the *Wall Street Journal* from his jacket. The headline screamed, "Maxxco Stock Price Plunges: Maxxco's Board Orders Its Lawyers to Settle and End Uncertainty after Billion Dollar Judgment."

The corners of Robert's mouth seemed to move upward, if only for an instant. "Anyway, Maxxco got a new lawyer. And guess who they hired? Francel Williams."

They both made feeble efforts not to gloat at Maxxco's, and Jimmy's, misfortune. They made efforts, but they were unsuccessful. Even in the middle of all this chaos, Robert looked upbeat for a moment, and Maria actually smiled.

"Wow," she said again. "First, Jimmy Coleman gets fired? And then, millions of dollars worth of legal business gets yanked out of Booker & Bayne? And then, Francel Williams takes over for Maxxco? Robert! This is like waking up from a bad dream."

"Yes, that part is wonderful. And it gets even better. Francel and I settled the case for eight hundred million dollars. It's a great settlement for my clients. And it lets Maxxco start fresh. You see, Maxxco's like any big company. It doesn't admit fault easily, but when it does, it cleans house. Frankly, they were sick of Jimmy Coleman and that scorched-earth style of his."

"Why did you settle the case for eight hundred million after you'd won a billion? I'm just a prosecutor, and don't know diddley-squat about how you handle a big-time civil case."

"Oh, it's not unusual to settle a case like this, even after the verdict. Remember, it was a hard case against Maxxco, and that usually means the other side has grounds to appeal. Like the statute of repose. Or the judge letting that juror, Hartley Rehm, testify about the death trap. Heck, Maxxco's even got a possible argument that we shouldn't get any punitive damages, and if they won that argument, we'd be left with only two hundred and fifty million. Settling for eight hundred million was absolutely the right thing to do."

"Well . . . I guess it makes sense."

"Besides, some of the plaintiffs are elderly. If they had to wait five years for the appeals, well, some of them wouldn't live to see it." He relaxed slightly and leaned back in his chair. "Thank goodness for the common sense of Francel Williams."

"Yes. Robert, I'm so happy for you!"

He hesitated. "But then, the next problem was, a bunch of the plaintiffs would only settle if I signed a document that says they still have the right to sue their attorney, namely me, for malpractice. And some of them went to see Jerome Mabray about representing them."

She screwed up her face in disgust. "Jerome Mabray's a scum bag, too." Jerome Mabray made a living suing other lawyers for malpractice, and he had a reputation for sharp practices. "Robert, that's awful."

Robert shrugged. "But unlike choosing that alleged scum bag Saw Mill Davis, I wouldn't necessarily get to choose whether my former clients would hire that other alleged scum bag, Jerome Mabray. Because they're the ones who get to decide whether to sue that third famous scum bag, me.

"But anyway," he went on, "some of my clients didn't believe the eight hundred million was reasonable, and they didn't trust me after Jimmy's motion for new trial. That's why they hired Jerome Mabray."

"What will happen with that?"

"Well, I heard that Jerome Mabray actually met with all my dissatisfied clients, and I heard he was great. He told them, point blank: 'Look, you don't have a case.' He said, 'Herrick represented you as well as anybody ever could have.' And he refused to file any kind of suit against me."

"Wonderful! Maybe there's honor among scum bags." Maria was ecstatic. "Robert, we've both come through all of this. We've managed to tell the truth and come out with clean reputations!"

He frowned. And from the way he frowned, she could tell that there was more to it. Much more.

"Haven't we come through it, Robert?" She sounded plaintive, frightened, and almost desperate to believe what she was saying.

But a war was going on in his face, and Maria felt her stomach heave. This whole sorry mess was like the layers of an onion. You could peel back one problem, but you'd immediately find another one underneath it, just waiting for you to stumble into it. It was all so tangled, so confusing, and so scary. That was why she had wanted to keep him out of the propane truck case in the first place.

But why was Robert so angry, now? Why now, when everything seemed to have turned out right?

"What is it?" She held her breath. "What? What?"

The ridges in his forehead drew tighter, and so did the ice around Maria's heart.

"Well, I'm sorry, but there's one more problem," he said finally. "And it's the biggest one of all."

He said it slowly, but firmly. "And that is, I found out about what was done to me by the woman I loved."

She looked at him through half-closed eyes, but all she could do was wait.

He turned to stare directly into her face. She had never seen him so angry. "Maria, at least you could have used a less obvious newspaper than the *Texas Lawyer*."

She looked back at him, searching his eyes.

And finally, when she was sure that he knew, she looked away.

"Maria, they got your fingerprints from Austin, from when you had to be fingerprinted before taking the Bar Examination. And your prints were all over the sHYsTer letter. How'd you expect to get away with this?"

"I guess I didn't." She was looking down at the floor. "I probably meant to get caught. I just wanted you to get off the propane truck case. I wanted it so, so badly!" Her words came out one at a time while she struggled for air. "I would've told you about it myself, sooner or later."

"Well, at the risk of asking the obvious, what on earth possessed you to do this?"

"I–I don't know." She was fidgeting like crazy. "I had this awful feeling about the propane truck case from the beginning, like I knew this case was going to tear you apart. Don't ask me how I knew. Maybe it was because of that spooky Transco Tower, because I always felt like that thing was . . . trying to tell me something. And I knew you wouldn't listen to that kind of weird stuff. And I was in love with you."

She pursed her lips. "I hoped this cut-up-newspaper letter would get you to drop the case."

"How'd you figure that?"

"If you wouldn't listen to me, maybe you'd listen to someone who threatened you. I know it doesn't make any sense, now! But a Cuban would understand. I was functioning on intuition. I loved you. I was scared to death."

Her voice was cracking all over the place. But he needed to know, and so he still asked.

"No, Maria, it sure doesn't make sense. And I'm not going to let you off the hook that easily. There's got to be more to it."

She bit her lip. "Damn you, Robert, for acting like you're a lawyer cross-examining a witness one hundred percent of the time!"

He waited.

When she finally went on, Maria's eyes were angry and pleading and apologetic, all at the same time. "Yes, there was more to it."

He was astounded to watch her fall apart. Maria had always seemed poised and perfect, a refined Latina lady who just happened to become an assistant district attorney. He had never seen her cry before.

"It's my little sister," she whispered, in a voice as hoarse as Jimmy Coleman's. "You know, Elena. My little sister."

"Your sister?" That threw him. "What does Elena have to do with this?"

Maria's voice thickened. "Elena bought—she–she bought cocaine from the case runner. From Esparza. From that same guy you did business with."

She saw how puzzled he was, and she explained again. "Elena was Esparza's customer, too, only it was a different kind of illegal business."

Now his mouth was even wider. "How did— . . . How . . ."

"How did I find out about your deal with Esparza? That's easy." Maria's disgust twisted her face into knots. "Esparza was so proud of running the propane truck case to Robert Herrick that he bragged about it. In fact, he blabbed to everybody who'd listen, including Elena. And Elena told me. And I didn't want to believe it, but Robert, you immediately turned up representing all the plaintiffs. You had snagged this big-money lawsuit, and it came from the same guy who was ruining my sister's life!"

He was so astounded that it made him ask stupid questions. "But–but why didn't you do something to stop her? Or get Esparza arrested?"

"And turn in my own sister? I tried everything. She just got deeper into that horrible stuff. And then, Robert, you showed up in the propane truck case! I realize, now, that you didn't know Esparza sold cocaine, and now I know about Icky, but I didn't know any of that back then."

"Why didn't you talk to me about it?"

"I did. A hundred times. I asked you every way I knew, 'please dump the propane truck case.' I didn't get into the thing about Elena and Esparza, because I knew it wouldn't do any good, and I'd just have ended up exposing Elena if you hadn't handled it right."

"Okay. Okay." He was still trying to absorb it. "But why the letter? And why did you send that thing to me right when Squint was trying to kill me?"

Her anger disappeared. "I'm sorry. You see, I didn't know about Squint, and I didn't know what was about to happen. I didn't want to tell you about Elena, and I didn't know whether to believe that story about you being mixed up with Esparza. That stupid letter was the only thing I could think of. In fact, I'm not sure I was thinking at all."

Robert's mind was spinning. Derrigan Slaughter's hunch, way back then, had been right. "It might even be, that whoever's prints are on that letter has no connection to Squint . . ."

But as for Maria, she was thinking about Wendy Bachman's warning. "You keep pretending you're some kind of friggin' actress, and you're gonna get your ass in big-time trouble."

Wendy was right.

"I'm such an idiot." Maria had to choke the words out now, because she couldn't stop crying. "My friends told me this would happen. It's a bad habit I've always had, pulling stunts like this. And I just didn't see this sHYsTer letter as much more than . . . a prank, like impersonating a supreme court justice. I did it without realizing how much pain it would cause. Obviously, I've found out since."

"You thought the sHYsTer letter was . . . a prank?"

"No. Of course not." She looked up, surprised. "Well, sort of like a prank, but more serious. It was a devious way to get you off the case. A stupid thing to do. But I did it."

By now, of course, he felt sorry for Maria. But after what she had done . . .

"Well, Detective Slaughter says he's not going to arrest you. Turns out, it's not a crime to send an anonymous letter. Not even one that's intended to scare the ever-loving fool out of the guy you're sleeping with."

"I'm sorry," she whispered. "I'm sorry. I know it's not enough, but I am. I am sorry."

And with that, they both looked out the window toward the west.

"It's ironic," Robert said finally. "I've sued careless people ever since I first started out as a lawyer. I've chased after careless people, and I've investigated them, and I've dug up the evidence to prove how careless they were. You see, careless people cause more injustice than people who do it on purpose. They hurt the victims worse. I can almost hear myself saying it to a jury, because it's exactly what I've told a hundred juries."

And for an instant, in his best courtroom voice, he said it the way he'd have said it to twelve citizens in a jury box. "It's not the conspirators who do the most harm. It's not the white-collar criminals. It's the negligent, oblivious, careless people, the ones who get blinded by their own selfishness. They're the ones who hurt other people the most."

He turned and looked directly into her eyes. "Well, Maria, this time it's you and me who have been careless. We've hurt other people. We didn't mean to do it, and we didn't conspire to do it. We just forgot what was right and wrong. We got caught up in our own self-centeredness. Truth is, I didn't really need the propane truck case that badly. And Maria, you didn't need to keep me out of the case that badly."

He put his index finger in the corner of his eye, as if something had gotten stuck there. "And I just hope I've realized all of this in time. In time to keep from destroying Pepper, and Robbie, and the baby, and, also, everybody who works at the law offices of Robert Herrick and Associates. Not to mention you and me."

Another long pause, with nothing but the magnificent view.

And then, quietly, Maria said: "So . . . what are you going to do now?"

"I'm going to get back to basics," he answered immediately. "I'm going to devote myself more than ever to my clients. I've been lucky. No disbarment suit, no malpractice claims. I'm just grateful to God and to our system of justice."

"Well, but . . . Robert . . . you and me . . . ."

"And that leaves the personal side of my life, which is what I've messed up the most. I'm going back to basics there, too, and I'm going to try to get my family back. As for you and me, Maria, it has to do with trust."

Slowly, silently, the restaurant rotated, and finally, they both stood up. They said good-bye, and they walked away in different directions.

Two hours later, back at the office, Robert tried to concentrate on the files that were piled on his desk. Files about upcoming trials. They were lawsuits about foam-covered breast implants, actually. All of them were cases for women who had serious injuries, persistent pain, and ruined lives. These women thought that he, Robert Herrick, was their best hope for justice, and if there'd ever been a time when he'd taken the trust of his clients for granted, he didn't now. He felt humble. He wanted to do his dead-level best for them.

But his mind wandered, and he couldn't work. Finally, he gave up and just looked out the window.

He desperately needed somebody to talk to.

Almost involuntarily, he picked up the phone. He dialed half of Maria's number before he realized what he was doing. Slowly, he put the receiver back into its cradle. And even more slowly, he stood up and shouldered his jacket. When the door to his office slammed behind him, he turned toward Donna DeCarlo. "I . . . think I'm going to call it a day."

"You told her what?" Tom Kennedy's look was incredulous. "This is the first woman you've been able to get along with in years. And so all of a sudden, you just told her to get lost?"

It was the "morning after," now. The morning after the breakup. Robert still couldn't work. He couldn't even pretend to work. He told Kennedy he needed to talk about the breast implant cases. But what he really needed was to talk about Maria.

And right away, here was Kennedy yelling at him about how foolish he was.

"What else could I do?" Robert was miserable, but determined. "After finding out about that sHYsTer letter, I couldn't believe anything she said. Ever again."

"Oh, Robert, that's not true." Kennedy's incredulity turned to disgust. "You've told me a million times how our clients make innocent mistakes when they hide some key fact from us. They do it because they're embarrassed, and maybe they don't see how damaging it is. But our clients are usually good people, and you've drummed it into my head. 'One mistake doesn't mean you can't trust them.' Those are *your* words, Robert. Not mine."

"Yes . . . well . . . but this is different. What Maria did is bigger, and it's worse."

"She screwed up one time. One time! And the reason she did it was because she cared about you."

"It's a pretty big screw-up, if that's what you want to call it."

"Okay. It's a pretty big screw-up. But it's only one screw-up. The district attorney's managed to forgive her. Why not Robert Herrick?"

Robert's thoughts already had been tumbling painfully and fast, and all he could do now was to turn a blank stare back at Kennedy.

But his younger associate wasn't about to let up. "Robert, did you ever hear that old saying about cutting off your nose to spite your face? Well, it sure fits what you're doing. You're standing on principle. Congratulations. You're a man of principle."

"I've always tried."

"Well, try this. Principle without forgiveness is meanness."

Robert struggled to put his betrayed feelings into words. "But how can I let it pass, after what she did? How?"

Kennedy's answer was harsh. "Just by doing it! By saying to yourself, it's just one screw-up, and you shouldn't blow it out of proportion. You're worried you can't ever trust her again, but there's got to be another part of that brain of yours. And that part knows, everybody makes mistakes!"

"Yes, but . . . ."

"And I hope there's still one more part of your brain that understands what you're giving up. I've seen the way Maria makes you feel. I've seen the way you look at her. I've seen the way your face changes whenever she walks in the room."

"But I can't put up with what she did."

"So, don't put up with it! She already knows you're not going to put up with it." Kennedy's voice was rising. "Hell's bells, Robert, she isn't even trying to get you to 'put up with it.' She knows she screwed up. And she admits she screwed up!"

Robert was silent. Kennedy was out of breath. They both looked down at the fine grain in the big mahogany desk.

It was Kennedy who broke the silence. "So I guess you're determined. You've decided, huh?"

"Yes, I have." But there was a struggle going on in his face.

Kennedy's voice oozed with sarcasm. "It's sort of like that movie, *Casablanca*. And Robert, you're like Humphrey Bogart, saying good-bye to Ingrid Bergman. She's the love of his life, but heck, old Humphrey—he's got principles. Of course, that was in the movies. But you, Robert . . . you're going to do the same stupid thing in real life."

Robert felt the ghost of a smile cross his face. The comparison to Humphrey Bogart was just extravagant enough to be funny.

And at the same moment, the tightness in Kennedy's face relaxed. It was as if the wheels in his head had stopped turning, because he had hit upon the ultimate strategy. A strategy that would shock his boss into forgiving Maria.

"I'll tell you what, Robert," Kennedy announced finally. "This is going to sound strange. But you'll understand why I need to say it."

Robert was torn between numbness and curiosity. Kennedy was acting very strangely, with a dramatic edge in his voice.

"I've always been crazy about Maria Melendes myself," Kennedy said matter-of-factly. "I always admired her from afar. And so I'd like to take her out, myself."

Robert just sat there, dumbfounded.

"So, I need to ask you. Do you suppose, Robert, that it'd be all right . . . if I asked Maria out?"

Robert stared.

"It shouldn't matter to you, since you're not going to ever see her again. And I think she's fantastic." Kennedy's eyes were level with Robert's. "And maybe I don't have umpteen million dollars, but I don't think the money was ever the biggest thing on Maria's mind. Maybe, just maybe, she'd get along with me, Tom Kennedy."

It was a familiar ritual, one that Robert recognized. Etiquette among men, about women. Every guy over sixteen years of age knows that it's bad manners to take out a friend's old girlfriend without asking permission. Even if they've broken up, even if they're never going to see each other again, there's an unwritten rule. You're supposed to ask.

And in spite of his numbness, Robert remembered the rest of that unwritten rule: When you're asked, you have to give permission. If you're not going to see that old girlfriend again, it is ungracious to be a dog in the manger. You're supposed to smile, and feign magnanimity, and say, "Oh, sure. That's fine."

So now, Tom wanted to chase after Maria Melendes? And he expected Robert to give his blessing?

Robert sat still until the idea sank in. And then, he did the only thing that made any sense. He went ballistic.

"Tom, I asked you to come in here so we could work up these damn breast implant cases!" He waved his arms. "But instead, you end up ragging me around about my girlfriend."

He gripped the desk until the mahogany shook. "And the answer, Tom, is No! What kind of garbage is this? My relationship with Maria is just barely dead, and you want to hijack the body before it's even buried."

Kennedy looked stricken. He stood up and stepped back.

"You could've at least waited!" Robert didn't realize how loud his voice was.

Kennedy stood still. There was a very long silence.

"I think we'd better end this conversation here." Robert had stopped shouting, but he gripped the desk as he faced his newly-minted rival. "The breast implant cases can wait."

He looked out the window and fought to get his temper under control.

Kennedy straightened himself and headed for the door. But beneath his wounded dignity, he wore the look of a man who had accomplished his mission.

It had always been his job to be a sounding board for the boss, and if Robert went off in the wrong direction, it was Kennedy's duty to say so. Gently. Or not so gently. And this matter of Maria Melendes was one of the most important problems that he and the boss had ever faced together. It called for drastic measures. Kennedy had done what he had to do, and he only hoped it would work.

EPILOGUE

Robert didn't know how many weeks had passed. He hadn't been counting. He tried to throw himself into his work and turned out plenty of paper. But he had the sense that he hadn't accomplished very much. And the worst of it was, he just didn't care.

He also drank more than usual. The only thing that kept him going was his clients. They trusted him. These women in the breast implant cases looked up to him, confided in him, and followed his advice, and he would never take his clients for granted again.

He had even been able, after a few days, to work with Tom Kennedy. Neither of them had mentioned that disastrous conversation about Maria. It was like ignoring a pile of explosives in the room, but both of them managed to swallow their words, their feelings, and their pride, as if a single remark might act as a detonator.

The puffs of clouds were in perfect rows today, as he knew from staring at them. "But what the hell," he thought. "I'm tired of beautiful days."

"I wonder if I can just call her and say, 'all is forgiven.' It would be such a relief, it almost would be like forgiving myself." He reached for the telephone, then hesitated. "The propane truck case—what a load of misery it brought to both of us. She made a mess out of it. Looking back, I didn't handle it very well, either."

Tom Kennedy was right. Principles without a sense of proportion were too costly. And suddenly, he understood Tom's strategy. Tom wasn't really planning to ask Maria out. Tom wasn't really trying to get Maria. Could Kennedy's ploy have been just a way of persuading Robert?

But he reminded himself that he had long since decided about Maria. He put the telephone down. And he wrenched his thoughts away from her.

It was a distressingly short time before he caught himself daydreaming again.

The truth was, and he might as well admit it to himself, he missed Maria all the time. Nonstop. But he had no choice. After that crazy letter, what else could he do but break it off?

He and Maria were so different. What else could he have done?

Now, weeks later, he was astonished by how constant the pain was. How much it still hurt, from moment to moment. Why couldn't he just call her and make all of these problems go away?

"Life is nothing but a bunch of last-minute guesses," he said to himself. "Our choices seem more deliberate than they really are, because it's only in the last instant of indecision that our thoughts crystallize. And we can only guess about the future." If he had known then what he would feel now, if he had been able to see how his outrage would give way to the realization that she had only loved him in a clumsy way, then maybe, just maybe, the last second of decision could have tipped the other way.

And what of the world behind that choice, the choice to forgive Maria? Would it have been a better future?

Kennedy had seen it. That was what his gambit was all about. Kennedy had pretended to be a rival so that Robert would be forced to feel the loss. Robert's anger melted into regret as he realized he had misunderstood his friend completely.

"Maybe if Kennedy had been just a shade more effective, or maybe," Robert thought ruefully, "if I had been a touch less hardheaded, maybe then the decision could have been different. And it surely would be less painful now." He wondered whether he'd ever have another instant in which to make a decision like that one, only different.

Or whether he could create another chance. Just by calling her. Now.

Suddenly, the telephone rang. It startled him.

He picked up the receiver like an automaton, and several long seconds passed before he spoke into it. "This is Robert Herrick."

"Hi, Robert sweetheart," said the familiar voice, haltingly.

He paused, surprised, and his heart jumped. Then, warily, "Hello. Why are you calling me? What's up?"

She hesitated, too. Then, she blurted it out, as though she'd decided the only way to say it was just to say it. "I know how much you like the ballet. Well, the Houston Ballet is about to do *Cinderella* this Friday, which is just about my favorite ballet of all time." She laughed nervously, with her little-girl laugh. "And anyway, I wanted you to take me to it. That is, if you ever actually go to these overly cultural events, like ballet."

It was just like Maria to deal with a breakup this way. To call back and make him laugh as a way of patching things up. At least this time she had the good taste to spare him that lame justification that she'd used so often, the mocking excuse that "I'm Cuban, and I have red hair!"

"I truly am sorry," she said slowly. "I wish I could take it back. I wish I'd never done it."

He felt the quicksand in his stomach. He almost panicked, and he wanted to run away. The last thing he needed, now, was to get involved again with the same woman who had betrayed him, right when he was struggling to sort out his love for her, and the anger, distrust, and bewilderment he felt.

He realized that his own behavior had been less than perfect. And for that matter, nothing's ever perfect, certainly not in relationships between men and women. She must have been under incredible pressure when she sent that stupid letter. Good intentions, maybe.

But knowing that this was how her love was expressed almost made it worse.

In that frame of mind, Robert hesitated. And then he knew what to do. He was certain of the decision, even though instinct was all he had to go on. In that final instant, he reminded himself, is there ever anything more to go on?

"Sure," he said to Maria. "The ballet? Where's it playing? Your place or mine?"

He liked the way she laughed at that.

POSTSCRIPT

wanted to write this story so that the lawyering was real.

   In a book of fiction, the action should create more excitement than real life. It's supposed to grab the reader. But still, I wanted this story to be an authentic reflection of the way that lawyers handle real lawsuits.

   I've drawn on my own experience to do this. For example, the statute of repose, which Jimmy Coleman uses to attack Robert Herrick's case, is a shortened version of a real statute in my state. The cases that Jimmy cites to the judge are real. The lawyer who lost one of these cases in the state supreme court was that supposedly eminent authority, me.

   But the most surprising thing that happened while I was writing this book was that there was new construction at the site of the "propane truck disaster." After I had written several drafts, but before this book was published, the ramp was redesigned. The very same ramp that Louie Boudreau drives onto! None of the other parts of the interchange were altered, just this one. Today, the real ramp is bordered by concrete blocks instead of guardrails, just as Robert's "expert witness" testified it should have been.

   This is a work of fiction, and it's not important how or why the real overpass was changed. And I don't pretend to know the companies that were involved in the construction. Unlike Maxxco, they may be very fine firms. Still, it's odd that this ramp was the only one chosen to be redesigned. It's almost as spooky as the Transco Tower in bad weather.

   In trying to be realistic, I wrote a letter to my friend Dan Luss, who is chairman of the chemical engineering department at the University of Houston:

> Dear Dan:
>   Here is a copy of my book. Would you please look at the first couple of chapters, which describe an accident on the Southwest Freeway, and tell me whether my description of how it happens is plausible?
>
> Sincerely,
David Crump

After reading about the explosion, Professor Luss graciously pronounced it plausible.

Then, Judge Caprice Cosper, who was assigned to the death penalty duty when she was an assistant district attorney, looked at the chapter about the execution of Johnny Ray Garrison. It would be unusual, she says, for three judges to hear a stay of execution by conference telephone, but it could happen. The prosecutor wouldn't necessarily go to the prison, but she could. The Supreme Court decisions that are cited in that chapter, such as *Herrera v. Collins* and *Penry v. Lynaugh*, are among the hottest capital punishment cases today. I collapsed two roles into one, because part of the prosecutor's work would be done by the state attorney general.

But some of my early readers had a different problem. They wondered whether a death penalty prosecutor really would have considered agreeing to a new trial, as Maria sometimes did. The answer is a resounding yes. Prosecutors do that when the occasion calls for it, and the good ones are aware that fairness to the defendant is a first requisite.

The chapter about the divorce courts owes some of its local color to an article called "A Day in the Life of a Family Court Judge," written by Judge John Montgomery. Better than I ever could, Judge Montgomery shows just how difficult it is, and yet how important it is, for lawyers to keep their heads screwed on straight in that tragic environment. When they do, it's less like a zoo than I've made it out to be.

I had to make several changes in the chapter involving the flight of the Gulfstream II to San Francisco. My friend, Captain Bill Harger, read the first draft, and he warned me that my flight plan was not permissible "unless you are Air Force One." Being a professional pilot, he also objected to the way I had the wheels "bounce" on the runway. I rewrote it so they "glided."

Some of the dirty tricks that Jimmy Coleman pulled have been pulled on me. The focus group's behavior is adapted from a story told by my friend Don Vinson, the world's champion jury consultant. As for Hartley Rehm, the jury panel member who became a witness, he is an echo of a witness in a real case, a potential juror who announced to a hushed courtroom that he knew the accident scene, and it was dangerous as all get out! He got disqualified, and the plaintiff's lawyers called him as their first witness. They coasted to victory.

Jimmy Coleman's "motion to dismiss or for summary judgment" is a concession to my friends and critics. To get technical about it, the most likely procedure would have been a "motion for summary judgment," and I wrote it that way the first time. My wife, Jill, said this would stop everybody cold. And it did. "What on earth is this, a 'summary judgment?'" But then I discovered that they all understood a motion to dismiss. It is unlikely that Jimmy could have hoped for a dismissal, but sometimes a motion to dismiss and a motion for summary judgment are joined together, and so I had Jimmy do it this way.

To get even more technical about it—and I admit, this is really technical—a motion to dismiss is called a "special exception" in my state. But to make matters more complicated (and this is really, really technical), there are some situations in which calling it a motion to dismiss still can be correct. I decided to just go ahead and call it a motion to dismiss.

Jimmy tries to get his case filed in front of a friendly judge. Frankly, every trial lawyer hopes for that. The difference is, most of them don't use unethical methods. But the temptations are powerful, and it occasionally happens that a lawyer uses influence in the clerk's office for "judge shopping." I talked this part over with *Houston Chronicle* Reporter George Flynn, who once covered a story about an errant clerk who used a slightly different method. I didn't want to write a blueprint for those kinds of people, and so I set up Jimmy's method so that it won't really work, unless the docketing system gets changed so that it's like what I've described.

I also need to say thanks to everybody else who helped write this story, including Barry, Catherine, Carolyn, Connie, Dan, Don, Elizabeth, Gail, Gene, Harriet, Hull, J.D., Jerry, John, Kim, Karen, Kristi, Mary, Paul, Rob, Terry, and Yocel. And especially to Mary Jane and Jean-Louis, thanks for seeing it through. As Francel would say, "You were won-n-n-n-derful!"

As the usual disclaimer goes, my story is a work of fiction, and there is no intended reference to real persons.

But so far as fiction allows, this is an authentic picture of what can happen in a lawsuit. And also, it shows the kinds of chaos and fear that are everyday companions in the life of a trial lawyer.

Not all big law firms are like Booker & Bayne. I've been privileged to practice inside a couple of them, and most of their lawyers are fine people, not crooks like the ones in Booker & Bayne. On the other hand, I've been acquainted with a few lawyers who resemble Jimmy Coleman. The win-at-any-cost mentality. The influence-peddling. The whole bit, right down to Jimmy's trick of reducing his opponents to sub-humans. The challenge to my profession is to write the rules so they don't give any advantage to the Jimmy Colemans. I think our system succeeds at that most of the time.

There is one other detail that has sparked a lot of comment from my friends, and that is the way that Robert Herrick is nervous—not just nervous, but scared—at the beginning of the trial. He's a professional, my friends argue. He would be cold and logical.

But Robert's fear is something that all trial lawyers can identify with. When you go to trial, it isn't interesting. It isn't fun. It's war. Ask a trial lawyer how he feels just before going to trial, and ten to one, the answer will be, "scared," or some variant of that word. I didn't understand it when I was in law school, but I did when I started my first trial. There are many trial lawyers, including some of the best, who have to suppress the urge to lose their breakfast every time they face a jury.

And so I believe that this detail is realistic, too. Just ask a trial lawyer!

— David Crump